Growing up in a dead-end, Thames Valley town like Marden Combe, Kai knows there's no escape without a lot of talent, hard work—and luck.

Two weeks before the Clayton Paul Blues Band plans to set out on tour to Germany, their singer quits, and drummer Kai takes matters in hand. With bandmates Jake and Jamie, they recruit a talented new singer—the enigmatic Dominique—as the new face of the band and set out on the road to Berlin in a rickety white van.

Dogged by mishaps and under-rehearsed, the band stumbles through their first shows, zig-zagging between chaos and brilliance. But as the first gig in Berlin draws near, the band begins to gel. They're clicking with their audience, and even the stone-hearted Kai starts to crumble under the spell, first of Dom and then…of Lars.

As the end of the tour approaches, Kai must make hard choices. Dom? But she's keeping a dark secret. Lars? Not after the acrimony of their last parting. The band? Or will that dream crumble too?

TEARDOWN

WILLIAM CAMPBELL POWELL

A NineStar Press Publication
www.ninestarpress.com

Teardown

First Edition, December 2024

ISBN: 978-1-64890-826-2

Also available in eBook, ISBN: 978-1-64890-825-5

CONTENT WARNING:

This book contains adult language, discussion of a deceased family member (in the past), past trauma, death of a prominent character (off page), and depictions of alcohol consumption and drug use (off page).

The song 'Whiskey in the Jar' adapted from the traditional song Roud 533, original lyrics © 2024 William Campbell Powell

To the fabulous Ken Wood and the Mixers

Chapter One

Sunday, September 18, 2016

The Band Hut, Marden Combe

THE BUS STANK of commuters. It wasn't like a night bus, granted, but the mix of sweat and cheap scent — and the pungency of diesel — was another reminder of how much I hated Marden Combe.

A Thames Valley town like every other Thames Valley town, Marden Combe had a posh, blingy bit, where the bankers, footballers, and celebrity chefs lived. The rest ran the spectrum from dilapidated through demolished to barely affordable modern rabbit hutches. The old town centre was closing down, and the new shopping centre was gridlock hell.

The bus lurched and swung left, past a school named for a long-dead parliamentarian. Or possibly a royalist. I ought to know; it had been my old school till I'd turned sixteen. But it had all seemed irrelevant to the more immediate problem of not getting picked on for being different. There were a dozen ways and more to be different, whether it was for being too ugly, too geeky, too slow on the uptake, too shy, too dark, not dark enough, having a funny accent, or a fundy religion, or being neurodivergent, being too posh, being too poor, liking the wrong music, or football team, or playing oddball sports, or using last year's tech; not liking girls, not liking boys, not liking either, liking both. Plus others, plus combinations. By more than one marker, I was weird, and I hadn't always kept my head down. But there'd definitely been no bullying at Sir Long-Dead-Parliamentarian School. Or Royalist, as the case may be. Oh no.

That didn't come close to summing up the suffocating, hope-crushing, soul-sucking, shit-brown hole that is Marden Combe. I needed to escape.

If I had a plan, it was that music would save me, as currently embodied by two pairs of drumsticks in my backpack and the cymbals in their hardcase. I'd found a few other muzos with a similar plan, and I was heading for the weekly escape committee meeting.

*

THE BUS CRAWLED through the town centre—the closing-down bit, where the last of the character pubs struggled to keep their doors open with, as always, the pressure on the landlords to boost profits, cut costs, and serve salmonella-free food, or be booted out with a mountain of debt.

I gave it a nostalgic glance as the bus passed the Lord Nelson, boarded up and awaiting planning permission for conversion to flats. Once, the very bricks had rung with rock and oozed the blues. Once. Now, it was just another live music venue, dead and gone forever.

Still clinging on: the Cherry Tree, where we played a one-in-four Saturday night residency, alternating with rivals the Dave Green Blues Band, the twice ill-named Silent But Deadly, and a guest out-of-town band for the final Saturday. That residency was our lifeline, our oxygen, dependent on our ability to bring in the punters and dependent on the other bands too. Rivals we might be, but every band had to pull its weight.

Last night's gig had been borderline, thanks to the competition from freshers' week at the uni. Jeff and Simon had shown the strain as they'd sat us down after the gig to pay us. A dear old couple, they did what they loved for bugger-all profit. Simon, a long-term AIDS survivor, was a respected leader in Marden Combe's tiny LGBTQIA community. They were never less than friendly to us as a band or to me personally, but yesterday, Simon got as near to reading the riot act as made no difference. Times were tough, and if our audience numbers didn't pick up…

We got the message.

The lights changed. The bus lurched into motion, taking us up the hill, towards Marden Combe's main industrial estate.

*

THE BUS PASSED an abandoned car on the grass verge. Last week, a sign on the windscreen said Police Aware, but evidently, not so aware that someone couldn't set fire to it in the interim. That was my cue to get off. I rang the bell, and the bus pulled to a halt about fifty yards short of a block of single-storey industrial units. It had been built in the 1960s, and the brickwork left much to be desired. Ditto the ironwork and the paintwork. Don't even think about asbestos. The third unit along was the one I was looking for. The sign read The Band Hut, and it fit right in with Marden Combe…

I pushed open the door, and all was gloom within. Thick cardboard and felt covered the windows. I called "Hi" to Wally at the front desk, hunched over his phone, and the autopilot grunted back. I moved past room 1 (a folk-metal trio), room 2 (empty), and into room 3, signed with gloss white paint roughly slapped over its matt black outer door.

Usually, with great rock stars taking interviews in their home studios, there wasn't an amp in sight unless it was some boutique marque they'd been paid to endorse. The studio would be airy, bright, and wood-panelled in glossy pine, with walls featuring three or four iconic guitars. Double-insulated patio doors would lead onto a beautifully manicured lawn, the whole set tastefully in the Cotswolds.

In Marden Combe, they did things differently. Black felt covered the walls and ceiling of Studio 3. Underfoot, recycled carpet tiles clung to my shoes, sticky as only years of spilt beer could accomplish. Worn and curling patches showed where the bass drum spikes had caught between two tiles and where the studio's cobbled-together frankenamps had been dragged too many times. Gaffa tape glinted under fluorescent lights, hasty repairs crisscrossing the floor. Other marks — cigarette burns mostly — clustered round the amps; the still-potent reeks of ancient tobacco and stale weed lurked at the edge of awareness. A tired but eclectic collection of posters hung on the walls, providing a potted archaeology of Marden Combe's indigenous music of the last half decade.

Jake was already set up and sitting on a Band Hut amplifier, cradling his beloved Fender Stratocaster. He didn't look up, but I didn't expect him to. He hunched over the fretboard, fingers spider-dancing their scales. Half in shadow, he was a little spiderlike himself, all spindly limbs that gangled and writhed. His hair, too pale for a spider, was cut short and neatly combed.

After a minute, he finished his phrase, and we nodded to each other. Jake wasn't a great conversationalist, so I didn't push him out of his comfort zone. It was called 'letting the music do the talking'. It suited both of us.

It took me about ten minutes to get the studio's drum kit set up the way I like it, with my own cymbals in place. All the while, Jake happily noodled on his Strat. Clay breezed in just as I was finishing up.

Clay was the kind of guy you'd want fronting a blues band. Beautiful, with ebon-black skin and close-cropped hair, he had a solid baritone voice with a growl that went up to eleven. Today, he wore jeans and a T-shirt from a Kyla Brox show, but on stage, he was sharp-cut suit and *moves*. Twenty-six years old and — speaking entirely in my capacity as detached observer — hot and classy as fuck.

"Hi, Clay," I called.

"Hi, Kai. Where's Jamie?"

"He said he'd be a few minutes late. The boss is making him do overtime."

Which, given that it was Sunday, was brother Jamie's standard polite fiction for his housemates roping him into cleaning the kitchen. A little unfair, given that Jamie is possibly the tidiest human being on the planet. If Clay had been thinking, he'd have remembered that.

"That's a bugger," said Clay.

"Yeah. Tell me about it."

But then he just stood there. Like a kid busting for a pee but afraid to ask the teacher.

"D'you need a hand getting stuff out of the car?" I asked.

"No." He held up the flight case that held his mic and harmonicas. "How long do you think he's going to be?"

"I don't know. He said a few minutes, but I've no idea what that is in real minutes."

Clay sat on an amp, then got up and walked over to the soundproof door. He opened it and the second door beyond it. He peered through the gloom. I could hear the folk-metal band getting into their groove, and good luck to them, but I was glad there would be a vacant studio between us and their sawtooth D minors.

No sign of Jamie though.

It was like something was up with Clay. I was almost tempted to ask him if he was okay. But what if he said no? That was why I didn't ask personal questions within the band. We played blues together, and we planned escape. We memorised the names of one another's significant others so we could be polite if they showed up at a gig. Clay's significant other, Sirelle was—again, in my capacity, et cetera, et cetera—hot, but she was also Little Miss Disdain. Jake did not have a significant other that wasn't made of wood and didn't have six strings. Jamie had been a sore test of memory up until Louise, but he was currently unattached. That was it.

Clay was making me nervous though. So:

"Are you going to set your mic up, Clay? I'll help you set levels so you're all ready to go when Jamie gets here."

No reason he couldn't do it himself, but I was also music tech, so I was allowed to ask.

"Uh, no."

Then, he expelled a deep, doom-laden breath, and I knew this day, which had started only medium crap, was going to end full-on shitstorm.

"I can't wait for Jamie," he decided. "Ah, guys…I've got an announcement to make."

Jake looked up but carried on playing irritating little shreds.

"Good news?" I asked, more in forlorn hope than expectation.

"Well, yes. Sort of. I've got a new job."

That doesn't happen a lot in Marden Combe. Let's not piss on the parade just yet.

"That's good. Well done. So, what's not to like about that?"

"It's…in London."

"Good pay, then, I guess. But I don't fancy your commute."

"Oh, it's not Central London. It's in Acton. But you're right about the commute. Apart from that, though, it's a pretty good job. It's a real step up in my career."

It was my turn to take a deep breath. "Okay. So why aren't you dancing for joy?"

"Well, it's a big project, and they need to get started right away. So, I'm starting next week. There's no flexibility on that date. We're up against the wire."

"Right. What happens when you go on holiday the week after? Are they okay with that?"

"That's just it, Kai. This is a huge project. It's a fantastic opportunity. I'll be in right at the ground floor. I need to be there. I've promised them I'll be there."

Ah. This is goodbye, then. Why can't you just fucking say it?

"So what happens to the Clayton Paul Blues Band? What happens to the tour? Köln, Aachen, Berlin? All those German punters waiting to see us two weeks from now?"

Clay wouldn't meet my eye.

"I can't pass this up, Kai. It's a dream opportunity for me."

"And you can't wait?"

"*They* won't wait. I aced that interview, but there's a bunch of guys almost as good, ready to start tomorrow. *White* guys."

"That shouldn't matter. There are laws…"

"Shit, Kai. Don't tell me *you* don't know how discrimination works. The manager liked me, stuck his neck out to make the offer. But if I start pissing them about, making conditions… It wouldn't be *discrimination*, no sir. But it *would* be 'we need someone who can start immediately'—that's what they'd say."

I nodded. I did know. *White male privilege, Kai.* "And the band? Your band. Us. The Clayton Paul Blues Band that goes on tour in two weeks?"

"I don't know." It was a scream of desperation, and it made Jake stop shredding. Something had gotten through to him.

"I don't know," Clay repeated, quieter. "It's just a tour. It's not the fucking Beatles going to Hamburg to find their destiny."

"No, it's not. In the great scheme of history, it's just a piece of fun."

"Well, then. You'll get over it."

Eyeroll. *Do you know how crass that comes across, Clay?* And a deep breath.

"With the greatest of respect, Clay, fuck you. I do not plan to 'get over it'. I said it's just a piece of fun, but that's why it matters. Marden Combe is a shithole of the first water. Nothing happens here. Nothing good has ever come out of here. If we stay here all our lives, dying will be the best thing that ever happens to us.

"So yes, it's a piece of fun. And no, it's way more than that. It's the hope of escape. It's the dream in our waking lives that makes all the crap worth enduring—the crummy job or the even crummier no-job."

A father who was too distant. A step-mom who was too close. But I didn't say it. Nobody else's business.

Clay shook his head. "I can't be responsible for the crap in your lives, Kai." It was a whisper.

Jake turned back to his guitar and started adjusting his pedal board. He wasn't going to get involved if he could help it.

"Okay," Clay continued, "you'd better cancel it—"

"Your band. Your tour. Haven't you got the balls to cancel it yourself?"

"I thought…you could find a stand-in for the tour. If you wanted it that much."

"A stand-in? And keep the band going afterwards, Clay? Is that what you want? This band as your bolthole, waiting for you to return when the new job settles down?"

I let that sink in, then asked him, "Can you commit to that?"

"Shit! I don't know."

"Don't know? Or don't want to tell us?"

"Put it on hold. We can put the band on hold, can't we?"

"How long for?" I asked him.

"I don't fucking know! I'll be flying over to the US quite a bit. And there's a bunch of guys in Japan I'll need to work with. Six months, maybe?"

And then it hit me. I knew why Clay couldn't meet my eye.

"The Cherry Tree. You must have known about this last night, and you didn't say a fucking word. We're already in the Last Chance Saloon. This is Boot-fucking-Hill."

I'd struck true. His mouth hung open, and the longer it stayed that way, the more certain I was.

"Y-yes, Kai. I had the offer, but I didn't know if I was going to take it. Honest, guys. But I thought it over, slept on it, and knew I had to take my chance."

Well, it *might* be true, but my money was on Clay being too chicken to stuff the band in front of Simon. It had been too long a pause, while he crafted a damage-limitation lie.

"This'll cost us our Saturday slot," I said. "You know that, don't you? Simon knows we won't find a new singer in time."

"One of you could—"

"Simon's already got a plan to fill our slot, else he wouldn't have given us 'the talk' last night. He's a lovely guy, but he's a businessman too."

"He wouldn't do that to you, Kai. You're one of his golden… kids."

Well, it was true, about being a 'golden kid' at least. Simon had taken me under his wing when I first got the notion I might become Kai. But that didn't change a thing because Simon taught self-reliance and owning the consequences even while he was still putting the pieces back together, with himself as the prime example.

"You know better than that," I said. "He owes the band nothing. He owes me nothing. And neither of us would have it any other way."

But I did owe Simon. Maybe what I owed him was enough notice to give another band a clear shot at the residency.

Which was all very noble but not the issue at hand. *Time to wrap this shit up, Kai.*

"You said six months," I began.

Six months. Six months without a band. I felt the dread rise up like a wave, ready to pull me under. The Clayton Paul Blues Band was my life.

Had been my life.

Six months though. Six months was more than enough time to build a *new* band. If I could pull the rest of the guys through.

Jake was in shock, biting his lip. His eyes darted about the room, to me, to Clay, back to the fretboard, where spider fingers shaped chaotic chords.

"No good. Jake, you don't want to be six months without a band, do you?"

Jake put on his best rabbit-in-headlights gurn.

Bad move, Kai. This isn't 'pulling the guys through'.

But maybe I hadn't screwed up. Maybe Clay sensed that the worst was over.

"No, you're right," he said. "It's not fair to ask you to wait. It's been a blast with you guys, but all good things come to an end."

He held out his hand. "Kai? No hard feelings? Maybe play

together someday when all this is done?"

I shrugged. But…why burn bridges? If I'd had the chance, wouldn't I have done the same?

"Maybe." I shook his hand. "Good luck with your escape from Alcatraz, Thames Valley. And don't cancel the tour. I want to think about that."

He shook hands with Jake too. There was an awkward silence. Jake went back to his guitar and began dabbing harmonics.

"Look, guys," Clay said. "I'd like to stay and say goodbye to Jamie, but I guess you'll want to talk over what's next, and you won't want me around for that. I've paid the Band Hut man, so the room's yours till ten o'clock anyway. Least I could do. Okay?"

The Band Hut man. *Clay, his name's Wally. He's been the set-up guy for two fucking years here, and you can't be arsed to remember his name.*

Clay's harmonicas and microphone were still in his flight case, unopened. He picked the case up, squared his shoulders, and left the Band Hut, leaving us to pick up the shards of a blues band.

Fuck.

*

JAMIE WASN'T BEST pleased when he arrived a few minutes later.

"No Clay? I thought I saw him driving past as I got off the bus. What happened?"

Jake let me do the explaining. When I'd finished, Jamie's comment was brief.

"Stupid bugger."

Huh? I expected more support from my brother than that.

Jamie saw my worried frown.

"Easy, Kai. I didn't mean you. You were right to force the issue. He wants us to give him a free pass back into the band if it all goes tits-up. No dice. Shame about the tour—"

"Yeah. Shame Clay's going to miss it."

Jamie started to say something, but I rode right over him.

"I've been thinking about it, guys. We've put a lot of work into rehearsing for this tour, and I don't want it to go to waste. It's a vital part of the Plan."

The Plan, which was to practise like crazy and hone the set with a tour—yes, like the Beatles, but in less time. We had Deller Studio A booked in Oxford for our return, ready to record a sizzling demo to impress the A&R men in London. Get a record deal. Spend the rest of our lives playing music and counting money. And spend it somewhere that was not Marden Combe.

Meanwhile, Jamie was being practical. "But we've got no singer, no van, and no driver…"

"Hey, we can fix that stuff. Advertise for a singer. Find one who can drive a van. Hire a van."

"That takes time, Kai."

"We've got two weeks. One of us could sing."

"Not like Clay."

Jake perked up. *Shit! The slumbering giant awakes…*

"Yeah. What Kai said. One of us could sing."

But not you, Jake. Please, not you. Behind Jake, Jamie rolled his eyes. One thing we agreed on.

"There'll be a lot of admin too," said Jamie.

"I guess that's mostly me, then," I replied. "You guys have got day jobs."

Jamie nodded. "Jake—anything else on your mind?"

"Yeah. Can we play now, bossman?"

"Yeah. I think we need to."

I fussed around with the drum kit a bit for the sake of something to do. Jamie plugged his bass into the studio's amp and twiddled a few knobs until it sounded okay.

No microphone. Clay had taken his away with him. So I begged Wally, the front desk guy, to find us a decent mic.

And, of course, with budget rehearsal studios, nothing's free; everything's an extra. Wally played hardman with me. He took the tack that, yes, Clay had paid, but that didn't include unlimited mics. He pointed to the price list on the wall.

"Ten quid, Wally? You cannot be serious. Show me something that's worth that much."

So, he reached into a drawer and pulled out an offering. "It's a Shure. Top-line mic."

I shook my head. "It's a fucking museum piece. Look—the windshield's dented. Somebody's dropped this, hard. And the lead's missing a grub screw. You can't charge ten quid for this shit."

He opened his mouth to reply.

I wagged a finger at him. "Here's five quid and a five-star review for your customer service. Promise. Okay?"

"Done."

I set up the mic—it crackled, and I wondered whether I'd sold my review too cheap. We argued about who'd go first, and Jake won.

Live, we always set up a special mic for Jake to do backing vocals. I mixed it up, prominent in the stage monitors, but it didn't go anywhere near the main bus. We endured it so the audience didn't have to.

That trick wasn't going to work in the studio though. We had to be fair; we had to let him try. Jake gave it his all.

"'Serves You Right to Suffer', guys," he said, grinning and bizarrely aware of the irony of his audition choice. "John Lee Hooker."

Indeed, a prophetic choice. Jamie and I set up a slow blues pattern, and Jake dived in on guitar, catching the groove. He took the guitar down to nothing and growled the opening lyric. Then he searched for a pitch, found a note he liked and hung on to it, while Jamie struggled on bass to find the key he'd chosen. Then Jake played a riff in the original key, clashing horribly with Jamie's bass. Jake glared at Jamie, who reverted to the original key.

Jake choked the guitar back again. His voice found another note he liked. This time, Jamie stuck to the original key and earned another black look from Jake. It went on like that a long time, back and forth between random keys, and whatever Jamie did was wrong. After a couple of verses, Jamie launched into an unmistakable this-IS-the-end-of-the-song fretboard run before Jake had a chance to start a new verse.

Jake turned to me. I guessed Jamie was in all kinds of bad books for pissing about with the bass line.

"How was that?" he asked, puppy-dog eager to start his new singing career.

"That was…astonishing, Jake."

It was all I could think of to say. It was even true. Technically 'astonishing' could mean bad as well as good. But as I saw a puppy-dog joy fill his eyes, I knew I'd said the wrong thing. The unvarnished truth would hurt him deeply.

Jamie saved me. "What happened to the guitar, Jake? I don't think I caught much guitar."

"That? No. I guess it was a bit sparse."

"We do need your guitar. Very much."

"I'm not sure I could do both. I could learn."

I jumped in. "Let's make it our plan B." By which I meant our plan Z. "Your guitar is too important to our sound. Jamie? Did you want to try?"

Jamie liked to bounce about on stage, so I couldn't see how that was going to work, live. Despite that, he wanted to try out, so we ran through a couple of numbers. He wasn't bad — we already knew his pitch and timbre were good enough for backing vocals — but he wasn't happy.

"You don't have to tell me, guys. That was shit. I can't syncopate against the bass line. I can't put any feeling behind it. Not the way Clay could. Your turn, Kai."

So I pulled the mic stand around to the side of the kit, set it up so it didn't get in the way of the hi-hat, and we gave it a go. I picked 'I Come from the Blues', which was one of Clay's compositions. It had fallen out of the set sometime in the last six months, but I loved Clay's soft, jazzy butterscotch vocals on it. If it had been up to me, it would still be in the set, but Clay had said he wanted to move on.

Where did I come from? I come from the blues.
Where am I going? I'm going to lose.
Where is my future? I'm sure I have none.
Where is my hope? My hope is all gone.

I've always sung along — off-mic and under my breath — so I didn't have any trouble fitting the words in the right places. And I've got decent pitch and rhythm. So I think I did all right.

Now, Jamie wouldn't meet my eye.

"What?" I demanded. "What was wrong with that?"

He mumbled something.

"I can't hear you, bro. What did he say, Jake?"

Jake looked away. He didn't want to get involved in any squall between me and my brother. Besides, he'd used up all his words for the day.

"I'm not sure how to put this, Kai. You've got a good voice. It's, well…not very, well, rock'n'roll. No…grit. Too pure. Sorry."

"I see."

"Look, we'll ask around our friends. Social media. There's got to be something online."

I didn't say anything. I was thinking lots though. About how I'd discovered that this was something I really wanted to do. And could do. All that bullshit about 'too pure' — no, my voice was good. Damn you, Jamie. I will sing. In this band, if possible. If not…

The rest of the practice was conducted with icy politeness. We mostly played instrumentals. Jamie sang the few bits where we absolutely needed the vocal cues. I sat behind the kit pretending to be okay.

It was crap.

Chapter Two

Monday, September 19, 2016
Shakeup + 1

FIRST THING THE next day, I made the call to Simon from my bedroom, better known as the Kai-Zone. It was also my recording studio and basically where I lived. At its heart sat my no-squeak command chair and a fanless PC running Ubuntu Linux. Add a decent condenser microphone, pop-shield, and over-ear headphones, and that was the basic recording set-up. Because real soundproofing was fucking expensive, I'd hacked together an aluminium frame — the Cage — with pegged-on duvets, blankets, rugs, wraps, throws, curtains, and whatever else I could scrounge to make it as soundproof as possible. I sometimes thought of it as my Bat Cave minus Bruce Wayne's wealth. It was as private as possible to get in Dad's house.

So, yes, I called Simon, feeling more than a little nervous but bolstered by the warmth and gloom of my cage.

Jeff answered the phone, happy to chat about the weather, the upcoming Germany tour, and the new guest beer they were getting in.

But I stopped him: "I've got something important to talk about."

"I'll get Simon," he replied.

Simon's style was to listen and to ask a question or two. He almost never gave advice, even if you asked for it. Especially if you asked for it. So I didn't.

By the end of the call, and without a word of advice from Simon, I'd turned a bunch of half-baked ideas into a plan that had all the major pieces blocked out and a couple of pages of ideas that had sprung out of his questions. Somewhere in there, I'd also given him my thoughts on a couple of upcoming bands who might be able to fill our residency. And we had two months grace to get our act together—kind of a reward for giving him proper warning.

"I don't know why you called me, Kai," he said. "You've got everything covered. But you know you can always call for advice if the need arises. I'd wish you good luck, but you won't need it. Have a good time."

*

STILL IN THE Kai-Zone, I booted up the PC as a digital sound recorder and sang at the top of my voice, trying to inject some gutsiness. Dad was out at work. Cassie was just out. So, I could make as much noise as I liked.

I alternated that with listening to my top ten great voices. People with names like Redding, Franklin, Sledge, and James from my dad's collection. Newcomers with names like Kyla Brox and George Ezra from my own. Male, female—I didn't care. I was looking for anything I could use. Timbres, phrasings. Anything.

Frustration wasn't the word for it. Sadly, I wasn't born with a voice like any of those guys. Jamie, damn his cotton socks, was right. My voice lacked distinctive timbre.

After a couple of hours, I thought I was getting there, but my voice had started to pack up. I hadn't warmed up, hoping it might help me get that roughness. More internet searching followed, looking up remedies for a sore throat: rest, plus stuff we didn't have in the house. So, I made myself a cup of black tea and sang 'Walking in the Air' in a fit of contrariness.

Soft and pure, that's your voice, Kai. Better learn to live with it. If you want to cause sonic mayhem, stick to your drums.

*

I GOT A DM from Jamie:

JAMIE: *Have u tried our website?*

KAI: *Whats up?*

JAMIE: *Just try it. lmk*

Downstairs in the kitchen, I switched on the family laptop and opened up a browser. Clay had always done a good job with our social media; he was a programmer, websites his bread and butter.

I wasn't sure what I was looking for—the banner came up fine. Looked like Clay had posted a few news items in the last couple of days. Then I looked closer.

KAI: *Wtf???*

JAMIE: *Yeah. Hijacked.*

KAI: *Clay?*

JAMIE: *Has to be. Link to some new band. Follow it.*

I clicked through:

KAI: *scheming bastard. thought he had new IT job*

JAMIE: *Nope. Boyband.*

KAI: *Sellout*

JAMIE: *Can u login?*

Good idea. I had admin rights too. Jamie didn't.

KAI: *No. Fckrs changed the pwd*

JAMIE: *Tried other sites. Same.*

The long and short—Clay had linked all the old social media accounts to new ones, promoting his new career in a new band. And locked them down so we couldn't post to them.

The one exception was our YouTube channel, where we kept gig footage. That had been nuked outright.

The new sites were slick. Some serious work had gone into

them. This wasn't an overnight hack job. He'd known, and he'd put long hours into creating his new brand. When the moment had come, he'd just had to flick the switch.

But us? It would take months to build up a social media footprint from zero. We had two weeks.

KAI: *TL;DR. We're fucked.*

JAMIE: *Yep. Ideas?*

KAI: *I'm not giving up*

JAMIE: *Never give up. Never surrender ;-)*

KAI: *?*

JAMIE: *Never mind. SciFi reference.*

KAI: *First thing is a website.*

JAMIE: *Can u set up websites now? I'm supposed to be working.*

KAI: *We need a name, quick*

JAMIE: *We need a singer first*

KAI: *I volunteer*

JAMIE: *Bet you've been singing all morning. How's the voice?*

KAI: *Shot. Fair cop.*

JAMIE: *Hahahaha*

KAI: *John Smith Blues Band*

JAMIE: *What if the singer doesn't turn out to be called John Smith?*

JAMIE: *Oh, right. Pink Floyd. Which one's Pink? None of them.*

KAI: *John Doe?*

JAMIE: *Could be. Why do we need Blues Band?*

KAI: *Coz we're a blues band. Duh*

JAMIE: *I mean, we could do something like Blues Ocean*

KAI: *We're a jazz band now? And what have you been watching? Heist movies?*

JAMIE: *Never mind. Boss is prowling. Choose a name, I'll support u.*

JAMIE: *Cul8r*

Busy.

I went for John Doe's Blues. And I nabbed johndoesblues.com, plus all the obvious social media accounts to go with it.

Oh, and Clay's new band was a soul band, not a boyband. He might have been a weasel, but he was at least a classy weasel.

*

I GOT BUSY setting up those accounts—following other local bands, pushing out invites, asking anybody and everybody to link to us. I built a vanilla landing page, stuck some band photos on it, and the dates of our tour. Cross-linked everything.

Ding!

An email. From Clay.

Hi Kai

Sorry about yesterday. I didn't handle it very well, and I feel a bit bad. You guys are OK.

I guess you'll have seen by now that I've reclaimed my media presence. It's <u>my</u> name, you see, so I still control what goes on there. No choice. It's part of my contract, so it was never going to be up for discussion. No hard feelings, eh?

I'm kind of glad you want to carry on with the tour. But you really can't use my name. I'm going out on a limb here, 'cause I haven't contacted the venues yet, and I really ought to have done. Gives you a few days to sort out a new singer. Anyway, I've attached a list of contacts, so you can tell them about the change of line-up and your new name. Whatever you choose so long as my name ain't there.

Clay

Thanks, Clay. You're still a weasel.

And @JohnDoesBlues has twenty-three followers on Twitter. No, bugger me, it's twenty-four. Clay was following us. *Thanks, weasel.*

*

JAMIE SHOWED UP after work. He spent ten minutes being pleasant to Dad and Cassie, while I hopped from one foot to the other. Duty done, we grabbed a couple of beers from the fridge and headed for the Kai-Zone.

Leaving aside a minimal wardrobe and the bed, where Jamie parked his butt, the Kai-Zone was mostly the Cage and barely enough space for my acoustic guitar, some MIDI drum pads, and a couple of small-but-effective studio monitors mounted on the wall. I used the Cage for my voiceover work — audiobooks for self-pubbed authors and advertising for local company websites. It wasn't a proper job; I couldn't live on what it brought in, but my voice *was* good at it, and it had paid for quite a bit of my gear.

Aside from all that, there was just room for a bedside table, now holding Jamie's beer. I hooked back the Cage's curtains and twisted the command chair around to face Jamie. I took a swig of my beer and set it down on the computer desk.

"So, have you found a singer yet?" Jamie opened.

"No, Jamie, I have not. I have been spending most of the day trying to build up our social media presence from absolute zero. It feels like I've reached the boiling point of nitrogen."

"Which is?"

"Never mind. Chemistry jokes aren't funny even the first time. Suffice to say, it's hard work, and I'm nowhere near where we need to be. I was going to go down to the student union tomorrow and put up a Singer Wanted notice."

"That's a long shot. We're about two weeks into the academic year, if that. Do you really think we'll find anyone willing to bunk off lectures for two weeks?"

"It's as likely as finding somebody working and willing to

bunk off."

"Fair point. It might be worth putting notices in music shops if there were still any music shops left in Marden Combe."

"You're saying we're screwed?"

"No. Just that we're not going to find anyone local."

I had an idea. "How about we ask Dave Green?"

Jamie's eyebrows rose. "It's an interesting thought."

"Well, he's local. He's in a band. He can sing."

"He's in a *rival* band."

"Now is the time for statesmanship. Let us extend the hand of friendship." I could fake pompous.

"But he's an asshole."

True, but… "It's only for a week."

"Ten days, plus travel time."

"I get your point. Ten days in a van with an asshole. I'd kill myself."

"No, you wouldn't. You'd kill him."

I grinned. "You know me too well, brother. Can I offer you another beer?"

He nodded, and we went down to the kitchen. Dad and Cassie had decamped to the lounge and were presumably channel surfing, so we had the kitchen to ourselves. I'd followed him, partly so I could choose my own beer but also because it was a lot less claustrophobic for two people than the Kai-Zone.

"So what do we do?" Jamie asked, settling at the kitchen table. "Have you put out the word on Twitter?"

"Yes. I figured we had to make a start there, but nothing. Is there such a thing as a singers wanted website?"

"It's the internet. Of course there is. We just have to find the one that everybody is using. Google is our friend."

Other than at mealtimes, the family laptop was always ready on the kitchen table, but Jamie opened up his high-powered work laptop and indicated for me to take the family antique.

*

GOOGLE WAS INDEED our friend but lacked discrimination. We found a dozen marketplace sites, so we registered with the first, then argued about the wording of the ad. Some sites charged money to advertise.

"What the hell—do we really have a choice?" Jamie asked and paid up.

"'Blues singer wanted for imminent tour and recording. Must be available to travel to Germany. Harmonica preferred'. You sure about that, Kai?"

"No. Make it 'instruments would be a plus'."

"And I'll mention the driving. And a van."

"As a plus."

"Agreed. We're asking a fuck of a lot, Kai."

"Yep. You know what they say. 'The impossible takes a little longer'."

I hit submit. "First one's done. I say we do the next three on the list. The rest look like they're US, or minor players. Then we wait."

Chapter Three

Tuesday, September 20, 2016
T Minus Nine

TUESDAY. NINE DAYS to go. Scene: the kitchen table.

We'd got a ferry crossing booked for a week Thursday, with a gig the same night. And a return ferry for two Sundays after that. Clay knew social media and computers, and he'd worked his ass off to fill the time between with paying gigs. Not just Clay. To be fair, Jamie had also found us a gig. Out of a potential ten evenings, we'd got nine confirmed gigs, with just one day off on the Tuesday. Even there, we had a possible lead; one venue hadn't said no. We also had a hell of a lot of driving all over Germany to get us from gig to gig and a long drive back, Saturday night through Sunday morning from Berlin to the coast.

Accommodation-wise, none of the venues offered anything.

Hotels were out—too pricey. We'd be camping or sleeping in the van. With luck, we might cadge a fan's floor to sleep on. If we could find any fans. Maybe that was the real reason Clay had looked for another band. He was a pampered city boy who couldn't slum it. No rock'n'roll in his soul.

I ran another search for lodgings. Half an hour wasted trawling Airbnb for places that would accept a band. No luck.

So, I went back upstairs to the Cage and switched to editing our rehearsal tapes from Sunday to see if there was anything good enough to put up on our new website. Some of the instrumentals were okay, but okay didn't get you gigs.

Then I had a rummage through our back catalogue. Like most bands, we'd recorded a few demo tracks in a pro studio with an engineer who knew what he was doing. And we'd got the individual 24-bit instrument tracks, so we could remix or record. All sitting neatly organised on a portable hard drive.

You'd think I'd have learned, but I gave it another go, not pushing my voice this time. Clay's vocals in the phones gave me my guide track, and to be honest, I'd played these songs often enough that I knew Clay's part as well as my own.

After a couple of hours, I had passable versions of the much-covered 'Walkin' Blues' and Elmore James's 'Dust My Broom'. We'd picked the keys to suit Clay's voice, so it wasn't my best register. But I'd gone for a breathy, close-miked sound that didn't require strenuous dynamics.

My voice plus digital FX plus Clay's backing band equals John Doe's Blues, mark 1.

Our first recorded tracks.

Up they went.

I DM'd Jamie: *Check out the website.*

Then I sat and chewed my nails. Even if he'd seen my DM, Jamie mightn't get to listen to the tracks for a couple of hours, depending on when he next got a break. So, I didn't literally chew my nails, but it was at the back of my mind while I recorded a voiceover track for a local bridal wear shop's promo video. And when my phone buzzed, I happily blew the take to find out what Jamie thought.

JAMIE: *You did those? Remixed Clay trax? Good job.*

KAI: *Thought you'd be angry.*

JAMIE: *Was. Thought it through. We need media urgent. It's a start.*

KAI: *Thanks for faint praise.*

JAMIE: *Welcome. We've got old backing tracks for you to do a couple more.*

KAI: *This evening?*

JAMIE: *Don't wait for me. We need to get stuff out there.*

KAI: *Got it.*

*

BY FIVE IN the afternoon, I'd got a couple more tracks mixed and uploaded, but it felt like I'd pretty much exhausted those resources. I'd switched back to the Rainbow Brides voiceover and was pretty much there when my phone buzzed again. It was a text from Jake. Jake was a fan of all things retro, especially guitars, and had no social media presence. So, a text from him was an event. This was brief and to the point. Like his speech.

JAKE: *Barrel Orange 8*

Never trust predictive text, Jake. I would go to the Barrel Organ at eight o'clock tonight.

*

THE BARREL ORGAN had been many things in its time. Trendy had never been on the list. In past times, it must have been thick with smoke, badly lit, with a beer-sticky tile floor and cigarette butts underfoot. If they hadn't demolished and rebuilt it as part of a brownfield renovation, the original building would actually have come into vogue. But some pubs were destined to always miss the parade. Its latest incarnation was still badly lit — fluorescent tubes, like a motorway café — and someone had decided the walls needed to be painted in a red that was closer to burgundy than to blood.

So why the Barrel Organ? It definitely wasn't the beer. My money was on Jamie's influence. If my brother had had any say in the matter, we were there because of the bar staff. The landlady, a short Polish woman for whom the word buxom had been invented, seemed able to hire any number of Eastern European barmaids willing to wear tight black tops cut low. I didn't complain; the more aggressively male punters left the tables free, tending to cluster around the bar. There, they would chat with the barmaids about how much they loved Poland or Bulgaria on the flimsy basis of a stag do in Budapest five years previously. It could be quite a struggle to actually get close enough to the bar to buy drinks, but brave Jamie always bought his round at the Barrel Organ.

I was a little late getting there and found Jake with Jamie at a table near the door. They sat with an older guy with a florid complexion and curly fair hair, all with glasses nearly empty. Jake saw me enter — the other guys watching the show at the bar — and waved me over. He introduced me as 'our drummer, Kai', and the older guy as Neale. Neale, whose age I guessed at forty-ish, drained the last of his Guinness and pushed his glass over to Jamie, who immediately headed to the bar.

I waited for 'the Look'.

Neale obliged. The Look had three parts, the first, a long inspection of my face. I had high cheekbones with a good line down to my narrow jaw, and I kept my hair quite short but well-groomed and was very careful to eliminate what little facial hair I had. The second part was a flicker of the eyes down to my chest and then hips. The third part returned to another inspection of my face, looking for details such as whether my hair was dyed or natural.

During all of this, I tried to stand still without posing and always smiled, making sure to include my eyes in the smile. Anything else would be rude.

The Look was short, as they go. Neale stood and offered me a hand to shake, his skin firm and dry but rough. Manual labour? He seemed a little unsteady for only eight-fifteen — a possible warning bell.

Jake rose to the occasion and introduced us. "Neale, here, is a fiddle player. And a driver. He owns a van."

Ah. I'd better smile, then. But, fiddle? We weren't a folk band all of a sudden, were we? I took a seat facing him.

"Hi, Neale. Pleased to meet you."

"The pleasure is all mine…Kai."

Little pause before my name. Optional part of the Look.

Pleasure? Perhaps. But his eyes kept slipping back towards the bar, nevertheless. They must have had a riveting conversation while waiting for me, Jake the mute plus two guys obsessed with the barmaids' racks.

"You're from Ireland if I'm not mistaken."

"And there's no hiding my accent from you, Kai. I'm a Dubliner by birth, but I've been living here these last fifteen years or more."

"Hence your fondness for the stout tonight."

"I wouldn't call them stout. Buxom." He twinkled.

The gods preserve me from Irish wits. Move on.

"So, what's Jake been telling you?"

"Ah, he's told me that you're in a bit of a corner, he has."

"Well, I'm not sure I'd put it quite that way, but yes, we've a tour set up that we'd rather not cancel, and we've been let down by a former band member."

"Rather not cancel? Penalty clauses? Money on the line?"

"No, nothing like that. There's not a lot of money involved. It's more a matter of reputation, of keeping up the momentum. A bit of pride at stake. And we've got some plans to do some recording when we get back. We've got a studio booked over in Oxford. We could cancel, but doing the tour would really sharpen our playing."

He smiled and leaned back. People's eyes *don't* twinkle with mischief. But…

"Well, it happens I'm at leisure for a week or two, and I'm up for the *craic*. I've been in the business a few years, and I like to help the youngsters just startin' out. But I do have my expenses to think about. Fuel, of course, and meals. That's food *and* drink, of course. I don't play dry."

"So, you're expecting to play? Has Jake told you what *kind* of music we play?"

"Oh, yes. I'll be able to fit me fiddle around whatever you want. And I can use a mixing desk, too, if I'm not playing."

An instrument that we didn't need, and a skill I already had in spades…

"That all sounds very useful, Neale. But we're racing ahead here. How did you come to find out about us?"

"Ah, well, I was Jake's guitar teacher briefly. I don't only play the fiddle. It happens that, right now, I don't have a guitar to me name, but that'll not be an impediment."

"It was a choice between the guitar and his fiddle," Jake put in helpfully.

Now it was Neale's turn to look annoyed. "A little matter of a debt incurred that needed unexpected settlement. I don't think you really needed to bring that up."

"So, the chance to earn a bit of cash," I said, stepping in, "and perhaps not be in the country for a few days—that comes at a good time for you?"

"I don't say it will. I don't say it won't. All I'm sayin' is I think I can help you."

Where the hell was Jamie? At this rate, I was going to have

to negotiate this on my own.

"And we can help you," I continued. "I'm sure we can pay for fuel. We'll be self-catering on the food for the most part. Eating in posh restaurants is outside our budget."

"And the drinks?"

"Whatever drinks the management provide, we'll share equally. No favourites on this tour. I hope you can live with that."

"Well, maybe."

"I tell you what, Neale. Midtour, we have a day with no gigs. We could do some busking to drum up some custom for the gigs and hopefully earn a bit of cash. Play your fiddle, and we'll earn a lot more. That'll top up the drinks fund. Okay?"

"I suppose so. All right, it's a deal."

"Great. In principle. You need to rehearse with us as well."

"Oh, sure, sure."

Hmm. Could have been worse.

Jamie returned with drinks. We got down to talking about music: What was in our set. What he could play on. His solo spot. Yes. A few jigs and reels. Just what our rock'n'roll audience would be looking for. Shall we play 'Stand by Your Man', too, while we're about it, for all the country and western fans in our audience?

If I'd bitten my tongue any more, I'd have swallowed it.

Chapter Four

Wednesday, September 21, 2016
Cancellation

STILL BREAKFAST TIME, and I got the first DM of the day. From Clay.

Hi Kai

You need to know the cats out of the bag. Got a DM from the guy at Wiesbaden. Said he'd seen the new website and wanted to confirm my new band would still be doing the gig. So I told him no, but the backing band would be interested…

I stopped reading and said, 'Oh crap', which wasn't a good idea as Cassie was at the table with me, drinking coffee.

"Mind your language, Kai. Your father would not approve."

"Huh? Did I say something, *step*mother, dear? Must have slipped out. Dreadfully sorry."

She sniffed, not remotely deceived by my reply. Our normal conversation ranged between icily polite and carelessly insincere. Our extremes involved shouting, storming about the house, and slamming doors, while Dad metaphorically wrung his hands.

I tried to be normal with Cassie, with distant being the preferred variation. I did try to love her, even, at first. After all, she'd saved Dad from alcoholism, and maybe worse, when Mum… wasn't with us anymore. And she'd helped me and Jamie because we were part of the deal.

But I couldn't love her. Not like I loved Mum. That wouldn't be right. So instead, I did try to be polite. Normal. Jamie was a hell of a lot better at it than me. But he had a regular job and lived under a different roof.

She tried a different tack. "Something's wrong. Can I help?"

"It's okay. I can deal with it. It's just band stuff."

"Well, I know the band is important to you. So, it's important to me too. Just tell me what's troubling you. Talking helps."

"I know that, but, really, it's not a big deal. Please, leave it. I'll sort it."

My phone vibrated in my hand. Sharp-eyed Cassie saw my momentary glance.

"Well, I can see you're busy," she said, "so I won't keep you. See you later."

She stood up and left, taking her coffee with her.

*

CASSIE'S INSTINCT WAS bang on. It was bad news. Wiesbaden had cancelled via a very polite email:

> *Esteemed Blues Band minus Clayton Paul. Your engagement September 30 is cancelled for cause of band break up.*
>
> *We are understanding and will not seek reparations as reliable local musicians already engaged.*
>
> *Dieter Juch.*

I responded to Dieter's scuzzy English in my own scuzzy German, the gist being that we had recruited a new singer and would be honouring our tour commitments. We appreciated that Dieter had filled the gig, but if the reliable musicians were to let him down, John Doe's Blues (link to website with two demos) would be happy to step in.

Fat chance.

*

THE REST OF the morning's news was better. At least no one else called to cancel, and when we'd got a few bites on muzomart.com, I'd looked closer and decided no. One, an Elvis wannabe — Costello, not Presley — looked great, but his voice wobbled all over the place. A couple of singer-songwriter types had posted, looking for a platform for their own songs. The best of the bunch was an old guy, about sixty, wearing shades and a *Blues Brothers* suit. Yes, he had a great voice. Yes, he played a great harmonica. But how would a sixty-year-old, bald white guy cope with life on the road? What if he forgot to take his meds, or worse, forgot the words?

Then, I got a text from Jake:

Can I help?

Sweet.

But Jake, you still used texts, FFS. How was a noob like you going to solve the internet and find us a singer from zero?

Still, what harm could it do? So, I called him. Rather, I texted him, and he called me back when he got a break at work. I started to explain about the internet to him.

"Yes," he said. "I know all that stuff."

"But you don't do social media or anything…"

"Not anymore."

"Oh?"

"Long story. I got hooked as a kid. Fourteen, fifteen years old. Online gaming, mostly, but social media too. I spent hours a day, every day, surfing. But I was careless, used my dad's credit card, and before I knew what happened, some bastard stole both my identity and my dad's and siphoned a shitload of money out of his account. I was devastated and went through rehab. Voluntarily. Bottom line now, I don't put myself in temptation's way. But this is important."

My preconceptions shattered. Little fragments of assumptions rolled around the floor and disappeared under the kitchen cupboards.

I began a sentence, hoping the ending would come to me. "Yes, but what if you, you know…"

"Get hooked again? I don't think so. I'm not a child anymore. That kid is gone, and the urge to surf is gone with him. But I remember everything he used to do."

So, I explained what Jamie and I were up to. Told him about the Wiesbaden gig being blown out.

"Yeah. That all makes sense. I've got a few ideas that won't conflict with what you're doing. I'll let you know if anything turns up. Okay, bye, Kai."

And he hung up.

Wow. The things you discovered about your bandmates. Still waters run deep. Wasn't that what they said?

*

TWO MORE EMAILS, two more gigs blown out. Shit. And shit squared. I shared the joyful news with Jamie.

KAI: *There's a big hole in the middle of the week.*

JAMIE: *Not good. How's the balance sheet?*

KAI: *We're in the red. Going to have to make some cuts.*

JAMIE: *Think of it as a holiday, with gigs thrown in. Nobody minds paying for a holiday.*

KAI: *Nobody with a job, you mean.*

JAMIE: *Hey, I'll tide you over.*

KAI: *That's not what I meant. I don't want charity.*

JAMIE: *I'm not offering charity. You'll pay me back.*

KAI: *Wouldn't have it any other way.*

JAMIE: *OK. I'll keep looking.*

KAI: *Thanks. See ya tomorrow to check out the van.*

JAMIE: *Sure.*

*

AND LATER:

JAMIE: *Hey, meant 2 ask, what dyou think abt Neale?*

KAI: *Did you brief him?*

JAMIE: *The Look?*

KAI: *That.*

JAMIE: *Just the Official Line. Name. No Pronouns.*

KAI: *Thanks. Standard inspection. Well-behaved.*

JAMIE: *Good. I was trying not to watch you two.*

KAI: *Of course. You see Gosia?*

JAMIE: *Don't know who you mean.*

KAI: *One of the bar staff. Female. From Łódź.*

JAMIE: *How dyou know?*

KAI: *I talk to her. She thinks you're cute.*

JAMIE: *Really?*

KAI: *No. But you might be cute, she says, if the crown of your head is any guide.*

JAMIE: *?*

JAMIE: *Oh. Ygot me. Am I really that bad?*

KAI: *You could always drink at the Star if the display of flesh bothers you…*

JAMIE: *The Barrel Organ is fine. And I was asking about Neale.*

KAI: *I'm still working out if that's the real Neale or just an act.*

JAMIE: *I thought he was okay. Just worried for you.*

KAI: *I can handle Neale.*

Chapter Five

Thursday, September 22, 2016
Van

THE VAN WAS okay. It was a van. It went, and it had a fairly decent space in the back for all our gear. A bench seat in the front would take three, maybe four, if two people didn't mind sharing a seat belt. Illegal, I knew. I was pretty sure the same was true of Neale's great plan to put one of us in the back with the gear. No seat belt. Still, if we did have a smash, we'd all be crushed by half a ton of stage gear, seat belt or no.

The van was white, with no logo. The sort tradesmen use. So, I'd been broadly right about Neale, though whether he was a plumber, a carpenter, or a general handyman, I couldn't tell. The van had a stonking great toolbox bolted to the floor.

I pointed to it. "No tools kept inside overnight. That what it says on the back door, Neale?"

"Yeah. I lied. That's evil of me. Some bugger wants to steal my tools, that's evil too. Fight evil with evil."

"You ever had a break-in?"

"Few times. The locks on these vans are a bit shit."

Right. So, we would store a few thousand quid's worth of gear in a van with 'bit shit' locks. Jamie was onto it. He waggled the handle. It spun too easily. He took his hand away, and the rear door floated open.

"Careful!" said Neale. "I've not got that fixed yet."

"Is it going to be fixed before we go?" Jamie asked. "I've got some nice bass gear I'd be really sad to lose."

"Trust me, it'll be okay. I've got me own fiddle in there too. I'm sharin' the risk with you."

"That's not the point. It's not even slightly secure. What if it opens while we're driving?"

Neale held up his hands. "I'll fix it. Don't worry."

He smiled, and I thought of leprechauns, rainbows, and pots of gold. And maidens gulled by the promise, *I'll pull out in time. Trust me.*

Chapter Six

Friday, September 23, 2016

CASSIE CORNERED ME when I came down for breakfast.

I groaned, but she pretended not to notice. It was catch-up time. Our weekly tête-à-tête as decreed by Dad. Part of us all 'being one family' and 'keeping the communications open'. Something he or Cassie had found in an American step-mothering book, I guessed.

"You seem very busy this week," she began. "Anxious."

I let the silence grow, then answered, just when she took a breath to ask again. "Not really. I mean, I don't really do anxious. But it's just normal stuff. Band stuff."

"Your grand tour."

Not sneering. Not condescending. She managed to insert a trace of awe, even. As if it were the eighteenth century. 'American

Stepmothering 101: Respecting Your Stepchild's Enthusiasms'.

"It's fine, Cassie. A little wobble, but Jamie and I are sorting it."

"Your singer quitting is just a wobble?"

That surprised me. But no snooping required. Jamie would have been okay with telling her. So, roll with it.

"Yes, it is just that. A wobble. We're a blues band. There's a lot of standard repertoire with the blues. We can adapt to whoever comes on board — play the songs they know."

"I do know about the blues, Kai. Jazz is more my thing, but I take pride in the blues too."

My people invented it. She didn't say it, not this time, but I heard it anyway. And that was genuine Cassie. She did love jazz, and she was, at least, very good friends with the blues.

*

It was just after…

It was just after Cassie had come on the scene and had begun to take Dad in hand. And Jamie and me. Because we all needed fixing.

We were all looking for something to fill the Mum-shaped holes in our lives. Jamie was sneaking into the drinks cupboard, thinking no one would notice his little thefts against the bigger backdrop of Dad's self-destruction.

Jamie said Dad was heading for huge smash, but then, so was Jamie. He'd been excluded from school for being drunk. Dad was on the verge of losing his job, but the union fought in his corner and convinced management to put him on garden leave for two months. Me, I learned to lock away all those difficult emotions where I didn't have to feel them.

Then Cassie showed up.

Cassie had known Dad since schooldays. Maybe she'd been Dad's first love? I don't know. Anyway, she'd heard the news about Mum through the internet grapevine. One day, she called up Dad out of the blue and sized him up in a long heart-to-heart. She showed up the next day and made it her mission to sort Dad out. That also meant sorting out Jamie and me because we were part of Dad's problems. None of us got much of a say in the matter.

Cassie saved Dad. I'd give her that. The first thing, all the booze went down the sink. The next, we all found ourselves on holiday, walking the north Cornish coastal path and camping each night. The weather was kind, and Cassie kept a smart eye out for any alcohol.

Jamie and I knew the drill — we were both in the Scouts — and between sunshine and exercise, Jamie turned himself around. I didn't think he'd ever stopped yomping since those days. Then, in one of those freak occurrences that shape your life, we found ourselves at an open-air summer festival at Polwithen. It was the first time either of us had seen a live band, and the first act we saw had been a local band.

At first, I just thought it was a bunch of old men, playing old music. But it wasn't Cassie's jazz. It was blues. The Blues. The singer sang about love gone wrong and played harmonica so haunting I felt my soul shiver. Then, the guitar came in, played slide-fashion, bittersweet as heartbreak, and I was home. Home with the blues.

*

"CLAY WAS GOOD," Cassie continued. "I just hope you can find someone else as good. You don't have much time."

"I know that. But we have the internet to help."

"And I do know about the internet. Your generation may have made it your own, but *my* generation created it."

I thought for a moment she was going to pat my hand, but if so, she thought better of it.

She changed tack. "Are you working today?"

I thought about it. There were about a zillion band things I ought to do, but earning some cash was certainly up there.

"Yes, there's an audiobook project I need to finish off. An indie author, willing to pay something close to the going rate. Four or five hours should do it."

"You'll take a proper break, won't you?"

"If you mean 'when can I run the vacuum cleaner?' then yes, I'll do about ninety minutes for starters. Is that okay?"

In other words, I'd like to go now.

*

IT'S AS WELL Cassie didn't ask what I was recording. She wouldn't have approved of the YA romance novel. *Young* Adult, so nothing too explicit. But Cassie had a blind spot about anything that wasn't pure M/F. She couldn't see why women couldn't just love men, and vice versa, 'like they're supposed to'.

And into the Cage I went for an interesting insight into the imagined lives of high school teens.

I just wished…

I wished someone would write a book about people like *me*.

Chapter Seven

Saturday, September 24, 2016
The Band Hut

WE WERE COOKING.

Instrumentals. Or rather, our normal songs minus the vocals. I had to say we were a pretty decent backing band. We'd run through a half dozen numbers, and I was feeling pretty pleased with the sound. All the iciness of the last practice had gone.

A final crash, and we'd wrapped up 'Hellhound on My Trail', a fine old blues number. Robert Johnson.

I looked over at Jamie, and he was looking back at me. I couldn't read his expression.

"What?" I asked, peeved.

"Set yourself up a mic, Kai."

"Why?"

"I was watching you. You were singing all the way through, weren't you?"

Well, yes, I had been. That was how I knew where I was in the song, by singing. Jake had been doing the same, inaccurately, but I'd tuned him out of my mind.

"I'm not trying to muscle in, Jamie. You said my voice was too pure."

"Well, I did, and it is. Let's make this our plan B. You're the only one who can sing without screwing up your instrument. So we have to roll with it."

"Just roll with it? Not rock?"

He smiled back at me. "Nope. Angel voices only get to roll."

"But I get a mic?"

"Yep. You want to do it, and we have to plan that you may do it. I know I didn't let you do it the first time. I was annoyed that I hadn't been able to do it myself, so I suppose I took it out on you. I'm sorry."

"That's okay. Thanks for coming round."

So, Jamie set it up for me and messed around with levels while I sang and got frustrated; Jamie didn't do tech well. It was *my* job, and I could have done it in half the time. But he'd just been really gracious; I swallowed my annoyance and said nothing.

We did 'Hellhound' again, and I messed up a couple of times because my voice was so much louder it was putting me off. But we played through and recovered, and everybody looked a hell of a lot happier.

A couple more songs and halfway through 'Rollin' and Tumblin' — Muddy — there was an interruption.

Neale. Forty minutes late.

"Don't mind me," he yelled across the chorus. "I'll just set up me fiddle here."

Which he did. And I lost my line of sight to Jake. At least I could still see the bass, but Neale's girth was a serious obstacle guitar-side.

From all the time he took tinkering and tweaking, I had to conclude the violin was a more complex piece of musical engineering than a drum kit. He scraped and sawed — gently, of course, not cutting across the music, no, no, no — and then adjusted and repeated.

I lost the plot. 'Rollin' and Tumblin' became crashing and burning as the song trainwrecked around me. I got a horrible glare from my brother. I didn't know what Jake made of it all; suddenly, I was thankful I couldn't see him past Neale's thick frame.

"Don't stop," called Neale, oblivious to the mayhem he'd caused. "I was enjoying that."

My mouth hung open for a long moment. It would be *so* tempting to kill him. I hadn't killed anyone before, and I did know that killing people was wrong, but it had become a surprisingly attractive idea. I reminded myself he had a van, and he could drive.

Smile, Kai. Smile.

"Glad you could make our practice," I said to him. "Shall we start again from your fiddle obbligato?"

"No, no, that was me tuning up. But sure, I could do one if you like."

Jake bent his head around Neale's belly and caught my eye. He made 'no-no-no' motions, waving his hands horizontally, palms down, and looking very worried.

"Ah, I think Jake is trying to say that 'Rollin' and Tumblin' is his guitar solo, Neale."

"Oh, that's no trouble. We could add another verse if you like."

"Like f—" And then I saw the glint in his eye. *You had me soooo wound up, you bugger.*

"Forgive me, gentlefolk, forgive me. It's a Gaelic wildness that takes me, that I need to test the humour of the new band. Well, I know you now; I'll stay the right side of the line."

Cleverly said. *Do I trust you, Neale, like my gullible heart says, or are you the con artist my head insists?*

He behaved himself. He tuned up in a few moments, set up a mic stand overhead, mic pointing down at the fiddle. Got it balanced and mixed on the desk as quick as I could do it.

"Slow blues," he said. "Key of A."

"'Stormy Monday', then," I said, and we slid into that tune.

Goosebumps. It was instant. In four bars, I was in territory I'd never been before, with plangent wails tugging at my soul. Just in time, I remembered to come in for my vocal, and then he was weaving around, over and under my voice, like a cat walking in and out between your feet.

Without warning, he disappeared, and my voice was out on its own. In the background, a gentle underpinning of my own rims remained, with Jamie stroking a soft shuffle down on the bottom string. Jake was mute, stock still and rapt. He rolled his eyes up, like he was reaching for…

A note. Lightly overdriven, it balanced the purity of my vocal. You got it, Jake. In the groove. Sweet.

*

IN THE PUB afterwards, Neale was in. No doubt.

Chapter Eight

Sunday, September 25, 2016
A Crash of Dreams

THE SOUND OF my dreams, crumbling.

She, yes, she has a gorgeous voice.

Jamie had just played me the demo track, a cover of Sting's 'Fields of Gold' that brought tears to my eyes.

"Are they all like that?"

"Mostly. There's some overlap with our own set. A couple of Robert Johnson standards. She sings a bit of everything, but blues and jazz are well covered."

"Okay. And she's available for the tour?"

"Yes."

"And afterwards? The recording in Oxford?"

Jamie shrugged. "She doesn't say."

"Well, what does she say? What's her name? What does she look like?"

"Not much. I mean, she's using an alias. No picture. But I think she's French."

Yeah. That could have been a trace of an accent in the Sting song. But it could have been put on.

Something was bothering me.

"No picture? I mean, this is all about performance in front of an audience. Why's she hiding what she looks like?"

"Ashamed of her appearance, are you thinking?"

"Something like that. I mean, nobody's going to worry if she's a huge big-momma type. Why wouldn't she post a picture of herself?"

But I was thinking 'disfigured'. And I was ashamed of myself for thinking it because, for all the prejudice I'd suffered at Sir Long-Dead-Parliamentarian School, I didn't know if *I* could handle that.

"I reckon she's a stunner, but she wants to be judged on her voice," Jamie said.

"Hah! Dream on."

He huffed. "Leave it alone, Kai. I am what I am. And you are what you are. I happen to like pretty, sexy girls. But I *desire* that voice. I want that voice to front our band."

"And what if she's neither?"

"Huh?"

"The world is full of women who aren't pretty or sexy, who aren't big-Black-momma. They're just plain Jane, flat-chested, more banjo clock than hourglass, all the way to princess-Fiona-looking and beyond. Do you still want that voice if the face or the body doesn't match the dream?"

Jamie made a face as though I'd broken his favourite toy. I wondered if I'd gone too far.

"Fair challenge," he said at last. "It would make a difference. I can't pretend it wouldn't. But she's got a hell of a voice. And she's the bird in the hand. We've got four days to the first gig. Princess Fiona is hired."

"Hang on. What about the rest of the band?"

"They aren't here. We need to make a decision now."

"What about me..." I began.

I glanced at Jamie, who wasn't saying anything. He was looking I-want-this right back at me. Maybe I could push Jamie on this, but was I willing to pay the price?

"Play me another track," I said. "Something blues and ballsy."

Nobody loves you when you're down and out...

*

CHANNELLING BESSIE SMITH, of course.

I let it flow over me and through me while it washed away the vanity of my dreams.

Soft and pure, Kai. That's your voice. Just be glad you can hit the notes.

Jamie had the grace to sit absolutely still while it played, and after that, long after the sound had faded, the only echoes were the ones in my soul. Finally, I took a deep breath.

"Type," I said. "You know what you want to say."

After a while, he looked up. "Do you want to read it?"

"Fuck it," I sighed. "Just hit send."

*

SO, I'VE SEEN Dominique, and she was Jamie's wet dream. But she stays Princess Fiona.

Backtrack.

A couple of hours after Jamie hit send, we got a reply.

I want to talk to Kai. Privately. BluesLady7130.

Jamie raised an eyebrow. "D'you know what this is about?"

I shook my head. Jamie's eyebrow stayed where it was though.

*

SHE CONTACTED ME on Hangouts.

DOMINIQUE: *Hi, Kai.*

I looked across at her profile on muzomart.com to make sure I got it right.

KAI: *BluesLady7130?*

DOMINIQUE: *Yes. I'll get to the point. A van. A band. A lone woman. Danger.*

KAI: *I see. So you call me.*

DOMINIQUE: *Yes. I need your perspective.*

KAI: *Because I'm different.*

DOMINIQUE: *Of course. You weren't hard to find on social media. Trust has to start somewhere.*

KAI: *I guess I should be honoured. But I understand your caution.*

KAI: *So what do I say to reassure you?*

DOMINIQUE: *Tell me about yourself.*

No. Not that. I was the Great Listener.

DOMINIQUE: *Kai?*

DOMINIQUE: *Kai? Did I say something wrong? It's so hard to know. I don't want to offend you.*

I realised my thoughts had wandered into strange places, and more time had passed than was polite.

KAI: *No. It's fine. But it's hard to open up to a keyboard.*

There was a long pause on her side. Then the video window opened.

Ah. She was in shadow. But she couldn't hide her bone structure, her complexion.

I turned on my own video.

"Hello, Kai. Pleased to meet you."

Shivers. A lot of sexy wrapped in a French accent.

"Hello, BluesLady7130."

"Please, call me Dominique."

"Dominique. That sounds like a stage name."

"It is my name. Just as your name is Kai."

Fair point. Kai is not the name on my birth certificate. But Kai is my name. Even Cassie calls me Kai.

She continued, "You are quite striking. The contours of your cheekbones are to die for. Your photographs on the website do not do you justice."

"We were in a hurry. We didn't have time for a photoshoot."

She leaned across towards the edge of the screen, and the video whited-out for a moment as bright light flooded over her. Then the camera adjusted, and the colours arrived.

Fair hair, blue eyes, Gallic features. By which I mean a Gallic nose. But it belonged. On her face, it was right.

"You are very attractive, Dominique. You're right to be cautious."

She sniffed.

"*C'est souvent difficile*. It's often difficult."

I smiled. Sympathy, not humour. "*Vraiment*…really."

"You have experienced harassment?"

The Ghosts of Sir Long-Dead still walk…

I nodded. "Doesn't anyone who doesn't conform?"

"Perhaps."

I decided to change the subject. "So, tell me, what are you hoping to learn from this call? What will convince you to get into a van with me and Jamie, Neale, and Jake?"

"Just tell me about yourself and the band. How you came together. What makes you tick. How you became a drummer. If it helps, start with that."

It should have felt like every nightmare job interview rolled into one, but it wasn't because she was smiling, and I knew that she cared.

"Well, you know my name, and I turned twenty-two back in May. My brother, Jamie, is a couple years older. Jake and Clay were the year above him at school, but they all went on to sixth-form college together."

"Clay? This is your previous singer, yes?"

"That's right."

I wondered what to say about Clay. I guessed some of the anger had gone because I began to tell her about some of the good times. About Clay's own musical background, the artists he'd introduced me to. His voice. And his gutsy, bluesy harmonica playing.

"Okay," she said when I was about done. "I understand something of how he shaped the band. But he is gone to follow his own dreams. I do not play the harmonica, but some of those artists, they are on my greats list too. You were telling me about Jamie being at college with Jake and Clay…"

"Right. I wasn't part of that group—I was still at school. I finished off my GCSEs, then I wasted a year doing A levels. It was a mistake; I knew that almost from the start. Come the next year, I switched to the Music Technology BTEC at the local sixth-form college and passed with pretty good grades. When Jamie and Clay put the band together two—no, three years back, Jamie was quick to pull me in."

"So that was you, Jamie, Jake, and Clay, right?"

"Ah, not quite. Jake was our second guitarist; he'd wanted to join from the start but failed the first audition, so another guy got the gig. He left six months later. Musical differences. We decided he was an asshole. He probably felt the same about us. So, the guitarist gig was open again. Jake had been taking lessons and practising in the interim. He'd got really good, and we brought him in. Aside from his backing vocals, we've never regretted it."

That caused a raised eyebrow, so I told her about Jake's voice, and that got a smile.

"Yes, I have known musicians like that. You will have to address that, one day. A *coeur-à-coeur*. Straight talk. Else it will damage the band. *Eh bien*. So. Jamie. He is your brother, of course. You are close?"

"Well, he doesn't live at home anymore. Jamie moved out when he finished college and got a job. I'm still living with my dad and his partner, Cassie, because I haven't yet found a job and because we can still tolerate one another. Jamie's sharing a house with a couple of other blokes. Nonmusicians, but they put up with one another. I visit, get on with them okay."

"That is not what I meant. When family is good, it is a source of strength in a band. When family is bad…" She left the question in the air.

"We are close…" I began. There was so much I couldn't put into words.

But Dominique didn't say anything. She was waiting. Somehow, she'd found this and knew it was important.

"Tell me," Her voice was so calming; it wrapped itself around my fear.

"He…was there for me. When I began my journey to Kai. Nobody else was. Dad had no idea what was going on with me. He was too wrapped up with his own loss. Cassie was on the scene by then. To the extent she was aware, she disapproved. She just thought fresh air and exercise could put everything right. To be fair, it had fixed some things…"

The four of us, walking the north Cornish coast…nowhere for anyone to hide a bottle of booze…and finding Polwithen…

"And Jamie?"

I lurched back to the present.

"Jamie saw what was going on. And he tried to understand right from the beginning. He was my fucking *rock*, and he never, ever let me down."

I gulped and let the silence stretch out. A telltale sting in my eyes betrayed me, a great tear gathering, ready to roll down my cheek.

I clicked, and the video feed was gone. When I clicked it back a moment later, the tear had been smeared to nothing over the ball of my thumb, and my composure was restored.

"You are okay?" she asked, concern welling in her eyes.

I nodded but moved on. "I don't see so much of him now that he's moved out."

"He is sharing a house, you say, with two other men?"

"If you're asking if he's gay, no, he isn't. There've been a fair few girlfriends over the last few years, but since he broke up with Louise six months ago, there's been no one."

"Should I worry?"

"I don't think so. He'll stare down your cleavage, and he'll catch himself, and then he'll look you in the eye and dare you to say he was ever looking anywhere else. But 'look' is as far as it goes. He tries as far as any male can to be a decent human being."

"And you?"

The question came out of the blue, though I should have expected it.

"Me? No. I'm…Kai. I come attachment-free. No significant others. By design."

Again, that raised eyebrow, and I felt compelled to explain.

"Look, my teen years are behind me. I won't say I was wildly sexually active, but I wasn't a total celibate either. You called me striking, and I do know it. I don't have to steal kisses. So, I'll admit to a few *offered* kisses and the like, but they belong to the past. I'm happy to leave them undisturbed at the bottom of the memory closet. My hormones are fine. Currently, I'm waiting to see who and what life throws my way."

There was a long silence after that. I couldn't tell what was going on behind Dominique's poker face.

Finally: "I'll see you in four days. There's an *aire* on your route. I'll send you details; I'll be waiting for you."

Was that it? I thought back over my ramblings, wondering what I'd said to clinch it.

But all I said was: "Anything we should do to prepare?"

That brought a huge smile. "No. There's nothing you can do to prepare."

Faint emphasis on the 'you'?

Then she winked and broke the connection.

Oh. And what did she mean by that?

Chapter Nine

Monday, September 26, 2016
Sleeping Arrangements

A PHONE CALL. A mobile number I didn't recognise.

"Just by the way, Kai." Neale's voice. "Do I get my own room, or am I sharing with one of youse?"

Ah. The elephant in the room. Had it slipped my mind, or had I subconsciously avoided that particular pachyderm?

"Hmm, there's not a lot of budget for accommodation, Neale."

"Twin rooms, then. I can manage that. Would that be sharing with Jamie, Jake, or with your good self?"

Over my dead body. No. Why should I make the sacrifices? Over *your* dead body.

"That's not what I meant," I said. "By 'not a lot' I meant that we're camping where we can, cadging floor space where the opportunity arises, and sleeping in the van if all else fails. Somebody always sleeps in the van to keep an eye on the gear."

There was a long silence.

"Are you still there, Neale?"

"Yes. I don't see how that's going to work. Have you ever slept in a van? It gets bloody cold, and you really don't get enough rest."

"We can't afford…"

The line went dead.

About ten minutes later, the phone rang again. I didn't have to look at the number to know it would be Jamie.

*

WE HAD TO compromise. Some nights would have to be camping. One or two, we'd have to cadge what we could. But Jamie had persuaded me to try alternative accommodation options on the internet. By persuaded, I mean 'shouted a lot down the phone at' until I caved-in. Some of them were prepared to take on a bunch of musicians. Them being the small B & B businesses trying to survive on the leavings of the budget (but still-too-expensive-for-us) hotel chains.

The first couple of nights would be the hardest, but then we'd have some chance to recuperate and freshen up. I opened my spreadsheet and typed in numbers. It didn't look good till I remembered the good news. Jake had found us a paying gig in Aachen to replace the lost Wiesbaden gig. So, pigs do fly.

But we were still heading for a loss unless we did well on our busking.

And while I did all that, Jamie took care of the persuasion. He didn't think I had "the right rapport with Neale". True. He was a great fiddle player and a definite asset to the band. But I might yet kill him.

*

I GOT BACK to remixing our rehearsal session to send to Princess Fiona to learn our arrangements. Yeah, I'd told the band her name was Dominique, but she was PF between Jamie and me. So he didn't get too much of a hard-on.

I also downloaded all her demo tracks as MP3s and shared them with the band. There were a *lot* we could use in the set: a stripped-back version of Susan Tedeschi's 'Midnight in Harlem', Sam Cooke's 'A Change is Gonna Come', Etta James's 'I'd Rather Go Blind'. *Loads*. I told the band I thought Dominique was French — that aire she mentioned was a rest stop on the way from Calais to Köln, which made sense if she was coming up from, say, Paris.

The challenge was that we wouldn't get to meet her until the day of the first gig. That meant no rehearsal, just learning one another's material and putting it all together on the night.

Chapter Ten

Wednesday, September 28, 2016
Getting Ready

AND THEN WEDNESDAY was on us. Specifically, ferry-tomorrow Wednesday. Get-your-van-over-here-Neale Wednesday. How-the-fuck-do-we-fit-all-this-in Wednesday.

Where should I begin?

Tents? Or Security?

Yes, security. Neale's idea of fixing the van's rear doors was to string a couple of large bungee cords from the door frame and hook them to the seats. That was good, Neale. Couldn't you have found a crowbar to wedge the doors shut? No? Probably just as well because while I wasn't a violent person, I might use it on you. Gah!

Tents. Followed on from security. Someone would have to

sleep in the van. Maybe two people. So, the other three needed a tent. At six foot three and built like a marine, Jamie was the kind of guy who always thought it'd be fun to go hiking up Snowdon in winter. He had a cosy two-man tent, designed for sharing with a very close friend. A two-*person* tent, I should have said. I'd long assumed he used it as a sort of final compatibility test for his women. He kept trying, but I didn't think he'd passed yet.

Jake, on the other hand, said he wanted to bring his dad's tent-in-a-crate. At about the size and weight of an adult coffin, the tent unfolded to the size of the Albert Hall. It was army surplus, made of lots of identical segments that buttoned together. So waterproof. The military mind was so inventive. The tent would be split up between everyone in the platoon, and everyone who hadn't been shot during the day contributed their piece come nightfall. I didn't know which tent frightened me more, but apparently, we were taking both. Maybe Princess Fiona would get the Albert Hall to herself.

Jake said we could also use the crate for a seat. Yes, Jake. Our PA system included two large full-range speaker cabs and three backline amps that we could use for seats. So, I made a phone call and redeemed a favour and borrowed a modern four-man tent. The button-together Albert Hall would be staying home.

We still had those two PA cabs and three amps, plus guitars and my drum kit. Of course, nobody wanted their precious instrument underneath anything else. As drummer, apparently, I didn't get a vote, even though it made no sense to put round drum cases at the bottom if you were trying to pack efficiently and have it all stable. At least Neale had unbolted and removed the toolbox from the van.

Camping stoves. Cutlery. Jamie had a posh rucksack. The rest of us had soft bags. Plus, massive sleeping bags, again excepting Jamie, whose sleeping bag' compressed to the size of a packet of biscuits yet would keep him warm and snug in the Antarctic.

I might exaggerate due to the stress of organising things. No one else seemed to worry about practical things such as whether it would all come crashing down like a swatter on a mosquito the first time Neale took a sharp bend at forty mph. Everybody had packed way too much gear.

But it was all in. And so was I.

I wasn't quite sure which laws of physics I'd broken, but we were there, all the gear somehow inside the van. We had a bench seat made out of the PA speakers with a sleeping bag unrolled across the top 'for comfort'. The light was fading, and everyone had buggered off to the pub, leaving umpteen thousand quid of gear secured by a bungee cord parked outside the parental home.

I'd had a guitar stolen once. I'd left it in a mate's car. They broke in to steal the radio—an expensive sound system—but they'd found my guitar under the blanket on the back seat. It wasn't particularly expensive or good, but it was *my guitar*. This was before I switched to drums, and it had been my very first instrument bought with my own money. I'd earned it with months of slogging a paper round. The police said it had probably been kids, stealing to fund a drug habit. They didn't even want the guitar for itself, which I could have forgiven. No, the bastards just wanted stuff they could sell for a quick high, over and gone. That hurt.

So, I sat with the van, tired after all the lifting and packing. After a while, it started to get cold, so I climbed into a sleeping bag and drifted off.

I woke up about eleven o'clock, still cold and with the corner of an amp sticking in my back. The others were still down the pub, and no one had tried to break in and steal the stuff, so I guessed my guarding had kept thieves away.

I went back in the house, where I spotted an old umbrella in the cupboard under the stairs. Not as good as a crowbar, but slid through the handles, it would help wedge the doors shut. I dug out a nice thick jumper from the back of my wardrobe and a pair of woollen gloves.

Back in the van, it was almost warm enough with the extra clothing. And I managed to find a way to lie across the cabs without impaling my back on the corner of Jake's guitar amp. If it had been a couple of degrees warmer, I might have slept.

Chapter Eleven

Thursday, September 29, 2016
Travelling and the First Gig

BUGGER.

We were going to miss our crossing.

It was my fault, tired, after a night almost-sleeping in the van. We stopped for fuel, and I put unleaded in the tank. Yeah. I didn't fuck up often, but when I did, empires crumbled.

The engine started to falter a couple of miles down the road. Neale seemed to know almost immediately that I'd misfueled his *diesel* van because he pulled over as soon as the van started to lose power. He glared at me, then swore.

"What did I do?" I asked, still dopey from lack of sleep.

"What did you put in the tank?"

"Just petrol."

"From the green nozzle?"

I nodded.

I was, apparently, a fuckwit. Lots of other things too. But definitely a fuckwit. *Okay, tattoo it on my arm. Humiliate me. Beat me up. No, I'll do that myself.*

So we spent an hour—I was told we were lucky—just an hour waiting for rescue by the RAC. Then another hour to drain and flush the fuel system. Quite a large bill to pay. Another glare. From all the band.

And then we were on the road again. Taking it very easy. The engine would run fine for a time, and then there'd be a judder, and the van would lurch. The first time it happened, there was a collective "Fuck!" from everybody in such perfect unison that it would have been funny—if we hadn't been sure the engine was about to seize. The engine settled down over the next twenty minutes, but it wasn't *right*. We didn't trust it.

Then we had a difficult moment when Jake decided he needed a loo break. We were already on the motorway with no services for miles.

"We can't afford to stop. We'll miss the ferry." That was Jamie.

"We're going to miss the ferry anyway." Jake.

"Not if I can help it." Neale.

I said nothing, being a fuckwit and not entitled to contribute.

Neale put his foot down and was rewarded by a lurch—a deceleration that threw us all forward. The van didn't pick up speed. Cars were beginning to bunch up behind us, earning us black looks from drivers passing us.

We had no choice really. Neale pulled over onto the hard

shoulder, and the van rolled to a stop.

The door practically flew open. Jake got his loo break.

There was a scrunch of gravel. Footsteps. I wasn't able to see, being the fuckwit in the back seat, but Neale could.

"Oh shit. The pigs. Get down, Kai. You're not here."

Right. Four in a van with only three seats. I got down. Jamie helpfully swept the sleeping bag off the amps on top of me. Then he lowered one of the big carry-bags on top of it. Then a guitar in its hard case. Ow.

I could hear Jake outside, trying to muster enough language to explain that the van really had broken down, and he'd simply taken advantage of the stop "to have a pee, Officer."

"What's wrong with the van, laddie?"

"Kai put the wrong fuel in. Engine's buggered."

Footsteps. A voice through the open passenger door. I pictured a monobrowed head with military hair.

"Which one of you guys is Kai?"

Silence.

"The pillock who put unleaded into a diesel tank?"

"Ah, that would be me, Officer. The RAC helped us out" —I heard Jamie rustling an incident sheet—"and towed us to a garage. We got it flushed out, but the engine still isn't running right."

"Start it up, driver. Let's have a listen."

Neale obliged. The engine caught, ran smooth, missed once, caught again, and settled.

"Sounds okay now. I'd suggest you pull off at the next junction and stay off the motorway. If you do break down, it'll be easier to get rescued. Where are you lads going? A gig?"

"Yeah, we got a tour. Germany."

"You got a lot of gear in the back. Guitars, drums. I used to be in a band myself. Drummer. Who's the drummer here?"

Silence.

"That's me, Officer."

Smart, Jamie. You're playing a dangerous game though.

"Right. Kai the pillock. Black nozzle, remember? I don't suppose your mates'll let you forget, will they? So what do you play? What's your kit?"

"Uh, it's a bit of a mix. Mostly DW."

The engine missed again.

"They make nice gear. But you guys need to get moving and get off the motorway. I'll drive behind you till you reach the next exit so you won't get idiots flashing you or driving too close."

I heard Jake climb in. The door slammed shut, Neale put the van in gear, and we moved off. The van lurched. Something slid and landed on the pile that had me at the bottom. I said, "ow," more in surprise than in pain.

"Shut up. He's following us."

"Thanks for asking how I am. I'm fine. Other than being the poor fuckwit buried at the bottom of a pile of gear."

"Language, dear…" Jamie's voice.

After a while, the van began to labour, and the weight shifted a bit on top of me.

"Is everything all right?" I asked.

"Yeah. We're on the exit ramp now. The cops are still following us… Neale's taking the A-road… The cops have got back on the motorway… How nice. He flashed us good luck."

"So, any chance we can stop and get all the crap off me?"

I wasn't in the best of moods. But Neale found a lay-by and

pulled in. Jamie hauled the guitar and the bags off me. We spent five minutes getting stuff back in place and secured again.

Jake asked what all the shenanigans had been about. Neale explained.

"It's a nitpicky, nanny-state sort of thing, having enough seats for your passengers. But it's the kind of thing that coppers can use to meet their arrest targets if they've had a bad month."

*

A LITTLE LATER, the road took us alongside the motorway for a few miles. The traffic wasn't moving. We saw blue lights flashing.

"Silver lining, eh?" said Neale. "We're not in that mess at least."

The van was running smoothly now. A few miles down the road, we saw the motorway again with handful of cars on it, the blockage now behind them.

"Shall we try the motorway again?"

Assent.

The motorway stayed clear. Better, the atmosphere in the van cleared up. Everyone was calling Jamie "Kai the pillock." And telling drummer jokes about him. But that was okay. Drummer jokes were way better than some of the vitriol that had been flying around.

*

WE ARRIVED IN Dover smiling. The sun was shining, though there was a chill, and we kept the heater running. We ended up in a loading area, a car park where a woman in a hi-vis jacket directed us into a lane with other vans. I thought we'd get grief when we showed our ticket for a ferry that had already sailed, but nobody dockside gave a toss.

I asked the woman who was marshalling the vans, "How long?"

"An hour. Bit longer?"

"Do we need to stay with the van?"

She waved her clipboard at a low building. "You can get a coffee over there. Or something to eat."

Neale asked if there was a bar, but she'd moved on.

So, we had an hour to kill and a café to kill it in. It had been an early start and an awful long time since breakfast. Jamie offered to do guard duty in the van; the rest of us trudged over. Halfway there, I realised I'd left my wallet in the van. I headed back, but as I approached, I saw Jamie had got out and was making a call on his mobile. He had his back to me, concentrating on the call. There was enough of a sea breeze that he had to strain to hear the caller and raise his voice to be heard. I caught a few words.

"…running about three hours late. I'm sorry."

He turned at that moment and saw me. For a moment, I saw fear in his face. Then it was gone.

"Got to go now. Bye." He turned his attention to me.

"Sorry," I said. "I didn't mean to surprise you. Who was that?"

"Oh, just…Dominique."

"Ah. She gave you her phone number."

"Yeah. Letting her know we'd missed the planned ferry. Courtesy."

I raised my eyebrows. Just a little. "And you didn't share the phone number? There were a few times this week I'd have really liked to call her direct. Sending messages through Hangouts was getting clunky."

"Well, I said I just wanted it for emergencies."

"Sometimes, I think this whole fucking week has been one long emergency, Jamie."

"I'm sor—"

"Never mind. Water under the bridge. We'll share contact info when we're all together. Is she on track for meeting up?"

"Yeah. She'll be there. Anything else?"

I shrugged. Jamie said something about needing to take a quick piss, tossed me the keys, and started walking towards the café.

I called after him. "Courtesy is good. I'm not criticising you, and I'm not spying on you either. In case you'd forgotten, I came back to pick up my wallet."

I opened the passenger door and grabbed my wallet from the back bench. By the time I'd locked the van, Jamie was fifty yards away and moving at full steam.

Sod him.

*

EVENTUALLY, WE WERE loaded onto a ferry. A guy in a hi-vis jacket waved us aboard, leapfrogging a bunch of cars that had been waiting longer than us. There, another hi-vis type directed us into an our-van-sized space. We were right at the back of the cargo deck, hard against a wall.

We climbed out on the passenger side and stretched our legs. If a ferry had tracks, we were on the wrong side of them, our scruffy, dented van parked in a dingy corner with all the other scruffy, dented vans.

The crossing was short, with barely time to grab a meal in the restaurant. Alternatively, we had more than enough time for a sandwich in the cafeteria, followed by a beer or two in the bar. We opted for the bar, mostly at Neale's insistence.

Yep. A beer or two turned out to be two. Neale was up for a third, but we reminded him that we'd be disembarking in a few minutes.

"Whisky chaser, then. That won't take long."

I mentioned that he was the only driver, and he'd be driving on the right side from here on. He looked put out, shooting dark looks my way in particular. Apparently, I was the sensible one, so it was my fault.

I climbed in and over onto the minimally padded PA cab in the back. Neale, Jamie, and Jake took their seats in the front. After an age, all the cars in front of us were off, and we were ready to go. Neale started the engine, which happily caught, but there was an ominous scraping sound.

"Fuck," said Neale. "Did those bastards move the van after we left it?"

"Did you put the handbrake on properly?" asked Jamie. "I think it may have rolled and caught the driver-side mirror on that stanchion."

"Smartarse." It was more of a grunt really.

So now the mirror was bent at an angle. Neale did something with the gearbox, moved the wheel, and let the clutch out. There was another scrape, louder and with a touch of metallic rip. Neale effed some more, moved the wheel in a different direction, and this time, there was no scrape. But the mirror was now dangling, supported by a couple of cables.

"There's something wrong…" I began.

"Shut your mouth. I've half a mind to sue the buggers for negligence, but we're running late, and they're lyin' bastards who'd never admit a thing. And I most definitely put the handbrake on, and that's God's truth, or are you callin' me a liar?"

No one called him a liar. One of the deck hands had got very interested in us and yelled at us to drive off the boat now. Then, he must have seen the mirror because he pointed at it and called something in French.

Neale gave him the finger as we drove past. "Wanker!"

But I didn't think the deckhand heard. He shrugged, Gallic-fashion. He'd seen it all a thousand times before.

We passed through the rest of the port without incident. Just as well because Neale was gearing up to give a mouthful to anyone who stopped us.

For a moment, we drove on the left of the road.

Jamie squeaked something that was probably "Right."

Neale growled back, hauled the wheel over, and said, "I knew that."

I didn't think any of us relaxed until we'd cleared the town and were on the *autoroute*. Neale muttered steadily as though the whole French nation had conspired to rip the mirror off and were driving on the wrong side of the road to spite him.

After about half an hour, I noticed a certain amount of wriggling in the front seat. *Loo break coming up.* Not me though. I'd taken care of personal needs before leaving the ferry. Well, I was the sensible one, recent cock-up notwithstanding.

On the current showing, Neale would probably have a different name for me.

Smartarse.

*

WE WERE ALL glad to stop at the next aire—the last before Belgium—which became a stampede to the bog, led by Jamie. I was glad to stretch my legs and buy something to read. Yes, it was in French—a magazine full of current affairs and somewhat left-wing, as far as I could tell from a skim of the first few pages. Refreshing after the right-wing monotony of the British press.

*

BACK ON THE road, it began to rain. Drizzle, really. There was spray from the road, and Neale eased up on the throttle. The van was running well. We'd been listening to Dominique's demo tracks, getting them in our heads, but about twenty kilometres down the road, Jamie reached forward and turned off the sound.

"D'you mind if we have some quiet, guys?"

"Are you okay?" asked Neale. "D'you want me to pull over?"

"No. It's fine. I'm just feeling a bit nervous, to be honest, and the music isn't helping. I mean, she's fucking brilliant, and we're just a bar band from nowhere."

"She approached us," I reminded him. "She thinks we're good enough."

"But you mixed the hell out of those tracks, Kai."

"GIGO."

"What?"

"Garbage In, Garbage Out. I can't make a silk purse out of a sow's ear. Pick your own proverb, but if the quality isn't there to start with, I can't fake it in the mix. At least, not with the tech I've got."

But I was nervous, too, and so were Neale and Jake. Whatever, we rode in silence while the van carried us the last ten kilometres to the aire.

The exit sign loomed.

"This is it," someone said unnecessarily. It might have been me.

We slowed. It was hard to see anyone clearly in the drizzle.

"A tall girl in a dark blue waterproof," said Jamie. "She'll be carrying a large rucksack."

"How tall is tall?" I asked.

"She says one metre seventy-five. What's that in feet and inches?"

"About five foot seven or eight."

She was by the café, standing alone. By the time any of us saw her, she'd already spotted us—white van, English plates—and was waving and walking towards us.

We pulled up, and we would all have got out to meet her, but she walked briskly around to the passenger side.

"Hi," she said. "You are John Doe's Blues, yes? I am Dominique. Pleased to meet you. There is room in the back for me, yes?"

Jake stepped down anyway to let her climb in past Jamie and onto the back bench. Jake passed her rucksack to me and climbed back in.

"Please, drive," she said. "Unless someone needs to piss.

Why is it always fucking raining in Belgium?"

She turned to face me, her blond hair matted and plastered across her cheeks. There were those wide-set blue eyes, and she was smiling.

I smiled back. "Hello, I'm…"

"Kai. You're the drummer; I have not forgotten. Would you help me get my coat unzipped, please? My fingers are frozen."

I was conscious that Jake and Jamie were craning their necks to look at 'Princess Fiona'. By unspoken agreement, *Dominique* and I tuned them out. Her white fingers fumbled with the fastenings of her coat. I lifted them away gently and began to draw down the zipper, conscious that she was watching my face — only my face — and talking.

"I know your voice from the demos. It is very fine, precise. You can sing at the same time as playing drums, I think."

"Yes."

The zip had stuck, and I wrestled the fabric out from under it. From the corner of my eye, I was aware of Jamie watching the process very closely. *Yes, Jamie, you are what you are, and Dominique is everything you were hoping she would be.*

"And you can harmonise?"

"Yes, I can find harmonies."

"*C'est bon.*"

I freed the pesky zip at last and drew it down. Beneath the outer raincoat, she wore a thick brushed-cotton blouse, open at the neck. Sensible for autumn travelling. She wriggled her arm and turned so I could pull her jacket free. For the first time, she broke eye contact and took in Jamie and Jake.

"Hello, gentlemen. Jake. Jamie. And Neale — I promise I will speak with you later, but I am sure you wish to concentrate on the road."

As she had with me, she held her gaze on the face of each of them while addressing them. It reminded me of a politician or royalty, meeting admirers, putting them at ease with well-chosen words so they would open up. The difference here was that, twisted half around, with me still holding the arm of her jacket, her blouse was stretched tight over her breasts.

Deliberate, I was sure. She was testing us, me included, to uncover the tensions and the temper of the band. I wondered if the hand I couldn't see held Mace.

But after a minute, she relaxed and let me remove her coat, so I guessed we'd passed, or else that at the next stop, she'd simply fade away, leaving us singer-less and un-Maced.

*

SHE NOTICED THE magazine I'd been reading. "*Tu parles français?*"

'*Tu*'. I was already the familiar 'you'. And since she was asking if I spoke French, I assumed the threat of Mace had receded.

"*Oui, mais pas récemment,*" I answered, then translated for the others, who were obviously listening in: "Yes, but it's been a while." And then back to French: "*Est-ce que tu es française, ou peut-être tu es belge*? Are you French or, perhaps, Belgian?"

She also slipped back into English, making it less complicated. "I was born in Brussels, but I live in Paris."

The kilometres rolled on while we chatted, mostly in French with only an occasional lapse into English. (*Sorry, Jamie. You should have studied harder; your French is crap.*) I told her a bit about myself, and she told me about her life in Paris, a humdrum job selling fragrances in a minor department store. Then she asked about the band, going deeper than our Hangouts conversations into quite a bit about Clay and our other influences.

So, I asked her who her icons were. Billie Holiday, of course. Etta James. And Aretha Franklin. No surprises there, but she also included some more modern singers. Bonnie Raitt. Annie Lennox. And Adele from the latest crop of divas.

Jamie turned around. "Sorry to butt in, but it sounded like you were discussing blues singers."

"Yes, and Kai was telling me about the band. But I think it is time we made music together. It is not so far to Cologne, so I will ask Jake if he has some blues on his smartphone."

"We were listening to your demos," Jake said.

"*Non,*" she replied. "Nor your own demos. Just something that we can join in on."

"I heard you mention Bonnie Raitt."

"*Parfait!*" she exclaimed and clapped her hands.

It didn't take long. Jake fiddled a bit, found a 'best of' collection, and ran it from the start. That got us singing till third track up when we had 'Women Be Wise' blues shuffling out of the speakers. That was the key that unlocked Dominique.

She nailed it.

Was it possible to fall in love with a voice alone? Yes, the demos had been fantastic, but that wasn't the same as falling in love. I did, right then, in the back of a van rolling down the E40 towards Köln. I was pretty sure the rest of the band had around the same time.

It hurt, sure, the certainty that I was going to be eclipsed in pretty short order. All my hard work on the vocals, gritting up my too-pure voice. All that brainwork, mixing in singing with the already complex coordination of drum playing. Wasted.

And yet, not wasted. If that was what it had taken to get us out on the road, so we could be the planets orbiting Dominique's sun, then that was what it had taken. Faustus had paid more for a momentary glimpse of Helen of Troy. We were going to *sing* with our Helen.

*

WE ARRIVED IN Köln late afternoon, and Neale's satnav took us straight to the Club Lorelei.

It was a mistake to arrive at a venue in the daytime. In the daylight, any rock'n'roll club looked like the second half of *Platoon*. This club ran true to form, with peeling paint and grimy windows. It was locked, and nobody answered when we rang the bell or knocked.

From knocking, we progressed to banging. Then Neale climbed up onto a ledge to see if… I didn't know what was going on in that Irishman's brain. At that point, it was no great stretch of imagination for a neighbour to take a dislike to a scruffy rock'n'roll band making noise outside their apartment

Whatever. Well under five minutes later, I became aware that we weren't alone. People in blue-black uniforms and stab-proof vests appeared. The uniforms bore the word *Polizei* embroidered on the right breast pocket flap. And each cop had a neatly holstered pistol strapped to their thigh. The man raised an authoritarian finger to his lips, and we could not move a muscle. I wasn't sure we could even breathe. The woman glided to a spot just behind Neale.

Neale hadn't noticed. He was investigating plant pots. Checking for hidden spare keys, I supposed.

Dominique, Jamie, and I still held our breath, waiting for disaster to strike.

"*Stop* what you are doing!"

The policewoman had spoken softly, but there was hissing steel in her voice, and Neale leaped about a foot in the air, swearing all the way. He twisted around as he came down and balled his fists. The policewoman had glided back a couple of feet beyond his reach. Her colleague had positioned himself off to one side, his bodycam presumably taking everything in.

It was sinking in, now, and Neale had turned pasty white.

"That is better. No need to startle. *Ssso*, tell me, what were you doing? Not breaking in, I hope."

"We're the band, Officer." Neale pointed at Jake, who was miles away playing little blues runs on his acoustic guitar, oblivious to our little drama.

"And that is why you were climbing all over this building? And searching for what? An open window, a—what is the word—*Schlüssel*, a…"

"A key," I offered helpfully, as talking was now permitted.

"*Danke. Ja.* Well. The club is empty. So, it is best if you drive away and come back when there is someone to let you in."

"But…"

"The neighbours are disturbed. You will be playing loud rock tonight; they deserve some peace now."

"You didn't think, Neale, did you?" I suggested. "We're all a little tired after a long drive, Officer. And we're probably not thinking straight."

She looked a little puzzled.

I translated for her in German that it had been a long journey, we were all tired, and apologised. I wasn't sure if it helped.

I turned to Neale. "Say you're very sorry."

"Ah. Sure. Yes, I'm very sorry. Sure I am. Sorry. Yes, sorry. But…"

"*Enough*! There is no 'but'. Your apology is sufficient. So, let me see your ID, and then you can all go."

Fortunately, Neale had his passport in his jacket pocket. Mine was in my gilet. And Dominique and Jake both had theirs. Only Jamie needed to return to the van and rummage through his luggage.

"Good," the policewoman said when we were all properly identified. She turned to Jamie. "Young man, I strongly advise you to keep your passport securely upon your person at all times. While it is not the law, it makes things easier in this country. Do you understand?"

"Yes, Officer. Thank you, Officer."

"And now you have no cause to stay. I have checked your IDs, so the neighbours will see that I have done my duty. The neighbours said you were hippies and were smoking drugs. I do not smell drugs, so I think they were just making mischief. However, I see there are five of you, and your van has only three seats, unless it has been specially modified. Shall I inspect your van to see if it complies with the law? Do you understand now?"

We understood. Passports on our persons at all times. And stay on the right side of the neighbours.

"Jamie, Jake, why don't you take Dominique and find a

coffee shop nearby? Neale and I will go and find the campsite and set up the tent. We'll meet you back here in an hour or so."

Jamie grinned like a fool. It was so obvious he'd been waiting for a chance to spend some time with our gorgeous new singer. Jake, as far as Jamie was concerned, was no competition. I wasn't so sure, myself. Jake could be a tongue-tied guitar geek most of the time, but he wasn't a eunuch. He had better self-control than Jamie, that was all.

So, I drove off with Neale. He said nothing on the way to the campsite. It took us about twenty minutes; we were lucky we'd not had to drive through the city centre.

At the gate, I had a short 'discussion' with the owner. We'd booked in advance, but he was having second thoughts. He looked askance at our van and the gaffa tape now securing the broken mirror. We were third-class citizens in the camping world. But I guessed the summer hadn't been kind, and the owner wanted our money more than he wanted us off his land — but not by much. He banished us to the far end of his campsite, past the shiny motorhomes and caravans with their awnings and well-maintained plots by the Rhine.

"It's bloody miles away," moaned Neale, his first words since we'd driven off together. He'd looked longingly at the bar as we passed it. It had been a long time since the liquid lunch on the ferry.

"We'll live. Just don't drink so much that you need to walk all the way back to pee."

That earned me another black look.

The gods smiled on us, that and some thoughtful packing of the van. The tent I'd scrounged — the favour I'd redeemed on packing day — went up in about half an hour without a drop of rain despite the threatening clouds. The good, modern-design tent, which I'd borrowed from a friend, had cost him about a hundred quid on eBay. It unrolled without fuss; we pegged it in about ten places, and with about four guy ropes, we were done. We moved the sleeping bags and travel bags inside, zipped up the door, and headed to Club Lorelei.

By the time we got back, about an hour and a half in all, the doors were open and the place lit.

We went inside.

No Jamie. No Jake. No Dominique.

Herr Rumpel met us. Though tall and chubby, he had a harsh face that lacked only a monocle to cast him as a silk-talking villain. But his voice was fifty-a-day rough.

"You're late. Are you going to be ready? And there should be four of you. I hired a rock band, not a duet."

Rock band? Hmm. I looked around at the posters of The Who and the Rolling Stones, but also Black Sabbath, Metallica, Muse, plus some (presumably) German bands I didn't recognise. Fair enough, we could pick some heavy blues that should work.

Rumpel waved at the stage — yes, even I could work that out, thank you — and stomped off without waiting for an answer. Neale and I got to work unloading the van. And work it was. We both had a fair old sheen on us by the time we were done, and I was seething, mostly at my brother who was doubtless still drinking coffee and chatting up Dominique.

We were nine parts set up when we heard English voices. Yep, it was Jamie, Jake, and Dominique. It didn't escape my notice that Jamie and Dominique were holding hands. All three looked bright-eyed and excited.

"It was great," Jamie bubbled. "We found a coffee shop, no problem, in a big square with a bunch of other shops and a load of shoppers walking past. Dominique said we should try to get some publicity for the gig. Jake had his acoustic guitar with him, so we started busking. I found a square of cardboard and wrote the name of the club on it."

He held out the sign: Club 'Lorrelie'.

I think he expected me to be pleased, and I sort of was. At least he hadn't wasted the time we'd been away. But 'Lorrelie'? No Jamie, it was Lorelei. The Maiden of the Rock. Hence, the sign outside the club of some weird rock chick in a low-cut chain mail fantasy of Rumpel's. The artist had given her a guitar, vaguely Gibson SG-like, but had lavished more care on the flesh-revealing cutaways in the chain mail than the cutaways in the guitar.

"…we told lots of people about the gig," Jamie was saying. "But we didn't have any handbills."

Oh, bugger. The handbills. We'd made up handbills for every gig, put them in the van. And I'd driven off with them. It wasn't my fault, I wanted to say. I was tired because we'd driven a long way. I was flustered because the police were moving us on, and I had a lot to think about, trying to stop her arresting us. But it *was* my fault. I'd done so much of the organising that, somehow, I'd ended up a kind of leader or, at least, a leader for all the boring admin stuff. And when stuff went wrong, the leader was the one who took the blame.

So, I was all ready to blast Jamie, and I couldn't. In fact, I was going to have to apologise.

"Well done, Jamie. Sorry I forgot to give you the handbills."

Taste of ashes.

*

AND, OF COURSE, being the drummer, I was the last to be ready. Never mind that I'd been lugging the PA, the guitars and amps, and all the cabling in from the van. What counted was that when everyone else was ready to go, I was the one still tightening wing nuts.

Herr Rumpel chose that moment to reappear. "I open the doors in five minutes. Five. No soundchecks after that. Good."

Then he disappeared.

I called out the first song that came into my head. "Dominique! 'Blue for No Reason'. You can do it."

I didn't have my floor tom secured, but what the hell? The song was a great, foot-tapping rocker that could survive worse than that. It had everyone in it, even Neale, weaving in and out on the fiddle.

I couldn't pretend it all gelled in that moment. It was distinctly rough in places. Dominique tried a run that took her voice where it wasn't warmed up to go. Jake's pedal array was crackling—a dying battery in there somewhere—and my floor tom drifted out, leading to an unintentional rimshot.

Neale skipped out to listen to the mix. He strayed too close to a speaker, provoking a nasty feedback howl. I gave him a black look, but everyone kept on going, and Neale found a place where the feedback died.

He detoured by the mixing board, provoking another howl as he passed the speaker again. There, he twiddled knobs and sliders for about thirty seconds, looked happier, and came back on stage.

I think he made it better, but a minute later, Herr Rumpel started the canned music, and that was our soundcheck done.

*

THAT FIRST SET was born in strife. Choosing the songs themselves was easy enough, but who should sing them? Well, Dominique, of course. Still, a part of me clamoured to take lead vocals. I had sweated blood to prepare those songs. And Dominique—she was untried. Yes, she knew the songs, but there was a huge difference between knowing the words and being able to perform them. Jamie insisted she could do it. He never once declared I wasn't up to it, but I could see him biting back the words that would have blown the band apart.

"Kai," Dominique said, "let us split the verses between us. You sing a verse, so I get the feel, then I sing a verse. We finish together."

She placed her hand on mine and looked me in the eye, completely open and sincere. She was a natural peacemaker, against whom I had no more defence than did Jamie. My anger drained away.

"No. That won't work, Dominique. You should sing. On your own."

I pulled my hand out from under hers, not roughly. Then I went for a walk. Away from her, away from the band. Out into the alley behind the Club Lorelei. Out into the chill night of the death of my dreams.

*

IT TOOK A good, long walk to let all the poison and nastiness out of my system. It needed doing, and if I couldn't find my way back to the club, then the band would be better off not having my nasty little ego on stage. I spent a fair amount of time leaning on the parapet of a bridge over the river, just watching the river flow, letting the bad stuff go.

Eventually, I decided I was fit to rejoin the human race. It took me about twenty minutes to find the Club Lorelei, which wasn't bad. I didn't want to know how long I'd been away, but the where-the-fuck-have-you-beens told me all I needed to know.

I smiled brightly to everyone to let them know I was fine. Jamie even smiled back, which showed I'd been right to take off. He knew me and my moods.

Dominique was dressed to hit the stage. She'd chosen a two-piece suit in dark blue pinstripe over a sky-blue shirt and black tie. The cut was odd. It fit her without being overly feminine, like a sort of inverse Bowie. I'd have expected her to show off her figure on stage, so this unexpected almost-masculine look bothered me. I meant... Well, I don't know what I meant. It messed with my head. I hadn't felt like that since taking the road to Kai.

I'd left it too late to get into my own stage clothes, as Herr Rumpel had told us we had five minutes to get on stage five minutes ago. Jamie was making signs at him to announce us.

The lights on stage dimmed—our cue to get to our places. Herr Rumpel himself took the stage, all sweat and pot belly, and gave us our intro.

"*Wollt Ihr Rock'n'Roll?*"

"*Ja!*" they all roared back.

"What's he saying?"—Neale's voice in my ear.

"*Wollt Ihr echten Blues aus England?*"

"*Ja!*" they answered.

"D'you want some rock and roll and genuine blues from England?" I gabbled, nearly missing what followed.

"*Und eine Jazzsängerin aus Paris, die euch umhauen wird?*"

"…and a jazz singer from Paris, to entertain you? I'm guessing '*umhauen*', colloquial, may be 'knock you dead'."

You'd think Rumpel would know his clientele better than that. This was a rock and metal crowd. 'Jazz singer' didn't get quite the enthusiastic response I'd hoped. But they hadn't seen or heard our French jazz singer from Belgium yet. She was going to leave Rumpel's cartoon fantasy in the dust.

I didn't catch what he said next, but it got a fantastic cheer, mixed with some coarse laughs. It was our cue.

Dominique stepped into the spotlight, and from behind the kit, all I could see was her silhouette. She looked good, and I could hear whistles from out front. If you were going to advertise your club with cartoon rock-chicks in chain mail, then your punters were going to whistle. At least, the male ones would. Dominique held her pose, got more whistles, let them subside. She…examined her audience, scanning from left to right, nodding her approval of what she saw.

"Hi, Köln. *Ich heiße Dominique.* I'm Dominique. *Je suis chanteuse de blues et de rock.* I'm a blues and rock singer. Are you ready to *rock?*"

"*Ja!*" was mixed with a few calls of "Yeah and *oui.*" They were going to have a tough time following her whimsical linguistic shifts.

We kicked off with 'Blue for No Reason', mostly because

we'd warmed up with it and had a rough idea of how to make it work. Jake had fixed up his guitar pedals while I'd been de-egoing around Köln. I slotted into the groove behind him, with Jamie plugging along on bass.

On the chorus, I doubled up with Dominique, adding a simple harmony mostly around the third, comfortably within my range. The vocal blend worked, too, my purer timbre adding a softness behind her blues growl. For a moment, Jamie looked up from his bass, caught my eye, and gave me a smile. Sorted.

"*Danke, Köln,*" Dominique said when it was done. They'd applauded a little, enough that Dominique's thanks came across as genuine. "That was a Bonnie Raitt song. And now…" She glanced down at the set list. "'Sitting on Top of the World'."

The Germans loved that. Jake went straight for the jugular with the guitar intro — a shameless Clapton homage — then pulled back to give Dominique all the room she needed to use her whole vocal range.

Third verse, she changed the lyrics and told the audience, "'If you don't like the peaches, don't shake the tree'," which earned her some more whistles.

Chapter Twelve

Thursday. Late

Köln, Club Lorelei Gig, continued

WE GOT THROUGH the set.

Nobody booed; nobody hurled anything. We got a reasonable amount of applause. Musically, the songs came together. There were a few rough edges — harmonies that didn't quite work, ragged endings, minor confusions over instrumental breaks. Inevitable.

Dominique?

Superb. I'd been practising the songs for weeks, but I couldn't have got close to her performance. With her talent, she could have snapped her fingers to get a backing band. So why us? It was the question I should have asked when we did the video call, but I didn't. How had John Doe's Blues from Marden Combe suddenly won the Dominique-the-singer lottery on muzo-mart.com? Where did she even come from? A singer that good should leave tracks. But I couldn't find her, and believe me, I'd tried. Of course, there were singers called Dominique around, but none of them was our Dominique. So, it seemed Dominique wasn't her usual singing name. Why was she using an alias? Was she some famous French *chanteuse*, slumming it on a whim, and she just picked us?

Bollocks.

Pure. Hollywood. Bollocks.

All this went around in my head while we sat drinking beers at a quiet table after the set. Plus, encores.

Herr Rumpel had cornered us after we'd come off stage for the third time.

"Well done, guys. They liked you. You're not so bad."

He leered at Dominique. She looked him right back in the eye, cold-stared him like she'd been ogled by middle-aged lechers so often it meant nothing anymore. He kept on leering to prove he didn't give a shit what she thought of him. Then, he remembered.

"*Ja.* Well, I got some bad news and some good news for you. The bad news is that I can't pay you now. It's been a bad week. It happens. That's showbiz."

"Riiight…" Jamie said, wincing at Rumpel's dire American accent. "What's the good news?"

"The good news is that it's getting busy. Really busy. Plenty of cash by the time we close. No problem."

"You sure of that?"

"I am getting to that. We need to keep them here. We need

to keep them drinking, of course. Listen. I have an idea. I will announce you will do another set. Then the customers, they twitter their friends in the other clubs. We get a full house; I can pay you."

"But that means we play twice. So, we get paid twice. *Ja*?"

Well done, Jamie.

"*Ja*, sure. I pay fifty euros."

"Fifty? But the deal was two hundred for the first set."

"*Ja*, but that includes your travel, right? For this set, you don't travel twice, cost less. Besides. You play same set again, same songs. Some guys get bored, they leave."

"One hundred. We've got other songs."

"Sure, but not so good. You've played your best songs already, I'm sure. But seventy, maybe. Good will, okay?"

Damn. He had us over a barrel. And how could he not afford to pay us, what with the price of drinks here?

Jamie haggled a bit more, but that was mostly over set length and when we'd start (not before midnight).

Herr Rumpel waddled off, taking his smug grin with him. We settled down to kill the time till midnight. We argued a bit over what new songs we could put into a set, came up with a bunch of standard rhythm and blues songs, *Blues Brothers*-style. Then, Neale suggested 'Whiskey in the Jar' and 'Wild Rover'. Both songs he could lead from the fiddle and that the audience would be able to sing along to. Dominique suggested a few more of her songs, stripped right back, because we didn't have a horn section.

"Oh, and we could do 'I Come from the Blues'," she added, which got my vote. With that, we had enough for our set.

The conversation drifted back around to the first set and its successes. Jake got into an argument with Neale about sport—the merits of rugby versus Gaelic football, or possibly hurling. I forgot which because that was when I noticed Neale's glass was full. Again.

"How many is that?"

"I'm not countin', Kai. 'Tis free, after all. I don't ask for them; the waitress just gives them to me."

I saw red. And maybe it was our balance sheet turning from black to red, but I was angry. Then I felt Jamie's hand on my elbow. That was right. I'd promised myself I wouldn't kill Neale until we were back to England. Unless I had a clear shot with no witnesses.

"There's no such thing as free drinks for the band, Neale. You should know that."

I held up the beer mat. It was well-decorated with little gates, each one with four vertical bars and a fifth diagonal. "You know what this is?"

He shook his head.

"This is how they run a tab in Köln. Every stroke is a glass that one of us has drunk. They're grouped in fives, so we've had…thirty-two so far. If you don't want another, just turn your glass upside down when you've had enough. If drinks were free, they'd not be checking them off. He's keeping a tab, no doubt. So. No. Free. Drinks. Got it?"

"Ah, fuck you, yer spoilsport."

But he said it like a kid who'd been caught with his hand in the cookie jar. Trying it on.

"Take it easy, Neale. That's all I'm saying. Else, we're playing this second set solely to cover your bar bill."

He growled. Not threateningly, only enough to let me know

he wasn't happy, but he wasn't going to argue either.

*

BUT IT WAS all too late.

Too late because it was half an hour after midnight before Rumpel gave us the okay to go on stage. Too late because the audience had peaked and was already dwindling. Too late because we were tired and had lost our edge. Too late because Neale had already drunk way too much beer and couldn't play, but not enough that he'd curl up and go to sleep in a corner somewhere, out of sight and hearing.

Yet it had started well enough. We kicked off with 'I Come from the Blues'. Yes, it was Clay's song, but it was made for Dominique's voice. Despite the title, it wasn't really a blues song, at least not classic twelve-bar blues. It was slow, moody-jazzy in a minor key. Something Billie Holiday might have sung.

> *My momma, she loved me, but she loved to fight.*
> *My daddy, he left her, and vanished from sight.*
> *So who can I trust to love me and care?*
> *I'm searching for someone, but nobody's there*
>
> .
>
> .
>
> .
>
> .
>
> *The blues never leaves me, it's deep down inside*
> *It laughs when I laugh, as it cried when I cried*
> *The blues is the singer, and I am its song*
> *I come from the blues; it survives when I'm gone.*

Neale was rapt, sitting off to the side of the stage, cradling his fiddle. I could almost believe there was a tear in his eye. But that was the song for you—it went straight for the soul. And the tear ducts.

If we'd had more like that…

…but instead, we'd picked 'Gimme Some Lovin'. It took the tempo up, and suddenly, Neale was ranging across the stage, lurching and sawing whenever he thought it was his solo. Smiling beatifically one moment, he bathed in the glory of his own genius, then snarled at the band's imagined foul-ups the next.

There was a moment in the *Blues Brothers* film where Jake and Elwood bail out of a gig, crawling down beneath the stage and fleeing back to Chicago. If there'd been a trapdoor in the stage that night, I'd have crawled down it. But there was no escape from the awfulness of that second set.

At least, not for us. The audience was bailing out pretty quickly. Rumpel was no fool. The moment he realised what was going on, he pulled the plug on us. The stage power cut. The sound and lights both faded in a couple of seconds, leaving me still bashing out a rhythm from behind the kit. I downed my sticks sharpish. That left Neale, still prancing and reeling in front of the few remaining punters.

He kept on going, cheered on by a lone, emerald-green-clad drunk in the audience. Finally—it felt like an hour but was probably only three minutes—Neale ran out of steam. He bowed at the drunk, swore at the rest of us, now off stage, and tottered into the darkness after us. He left to ironic cheers and catcalls.

Jamie had taken the lead in the negotiations over the second set, and now he bore the brunt of Herr Rumpel's anger.

"Ehr besoffenenen Wichser. Huck aff un kutt mir ja net widder."

His Cologne dialect made no sense at first. But I let the words roll around my head. I still couldn't make head or tail of the first bit, save that we were some kind of awful people. Drunk people. No — person. *Wichser?* Not in my vocabulary. *Net widder* was surely *nicht wieder* — never again. But the message was clear. We'd fucked up. Rumpel didn't want us around, and I couldn't blame him.

He didn't pay us for the second set, and that was no more than we deserved. Jamie tried to argue he should still pay us for the first set, which had been okay. So, of course, Rumpel pulled out our (Neale's) bar bill, which he claimed wiped out a big chunk of the fee for the first set.

It was going to get nasty; Jamie was starting to get riled. Which should have been my job. No, we could each be as bad as the other. Sometimes worse.

Dominique intervened and somehow persuaded Rumpel to settle on 175 euros. Which still worked out at fifteen euros a head on beer. I opened my mouth, ready to correct Rumpel's arithmetic, but Dominique caught my eye first.

"Let's go, guys."

Jamie stood firm.

"Come on, Jamie," said Dominique. "It's time to leave."

That did the trick. The words, plus her hand on his arm. Putty.

For a moment, I saw Herr Rumpel's expression soften too. Would Dominique work magic there too?

His eyes hardened.

And his eyes stayed hard as he watched us load the van,

checking that we didn't steal anything. As if.

Actually, he was right. Neale was all for nicking anything that wasn't screwed to the wall or, failing that, setting off the fire extinguishers. Rumpel took out his smartphone and made a point of photographing each of us as we passed him. He took a couple of shots of the van, making another point of capturing the registration plate. After that, he stood there, glowering, with his hand poised to speed dial the *Polizei*.

Telepathy prevailed. By unspoken agreement, we made sure somebody was with Neale at all times. The loading was slow and tense as a result. But at least Neale couldn't sneak off to wreak his own petty, pointless vengeance against Rumpel.

Neale shouldn't have been driving with all he'd been drinking. He took the drive through the streets of Köln at a snail's pace, swearing at every frustrated driver that flashed him from behind.

The gate was locked when we finally reached the campsite. There was nowhere to park, except right in front of the gate. I volunteered to sleep in the van to make sure no one broke in. Dominique offered to bring my sleeping bag back from the tent.

I watched Neale make a hash of climbing over the gate, heard a rip, and saw a flash of underpants through the parted seam. Jake and Jamie steadied him, helped him down from the gate. I thought Neale would lose his rag, but instead, he burst into hysterical laughter. Everyone disappeared into the dark. I fiddled with the keys to turn the headlights off but leave the sides and cabin on so Dominique would have something to aim for when she returned.

*

I WOKE TO find Dominique climbing into the passenger seat. Her expression was deeply disapproving.

"What's the matter?" I asked.

She told me how Jake had produced a tin of — mostly — tobacco and proceeded to roll a joint, which he'd then proceeded to offer around.

"In the tent? So you left them to it."

"Yes. Laughing like hyenas? Is that the phrase?"

I shrugged. "I get the picture. I've been there, when every remark is irresistibly funny. They'll be awake for hours. Assholes."

She held up two sleeping bags. I'd seen them already.

"So you're not going back."

"*Non.* I don't like drugs. I don't trust them. And smoke is bad for the voice. I hope you don't mind if I stay."

Mind? No, I didn't mind.

"Back or front?" I asked, pointing over my shoulder at the makeshift bench made out of two speaker cabs.

"Back."

*

NEALE HAD BEEN right — the metal shell of a van did bugger all to hold back the chill. I spent the next hour or so neither awake nor asleep. I could hear frequent rustlings from the back. Dominique was having as much trouble sleeping. I drifted and found an almost-dream in which I was on a narrow ledge, halfway up Everest. My fellow climbers were snug in their tents, but in the strange logic of dreams, I'd ended up tentless. Not only tentless, but without sleeping bag and, of course, naked. Snow had begun to fall. Then a large drift slid down on top of me, covering my face so that I couldn't breathe.

"*Je suis désolée, Kai*… I'm so sorry."

Oh.

I was awake and back in the van. Something warm and soft lay over my face. A sleeping bag. The next moment, it was removed.

Dominique was looking down at me. "*J'ai froid.*"

"Yeah. I'm cold too."

She slid over the seat and unrolled her sleeping bag next to me, head to toe.

"Y'welcome," I mumbled.

The other climbers were still snug in their tent. But I now had a warm yeti next to me. If it didn't eat me, and if we didn't tumble off the mountain, maybe I'd survive until the morning.

*

THEN I WAS waking up to someone banging loudly on the van. Dominique…

I sat up, feeling almost warm, looking around to see what was doing the banging. In the back of the van, Dominique sat up in her sleeping bag, holding a book open, but she wasn't reading. She was staring out of the window, eyes wide.

Another bang.

It was the campsite boss, wanting me to move the van and unblock the gate. Right now. On the other side of the gate, a car waited to get out. Damn. I needed Neale, and he wasn't around, probably still drunk, stoned, or both, back at the tent.

The manager was not pleased, and I was willing to bet he'd

boot us out if the van wasn't moved double-quick. The way our luck was running, he'd withhold our deposit. Two hundred euros we couldn't afford to lose.

So, I reversed the van away from the gate. Somehow, I managed to find the right gear and not stall the thing. It even started for me first time. Yeah, I didn't have a full licence. If I pranged the van, I'd be in a helluva load of trouble. I didn't prang the van.

The driver pulled out, towing a caravan about the size of a barn. He gave me a friendly, middle-finger wave, but I let it pass. I was still quaking inside, knowing the stupid risk I'd taken. Then, the boss was waving at me to come into the campsite. I put the van in gear again, stalled, and went to pieces, driving-wise.

"*Sois calme*," Dominique whispered, "Stay calm," and patted my shoulder. I turned back to catch her eye and got an encouraging smile in return.

I didn't trust myself to do more than park up next to the main building.

In daylight, the van looked okay. We'd packed it well, and there seemed to be plenty of room. Oh, right, the tent and bags were out, down at the far end of the site. Taking account of that, it all tallied. Nothing too major missing, at any rate.

"Shall we get some breakfast?" Dominique asked.

That suited me fine.

*

"THANKS FOR KEEPING me warm last night," I told her as we tucked into croissants and jam. "I dreamed we were on Everest, and you were a huge, hairy yeti. You were very warm, and you didn't eat me. Thank you."

She smiled, or almost smiled, as though I'd said not the right thing. Not what she'd hoped or wanted.

"You are welcome," she replied after a pause. And then, "It was quite cold. I…I changed around later on in the night. I hope I did not…disturb you. It was warmer that way."

"I didn't notice. You didn't wake me. It didn't seem as cold though."

She nodded. "I am glad you sang harmonies last night. You have a nice voice and a good ear for harmony."

"Thank you. I wasn't sure. A couple of times, it didn't quite work, I thought."

"Of course. But nothing terrible happened. It is part of music. You try things. Sometimes, they work. Sometimes…" She gave a Gallic shrug, head tilted, lips pouted, and a comic glint in her eye. "…not."

I laughed. It was so very French. All that was missing was a beret and pack of Gauloises. But no. Dominique was too concerned about her voice—she'd turned down a joint last night for that reason.

Thinking about that, my face fell. Jamie, Neale, and Jake. Drunk and stoned, most likely. What sort of a hangover were they going to have this morning? Especially Neale, given that we were going to be driving to Aachen for the gig tonight.

Dominique downed the last of her coffee. "We might not see the others for a while. I think they will be quite bad this morning. Their heads will not be pleasant inside."

Exactly what I'd been thinking. Dominique was *très sympa*, I decided—my kind of person.

"Do you think I have time for a shower?" she asked.

"I should think so."

Hmm. I'd been wearing the same clothes all the way from England, through one sweaty gig and through the night. I was probably pretty whiffy myself. Was Dominique dropping a gentle hint? I sniffed, and my nose confirmed.

"Hint taken. I'd better join you."

She raised an eyebrow at that. Part amused, part surprised, part something I couldn't quite make out. I blushed.

"It's okay," she said with a chuckle, patting my hand. "Separate cubicles. Sleeping together was necessary. Showering together..."

That Gallic shrug again. It could mean so many things, especially in tandem with a twinkling eye.

"I hope you're joking," I said.

"Yes. You are not offended?"

"No. I'm not offended."

"But you are under a lot of stress. The others, they are not very responsible. You do so much planning, and they think it is all a joke. I do not want to make more stress for you. So, my joke, it was a bad one. I am sorry."

"It's okay. Really."

"Perhaps. But I will get to know you better so that I know when to make a joke that you will enjoy."

Dominique grabbed a towel and some fresh clothes and disappeared off in the direction of the shower block. I stayed in the van, having told her I didn't want to leave it unattended. Now that I'd checked, I was all too conscious of my own stink. I hoped she'd be quick.

I had Dominique down as a thorough shower person, but

she didn't dally. She was back in ten minutes, bright and smiling, with a fresh white T-shirt, tight over damp skin, and no bra. No stress, eh, Dominique?

I bailed out quickly, heading straight for the shower. I *was* a thorough shower person. That could be a good thing when smelly and sweaty, but it was also a bad thing if one had too much time with nothing to do but think while soap and hot water dug out the sweat and grime.

I dried myself thoroughly.

*

THE TENTED THREESOME had yet to emerge. Dominique and I returned to the café, which overlooked the river, and ordered coffees. We found a couple of armchairs by the picture window. With the free Wi-Fi, I had my head down, deep in social media-land, looking for what the @ClubLoreleiKoeln punters had posted about the gig.

It was a mistake. We'd got some good tweets after the first set, but the second set had been panned. Footage of Neale, which might have been comic in other circumstances, was just a bit too raw, and anything I tweeted in my current frame of mind I would definitely regret later.

I put my phone away. Dominique was watching the Rhine traffic — working barges, pleasure cruisers, a coxed eight, whatever. She became aware of me watching her.

"You were looking at Twitter?"

I nodded. "It's not good."

"There will be no more like it."

"I hope not."

"There was so much that was good. Tonight, we will build on that. Now, you must put it out of your mind. Let the river take it."

That poor river. All of my bile last night and now the hurt and embarrassment of a crap gig.

I didn't see them approach, and Dominique was again completely lost in the river. But we heard them climbing the stairs, and I could catch their voices but not the words.

"They're here." That was Jamie, leading. "Hi, guys."

"Good party?" I asked.

No answer. Sheepish looks from all three.

"You all right?" Jake asked. If any of the three looked most guilty, it was Jake.

"Fine, thanks. Fresh air and a good night's sleep is good for a body."

"Right." Jake again. "Er, are they still serving breakfast?"

"Might be lunch, but go ahead and grab some. You've got time to eat before we head for Aachen."

Jake and Neale found a table and started on the breakfast buffet. Jamie hung back and asked Dominique if she was okay.

"Yes, Jamie. I am fine, thank you."

"You could have stayed. Last night. It wasn't…wild or anything. We…talked."

"Yes, I know I could have stayed. I can look after myself."

"Was it the…weed?"

"Yes. I don't do drugs."

"You disapprove, then."

"No. I do not judge you. I make my own choices. I drink a little wine, sometimes the beer. I do not smoke. I do not enjoy the smoke of other people. That is all."

"But you are all right? Not angry?"

"I am…fine. I am not angry."

"We are still friends?"

"Yes. We are friends. Now, if you please, go and get some breakfast."

The whole time Jamie didn't look at me once. He wanted Dominique's forgiveness, not mine. So, his attention was all for her, and I was free to people-watch. First, Jamie tried to meet her gaze, and then, he looked down in druggie-shame. He must have realised he was staring at Dominique's boobs, and he looked up again, ashamed for ogling her. And the whole cycle repeated.

Now, as he turned to the buffet, Jamie still wouldn't meet my eye.

"*Bon appétit*," I called to his back.

Silence.

"Oh dear," said Dominique.

Chapter Thirteen

Friday, September 30, 2016
Travelling to Aachen, An der Ecke

DOMINIQUE'S BACKING BAND wasn't speaking to me anymore. Hell, they weren't even speaking to one another when they were in my presence.

I should backtrack.

I wasn't angry with anyone. But I was disappointed. I probably didn't need to say a word, but I did anyway. I thought I'd come on this tour with three adults, but apparently. they'd left their wits at the border: *"Come on, guys, what the fuck are we doing carrying drugs? Do you even know what the penalties are?"*

And other words to the same effect. They didn't argue with me. They didn't defend themselves against my accusations of substance abuse and other sundry tomfoolery. Even Neale accepted my bollocking without a word of backchat.

So, I kept going. I wanted them to whimper, but they wouldn't. I overdid it, and it took a warning touch from Dominique to shut me up.

"Okay, guys. Let's get the show on the road."

Silence. But they moved. We drove from the café down to the far end of the campsite. Everyone got out and disappeared into the tent. After a few minutes, hands passed out packed travel bags and bundled sleeping bags.

Still not a word.

Then, the three mutes emerged and stood. Their expressions weren't defiant or long-suffering but very carefully blank.

If one of them gave a signal, I didn't see it. They turned back to the tent, started to take it down. On his own and sober, Jamie would have done it perfectly. Hungover, they fell short of perfect, but they didn't mess it up either.

Their silence was winding me up something rotten. And then I decided to play passive-aggressive too. I left them to it and went to stand on the far side of the van where I couldn't see them and get annoyed. Dominique watched what was going on, exasperated. We kept to safe subjects—the weather, the expected travel time to Aachen—speaking in hushed voices while the silence kept thickening.

Fifteen minutes later, the last banging noises ceased. I heard a clatter of people climbing into the van, followed by doors slamming.

I looked around. Neale sat in the driver's seat, Jake and Jamie in the back. I did a litter patrol of the pitch but found nothing left behind. No debris. No lost property. Not so much as a single orphaned sock.

They'd done a good job. Perfect. Naturally. Jamie had seen to that.

Dominique had seated herself next to Neale already, so I climbed up next to her and pulled the door shut. Without a word, Neale started the engine. It caught first time, behaving properly again as if my fuel folly had never happened. We drove back to the campsite gate, parked, and I went to the office to settle the bill. When I emerged, deposit refunded in full, the van was on the other side of the gate, exactly where it had been parked the previous night, now ready to drive away.

For a moment, I wondered if they would do that—drive away without me. It would have been a relief from the head games, but no. That wasn't how passive-aggressive worked. They waited for me, let me climb over the gate, and get back in the van. Then, we pulled away. In silence.

It would be a short drive to Aachen, relatively speaking. Google decided it was about an hour and gave me a choice of buses, trains, as well as a couple of routes by car. Neale followed signs to the *autobahn*, the main German highway. In total silence.

To give him credit, he drove well, given that his blood was still an interesting cocktail of psychoactive substances. He drove with a fierce concentration, hunched over the wheel and making acceptable use of the remaining wing mirror.

I played the same game—silence. I'd have happily chatted with Dominique, but she'd fallen asleep between me and Neale. I guessed the late night and the cold had taken their toll more than she cared to admit. If not, she was avoiding getting involved and faking sleep very well.

*

SOMETHING HAD TO break the deadlock, and it had to be me. But in my defence, I had no choice.

I hadn't slept well enough, either, but I did notice the white line in the middle of the road was now disappearing right under Dominique. I turned to Neale. His eyes were *closed.*

"NEALE! Wake UP!"

That might not have been my brightest idea, but his eyes sprang open.

He wrenched the wheel around to the left, taking us back into the path of the fastest traffic. A horn sounded, and a BMW sped past us on the right.

"Wrong lane, Neale! This isn't England…"

Neale still wasn't with it. But at least he hadn't hit the central barrier. Yet.

He braked, and we should all have died, stopped in the fast lane of the autobahn. We had the luck of the Irish, perhaps, because nothing hit us. I glanced in the mirror on my left. A Mercedes had screeched to a halt about three yards behind us, the smoke rising where it'd burned rubber. Behind it, a line of cars stretched back. I didn't know how far.

"What the fuck do I do?" Neale asked.

"Start up. Drive on. Hope that no one smashes into the back of that queue behind us."

He put the car into gear, and we moved off. Because of the weight in the back, it took a while for us to get up to speed. The other cars flashed us as they overtook on the right. If we didn't get out of the left lane quickly, we'd be pulled over by the next police car to come along. Surely, we'd already been spotted; there must have been surveillance cameras we'd passed.

Finally, a gap opened up, and Neale was able to get into the next lane.

I'd been checking the map. "Come off in half a mile."

I directed him to a small town with a petrol station and a café, where we could take time out and calm down. Dominique, Jake, and Jamie had been dozing and had missed all the fun. Neale and I, however, were still white with shock. On the plus side, he and I were talking, and neither of us was too fussed about who'd caved in first.

I didn't know if it was okay to have coffee after a shock. Too bad. We all had coffees. I needed one, and Neale needed something strong that didn't contain alcohol.

Jamie was getting nervous. "Shouldn't we be getting on?"

"*Non*, Neale needs to rest."

"But we've got to get to the gig."

"We can wait," Dominique suggested. "It's not far to Aix-la-Chapelle. Aachen."

Jamie wasn't happy, so I chipped in.

"Look at Neale. He's done in. Knackered."

Dominique surprised me then. "Do you want me to drive?"

"You?"

That was Jamie. So, he didn't know *everything* about Dominique.

"Yes. I can drive."

"What about insurance?"

"You weren't worried about him driving while drunk!" Dominique challenged. "Why are you so fussed about insurance?"

"That's not the same…"

"It's just the same. Both illegal."

"But you can drive? You're not simply making a point?"

"I can drive us, Jamie, and if it were an emergency, I would. But why? We aren't in any hurry. We simply need to let Neale rest."

Jamie looked thoughtful but said nothing. I could see him filing that information away. One day, it might be useful.

Through all of that, Neale said nothing at all. That was how much he was in shock, that he didn't react.

"Get some sleep, Neale," said Dominique softly.

We walked with him back to the van. He lay down across the front bench seat, and I covered him with a blanket. He smiled his thanks to me. It was a start. I was still hoping he'd apologise for being a drunken asshole. Someday.

We left him there and returned to the café.

Dominique stayed put in our booth, as the rest of us worked the pool table. Jamie sat with her first while Jake played me. Jake was actually quite good, and I wasn't, so he wiped the floor with me in pretty short order. I took Jamie's seat, facing Dominique, my back to the table.

"We should have a little chat," she said. "About the band, but about you too."

"Me? I'm nobody. Just the drummer."

"By choice? You spoke of joining the band at its beginning. You must already have had skills because you told me you auditioned guitarists."

"You remember when we spoke over Hangouts? I mentioned Cassie and her fixation with fresh air and exercise…"

"Ah, yes."

"I would have been twelve — no, thirteen. Dad was hiding in a bottle, and Jamie wasn't much better."

"And you?"

"That child wasn't Kai. Remember how I told you that Cassie decided the way to dry Dad out was to take us walking along the north Cornish coast path? She kept an eye on us, made sure nobody sneaked any booze along. Jamie and I were both Scouts, so camping was practically in our blood. Anyway, one afternoon, we stumbled into Polwithen. It's a tiny village, but it's set in a cleft where some glacier gouged out an arena. It made a great natural theatre, and a local entrepreneur put on a music festival that summer.

"I can't remember the name of the band now, but it doesn't matter. Whoever they were, they blew us away. Cassie saw the signs and seized the moment. When we returned home, Jamie and I were equipped with a bass guitar and a drum kit off eBay, and we started our journey into the blues.

"It wasn't a straight-line journey, at least not for me. I didn't get on with the drums at first, so I switched to guitar. Then my guitar got stolen, and about the same time, I came across Toto. They were way outside my normal orbit — that orbit being straight blues, as per the great Joe Bonamassa — but their drummer caught my imagination. I dusted off my old drum kit, got some more lessons, and never looked back."

"That would have been Jeff Porcaro — the drummer who inspired you, yes?"

"Yeah. It broke my heart when I found out he was already dead, and I'd never get to see him play. But I put heart and soul into becoming a half-decent drummer."

"That is what they call British understatement. You are more than that. And you have a lovely voice. You could be a singer in your own right."

"But not in a blues band."

"Perhaps not. But if you really want to sing, your heart and your voice and a muse will find a place to meet."

"My heart?"

"Of course. Once your heart learns to love, then it wants to sing."

"I love music already. As I told you, it's what I studied at college."

"I was not talking about loving music. I was talking about love. Of people. Have you learned to love people?"

"I'm not a virgin, if that's what you're asking."

She sighed. "Never mind. Tell me about Jake. He intrigues me. He loves the blues. He puts great feeling into it. Where does that come from?"

"Jake? I don't really know him. He doesn't talk much about himself. He's shy anyway. He listens a lot when we all go for a drink. Sometimes, he can be really funny — he'll pick the exact moment to drop in a witty line, and we'll all crack up."

"Hmm."

"Why are you asking this?"

"I'm trying to find the soul of this band, so I can work with it. Jamie has told me a little."

"You mean, when you met him at the aire? Or…before?"

"Before. We exchanged phone numbers. It was easier than using the muzomart dot com chat."

She caught my raised eyebrow. "Ah. You did not know? I am sorry. He told me you were working on getting me rehearsal tracks, so I assumed you were…the engineer, and he was the manager. I was very grateful for those tracks, by the way."

"You're welcome."

"But it is more subtle than that, wasn't it? You put so much energy into this band. Where does it come from? You wanted this tour to go ahead so much that I think Jamie was afraid of you."

"I was pretty pissed off with Clay."

"That I can understand. You are stubborn. You like the world to be just so, and you make your plans accordingly, and you do not like it when someone — what is it — *déranger*?"

"Disrupt. Yes. I get angry when folks change my plans. But I'm not a control freak."

"Good. You are aware of the danger. You went for a long walk last night."

I smiled. "Yes. I had a lot of poison to dump in the Rhine."

She laughed. "Very funny. There is a time for anger, and channelling it can accomplish much. But if you are always angry, it will destroy you. So, I make you this offer. If you feel the anger is growing, and you need to take a walk, I will walk with you. As a friend. Will you do that?"

I took several deep breaths. I saw only Dominique before me, knew that in some unearned way, she cared for me. And for the others.

"I will do that."

"And when the anger is gone, I would like to see the other, gentler emotions you do not show."

I nodded. A tiny little nod that was scarcely more than a

shiver of my jaw as her words shot past my guard and dove into my heart.

"The soul is hard to find. But last night, I began to see that soul. Clay's song—"

"I know. It's beautiful. And you made it yours. Astonishing."

"Thank you. I tried to do it justice. But where did it come from? Clay alone?"

"No. Clay came up with the words. But we made suggestions. Some he kept. Some he didn't."

"How about the opening verse?" And she sang, softly:

> *My momma, she loved me, but she loved to fight.*
> *My daddy, he left her, and vanished from sight…*

"That was certainly Clay," I answered.

Her face fell, only for a moment, and I got the feeling it wasn't the answer she'd been looking for.

"His parents did split up, though I think he made up the part about his daddy vanishing. I think they're both still living in Marden Combe or nearby."

"Never mind. I hoped it might have been more of a collaborative song, with your own experiences."

Not mine. But I said nothing.

"As I say—never mind. So instead, I will have to start with the physical appearance."

With a start, I realised she was talking about the band again. "You mean, on stage. You are going to make stage patter about our appearance. Jokes?"

"Something like that. But I will not be cruel. I promise. Last night, I talked about myself because I can always do that. I was playing around, mixing French, German, and English, but it was a gimmick, to help my nerves. Tonight, the focus must be on the whole band. I will try little things to see what does work. For us all."

"Clay wasn't like that…"

"I am not Clay, and he isn't me."

Behind us, Jamie and Jake were closely matched in their pool game. Jake usually had the edge, but this time, there was no victory cry from him. Instead, I heard the rattle of balls as Jamie racked up the new game.

"I would like to talk with Jake. This next gig is his, isn't it? The one he arranged?"

I nodded. "I'll try to keep Jamie busy." I got up and picked up the new game with my brother.

The gods were with me, and Jamie couldn't pocket the balls worth a damn that session. Neither could I, but for long minutes, I managed to hide the cue ball where he couldn't do much damage. When I wasn't taking a shot, I glanced across to Jake and Dominique. To my surprise, they were talking with some animation. I wondered what on earth had brought Jake out of his shell. I didn't think he had it in him to be so forthcoming, that he'd have been totally tongue-tied with such an attractive, downright sexy creature as Dominique.

Jamie managed a fluky cannon then. Two of his own balls went down, but he also left himself on for clearing the table. Seeing the end, I moved closer to Dominique and Jake, still watching Jamie, but now I could hear what they were talking about.

Blues guitarists. Of course. And Dominique was holding her own. She was telling him about a Clapton gig she'd been to a couple of years back in Paris, on the same tour that Jake had seen him. They were comparing set lists.

Jamie missed a pocket then, so I had to get back to the game. But I fluffed my shot and gave him the opening he needed to pocket the last of the 'stripes' and then the eight ball.

"Best of three?" I asked.

Jamie was all ready to head back and resume his conversation with Dominique. "What? But it's my turn… I mean, Jake needs to come and play you."

"Jake doesn't need to do any such thing, fatbrain. He's having a nice chat with Dominique, so leave them be."

"But—"

"But nothing. You'll get your chance to talk with her before the tour is done."

"But what if—"

"Cool it, Jamie. I know what you're thinking, so please don't say it. Stop thinking with your balls and give your brain a chance. I've had a couple chats with Dominique, and she's a people person, the sort who *has* to get to know people she meets. That's what she's doing now. I know it looks intense, but that's how she is. She's being friends. *Friends.* okay?"

I'd dropped my voice. If Dominique could hear us, it didn't matter so much; I was pretty sure she'd make sure her end of the conversation didn't falter. But I didn't want to disrupt Jake's flow.

Did I feel sorry for Jake? For his shyness and awkward nature? Yes, a little. And there was a little bit of devil in me who wanted to give Jamie a bit of competition. A bit of sibling one-upmanship in return for his overeagerness to get at Dominique on the tour. Not that I minded her being here now. But Jamie had been plotting conquest like a Caesar, and he needed taking down a peg or two.

Wearing a face that would sour milk, Jamie put a couple of coins in the slot. The balls thundered down, and we racked them up. He beat me. It was quick. I potted one, no, two balls. Jamie sent down the eight ball, gave me a mean look, and strode over to Jake and Dominique.

"Come on, guys," he said. "Neale's had enough sleep. We've a gig to play."

Jamie, you selfish git. You couldn't leave them alone, could you?

*

FROM THE CAFÉ, the satnav had taken us to the gig venue without mishap, but it was all closed up. We couldn't see a thing inside. Steel shutters blocked the windows and the doors. The dirty grey concrete buildings gave the neighbourhood a rough, industrial feel. I shivered, glancing back at the van to make sure nobody was stealing the gear.

I couldn't see any posters about our gig. Nothing with our name on it, at any rate. No passing trade. No one to ask when the club might open. So, we headed into the *Stadtmitte*, the city centre. There, in one of the lovely open squares that Germany does so well, six bronze statues surrounded a pool. I laughed out loud. They weren't the only statues there. I noted the other brilliant caricatures, art that was meant to be funny—with a sly dig—and to be touched. Articulated. Truly, a city with a sense of humour.

I fell in love with Aachen.

First stop was a coffee shop with Wi-Fi. Social media time; @JohnDoesBlues time. Time to look at the coverage from our first set and learn. We searched Twitter and Instagram, mostly. Perhaps I'd been a bit too hasty to condemn all our coverage; there were a few positives when we dug for them. Rumpel had done a big build up after our first set, and someone had posted a smartphone video on YouTube of 'Sitting on Top of the World'. It was handheld, so a bit shaky, and mostly centred on Dominique, but it captured Jake's solo. It wasn't flawless — on a smartphone, live music always sounds tinny and off-key — but we found a couple of other posts that weren't too bad, and we got to retweeting.

"Hey, Neale," I called. "Someone's labelled you '*Der hot Geiger*'."

He grinned, then looked worried. "What the fuck does that mean? Am I radioactive?"

"'*Der Geiger*' is German for a fiddler. Hot is probably just an autocorrect glitch."

"Hot? Fuckin' right I'm hot. And me fiddle-playin's fuckin' brilliant too."

That wasn't what the later tweets from the @ClubLoreleiKoeln punters were saying, but there was a time and a place for brutal honesty. This was the time and the place to zip lips.

Still, we had enough okay coverage to work with. We majored on Dominique's visual presence on Instagram. She looked fantastic, though it really should have been about the music. That second set hadn't cut it, and there was no avoiding it. In hindsight, I was glad I'd left the Lorelei's @JohnDoesBlues handbills in the van.

We left the café and found a spot close by the *Kreislauf des Geldes*, locally known as the 'money fountain', where we could busk to raise a bit of cash for our next bar bill.

Neale roved, and Jake and I followed him as he moved through the statues like the Pied Piper, enchanting the children trailing behind him. Neale posed with those statues, serenading them, wooing them, mocking them. And then he moved on again, springing high into the air one moment, crouching down low the next.

Jake picked up on the mood, and whatever Neale did at a particular spot, Jake did the same a step later. And I, yeah, I did the same. And bugger me if we hadn't picked up a whole conga line of passers-by, adults and children, all laughing and getting into the groove. Around we went, and then Neale hopped up onto the broad rim of the pool. And I wasn't quite sure if he paused a beat too long, and Jake just bumped into him, or whether Neale couldn't help pushing the boundaries, but there was a splash, and Neale was dancing in the pool, cackling and sawing on the fiddle.

And, of course, Jake followed. I hesitated for the space of one what-the-fuck and splashed in too. The English abroad, eh?

The children, I noticed a few moments later, did not follow. Nor did the adults. The water wasn't deep, wasn't dirty, but dancing in it was clearly *verboten*. The mood was broken, and the three of us were left capering on our own, our music and our frivolity quickly and awkwardly stilled.

Neale faced us and frowned. He gestured with his bow, motioning us to bend over, and as we bent, he teacher-stared down his nose at us and mimed a caning. Whereupon he struck up a mournful air and led us disconsolately out of the pool.

We didn't quite recover the jollity after that. The coins stopped dropping in the hat until our audience had cycled and our transgressions had swept away.

Nevertheless, we gave out many handbills with the name of the club correctly spelled and with @JohnDoesBlues prominent. *An der Ecke.* It meant 'on the corner', which it was. With those statues around us, the whole of Aachen felt like a neighbourly place for a gig. I quite forgot the grim appearance of the suburb of the evening's venue.

We rang the changes and brought Dominique in to sing. Jake lent Jamie his acoustic guitar, and the two of them did a few songs while we went in search of dry socks. Then, I held the fort in the van while Jake and Neale returned to busk once more. I didn't notice when Dominique left, but I did see when she returned — with Jake, carrying several shopping bags between them.

"Stage clothes," Jake said, a big grin on his face. "We found some charity shops."

The weather had been fine, though still a little chilly, and there was beer money in the hat. Dominique had sung, which had helped a lot, but Neale's fiddle had also gone down well. We'd found a couple of Irish-style pubs, relics from the Cold War. Back then there'd been a big American presence in Germany. Every Irish-American serviceman had been a sucker for stout made with genuine 'Liffey Water'. So, Neale's music, his jigs and reels, still touched hearts, even though there were few Americans around. Irish-American Germans, perhaps?

Jamie had been trying to call the owner at our venue, the An der Ecke, and he'd finally got through early afternoon. She told us we could show up at five.

"She sounds young," Jamie commented. "If her face matches her voice…"

"She'll be a dragon," I teased. "She'll be old enough to be your grandmother."

Jamie made a rude gesture at me, which I ignored because, out of the corner of my eye, I saw Jake listening closely and looking worried.

"What's up, Jake?" I asked.

"I'm hoping we'll do better tonight."

"Me too."

"Yeah, but this is my gig. The one I set up."

"It'll be better. Last night was learning to work together. Knocking off the rough edges. The busking is more of the same. Don't worry."

Dominique needed a break, and she went back to the van, relieving Jamie from guard duty. He convinced me to sing another folk song — 'Matty Groves', a nineteen-verse everybody-dies monster from early English folk-rock days. What the hell. But we were running out of material

None of us wanted to strain our voices, so we packed up around half three and arrived at the An der Ecke with three quarters of an hour in hand. I was, once again, struck by the industrial nature of the district. Someone suggested we take some moody, arty photos of ourselves in front of the club. We did have plans to record some tracks for an album when we got back home, and we needed an album cover. Those 'stage clothes' turned out to be for Jake — an all-red mishmash of drainpipe-narrow trousers, shirt, and a hat that turned him from scruffy guitar nerd to pro-axeman. *'Le Gentilhomme en Rouge,'* Dom called him. The Gentleman in Red.

Neale and Dom got into the spirit of things too. It was Jamie's idea to take photos, and it was his camera. *Brother, you are so transparent.* But Dom didn't seem to mind and even played along with some of Jamie's somewhat risqué ideas.

Dom? One of us had called her by this name, and she'd smiled and said, 'Yes, I can be Dom if you like," and by the end of the afternoon, it was like we'd never called her anything else.

Then, at the sound of keys in locks and the first squeaks of metal, the shutters rattled up into their casings. As they did, we observed two pairs of feet appear at the base of the shutters. More squeaking of metal and two pairs of shapely legs appeared, clad in spandex, bright-coloured stripes winding up. Jamie's jaw dropped in anticipation.

"Close your mouth, Jamie. Dragons. Grandmothers."

But he wasn't listening, and I had a feeling I would eat sawdust shortly anyway. Hips followed, and tight, bright, matching spandex tops. The odds were against either a dragon or a grandmother.

I'd guess the girl on the left was nineteen. Lustrous, ebon hair cascaded past her shoulders and splashed in arcs of night over the rainbow spandex below.

The other woman was older. She had the same aristocratic nose and the same set of the eyes, though she'd cropped and rainbowed her hair to blend with the top. Mother and daughter? Hers was a more mature glamour. Glamour was the right word because now Neale's eyes were popping when, for the most part, he'd managed to avoid ogling Dom.

The women exchanged glances and a quick smile. They knew the effect they'd had on their watchers. Their little show was done.

"Hallo," said the older woman. "Come in, come in."

And then it was all business. Unloading the van. Setting up on stage.

The stage was small, designed for a disco rig. That rig had been pushed off to one side but still filled too much of the floor for comfort. Every stage started like that, I reminded myself.

Neale stood facing the bar with a wistful expression.

"Eyes front," I said, sotto voce. "There's work to do."

His gaze lingered a moment, and he murmured, "Fine looking woman." Then he straightened his shoulders and—to be fair—made a decent job of wiring up the PA. A very good job, actually. Just like I'd done it the previous night. I let him get on with it and went back to drum set-up. When I was done, I checked everything over.

"Thanks, Neale. You've done a good job." I meant it.

He looked up from the faders, smiled like a naughty child caught helping an old lady across the road, nodded, and looked back down again. "'S'all right."

Then, he plugged his fiddle in, and instantly, a horrible mains hum emanated from the floor monitor.

"What the fuck is that?" he yelled. Then, "Excuse my French. I meant to say, where the bloody hell is that mains hum coming from?"

Some venues were like that. We'd wired every single cable the same as the previous night, but last night, there'd been no hum. Tonight, hum. We checked the power all the way back to the wall outlets and tried wiring everything through a single outlet. Still hum. We ran an extension over to a different outlet and took the power from that. Still hum.

I got the screwdriver out and disconnected the earth wire. It wasn't a good idea to do that—it wasn't safe. But I did it anyway. The damned hum wouldn't go away. I reconnected the earth wire. Still hum. We disconnected the fiddle. The hum went a bit quieter, but it was still there. So, I put in a low-frequency filter on the PA, which got rid of the worst of it but left a hole in the bass response.

While Neale and I tried different things, the rest of the band looked on bemused, like, shouldn't there be a switch to press to get rid of that noise? *Isn't that your job, Kai? Isn't that what tech nerds do?*

The older woman came over. "Hi. Is all in order? It sounds like you have a problem with the sound."

Neale stepped in, interrupting before I could answer. "Ah, darlin', we're picking up some interference, I think. I wonder if it might be from some of the equipment in this fine club of yours. Would you mind showin' me where the circuit breakers are, *acushla*?"

Acushla? Sweetheart? I let my mouth hang open as Neale took her in tow, led her by the elbow back to the bar, and out of sight. After a while, the lights went off in sections, then came back on again. Still hum. Then the hum stopped.

I yelled out, "Whatever you switched off just now, that was it."

I didn't think he'd heard me properly because the hum came back. So, I ran across to the bar where the nineteen-year-old stood, chatting with Jake in his smart new clothes.

"Where are they?" I asked.

She pointed to a doorway and steps leading down. "Five

steps below. There's a store-cupboard with the breaker panel."

And indeed, I found them standing in the store-cupboard, at the end by the circuit breakers. Mature Glamour had her back to me and was explaining something to Neale that involved quite a bit of headshaking and pointing. She must have seen Neale's eyes shift as I came down the stairs because she stepped away from him and faced me.

"Hi. Yes, we know what the problem is." She pronounced it 'pro-blayme' with a long *O*, the German way. "It is the machine — to cool the beer. When we turn it on — *hmmmmm* — the hum comes. We switched them off again — the hum is gone. But then, we have warm beer. So now, we switched them back on again. We are a club — so, we must have chilled beer."

"Can I have a look?"

"Sure thing."

She stepped out of the store-cupboard so I could take a look. Very cosy, that cupboard. I wasn't sure how two strangers could fit in it. Still, I sidled in next to Neale, who didn't make a lot of effort to give me any room.

"If you don't mind…"

"Ah, sorry, Kai." He squeezed out past me. Yes, 'handyman' Neale might know electrics, but that didn't require us to play sardines. My body, my choice.

They were right. The chillers were on their own breaker, neatly labelled *Zapfanlage*. Not a lot we could do.

So, we trooped back to the bar, Neale's hand on Mature Glamour's hip, a hairsbreadth from her butt. Dammit, he was a fast worker. Handyman, indeed.

*

THIS TIME, WE got a decent soundcheck. And Mature Glamour brought us a crate of bottled beer.

Jamie eyed her suspiciously. "Are those for us?"

She smiled brightly. Genuine. As if she wanted musicians for the music they played and not merely for the bar takings they brought in.

"Naturally. These are free for the band. If you want more, you pay at bar. But I think this is enough. So, relax yourselves. Don't get so drunk that you cannot play your best."

A little too close to home. We all looked anywhere but at Neale.

"Thanks," I said and realised I'd missed out on the introductions. "Thank you. Sorry, but I didn't get your name…"

"Bettine. My daughter's name is Lotte. And please tell me yours."

"Thanks, Bettine. I'm Kai."

"Weird names, these Germans have," Jamie said to me quietly.

"Lotte is probably short for Charlotte. But you'll come across weirder names yet."

"I'll stick to English, thank you."

*

IT WAS TURNING out to be a good gig. The audience seemed to build up from nothing to heaving in the space of about half an hour, and we hit the stage shortly after eight. From the opening bars, I knew most of the rough edges had gone.

There was that damned humming, of course, back in the mix. It didn't show too much, but it was there. Once or twice, it intruded in quiet passages, where it clashed with the song key, and Dom nearly wobbled off pitch.

For myself, I was relaxed, no poison, no nastiness. I'd been looking forward to singing with Dom. We'd used the busking to fix the few harmonies that hadn't worked quite right last night. And I was in stage clothes—not my sweaty, smelly street clothes, but my favourite gilet. So, it *felt* like a gig.

Dom was superb. She'd settled into our music, given it her own spin, and taken us with her. I fitted my backing vocals around hers and took the lead once or twice for the odd verses we'd agreed on. For her song links, she dropped the French, sticking to English with occasional German.

And Jake was astonishing. He was now '*Der Mann in Rot*', which meant 'The man in red', so almost the same as '*Le Gentilhomme en Rouge*'. He could be wild and unpredictable at times—a curate's egg of guitar. For that first set, though, he was inspired, whether by the name, or the clothes, or Dom, or all three. His rhythm work was driving, his solos soared, and in between, he wove ophidian obbligatos around Dom's vocals. He surprised even himself, finishing wide-eyed and did-I-play-that amazed.

I headed to the bar to get myself a water; I'd put a lot of energy into that set, and I was feeling damn pleased with myself. Lotte and Bettine were busy serving, and I had a while to observe them, waiting for my turn. They worked hard behind the bar, an efficient team, each helping the other. In the confined space, not a movement was wasted. It was like watching two dancers trained by the same coach.

Every customer got a smile, and the women greeted almost everyone by name. My ear for German was improving, even in this hubbub, and I caught some of the banter too.

"Hello, Kai. What can I get you?"

"Huh?"

Lotte had finished with the last customer and stood opposite me. I was impressed. I'd not been introduced, but she'd learned my name. And she was keeping track of which customer to serve next, rather than serving the loudest.

"A mineral water, please," I said. "A large bottle, if you have one."

"Sure." Lotte bent down beneath the bar and rummaged about for a few moments. "I'm sorry. No mineral water." She bobbed up, already apologising.

"That's okay," I assured her.

She called across to her mother, got an answer, a bit too quick for me to follow. Then she spoke to me again. "Can you just help me, please? There are so many customers, and I must a heavy crate from the *Kellar* bring…"

She shook her head, sending ripples the length of her hair. "Sorry, I can do better English than that. I've got to bring a heavy crate up from the cellar. If you could help with the doors, we will be quicker."

I nodded. "Sure."

Passing the electrics cupboard and with the door closed behind us, it was easier to hear each other.

"You got a great band, Kai," Lotte said, twisting a reluctant door handle and shouldering it open. "And you play drums real well."

"Thank you."

"Your singer, Dominique. She is French?"

"Belgian." I concentrated on not falling to my death down the steep, uneven, and ill-lit steps.

"She speaks German well, then. But she is fantastic. I want to sing like her. One day."

We were at the bottom now, and I was still alive. I started taking a bit more of an interest in Lotte's conversation.

"Yes, she's brilliant. We met her by chance. This is only her second gig with us."

Lotte didn't react. No cynicism, I guessed. Instead, she changed the subject.

"Your guitarist. Jake. He gives me shivers with his playing."

"Huh, Jake? He had a good night tonight. One of his best, I'd say."

"I would like to tell him so. But he acts so shy. He looks at me, and that makes me happy. But then he looks away quickly. Like he has not been with a girl yet. Is that so?"

Where did that come from? I unslacked my jaw and told her I'd never thought about it. But Lotte was blushing furiously.

"No, no, I did not mean to say that. Some men you can be direct with, but not Jake. I don't want to scare him away. I was wondering if he had a girlfriend."

"A girlfriend? Jake?"

"Yes. Does Jake have a girlfriend?"

Present tense.

"I don't think so. Why are you asking *me*?"

"Because you are the leader. I have watched you with them. They are like little children. They ask you what to do. They listen to you."

Hmm. It doesn't look like that from where I'm standing, Lotte.

"No. I think you are going to have to speak to Jake."

Her hand flew to her mouth. "No," she gasped, reddening again. "I couldn't do that. What would he think of me?"

"And you like him? Sorry, stupid question. You like him, but…you're shy? You?"

"Yes. I am shy," she admitted. "Do you look at me and assume 'pretty girl, sexy, full of confidence, sleeps with anyone she chooses'? *That's not me.*"

My turn to be embarrassed. "I'm sorry. You seem so confident behind the bar."

"That, I learn from my mother. *She* is confident. I copy her, and I pretend."

"I see. So, what do you want me to do? Give him a message?"

"Yes. No. I don't know. Find out if he likes me?"

Then it hit me. This was *Jake's* gig. "You and Jake…you used to know each other?"

She blushed but nodded. "We were much younger. We played online games. Jake was very good, but so was I. We were rivals, but we were also friends, and later, allies. I used to practice my English with him on the chats. I loved his sense of humour."

Yes. Sometimes Jake would crack me up. Not good at breaking into a noisy, fast-paced pub conversation, but in online chat…

"Online," I said. "I guess he could be really funny. So, the two of you got on well."

"Very well. Always. And I was growing up, but he was

older; I could tell. At that age, it was a big difference. Now, not so much."

"But then it stopped."

"He just disappeared," Lotte said. "I wondered if I'd said something wrong. Or if he'd found out."

"Found out what?"

"You're not a gamer?"

"No. I never got into it."

"This is not pleasant to recall," Lotte began. "Some of the gamers could be very cruel to girls. They'd form alliances and gang up on girls. Cyberbullying, you must know it, and it's really horrible. So, I never let on to anyone. Not even to Jake. Not that Jake ever bullied anyone. He was the opposite. He took time to help noobs—inexperienced new players—whether they were boys or girls. A lot of the abuse was verbal. Nasty, sexist stuff. But Jake would challenge anyone who got mouthy with a girl. If they didn't stop, there'd be a friendly fire accident. He broke up gangs if he saw one forming, and he had the skills to take down any bully. He had quite a reputation, and after a while, word got around, and the bad guys went elsewhere. Science fiction was another thing we shared. You ever read *Ender's Game*?"

I shook my head. "Crime and thrillers are what float my boat. Wasn't there a film?"

"Just read the book. The film misses out a lot. Anyway, Jake tried to be like Ender. A good player, but also a good guy who built people up. His gamer handle was FenderWiggin, which not many people got. I guess I could have told him I was a girl, shared my picture, even, but in battle, mistakes happen, somebody drops a pronoun… When he went away, I asked around, but nobody knew what had happened to him. Anyway, I think Jake was shocked when he saw the real me for the first time this afternoon."

I'd missed that. I'd been watching Jamie.

Lotte continued. "When he got in touch, last week, it came out of nowhere. FenderWiggin, back from the dead! Where have you been? I asked. What happened? He didn't say much, but he did say he was coming to Germany, and could I help him get a gig? My God, I wanted to see him so much. I would have knocked on the door of every bar in Aachen, but thank God, my mother booked him in here."

"He knew your mother ran a bar, then?"

"Oh, yes. I had told him many things about my life here. And then he arrives, and he asks me, 'Are *you* AacheNinja?', like he was expecting to meet me in my space armour, two metres tall and armed with a pulse laser."

I couldn't help it. I laughed and tried to turn it into a cough. Lotte looked upset.

"I'm sorry," I said. "But let nobody say that Germans have no sense of humour."

She continued, mollified. "We talked a bit, earlier, and he apologised for his rudeness. He sounded so very polite. He's not like the boy I remember. I don't think he likes me."

"Of course he likes you. Why wouldn't he?"

She said nothing, and I realised how stupid I was being.

"Sorry. Minus the sex thing, I have no idea. We're band-mates, nothing more. I don't get to see Jake's soul."

Her face fell. She bent down and heaved up a crate of mineral water.

"Look, Lotte, just..." I reached for some encouragement to

give her. "Don't give up on Jake. He's very shy too. But he's playing his heart out tonight like I've never seen before. You just might have something to do with that. Take the chance."

She didn't say anything, and I wondered if I'd overstepped the mark. The lighting wasn't good enough to be sure, but I think I saw a little glimmer of hope reappear in her expression.

She adjusted her grip on the crate. "Let's get back. I lied about needing a hand with carrying crates. But you can hold the doors if you don't mind."

As she led the way back up the stairs, I sneaked a look at the time on my phone, remembering her words. *"We will be quicker."* Right.

*

WE PLAYED A second set. A few repeats, some new songs. Some numbers were better, some not so good. Around the halfway mark, I started losing focus. I started worrying about the last problem of the night.

Where the fuck were we going to sleep?

We were due in Fulda on Saturday. Not an immense drive — three or four hours. But I'd been scared shitless when Neale had fallen asleep at the wheel. I wanted us to tackle the journey fresh.

I'd pushed the thoughts off to one side all through the setup and the first set. But it had started bugging me again as we prepared for the second set. Everybody else had closed their eyes to the problem. I remembered something Jake had said to Jamie in passing — what's Kai's plan for tonight? — and Jamie's response. Apparently, I'd sort something out.

Why was it my responsibility? Why Kai in loco parentis?

You're all adults, guys, so pull some weight. Even Dom had been letting me get on with sorting stuff out.

And then it was too late to worry. The canned music faded, the stage lights were on, and Dominique launched into the spine-tingling opening of 'Bell Bottom Blues'. As I said, some bits were better, others, the edge was missing. And then, I didn't know what time, but I could see the end of the set approaching, and the problem bubbled back up.

But Dom carried us through, and Jake, still on fire, played a couple of barnstorming solos that obliterated any of my mistakes. And then the lights were bright in my eyes as I came out from behind the kit and joined the line-up for our final bow.

*

THE VAN WAS loaded, near enough.

Most of the crowd had faded pretty quickly once Bettine had called time. Lotte excused herself from the bar and gave us a hand breaking down and carrying the gear out to the van. She was strong—I guessed carrying crates and shifting barrels was on a par with lugging Jake's Marshall cab or my drum ironmongery. But Lotte also had a good eye for working out what to bring next.

And then Bettine called me over, and I remembered it was pay time.

"Hi, Kai. You played good tonight. Everyone had a good time and spent lots of money at the bar. We made a profit, which is nice. And you made a few good friends tonight, who like you, like your music, and would like to see you come back again. So, this is what we agreed."

She handed me a wad of euros, and insisted I count it. It was all there, not that I doubted her. She was no Rumpel.

"Thank—" I began, but she stopped me.

"My daughter, I think she is now one of your friends. She was helping you load, which she doesn't do for any band, and she was talking a lot to Jack—no, Jake—at the bar after you came off-stage. She says you guys got nowhere to sleep tonight, right? The campsite is full."

Full to us at least. It had been our first stop in Aachen. Booking error, they'd said. Like fuck. They wanted posh caravans, not tents and scruffy vans with broken wing mirrors. So, true in essence.

I nodded. "We'll be driving across to Fulda. It'll take a few hours at this time of night. We'll stop in the morning, get some sleep—"

"No. You've been driving too much already. Jake said you had a bad scare this morning. You stay here."

"We can't impose on you—"

"Of course you can. When you have an accident, I will never forgive myself. We have an apartment above ours. You can use your own sleeping bags, okay?"

"Okay. Thank you."

"Good. One more thing. No messing about in this house. Do you understand? If I catch someone with Lotte, I cut your throats. Or your brake pipes—"

"Uh, are you *serious*? I mean, we're all adults here, including Lotte. I can't make promises for anyone but myself."

"Then have a nice drive to Fulda."

"Hold on, hold on. I'll ask the guys."

"Everyone. Not just the guys."

"Yes. Everyone."

Neale was blazing mad when I told them all. "I'll drive us to Fulda, so I fuckin' will, and don't you worry. That bloody woman, making eyes at me all evening, she was. And now she wants to lock up her daughter, like a bloody nun. Bloody hypocrite, that's what she is—"

"Easy, Neale. Let the others speak. Jamie?"

"I don't care. I was planning to volunteer for van duty anyway. Someone's got to guard the gear, and you've done your stint already."

"Okay. Dom?"

"It is offensive, her attitude. I will not sleep under this woman's roof. I will join Jamie in the van. He is a gentleman whom I trust."

That's telling you, Jamie! Keep your hands to yourself... But I hid my thoughts, saying only, "Fair enough. Jake?"

Jake looked so sad it almost broke my heart. "I'll go along with the others," he said, a wobble in his voice I'd never heard before. "Just... have we got to go right now?"

"No. We have a few minutes. I'll say goodbye to Bettine. Make sure you get Lotte's address. She's a nice girl. Shy. She likes you."

He looked surprised—of course, he'd already have Lotte's address. "Uh, yes. Thanks, Kai."

Chapter Fourteen

Saturday, October 1, 2016
Fulda, the Gaelic Club

JAKE WAS VERY quiet in the van.

Yes, Jake was always pretty quiet. This was different. His normal quiet was simply an absence of human conversation. This quiet was like he was sitting at the bottom of his gravity well, letting nothing escape.

It brought home to me how little I really knew Jake. We'd been playing in the band together for a couple of years now, which was one hell of a long time to not know somebody. When we went to the pub, he'd sit listening, laughing at the right moments. Every now and again, he'd say something witty. Always polite, always waiting his turn to speak. There was a keen brain in there, I was sure. And, of course, he had a solid knowledge of the blues. Half the artists in my collection I'd discovered through Jake. And he could *play* the blues.

For the first time, I was seeing him live and feel the blues without a guitar in the equation.

And a rose might bloom in a desert. Something *had* happened between those two. Maybe my half-time pep talk with Lotte had done some good. Maybe Jake had sprung out of his shell. I hadn't seen it, but then, I'd been keeping myself pretty busy since we'd arrived at the An der Ecke. And then there was Bettine's comment about them chatting post-gig at the bar. *She'd* noticed.

And now we were driving away, far and fairly fast, from the only female Jake had, in my experience, shown an interest in. Apart from Dom? No, Dom wasn't the same. They'd chatted intently about gigs and artists and stuff, but that was no more than Dom being democratic with her bandmates.

Still, it had been, at most, an hour they could have spent in each other's company. Were they Romeo and Juliet to fall in love at first sight? Scratch that; they'd been friends as kids, really good friends by Lotte's account, meeting for the first time as adults. What a strange roll of the dice.

I left him to his thoughts.

*

WE STOPPED AT a *Raststätte*, a rest stop, about a half hour beyond Köln. Jamie needed a pee. We all needed fresh air. Neale needed to rest. He stayed in the van, in the dark, with a woolly hat pulled over his eyes.

The fresh air was pretty chill, though, and Jake marched

over to the café, where there was hot coffee and terrible music. Dom and I started to follow, but halfway there, Dom placed her hand on my shoulder.

"Stay back, Kai. I think Jake will talk to me better alone."

"And why…" I shut up and nodded my agreement. No point in getting on my high horse when I'd already admitted to myself I didn't understand him. Dom, though, might have a chance, on the back of that long chat they'd had while Jamie and I'd been playing pool.

Wait here in the freezing cold though? Not bloody likely.

I was wrapped in my thoughts when I got back to the van. So, it appeared, was Neale. He'd shifted over to the passenger seat and was bent over, peering down at something. I raised my fist to rap on the window, then paused.

Neale's trousers were pulled down to his knees, leaving his thighs bare. He had a pen in his hand, I thought, poised over his right thigh, as though he was about to write on it.

No. He wasn't holding it right. His thumb was pressing the top end. And then it fell into place. He wasn't writing. He was *injecting*.

Dammit, Neale. I could wink at a bit of harmless pot. But this…

And I bottled out. I should have tapped on the window, challenged him there and then. But I couldn't take any more confrontation right then. I was washed out. Never mind that in half an hour, there'd be a junkie behind the wheel, driving us to a messy death on the autobahn to Fulda. The tour was doomed. I would accept whatever karma came my way.

I walked away, staying out of sight of Neale, then looped

back, approaching the van so he'd see me a way off.

The light was poor, but I inspected him as best I could when I climbed up next to him. I didn't know what I was expecting to see. I had no idea what a heroin addict looked like when under the influence. He was…unremarkable. His trousers were hitched up at least.

"Are you okay, Neale?"

"Sure, I am. A little tired. But that was a fuckin' good gig, wouldn't you say?"

"Aside from that cow Bettine."

"Ah, go easy on the poor woman. She's had a hard life, runnin' a bar and raisin' a kid all on her own."

"You're very generous all of a sudden."

"Well, I did talk to her a little."

"*Acushla*, you called her, as I recall. Sweetheart. In the electrical cupboard."

He smiled. A little sheepishly perhaps. "It was just blarney." And then the mischief returned to his eyes. "Not jealous, are we?"

I didn't respond. Dignified silence was usually best.

"Ah, loosen up, Kai. Take the ramrod out of your arse. But yes, she told me about her life. Some rogue took advantage when she was too young to know better. She had a little legacy, and he convinced her to invest in his bar. But he robbed her blind, hand forever dipping into the till, and he left her pregnant to boot. Then he cleared off with most of the money and left her with all his debts."

"Didn't she report him? To the police, that is."

"Yes, but the bastard had skipped out of the country. They never caught him. If they even gave a shit."

"Bastard, indeed. So she raised Lotte on her own, and now she won't let the poor girl be an adult."

"At nineteen, and with a body like hers, she's an emotional disaster waiting to happen."

"Don't be so judgemental, Neale. Not all teens are puppets to their hormones."

"Like you? Navigating yourself incorruptible through the ice floes of the flesh. Weren't you ever tempted when you were a teen?"

I guess I paused a moment too long there because he started to grin.

"Somebody has to keep their head screwed on," I said finally.

"It's not about yer *head*..." He laughed. An ordinary, mischievous laugh. If he was on psychoactives, I couldn't see any sign of it.

I took a deep breath. "Neale, I need to ask you something."

"And what would that be?"

"Do you use hard drugs?"

His mouth opened wide with surprise for a moment and then: "No. I bloody don't use hard drugs." His eyes narrowed. "I use life-saving, doctor-prescribed drugs, you ignorant little fuck. Insulin, to be precise."

"Oh."

"Yes, 'Oh'. Do you know about diabetes?"

"N-no. Not really."

And then the anger drained out of him. "Oh, fuck it. I'm sorry. I shouldn't have lashed out at you like that. It's not your fault. Unless you know somebody who's got it, why would you know what it's about? It's just never-ending needles, taking blood sugar tests, injecting insulin, eat, rinse, repeat."

"It doesn't sound good."

"If you don't think about it, it's not too bad. But always, always, there's a voice in the back of your head saying, 'Careful, careful now'. Even at the Club Lorelei, I knew how much I had to drink, and I injected to cover it. You can't ever let go."

"Why didn't you say anything? I mean at the Barrel Organ. Or later."

"Because people don't understand. Because I don't want to be a leper. I just want to be normal."

"I can understand that. But do you think you can do it?"

"Why shouldn't I? I'm not sure it's the best example, but your prime minister has type 1 diabetes, the same as me."

"*Your* prime minister?"

He laughed. "I'm Irish, and don't you ever forget it. My point is that most of the time, you'd never know the PM has diabetes. You probably meet a few diabetics day to day and never realise it."

"You're our driver. Should we be worried? Is there anything we should know?"

"I have good control. I know the warning signs, and I'll pull over if I have a low. There's orange juice and glucose tablets in my jacket pocket. If I ever look spaced out or dopey, give me one or the other, and I'll perk up. That's all you need to know."

"Will you tell the rest of the band?"

"I'll find a time. Maybe."

"I'll leave it up to you. *Our* prime minister, eh? Who'd have thought it?"

"Yeah. Thanks, Kai."

Jamie was the next to return.

"Did you see Dom or Jake?" I asked.

"Yes, but I let them be. They were talking over a coffee. At least, Dom was talking. Jake was staring out of the window like he wanted to be left alone."

No threat, in other words, so you didn't butt in. Why can't you be that considerate the rest of the time?

Neale was lying still in the back, resting, eyes closed, but not asleep. He piped up. "We ought to get going. I'm feeling pretty fresh and ready to drive."

"Give 'em ten minutes, Neale," I replied. "I'll fetch them if they're not back by then."

Five minutes later, Dom showed up, scowling.

"I cannot get through to 'eem," she said to everyone and no one. "I left 'eem finishing 'ees coffee. 'E promised me 'e would follow as soon as 'e could."

Her accent was breaking through. On stage, she used it for sexy, used it for sparkling effect. Now, all I could hear was tired and frustrated. In the last couple of days, I'd watched her come to care for the band every bit as much as I did. And hearing her frustration, I wanted to reach out and hug her.

My traitor mind followed that up with a memory of exactly what it was like to hug her. *Thank you, mind. We're not going there, okay?*

My ears were burning but not quite bright enough to pierce the night in the van.

Neale had moved to the driving seat, ready to roll. I joined him in the front, ready to get Jake if he didn't show. Dom had climbed into the back with Jamie and now leaned against him, half asleep. But that was none of my business.

Jake climbed up as though nothing was wrong. No 'thanks for waiting while I got my head in order'. But neither the old nor the new Jake had ever been much for words.

We set off. I had the map in my lap, mostly to keep it off the floor. The route to Fulda wasn't difficult, and Neale didn't need me to navigate. I just couldn't not navigate, using it as my shard of comfort while I adjusted to the new Neale and his curious condition. On the now-unlikely chance we all died in a horrific pile up, I would go to the afterlife with the tiny satisfaction of knowing exactly where we had died.

*

I DOZED OFF somewhere around Siegen on the E41.

I'd stopped worrying about the state of Neale's diabetes. His driving was, if anything, better than normal. It helped that the quiet night-time roads gave him less to vent at. The lights of the occasional cars and trucks didn't bother him, but I found the constant flickering white line hypnotic. I kept finding that my eyes had closed again, my thoughts disappearing into weird la-la lands. And then a thought would pierce the spell, and I'd sit up with a jerk. I'd ask Neale where we were, and he'd say 'coming up to Bergneustadt' or wherever, and I'd find it on the map. And then, the white lines would worm their way back into my head, and the cycle would begin again.

I awoke as we pulled into a *Raststätte*, a rest stop, a few miles beyond Giessen. Jake slept beside me, managing some strange contortion with either the headrest or his neck. He sat face-up to the ceiling, mouth wide open and uttering grunting snores. His smartphone, still in his lap, blinked an angry red battery warning, unheeded.

Behind me, Dom and Jamie also slept. Their arms had become somewhat entwined, Jamie's head resting on her shoulder and her head was against his.

Dom stirred as the van jolted over a pothole. Her eyes opened, and she took in her situation, Jamie's warmth against her. Her lips quirked a what-can-you-do smile at me, but she made no move to push him away. The van was pretty cold, and Jamie hadn't taken any liberties. He was indeed being 'a gentleman whom I trust'. *Take your warmth where you find it, Dom.* As I had been happy to do.

By common consent, we headed, shivering in the chill night air, towards a café and ordered ourselves hot coffee. Neale joined us but chose a hot chocolate.

"I'm going to have to crash," he apologised. "So I'll skip the caffeine."

We ignored his poor choice of metaphor and headed back to the van. There, we broke out the sleeping bags and tried to fit ourselves around the gear and one another. Jamie and Dom resumed station on the bench of speaker cabs. On the front seat, I decided that curling up with Jake and Neale would be too uncomfortable for any of us, so I chose the floor. I unrolled my sleeping bag and stretched out.

Stupid decision, of course. Even in my sleeping bag I lost heat through the floor like it was the South Pole. I lay there, cold and unable to sleep. It didn't help knowing that everyone else was warmer than me because they'd managed to pair up, and I was alone. Mostly, I was taunted by memories of an altogether warmer night with Dom. Even if she had been a yeti.

After a lot of thinking around and around in circles, I eventually did drift off into something akin to sleep. In that almost-sleep, my dreams and my thoughts and my desires gambolled crazily.

*

SOMEBODY WAS BANGING on the passenger door.

"*Sie können hier nicht stehen bleiben. Maximale Parkdauer sind zwei Stunden.*"

Some guy in a uniform waved a torch in my face. Police? And then the first nuggets of meaning emerged from my sluggish Kai-brain.

"Wake up, Neale. We've had our time. We've got to drive on."

"Huh?"

"We can't park here more than two hours."

And the next word was always going to be…

Zahlen. Pay up.

Oh, bugger. Not a policeman. A parking attendant or whatever. Of course, nothing was free. If you wanted to sleep, find a motel. It wasn't the Germans' fault, particularly. Same all over the world. If you wanted to sleep, you had to pay. *Zahlen.* The law of supply and demand at service stations. They existed to make money.

We, by contrast, existed to pay that money.

Zahlen.

"No," I said to the attendant and then tried in German. *Nein.*

Jetzt fahren wir weg. Unser Fahrer ist plötzlich müde geworden. Er mußte schlafen." We're leaving now. Our driver was too tired and had to sleep.

What the hell was the German for an accident? *Unfall?* Try that. Yes. It was an accident that we all overslept. Yes, we are English. We're on our way to Fulda, and we're late. Thank you *so* much for waking us…

Beside me, Neale climbed out of his sleeping bag, shivering in the cold air, wondering aloud where the bloody hell he'd put his effing keys. The others were stirring too.

Zahlen.

Wir fahren weg. Nicht zahlen.

We're going. No pay…

The engine coughed, and I felt fear. Now was not the time for the fuel gods to take revenge, please no. But the engine caught. The attendant banged on the van, then leaped backwards as we began to move.

Danke. Auf Wiedersehen.

Thank you. Goodbye.

And we were *Scheiß*-something. Ah. We were *Scheiß-Tommies!* Bloody Tommies! An anti-British insult dating back two world wars. I wondered how Dom would feel about that.

Goodbye *Raststätte.*

*

MORE MILES. KILOMETRES. Whatever. Endless thousands of white lines flicking either side of us, arrows flying out of our future to pierce our past. But Neale had it all under control. The van weaved through the storm, Baius holding course for Odysseus between Scylla and Charybdis.

Baius? Didn't end well for him… Hope that wasn't an omen…

Hmm, I think my mind needs putting in order. Sleep deprivation.

*

FULDA. OR AT least, a café in a village a few miles outside, serving breakfast. No coffee, please. *I want sleep, I really do. Food first though.* Sausages, onions. *Senf.* Mustard. A weak tea, a Lipton tea bag left to drown in tepid, milky water. *But it's liquid and that's enough.*

*

WE FOUND A park, still wreathed in coiling tendrils of morning mist. Scant warmth in the day yet, the sun struggling up from the eastern horizon, fighting through patchy grey clouds that promised rain later.

The new dawn still resting light on dew-soaked grass, we fetched the big groundsheet from the van and unfolded it. It felt so good to be able to stretch out.

*

A HAND TOUCHED my shoulder, and I jumped.

"I'm sorry, Kai. I did not mean to surprise you."

Dom. Her hand still rested on my shoulder.

"That's okay. What's up?"

"I had an idea. Some words. A song perhaps."

"So you woke me. Wouldn't it wait?"

"No. It's like smoke in the wind. If I don't write it down, it will blow away."

She leaned over me, a curious urgency, a tension I hadn't seen in her before. And that hand still on my shoulder. I wasn't a 'touchy' person, and Dom had kept her distance with the band, save for keeping warm. This was new. Not…unwelcome though.

I sat up, and her hand fluttered away. "You need some paper?"

"Yes. But I want you to help me write it. The idea came to me in English, but my English is rusty. I need rhymes and rhythms. Words that mean the same."

"Synonyms."

"*Oui.*"

I fetched a pad from my bag in the van, and a pen, and rejoined Dom on a bench a dozen yards from where everyone else slept.

"What's your idea, Dom?" Now it was my turn to reach down and rest my hand on her shoulder.

It didn't seem to bother her, for she held still a long moment, deep in thought. Then she turned her head and met my eyes.

"This," she said, and with her forefinger drew a sweeping X between her breasts. "It is a cross, yes?"

"Yes." But why draw it just *there*?

"And *traverser*, that means to cross, also, yes?"

"Yes."

"And cross is also angry."

I nodded. I thought I could see where she was going, plays on the word cross. I suggested a couple more.

"You can cross someone, which is to antagonise them. And

double-cross, which is to betray them."

"If I say 'cross me', what picture comes to your mind?"

And I saw her lying naked, arms spread wide in welcome, as someone moved to cover her…

I stopped the thought.

But she saw me blush. She'd been watching me too closely.

"I thought so. *Cross me*. It suggests much, does it not?"

"I…it does."

"Then we can make something of this. I was not sure that my idea worked in English. Thank you."

"For what?"

"For not getting angry or upset. Your words are always helpful, but I needed to see your emotions, your thoughts. You guard them well, and I made you reveal them. I hope I have not offended you."

"No." —Yes. Not offended perhaps. But she had disturbed me, and I was no longer entirely calm.

"Then sit with me, Kai. Work with me."

Words. Rough at first, not quite fitting. Crossings out. (Pun not intended.) But then we had a verse and our metre. And a sort of chorus. A refrain.

Don't cross me, cross to me.

The tune was harder, humming snatches. I wanted to fetch a guitar, to try out ideas, chord progressions, but Dom said no.

"I want to *feel* this song into being. It will not be like the other songs we play, so don't force it with guitars. It might *be* a voice…with soft bass. Or violin."

It grew. At some point, the song became solid enough to record on my smartphone. We were in a strange time, a little island of creativity in the madness of the tour. With different rules.

I'd written a few songs before, always alone. But writing with Dom was different. She worked with open heart and soul and mind. And body. I don't touch, but in those moments, I did touch. I didn't flinch when Dom pressed against me in the eagerness of creation. It sounded crass, too physical, but it helped us both find the necessary honesty. We were creating a song for Dom to perform. So, I was co-creator, acted upon and reacting, crossed and crossing. I was her first audience, delivering my emotional reactions. Unfiltered.

> *Alone in my mind, alone in my heart*
> *Wondering why love should force us apart*
> *Two bodies, no closer than*
> *Sun and the moon.*
>
> *Don't cross me, cross to me*
> *Cross my heart, sing my tune*

Caught on my smartphone. Saved—and bugger the hit on my data allowance—to my cloud.

*

THERE WASN'T A lot to Fulda. I didn't think I was doing it a disservice. The cathedral housed the tomb of Saint Boniface, or at least his head. There was also a castle, of which, apparently, "…some minor buildings might interest the dedicated tourist." Save those highlights, the rest of Fulda, as far as I could tell, was houses, shops, and office blocks.

We were due to play the Gaelic Club. In former days, it might have been full of American servicemen, bright-eyed and enthusiastic for a whiff of the 'old country'. And a taste of stout, made with the proper Liffey water.

Neale turned his nose up at the whole thing. "It's a fuckin' sham. A con. An Ireland that never existed. And the stout is shite. They don't serve it right."

But he drank it anyway. And then we got down to the business of working out how the hell we were going to fit our gear into any sort of coherent line-up. The venue, once we'd lugged all our gear up two flights of steps, turned out not to have a stage.

The space had been partitioned into booths on the ground floor—what could anyone do with that? A narrow, L-shaped mezzanine took up two sides, bounded with wrought-iron railings. We were told the bands played there. More stairs made the access so narrow—even after we'd shifted tables out—that the only place I could put my drum kit was right in the *L* of the mezzanine. The kit would block off the far end. In the event of a fire, Jamie and I would spring like Batman and Robin from the blazing balcony to save ourselves.

"*Quel cirque*" was Dom's comment— What a circus. She saw my raised eyebrow. "*C'est mal foutu*. It is useless. A mess."

"It's pretty crap."

"Yes, Kai. You are right."

She paused, then, "Tell me. Do we have a radio mic?"

"A radio mic? No. Clay had one. Our previous singer."

And why did I even need to mention that? Dom wasn't Clay, so why bring up the past? A little voice whispered to me, *and Cassie isn't Mum, so why…*

Shut up, little voice.

"I see," Dom continued. "Well, we must obtain one. I cannot play this venue wired."

"Obtain one? You mean buy? Or hire?"

"I mean buy."

"But they're expensive."

"Not so much. I will not need the very best. But I should have brought one. It's my fault."

Smartphones came out, and the race was on to find a music shop. I misremembered *Musikladen*, and Google coped. There were several. I eliminated the one that only sold recorders— *How can you make a living selling recorders and nothing else?* Only in Germany, I guessed. We played pass-the-phone, so between us, we could find out if any of the other shops had a model she'd be happy with.

It was a short drive—three of us—Dom to buy, Neale to drive, and me for my German. Jake and Jamie stayed behind to do setup.

Dom went for the Shure. She tried a couple of other equally reputable brands too. Not the very best, she said, but they were all in the five-hundred to eight-hundred-euro range. Out came a credit card in a very understated black. No quibble. And then Neale pointed at a feedback killer, and Dom nodded. Plus cables. Out came the credit card again for another two hundred and fifty euros.

For some reason, the credit card machine chose that moment to stop working.

It was the first time I'd ever seen Dom lose her composure. All the colour drained out of her face. But the store assistant just muttered '*Scheiße*' and marched off to fetch the manager. By the time they returned, Dom's colour had returned, and the manager was all apologies: *The card reader is new and is only causing trouble. Wait a moment, please, I am sure your card is covered.*

They disappeared back into the office and eventually brought out an antique credit card machine and some kind of form that they loaded into it over the top of Dom's shiny card. The assistant worked the machine, but it didn't work right, and it chewed up the paper. So the manager waved him away, and she had a go, and this time it worked.

Then they faffed around some more, trying to find a working ballpoint that would make an impression through carbon paper onto the bottom sheet and write out what Dom had just bought, the price, and a couple of more boxes to tick. Dom, who'd evidently done this before but not for many years, was now trying hard not to laugh as she signed.

And then we all smiled and thanked them and went back outside to Neale's ramshackle van, carrying our booty. Out of habit, I checked to see if anyone had tried to force the van door. But there wasn't much to steal, and in any case, there were a couple of cops in a *Polizeiwagen* just up the road.

"What was that all about?" I asked.

"Ah, and it takes me back to the old way, before chip-and-pin," said Neale. "I'm surprised they had a machine at all. Germany's supposed to be so modern."

Dom unfolded the slip, laughed, crumpled it and dropped it in the gutter. Neale opened the door for her, and she climbed in. I remembered the two cops, watching, so I bent down and very ostentatiously picked up the credit card slip and pushed it deep into

my jeans pocket. Maybe the cops wouldn't bother with a litter of-
fence, but maybe it was a slow day in Fulda, and maybe they really didn't want foreigners littering their beautiful, clean city.
Their clean city anyway.

So, Dom had just forked out the best part of a thousand euros on gear without batting an eyelid. And she sells fragrances in
a minor department store. Right. But I said nothing, and Neale
said nothing; he just started the engine and drove us all to the
Gaelic Club.

*

BACK AT THE Gaelic Club and up those damned flights of stairs,
we found Jamie, bless him, had pretty much finished wiring up
everything. I checked it, anyway, but it was fine. We plugged in
the new mic—that was fine too. No trace of hum on any channel.

At soundcheck, only a couple customers lingered, nursing
their stouts, and they both looked up as we tuned and got our
levels.

> *I've got the blues, I ain't worried*
> *I seen the last of my ol' man*
> *My last dollar in his pocket*
> *And a suitcase in his hand*
>
> *Headin' down the road to Memphis*
> *Headin' down the lonesome track*
> *He's a leavin' me with nuthin'*
> *And it's nuthin' I'll take back*

AKA, the blues version of 'everybody dies and goes to hell'. Yeah. Another one that Dom and I wrote in the park. Straight blues—no sweat. The muse was upon us. A very black, bleak muse. But never mind. If there was one thing I'd learned, it was that you didn't say no to the muse.

The 'Cross My Heart' song was trickier, but Dom stuck to her simple vision. Call it version nought point five—hell, we hadn't even settled on a title yet. It was a shoot, but a shoot that would grow with every playing.

Jake and Jamie decided they needed fresh air, so they cleared out for an hour or so. That left the three of us to set up Dom's mic with the feedback killer.

I had to say that was bloody good tech. It might not have been the best, but Dom could take that mic pretty much anywhere in the Gaelic, except right in front of the speakers, and it wouldn't howl.

And that was how we played the gig. Jamie and I were trapped up in our balcony, Neale and *Der Mann in Rot* managed little excursions, but Dom ranged far and wide. She prowled around the tables, weaved effortlessly through the crowds. She was Billie Holiday, and she was Spiderwoman. She climbed up on tables, scaled the balcony, and shimmied down the bannister. It wasn't quite a pole dance she did…but it skirted erotic.

No. It *was* erotic. The guys lapped it up. They whistled and roared.

And then she turned back to us and crossed a bold X between her breasts.

Alone in the night, thinking of what
If I were not so formed, we would not
Be strangers, but closer than
Threads in a loom

Don't cross me, cross to me
Cross the street to my room

With a brushed snare and a bassline that begged to be played fretless, Jamie did the best he could, fretted. I added a harmony, a third above, for the chorus. Version nought point seven. Spine-tingling stuff.

Dom had been weaving through the tables, past a curly-haired, Mediterranean-looking guy. He reached towards her tight-denim ass as if to pat her, but she gently caught his hand and raised it up for her lips to kiss. As the second verse came up, she looped around and planted herself in front of his short-haired companion.

Heat of the day, cool of the night
Alternate faces, nature to fight
'Gainst nature, far closer than
Lover do hold

Don't cross me, cross to me
Cross boundaries, cross me bold

Dom squatted, looked straight into the adoring gaze of the short-haired girl, and loved her right back.

And I hadn't seen it coming.

Hold the beat…

Was that Dom flirting? Acting out the words of the song? But…

Hold the beat…

…we wrote that song, Dom and I, about…

Hold the beat…

*…*Oh! girl on girl…

Hold the beat…

I held it and pushed that whole maelstrom back into the green room, where it would wait to assail me later.

*

AFTER THE GIG was done—and our fee was safely in my pocket…

"The best yet" was Jamie's verdict, and he riffled a small sheaf of euros to emphasise the point.

I nodded my agreement. "Yep, we're gelling now—not too many problems with any of the songs. Dom?"

"You are right, Kai. We're getting pretty good. Jake?"

"Yeah, sure. Neale?"

"Whatever." Uh-oh. "But this isn't what I signed up for. Where are we sleeping tonight, then, Kai? A campsite again? Or a service station?"

"It's a bed and breakfast, since you ask. It's cheap enough that our earnings will cover it. And it gets mostly three stars online, so there shouldn't be too many fleas."

"Smartass."

I guessed he was mollified as there wasn't too much antagonism in his response, so I added, "But we do need to get moving.

The place has a secure yard where we can put the van, but they want to lock up at midnight."

Neale looked at his watch and groaned. "Ah, fuck it, an' I was hopin' to enjoy a beer for the road. An hour to break down, load up, and find the place is cuttin' it a bit fine. How far is the place?"

"Ten minutes from here. We can do it, but there's no hanging around. So come on, guys. If we make it, nobody sleeps in the van tonight…"

Not the most motivational speech I've ever made, but that final point did the trick. Everyone pulled their weight. Everyone. And Dom got a few of the punters, including Mediterranean guy and short-haired girl, to muck in.

So, it was a quarter to midnight when we slammed the doors on the van and climbed in. I'd done my final inspection and picked up only a couple of cables and one of Jamie's plectra, which was the best result yet. Dom gave every one of the helpers a 'special hug' for thanks, and I fretted at the time it all took. One or two of those helpers had done bugger all as roadies but were eager as fuck to collect a special hug from Dom. And I'd have made some of them shower first if it had been me. A long shower with the most bristly brush possible. But I couldn't begrudge Dom's quick, three-way hug with Mediterranean guy and short-haired girl, who'd both worked like Trojans.

"Good work, guys. Thanks," I added and got a drunken chorus of *'tschüss'* (bye) and *'wiedersehen'* (see you again) and *'komm bald wieder'*s (come back soon) in return.

*

NEALE DIDN'T HANG about. The satnav did its stuff, and at about two minutes to midnight, we rolled up outside the B & B. Neale parked the van in the back while I registered at the reception, out of breath and still sweaty from loading the van.

The receptionist gave me the Look — the disapproving, sucking-on-limes variant.

I showed her the reservation on my phone.

"I have it. Yes, two rooms. Four guests."

Oh, bugger! I'd forgotten to change the booking for Dom.

"Ah," I began. "There are five of us…"

"Yes. I can see that. So, you will need three rooms. I am sorry, but we do not have any vacancies."

"Are you sure?"

It wasn't a large hotel, and she rolled her eyes upwards like she wouldn't know how many guests she had and whether all the rooms were full.

"Yes, I am sure. You see, we have a computer here."

So, I began to explain that one of us could sleep in the van — and guess who that was going to have to be — to look after the gear. But she wasn't having any of it. It was the law, and she would not bend. If there were five of us on the premises, we each had to have an allocated bed in one of her rooms. She didn't care if we slept in them or not, so long as she got paid.

At that point, Dom walked in. She knew at once something was wrong.

"Let me make a call," she said when I had explained. She patted my hand absently, oblivious to the dry-throat heat that bushwhacked me, then walked out of my earshot and took out her phone. She then read from a little piece of paper that she'd taken from her jacket.

It took no more than a couple of minutes, and she was smiling from the first five seconds into her call.

Returning to me, she said, "It is all sorted. I have some old friends here who will look after me. I will meet you back here tomorrow at nine. Sleep well, and do not worry about me."

She kissed me gently on the lips and walked out of the lobby into the night.

The guys arrived a moment later, after Dom's quick departure. We became busy registering, and it didn't occur to anyone to ask where Dom was. At one point, I noticed headlights sweep past the B & B and heard a car door open and slam, but there was never a moment to interrupt and tell the guys what had happened.

So, I got it in the neck when Jamie asked where Dom was. He actually asked which room Dom was in, not even which floor, which was pretty unsubtle. But he got away with it because I had to tell him that she'd left. For the next few minutes, he let me know I was a complete and utter fuckwit for letting her go off with strangers.

"She's not a child," I told him, but logic cut no ice. Only the receptionist, threatening to call the police if we didn't shut up, finally brought Jamie's carping to an end.

Just as well. I might have called Jamie out on his real motive for wanting to know Dom's room number. And if Dom wasn't a child, then neither was Jamie. None of my business.

*

I LAY IN the darkness for ages, dog-tired, with too much going on in my head to actually sleep. Jamie's accusations had taken root, and never mind Dom's assurances that she was with friends. I think it boiled down to three themes:

Was Dom currently being raped and/or murdered?

Alternatively, had she genuinely hooked up with an old flame—in my head I used her phrase 'old friend', but I knew what I meant—and was now enjoying full sapphic ecstasy?

And lastly, what had she meant by that gentle kiss, which had, nevertheless, set my whole body tingling?

Sub-point one: what would I do if the opportunity arose to repeat it in less frantic and more private circumstances?

Sub-point two: had anyone in the band noticed the slight lip gloss smear on my upper lip, now carefully tissued off and the evidence flushed safely away?

Jamie, I hoped, was oblivious to all this. At any rate, he spent most of the night snoring soundly. I know this because I lay awake for most of the night on the edge of sleep, replaying that kiss. Occasionally, I glanced at the alarm radio by the bed, obsessively calculating how many minutes had passed since the last time I looked.

I did sleep, eventually, but nowhere near as much as I'd been hoping for. I woke to the gabble of a German news program and the sound of Jamie in the shower. Bastard had set his alarm five minutes before mine and grabbed the bathroom. His clothing was strewn everywhere; his bed looked like a bomb site.

I packed what I could while I waited for the bathroom. The shower stopped, and then the shaver started.

"Can't you shave out here?" I called, but he couldn't, or

chose not to, hear me.

When Jamie finally emerged, scrubbed and beautiful, the selfish git didn't wait for me to finish my own shower but went straight down to breakfast. He hadn't bothered to pack.

The shower helped though. Lots. I felt mostly human by the end of it and arrived in the breakfast room as Jamie and the others were finishing.

"Best night's sleep for a week," said Neale. "Hope you slept okay, too, Kai. We're off to pack."

I gave them my best sweetness-and-light smile but said nothing because they'd already turned away. Coffee helped the re-humanisation process, but the traditional German breakfast of cold meat and plastic cheese didn't.

My mind miles away, I started at a touch on my shoulder.

"Hello. May I join you? The others said I might find you here."

It was Dom, of course. Fresh and smiling and no hint of having been murdered.

"Hi, Dom. You okay?"

She nodded and poured herself a coffee from the pot. She took a good draught, then studied me over the top of the mug.

"You look like shit, Kai. Pardon my language, but it is best to speak plainly. Are you not well?"

"Lack of sleep. Nothing to worry about. Your friends looked after you, I guess?"

I watched her right back, but her expression of solicitude didn't change one iota.

"Yes, thank you. Giulio and Karin are excellent hosts. But I *am* worried about you. You look exhausted after a night that should have been full of rest and healing. You are pushing yourself hard, I think. Too hard. And we have a long drive today. To Berlin."

"I'll be okay. We'll have a couple of days to recover after tonight's gig. I can get through it."

"It should not be a case of 'getting through it'. If you do not enjoy it, something's wrong. Will you tell me what is wrong?"

"I couldn't sleep, that's all."

I should have stopped there, but then I said, "I was worried about you."

"You were worried about me?"

"Yes. I was worried about you. You went off, and I didn't know who with. I didn't know if you were safe."

"Oh. But I said I was with friends. Did you not hear me say?"

"Yes, but—"

"But I did not tell you their names. Giulio et Karin, as I said. I am sorry you were worried. I am also sorry you did not trust me. I'm not a child, Kai!"

"I know that. But I tried to tell the band, and they were worried. And I picked up on it."

I tried to tell *Jamie*. Why was I bothering to shield my horny brother?

"Oh," she sighed. "I'm so sorry. I know how that is. I will speak to the band."

"No. Don't do that. It's not their fault. It was just my own mind, doing its own thing, getting itself in a stew over you. In the darkness, I didn't believe my own logic."

"Well, it is light now, and you can put the fears of the night behind you. Yes, my friend?"

I nodded. "Of course."

"Then let us go. The others are waiting."

She put her hands on my shoulders after we stood and looked me straight in the eye. "You will try to get some sleep, will you not?"

I nodded again.

"And you will tell me if there is anything else? I will listen, and I will not judge. I promise."

I smiled my thanks to her. The brightest, least-tired smile I could manage, and Dom rewarded me with a hug. After a moment of surprise, I squeezed back.

It was a good moment. The tiredness would hit me later, and I'd likely be a grumpy git too. But right then, I felt fully, wonderfully human again.

Chapter Fifteen

Sunday, October 2, 2016
On the Road to Berlin

THE DRIVE TO Berlin usually took four and a half hours by car. Add another hour for our slower van, an hour for lunch, and another for breaks. Tack on another hour for getting through Berlin traffic. Bottom line, we needed to get moving *now*.

With considerable reluctance, we headed out to the van. Fresh from our showers, we all noticed it had begun to smell.

"All aboard the stink-wagon for Berlin, guys. Home of decadence and fine music ever since the invention of Prussia."

Jake blew a raspberry at my description. He was grinning, though, as if the next eight-plus hours were his dream come true. That was fine by me. I'd take Jake blowing raspberries over morose Jake or ultra-quiet Jake. Maybe this tour, I'd find out which of them was the real Jake.

Dom, however, frowned. "That's not a joke. There's still a dark side to Berlin, as with all the great, old cities. It changes people."

"Really?"

"We'll be fine. We have money, and we're sensible. But it's not a place to be poor or to take risks."

"Ah, y're an old woman, Dom. Live fast, die young. That's me."

The look she gave Neale was unfathomable.

*

THE ROUTE FROM Fulda to Berlin was pretty simple. Drive north on an autobahn a lot. Turn right. Drive east on another autobahn a lot. Stop and unload.

For a while, we discussed the last gig. It had been pretty frantic with the loading up and then the distraction of where-did-Dom-go. There'd been no time to analyse how the set was gelling or how the new numbers—so to speak, they were all new—had performed.

I'd managed to upload some posts on social media for the last two gigs. A few people had published clips of us performing, though the sound was pretty awful. Better, though, we were getting traction with some hashtags. One made me smile.

"Hey, Jake, you've got your own hashtag. DerMannInRot. The Man in Red."

He looked up from his phone. "Yeah. Lotte told me."

"My, you have changed," I answered. "I've never, ever seen you use a smartphone so much."

He shrugged. "Don't pick on *me*. We've *all* changed. John Doe's Blues? Look at the material we're doing. We're not a blues band anymore. We're certainly not the band that Clay quit. We're not the same band that left England. We're not even the band that played Köln the same evening. Every gig changes us. Massively. I barely recognise some of these tweets, and they're only two, three days old. We're still John Doe's Blues, but not for much longer, if you ask me. John Does a Lot of Other Stuff Too. We're changing. We're Dom's band. I'm still getting used to it, but for the record, I'm okay with that."

That was one hell of a speech from Jake. For about a minute, there was no sound but the drone of the autobahn and the burring chug of the diesel as we digested what he'd said.

Jamie broke the silence. "Yeah. Me too. Neale?"

"I haven't turned the van around, have I?"

"We're on a bloody autobahn, you crazy Irishman."

"So? Still, since you've asked, this is the band I joined. Your past is not my past. I never worked with Clay. But then, I'm a hired gun, so your future is not my future either. As I said before, I'm in for the craic."

We all sat in silence for a bit longer. After a while, I realised they were waiting for me to speak.

"Oh, yeah. Sure. I'm in. I didn't realise we were voting. But it doesn't change anything. The tour is now. The future? Recording? Who knows? Let's just make the next week a success."

I looked over at Dom, in the back with Jamie.

She nodded agreement. "That is wise. I'm happy with what we have now. I will try to do my part."

And that rather drew a line under the subject. Everybody fell silent again, wondering what would happen when the tour was done. At least, I was wondering about that. After a while, Jake unlocked his smartphone and started thumbing around. In the back, Jamie was reading a book. Dom had closed her eyes, apparently trying to sleep.

*

AFTER AN HOUR'S silent driving, we broke for twenty minutes at a rest stop for Neale to get some fresh air and stretch his legs.

Dom took me aside. "This is not good. You should have two drivers. It is too much for one person."

"This is the last for a while. After Berlin, we have a couple of days break before the next gig. We can see the sights, get some rest. Neale won't have to drive, at any rate."

"It is still not safe. None of the rest of you drive though?"

"No. I'm still learning. Jamie and Jake don't drive. Jamie's a fit bugger, who cycles everywhere. Jake takes the bus."

"How did you manage before?"

"Clay drove everywhere, picked everybody up. When we practised, we used the studio's backline and drums. Plus, we never had to drive across Europe to get to our next gig."

"Hmm…then I will have to help. I should have done so before."

"Help? How?"

"I can drive. You know that. I simply need to contact my…*agent d'assurance*."

"Would you do that? It would certainly make a difference having two insured drivers."

"Of course. I will speak to Neale in private and ask his

permission."

I was expecting some fireworks, but no, Neale was willing enough. Relieved, I thought. So, Dom made the call, even though it was Sunday, and must have got the answer she wanted. I suspected she hadn't mentioned the slightly non-standard seating arrangements.

So, Dom took the wheel, though Neale claimed he was okay to do another hour.

"So long as the traffic isn't too heavy, the autobahn is a good road for me to learn to handle the van. I can drive many kilometres, so you will be fresher when we reach Berlin."

And then: "You bloody English. Always driving on the wrong side of your miserable little roads in your crappy opposite-way-round cars." But she was smiling as she said it, and she pulled into traffic faultlessly.

Neale, now sitting in the back, drifted off to sleep after about twenty minutes. He stayed that way until Dom pulled off the autobahn, shortly after we started heading east. We'd made decent distance and were ready for lunch.

Neale admitted the rest had done him good. "Dom, do you think you can drive some more? I'll take the last stretch into Berlin if that's okay."

"Sure." She pointed to a spot on the map. "We change over at Grunewald West. Okay?"

Which made it a substantial drive that Dom had signed up to, but she seemed fresh enough still. Half an hour down the road, though, she groaned as the tail lights illuminated on the cars ahead of us, and the traffic ground to a halt.

Far ahead, assorted emergency lights flashed. Nothing

happened for about half an hour. We sat there, in the middle of a sea of cars, not moving. Out came Jake's smartphone, of course. It seemed a reflex reaction to anything and everything these last couple of days. I hoped Jake had a good roaming deal.

When the traffic started moving again, it was stop-start motoring, crawling along at never more than five miles an hour. Grunewald West seemed as far away as ever, and Dom wasn't used to handling the van in slow-moving traffic. The gear changes with her left hand were still awkward, and her freshness was falling away.

And then the engine misfired, or something. At any rate, the van lost power, and Dom tried to give it more revs. We suddenly lurched forward, and Dom slammed her foot down on the brake pedal. The van stopped with a jerk a couple of inches from the car in front.

"*Merde!*" she growled in the same moment as a discordant thump sounded from the back.

"Fuck!" Jamie. "Watch that, Dom. That was Jake's acoustic coming down on me. Just as well it wasn't his amp. Could 'a killed me..."

"Give her a break, Jamie," I filtered. "The engine is playing silly buggers again."

Indeed, it was. Was my fuel fuck-wittery coming back to haunt us?

It appeared so. For the next fifteen minutes, Dom played a virtuoso performance on three pedals, keeping the van lurching along without crashing into the car in front or tipping any large amplifiers onto Jamie or Neale.

Finally, the traffic picked up speed, and we were making a

steady fifty mph. The engine had settled down.

We pulled in at the next *Tankstelle*, or petrol station, and topped the tank right up with diesel. If there was any petrol still in there, it should be diluted to the point where it wouldn't have any further effect.

Neale took over the driving after that, bringing us another hour closer to Berlin. The van didn't give us any trouble, which Neale claimed was down to 'knowing the boss was at the wheel'. But it behaved equally well when Dom took over again, driving as far as the Grunewald West rest stop and what we hoped would be an easy remaining stretch into Berlin for Neale. The A115 would take us through the Grunewald, itself, and then the long, straight road from the west through Charlottenburg into the heart of Berlin. The Grunewald was a forest between Berlin and the Wannsee, a large lake, very popular in summer and less so later in the year when it got towards winter, like now.

From behind the van windows and sharing the warmth of five people, it looked almost Christmas card pretty, though it still lacked snow. Which was fine by me. A few miles later, the forest came to an end, and we took an off-ramp. Blink. We were in Berlin.

There was no good reason for it, but if every car in Berlin wasn't on the Charlottenburg Road, I was a Dutchman. We joined a tailback at the bottom of the off-ramp and started crawling. After about ten minutes, the van started misfiring.

Neale swore. " — kwit"

I only caught the end of it, my triumphs already forgotten.

*

WHAT WAS THERE to tell about a tailback? They lasted forever while you were in them. If you tried to turn off into a side street, you'd hit a one-way system that conspired to take you back the way you'd come and laughingly disgorge you half a mile behind the place you'd tried to escape. Then you'd crawl back behind yourself, snarl at the so-promising side street you'd driven down twenty minutes ago, knowing you'd never catch yourself up. People who knew the lanes better than you hopped in — or out — in front of you, and a moment later you'd realise you were trapped in a lane that led to a goods entrance, or a bus lane, or to the ninth circle of hell. And all the while, the fucking van lurched and stalled and threatened never to start again.

Some or all of those things happened to us in the hour or so that followed. But especially the last.

After a while, the ninth circle became the eighth, and then the seventh. A little later, we passed a sign saying thank you for visiting hell; we hope you enjoyed your stay. Well, no. But the traffic did move a bit faster. And Neale stopped his Dante-inspired commentary. I would definitely go read the original.

The satnav decided it was now time for us to leave our current tailback and join another. It got interesting as we zigzagged through a series of GPS-dead junctions with ambiguous road signs. We got some right, others not, and then we'd go around the block for another try, still lurching and stalling, Neale's F-bombs accompanying.

A couple of alarming lurches followed. Neale swerved violently, and Jamie swore. An amp teetered, steadied as Jamie's hand slapped at it.

And we were stopped quite close to the kerb, to judge from

the squeal from one of the tyres.

"Did you mean to do that, my friend?"

"Yes. I. Fucking. Did."

There was a long pause. Icicles began to form within the van.

"Ah, sorry, Dom. I wasn't swearin' at you. But yes. The satnav says we're right outside the place. Me, I'm not so sure."

"Which one is it?" I asked, relieved to see the temperature climb.

"Well, that's a bank, or I'm a Protestant."

"It's a bank," said Dom.

"Well, Hail Mary, full of Grace, I'm still a Catholic!"

"The rest look like houses to me," I observed. "What's the number, Jamie?"

"Of what?"

"The house number of the venue, of course."

"Forty-seven. The bank is number fifty-one, for your information."

We twisted in our seats, trying to work out the street numbering.

"It's that house," said Neale eventually, pointing somewhere behind him that I couldn't see.

"Are you sure?"

"Not a clue, Kai, not a fuckin' clue. I'm making shit up because I've had a lousy fuckin' drive through nine circles of hell, and I can't be arsed to walk twenty yards and find out. What's your excuse?"

"I'll go take a look."

Forty-seven was indeed one of several ordinary-looking houses just up the street from the bank. Some of them had been divided into flats, but number forty-seven was, as far as I could tell, a single residence on three levels. No, four. There was a basement.

I went back to the van.

"It's an ordinary house, guys. Big. But it's no club. Are you sure it's the right address, Jamie? Did it have a name?"

"Sure. Chez Jurgen. To play a private party."

Jamie, of course, pronounced 'chez' with a hard *ch*, to rhyme with 'fez'. And 'Jürgen' with a hard *J*. I didn't bother to correct him because a nasty suspicion was forming.

"Have you still got the emails? On your phone?"

Jamie thumbed and swiped for a few moments, then held his phone out to me.

Hi Jamie,

I am glad to hear that you can play at my birthday party! You'll find Chez Jürgen at house number 47 (link). I am sorry there is no lift in the house, and you'll have to carry your equipment down some stairs. But me and some friends can help you to carry. We saw your YouTube videos and all liked your blues very much. After the gig, I'll invite you to have some beer? You are welcome to sleep for the night there on the floor if you wish.

mbw. J

J. Jürgen.

"Why did you think this was a club, Jamie?"

"The name. Chez Jurgen."

I winced. Hard *ch*. Voiced zed. And hard *J*.

"Sorry, Jamie. That means 'Jürgen's home'. It's in French."

"But he's German. Why wouldn't he just say 'at my house'?"

"I don't know. Maybe he's half French. Maybe he's just a pretentious twat."

And maybe he was trying to con the gullible Englishman.

"How much?" I asked. "How much is he paying us?"

I don't know why I asked, because I'd done the figures. But Jamie took his phone back, thumbed and swiped some more, and showed me.

Four hundred fifty euros.

That was good money. It was a big part of our 'avoid a massive loss' strategy for the tour, not least because accommodation was part of the deal.

But a private party? In the guy's home? It brought back memories of my first gigs, barely into my teens, with a guitar that was way too big for me slung around my neck. Before I'd been old enough to go to adult venues. Before I'd begun to love the blues or seen Joe Bonamassa touring the UK. And before I'd stumbled across Toto's Jeff Porcaro on YouTube and decided that I really, really wanted to play the drums after all.

They were not good memories, particularly. Standing elbow to elbow with Jamie in front of some fireplace, playing Robbie Williams covers to an audience that wanted to get back to listening to Now 74 or whatever number they'd reached back then. The pain of hearing the words 'Can you play some…?'" and knowing that whatever name came next, our answer would be "Sorry, no."

*

BUT JÜRGEN TURNED out to be a decent bloke in a sort of puppy-dog eager way. He answered the door and beamed as he said, "Hi…Kai. You are the drummer, yes?"

And then—without the Look—he grabbed my hand in a fierce handshake that caught me unprepared. Before I knew it, I was inside and the door had closed behind me. He beckoned me through, without giving me a chance to answer, and then my jaw dropped. Because Jürgen's pad was smart. Glass-and-chrome minimalist smart. Indirect lighting smart. Concealed storage smart. It all spoke of serious money. There was an exercise bike in the corner and a rowing machine next to it. Jürgen looked a healthy thirty, trim with a slight sheen of perspiration on his brow. He wore a black sports vest and spandex cycle shorts, plus an expensive-looking watch, that I didn't recognise, because who still uses watches?

A dark-skinned woman popped her head around the door, then disappeared. He must have caught my eyes flickering past his shoulder.

"*Meine*… Sorry, my…" He hesitated.

"Mother-in-law? Stockbroker? Masseuse? Give me a clue…"

He laughed but gently. "No. None of those. She is my office manager. My administrator. My major-domo. She is Turkish, but she also speaks German, English, Italian, and French. A very smart woman. I will introduce you later."

"Thank you."

This wasn't going where it needed to go. I held up my hand.

"Listen, Jürgen, we've come to play a gig. But this is a house, not a club. Is that right?"

"Of course. It is my house. It is my party. And you are my blues band, to help me celebrate my birthday with my friends. There will be music, and there will be dancing. There will be booze—fine champagne for the guests. And…more."

More than champagne? Did he mean drugs? Gentle chime of warning bells.

"And we're in the middle of Berlin," I said. "Is it okay to just throw a party?"

"Sure. No problem. My place is just a few streets away from the Alexanderplatz. Clubs everywhere. Loud music. Even some good music. All the time."

"Okay. It's your party."

"Yes. It is my *birthday* party. And *today* is my birthday."

"Happy Birthday, Jürgen." And then again in German, because a part of me hated being the monoglot English abroad. "*Herzlichen Glückwünsch zum Geburtstag, Jürgen.*"

"Hah! You sound like a birthday card. But thank you. So, is that all of your German?"

"I could use a bit of practice, but I can get by."

"And the band?"

"A mix."

"Well, you can tell them not to worry. Everyone speaks English, here. And I mean here—Berlin. Sometimes, it feels like German is a dying language, right here in the heart of Germany."

Practical topic needed. "Uh. The other guys, they're out in the van. Waiting to unload the gear."

"Oh, yes. Drive round the back. I show you, sure."

A curious guy; I couldn't make him out. Buzzy. Excited.

Intoxicated? I didn't think so. High? Or hyper?

*

WE WERE IN the basement. It was completely and consciously different from the rooms I'd seen. Those had all been like Jürgen's ground floor gym, sparse and elegant and new. A well-stocked bar flanked the entrance to the basement, a spacious, sleazy crypt-like structure, with alcoves to the sides and a wide central aisle. There weren't any actual tombs in the alcoves, but the brickwork looked old, and I guessed Jürgen had spent a ton of money to get it that way. At the far end was the stage, kitted out with recessed floor sockets for power and audiovisual. It even had a small set of stage lights clamped on proper scaffolding. Money again.

A dumbwaiter arrangement shifted equipment in and out of the basement. Jürgen stayed with us while we brought instruments and amps down. He chatted, dropping hints that he'd made his pile as some kind of software designer in the online gaming world. Well, good luck to him. He was generous with his money, based on what he was paying us. He spent time talking with us, getting to know us and putting us at ease. He made us feel like we weren't just the hired help but a valued part of the team putting together his party. Only one thing—he was cool with Dom, which surprised me. He seemed quite immune to her modus operandi. I got a mental flash of two prowling tigers avoiding each other.

Then, when we'd unloaded the gear, he gave us the grand tour around the rest of his pad, again, everything bright and modern in glass and chrome, with wooden floors and white walls. The centrepiece was his computer room, full of some serious hardware: two racks of servers plus five or six big gaming machines with a mix of plasma screen arrays and VR headsets. Nice.

He spent a few minutes bragging about uptime and bandwidth and redundant cloud-based data centres. As he talked, his screen saver cycled through holiday photos of somewhere hot and sandy. The photos showed a group of friends, men and women, laughing and drinking. Nothing I could quite put my finger on at first, but the camera seemed often to return to one of the men. I finally twigged that he and Jürgen were an item. A couple of frames later, up came a shot in which they were puckering up for the camera.

Jürgen's partner was as physically fit as him, Mediterranean dark, where Jürgen was fair, and carrying a two-day stubble. He had heavy eyebrows over narrowed eyes—smouldering was the adjective that came to mind. Park those thoughts.

With that, the tour was done. If that final stop-off was Jürgen's way of letting us know he was gay, then mission accomplished. He led us back to the crypt, told us to soundcheck before six, and hauled over a crate of mineral water for us to share.

"Beer later, guys. And if you want to try anything else, drink lots of water first. Okay?"

"Sure," we agreed.

I asked, "Is there somewhere nearby we can get something to eat? We've been driving a long while."

"Sure. There's a Döner round the corner if you want. But why not get some proper food? You wait. Gizem will bring you party food."

Gizem, it turned out, was Jürgen's admin, the woman I'd glimpsed earlier. She appeared about ten minutes later, carrying a tray of food, and I got a good look at her. Shiny black hair, coiled in a tight, business bun. Mid-brown complexion and eyebrows plucked to microscopic symmetry. Late twenties, immaculately made-up with a delicate palette from magenta through lilac. She wore a tailored two-piece iron-grey business suit over a white blouse, and her nails were painted lilac to match her lip gloss. I doubted she'd prepared the food herself.

She smiled with the ease of someone never, ever out of her depth. "Hello, I'm Gizem, and I'm Jürgen's assistant. Mostly, I deal with his business, but tonight, I'm helping ensure the party runs smoothly. I know Jürgen has given you a personal tour, but if there's anything you need, try not to bother him. Come and see me. It's my job to make sure Jürgen can relax."

I got the distinct feeling I wouldn't want to make Gizem's life difficult.

But right now, she was pleasant; she'd brought down a platter of rolls, cheese and cold meats, and—this being Germany— gherkins.

"Ach," groaned Neale, "what the fuck are those little green turds?"

"You have seen *les cornichons*, Neale, have you not?"

"Gherkins, Neale. They won't kill you."

"They're not going to bloody get the chance, Kai. Nasty looking buggers, they are. Is that what Germans eat?"

Gherkins, cornichons. Whatever. I was famished, and so were we all. By unspoken consent we broke off the set-up and pulled over some large beanbags into a circle. For the next twenty minutes, we sat, eating in silence. Save for Neale's occasional cursing of gherkins and everyone's mineral-water belches. Mine included.

The delights of a band on tour.

After the contortions of Fulda, it was a pleasure to set up on Jürgen's small but well-equipped stage. With all our gear, it verged on cosy but entirely adequate. Unsurprisingly, Jürgen's PA was better than ours, but we used our own desk.

We started playing a couple of numbers. Not a soundcheck, more like a chance to unscrunch after our long drive. About half-way through 'Blues with a Feeling' Jürgen appeared and parked himself on a couple of beanbags. When we finished, I let Neale tinker with the desk. For a gherkin-hater, he was a pretty good sound man. I was learning to trust him. When he was sober.

Next up, we dove into 'Whiskey in the Jar', Neale's tour de force. Fiddle, of course, but he also took some of the vocals with Dom. The performance owed as much to Phil Lynott as to Shane MacGowan. They'd tinkered with the words, so it would work as a duet. Dom sang Jenny, complete with a triple betrayal by the final verse.

> *And then came Captain Farrell to the room where I'd been staying*
> *His shirt a-splashed with scarlet from the man that he'd been slaying*
> *But I was gone with gold and jewels; for England I was sailing*
> *In London will I live a Lady's life with wealth unfailing*

At the end, Jürgen leaped up from his beanbags and

applauded wildly.

"*Prima!*" he called. "*Zugabe! Encore!* More!"

That was good news. There'd been a few nervous moments earlier, when he'd seen Dom and Neale.

"*Where is Clay?*" he'd asked, which was a bloody good question, considering his reputation as a party host was on the line. The band he'd seen on YouTube was a known quantity — an entirely decent blues band, if a little obscure. On the other hand, a fresh-formed and under-rehearsed band would turn his birthday shindig into a disaster.

And all of that weight of expectation would have been on me. My too-pure-for-blues voice would not have cut it alone. Not here in Jürgen's basement.

Now, though, Jürgen was on our side. His genuine enthusiasm would bounce around and infect his guests. Jürgen was a guy who took his friends with him, and it wasn't about his money. His whole pad oozed taste (as well as money), and his friends would take their cues from him. The gig *should* turn out to be a blast.

And then he dropped his bombshell.

"Look, guys. Do you think I could play saxophone with you on a couple of numbers?"

So why was the whole band looking at the drummer? Me. AKA Muggins, who'd have to make the hard call. If he was okay, then I'd be 'lucky'. If not, I'd be 'fuckwit' again, who'd not had the balls to say "no."

"Yeah," I answered before my brain had a chance to get involved. "We could do that. Got any ideas what you could play?"

"I play jazz, mostly. But I can do improvisation on blues."

"Okay, I'll have a think. Get your sax ready."

Jürgen disappeared back upstairs. For the life of me, I could only think of the *Pink Panther* theme. *Which isn't part of our repertoire and* never *will be.*

"Help me, guys. Any ideas what could take a sax part?"

No help. They looked at me as if I was speaking Finnish. *Uh, I don't.*

"Why don't we try 'Bell Bottom Blues', Kai?"

I let the idea swirl around my brain for a bit.

"Yeah. That could work. Thanks, Dom."

So we tried it, and Jürgen appeared around verse two and listened a bit. Dom called to him to start playing, but he shook his head, continuing to listen while we wrapped up the rest of the song. He fingered keys, just didn't blow. When we finished, he spoke.

"Give me an *A*, please."

Of course. Tuning up. The bane of bands working with acoustic instruments. We ran through 'Bell Bottom Blues' again, this time with Jürgen on sax. And he *could* play, which was a relief. He was no Charlie Parker, but he was competent.

Now that we knew what he could do, that triggered a few more suggestions. All fairly straightforward—we weren't looking for a new band-member. This was glory time for the birthday boy, a chance for him to show off in front of his friends and earn us a few brownie points.

We had three Jürgen numbers in the bag. That was enough, and he was wise enough to know it. We arranged a spot in the first set for him to do one number and a second spot towards the end of the second set for the other two. Sorted.

"Okay, guys. I'll see you later. The party starts at seven

thirty. Don't hide down here—all my friends speak English, so please go upstairs and mingle. They're pretty free and easy. Don't get too pissed. And…'don't mention the War'."

He grinned and left us.

'Don't mention the War', indeed. If Fawlty Towers had reached Berlin, then we should have no worries about speaking English at all.

A couple more songs completed the soundcheck, but Dom asked if we could do a little more work on 'Cross My Heart', now renamed as 'Cross, Don't Cross'. I got a little distracted—mental pictures of a short-haired girl favouring Dom with an adoring gaze—because I played right through a rest bar. I got a dirty look from Jamie. *Whoa, Kai*! I pulled myself together and started concentrating on the structure. No more snafus.

Then Dom asked if we knew 'The Hall of Fallen Angels'. I said I'd heard a version by Ry Cooder, and she nodded.

"Do you know the Eva Cassidy version?'

Eva Cassidy? The name was familiar, but I couldn't place it. Nobody else knew the song, so Dom borrowed Jake's Strat and ran through the whole thing. Then she handed his guitar back to him and sang, while he played the chords he'd learned. A couple of errors, but he'd fixed them by verse three. Jamie followed Jake's chord shapes on the next pass, and I got ready to add a drum part when they were done.

But Dom said no. "Okay, you know the chords, but now I want you to take it right back, Jake. No chords. Do light guitar fills over bass. Jamie, your pattern is fine, but make it smoother, if you can, like a fretless. Kai, no drums. I want you and Neale harmonising, thirds and fifths. Sing 'oo', for now, filling in the chording.

Then, as soon as you can, pick up the words, especially the last lines of the verses, and add them."

So we did it the way Dom said, and Jake picked up the fourth in the chords that Neale and I weren't covering. Dom sang but coasted, staying with the melody, letting Neale and me get comfortable with our harmonies. There were a few stumbles first time through—a major third for a minor, or vice versa—but we fixed those.

"You ready, guys?" Dom gathered us by eye and was in on the opening *A* chord.

> *There's a place that no one speaks of, at the end of Meeting Street…*

An arpeggio from Jake, and Neale and I both missed the cue. We should have been singing our backing line as she came in. Instead, we left it bare and came in at the chorus with the 'past mistakes' hook.

The song was about a cheating couple, meeting in secret at a cheap, by-the-hour motel, living in fear of discovery, and denying each other in public. Dom gave it everything, the guilt, the fear, and the delicious, addictive pleasure of the love-cheat all played out in the tremble of her voice. It was no longer Dom singing a song. It had become Dom's defiance of an immoral morality, drawing on, I know not what, personal experience.

And then, as Neale and I sang 'welcomed there', ready to softly switch to 'oo', she spoke over us.

"Kai, verse two. Sing it with me."

Dark angel calls to angel…

Dom dropped out, picking up my wordless harmony line, and I was out on my own, singing the other lover.

> *…and two hearts forbidden beat*
> *As one, and one draws closer, and passions flame and*
> *heat*

And back in she came…with me.

> *In secret rooms we threw off caution, and played our*
> *fantasies*

Well, back at you, Dom, and I dropped out, leaving her alone to sing…

> *And I crept home and filled my once-love's ears with*
> *hollow lies*

And now we knew the game in time for the chorus:

> *The new mistakes we're building, which you and I now*
> *share*
> *In the Hall of Fallen Angels, in the bed of I-don't-care*

You crazy boss-lady, Dom! But I was smiling. Just.
Until over the link she said exactly the same thing to Neale:

*The ones that we have left behind, the first loves we
now wrong
With lies that sound so sweet, but taste so bitter on the
tongue
A stolen hour at noon-time spent in passion on a quilt
The room keys shine like gold but all they open up is
gilt*

*The futures that we hoped for have turned to dark and
cold
In the Hall of Fallen Angels, where we count the love
we stole*

*

STANDING IN THE kitchen, beer bottle in hand, I was deep in conversation with an earnest young Dane named Lars, who'd said he wanted to try out his English on me. And possibly more — But for the moment, I kept the conversation to safe subjects. Currently under discussion was Lars's job as an administrator at Berlin's Stasi Museum. That suited me; I had no wish to offend one of Jürgen's guests, but Lars's conversation did veer off on odd tangents...

Backtrack.

After our soundcheck, I'd gone into the kitchen to find a beer. The basement had a bar, but Jürgen had set up beers and nibbles in the kitchen — two floors up and sans music — so people could mingle, chat without shouting, and then never leave. That was what kitchens were for, right?

So I wasn't too surprised when the guy in front of me

plucked a couple of beers from the fridge and thrust one at me.

"You want a beer, Kai?" he asked.

"Sure, thanks. And you are?"

"I'm Lars." He cocked his head as though it should mean something.

"Pleased to meet you, Lars."

"You don't make the connection?"

I shook my head. Then… "Lars? On Twitter? You're Vaegbryderen?"

He grinned and raised his bottle.

I clinked mine against it and said *"Prost."*

"Prost!" he replied.

It turned out Lars had started following the band pretty much on the day John Doe's Blues had gone public. Courtesy of Google Translate, I'd worked out that Vaegbryderen meant 'wall breaker', and it was Danish. I was a bit puzzled, though, how a Dane had found and followed a very obscure blues band from Marden Combe.

That had kicked off in interesting DM directions because it quickly became clear he knew that John Doe's Blues had emerged very recently from the ashes of the Clayton Paul Blues Band.

KAI: *So you were planning to see the band?*

LARS: *Yes. In Berlin. But I noticed Clayton Paul was doing his own thing, so I DM'd him, and he told me you'd split. TL;DR, I'll be coming to your gig in Berlin.*

KAI: *:-)*

From there, I'd headed over to @Vaegbryderen and commented on a tweet of his in German, and he'd followed me, and I'd FB'd him. But I'd always assumed he'd meant the Club Mojo gig on the last Saturday, not the private party.

Back in the present, in the real world—or at least in Jürgen's kitchen—we picked up on one of those Twitter tangents. Mostly in English because Lars said he got a lot of English tourists at the museum and needed the practice. But we had one of those very polite arguments that English linguists had abroad because we wanted to improve our (insert foreign language here) skills too. So we dropped into German from time to time.

"But you should learn Danish, Kai. If you can learn German…"

"*Schon habe ich Deutsch gelernt.*"

"Yes, you have already learned German. Therefore, you will find Danish not too difficult. It is the same family of language. Except Danes do not the crazy German leave-the-verb-to-the-end thing do."

"So what crazy thing does Danish do instead? If Danish were perfect, we'd all be speaking it."

"No. The Danes never tried to conquer the world."

"The Vikings tried, didn't they? They were Danish, weren't they?" I was on shaky ground here. My Nordic history extended to knowing the Vikings had crossed the Atlantic and that their helmets didn't actually have horns, but not much more than that.

"You're right about the Vikings. But they were traders, not conquerors…"

So, I didn't find out what crazy thing the Danish language did, though I did discover that the Normans were Danish colonists, and they'd conquered England.

…and later:

"I found your first demo," Lars said. "The one with you on vocals. I think you used some old tracks from Clayton Paul, yes?"

"Yeah. I dubbed my own vocals over the top because we needed to get something out onto the internet while we were looking for a proper singer. They weren't very good vocals."

"You mean they didn't sound like Clay's vocals? Of course not. But you have a good voice. And you are a very good drummer."

"I'm not fishing for compliments, Lars."

"Well, sometimes they jump out of the water anyway and land in your boat."

Maybe that was the tangent, or maybe it was another one we were travelling when we came to an unexpected stop in the conversation. We'd been rattling along, talking about anything and everything. And then there was nothing to say because…

Clarity. Congruence. Complementarity.

Two minds, drawing together. And as the minds, so…

Two trains running on adjacent tracks.

Two walkers approaching each other upon a single tightrope.

No distance…

Stillness.

His lips, slightly parted, were so close that I could feel his gentle breath upon my cheek, upon my own lips…

Fragility. A single way of harmony, battered by a million ways for it to spiral into chaos, flames, and destruction.

Then I remembered the Thunderbolt. The *colpo di fulmine. Hit by thunder. Love at first sight.* The phrase had stuck in my mind when I'd read Puzo's *The Godfather*. Michael Corleone struck by the first sight of Apollonia. And all the bloody reverberations of that moment.

Neither reading *The Godfather* nor anything else in my life had prepared me for my own moment, nor for the moment stretching. I didn't dare look at Lars's face, in case I saw my own looking back.

'Kai?' My name, softly enunciated.

I was a lock, and I felt the key turning inside me.

It wasn't something I wanted to face. Yet neither did I — wholly — want to flee. And so, I let my eyes meet his.

And time stopped.

*

I FELT A tap on the arm. I turned, expecting Gizem, wondering if I'd unknowingly transgressed. But no. A woman, but not Gizem.

"Kai? Sorry for interrupting. We have a visitor at the door. Would you come with me, please?"

Someone at the door? I wasn't sure what business that was of mine, but I went along anyway, promising Lars I'd be back.

I remembered the woman from Jürgen's screen saver photos — close-cropped fair hair and high cheekbones. White shirt and khaki shorts plus designer shades. I mentioned the photos.

She smiled and agreed. "Yes. I am Annika. We were on holiday near Barcelona. Such a perfect day for a grill party on the beach."

Beach barbie in Barcelona. Got it. And then we took the stairs down to the hall, and Annika cut short her reminiscence. As the hall came into view, we halted and Annika pointed at a figure in a heavy coat and a woollen hat, carrying a backpack. A girl, I decided, though her back was to us. She was with Gizem, of course, who was keeping her talking until someone could vouch for her. Gizem flicked her eyes towards us as we resumed our descent, and the girl broke off to turn and face us.

For a moment, I couldn't place the face, though it was strangely familiar.

Then she swept the hat from her head and called, "Hi, Kai!" She swished out night-black tresses from under her collar and smoothed them down over her breast. Ah.

"Lotte!"

… and…

"What the fuck are you doing here?"

… and…

"I mean, it's lovely to see you, and Jake will be pleased" — and *there* was a conversation I needed to have — "but does your mother know where you are?"

That last might have been the wrong thing to say as Lotte's face darkened.

Fortunately, Annika interrupted at that point. "This is your friend, yes? You vouch for her?"

I nodded. "This is Lotte." I decided I needed to make up for my gaffe. "She's a very dear friend of Jake. Yes, I absolutely do vouch for her."

That was good enough. Gizem vanished, while Annika beamed and turned to Lotte, defusing any explosion that might have been brewing. She helped her with her backpack and coat and tucked them into a closet. Then she fished out a comb and a mirror for her.

I judged a hug was in order, and Lotte hugged me back. My rudeness was forgiven.

"Kai. We'll catch up later; I promise. But I've had a long, shitty journey, all to see your guitarist. Where is Jake?"

I didn't know, but I took her by the hand and led her to where I'd last seen him. In the tide of people, he'd drifted a little and was now deep in conversation with a guy in an orange fedora and a T-shirt advertising a Berlin guitar store. I caught phrases like "…Gibson 335" and "…Les Paul." No surprise there, just two guitar nerds having a pissing contest, and it was still round one because they hadn't yet started trading specific years of guitar excellence.

I would treasure the memory of the next few seconds for a long, long time. Jake turned and saw me, and then his glance flicked to Lotte standing next to me. His mouth opened a fraction, and he tried to say something, but the words wouldn't come. His eyes brimmed with tears, and Lotte was suddenly next to him, arms holding him very, very tight. She was crying too. It might have been relief at the end of a long train journey halfway across Germany, but…

Whatever. One in the eye for Homer—Penelope had found Odysseus.

Orange fedora guy was still wittering on about models of B. B. King's 'Lucille' guitar and its many replicas and custom shop models. I took a deep breath, tapped him on the arm, whispered 'Can we talk about Telecasters?" and guided him somewhere far, far away.

I grinned from ear to ear, nodding with mock enthusiasm, while the complete history of the Fender Telecaster washed over me. It didn't matter. I was 'taking one for the team'. Perhaps I would bend Jake's ear later. But I wouldn't be the one to puncture his and Lotte's bubble of love. Or lust. Shush.

"Excuse me, I'm not the most sensitive of people, but I'm not sure you've been listening. I mentioned a Telecaster Quadcopter and the experimental Jellycaster, and you just nodded. I think you owe me an explanation."

Oh shit!

I tried to dredge up what he'd been saying, but nothing had stuck. Nothing.

"I'm sorry. You're quite right."

So, I told him about Jake and Lotte, and his face softened. And then he laughed.

"Yeah, I missed that. I'm not good at spotting some of those 'people things'. Thank you for telling me. I like talking to people in bands, but I know I can get a little intense. More than intense, if I'm honest. Too much for a lot of people. But Jake was good company for a while."

"I'm sorry I misled you. It was all I could think of to give them some space."

"Don't worry about it. He's lucky to have you looking after him. But you're not another guitarist, are you?"

"Huh? No. I play a little acoustic guitar. And I really would like to own a Telecaster if I could afford one. I love the sound, and they look so cool. I'd use it for writing songs on. But I'm the drummer."

"Interesting."

He pointed to his T-shirt. "This is my shop."

Ah. So much made sense when I actually read the name.

'Orange Fedora Guitars'.

He continued, "Just guitars for now. I buy used guitars, and I repair them, make them real good. Business is okay, but I want to expand. Start selling new stuff too. If I can find the right people, I would sell basses, keyboards, even drums. There's a basement in the store — I use it as my workshop. But there's more space than I need, so I could set it up as my bass department. Or my drum department. I don't know. It depends on the deals I can set up, and the people I can find. They'd need to know their instrument and be able to inspire people with their love for that instrument. That's what sells."

*

OUR FIRST SET was at nine, and we were ready to go about fifteen minutes before then. Jürgen ushered his guests down, so we had a full house or near enough. It helped that there was a bar too.

Lotte had stationed herself behind the bar, serving Jürgen's guests with speed and skill. Perhaps it was her thank-you to Jürgen for letting her crash his party. Jake tried to help her for a while, but he had no aptitude for the job. Dom had gathered him up early for a final tune up, and Lotte was much quicker serving after that.

We started with a couple of standards that set out our stall. First up was 'Rolling and Tumbling', setting a good, bouncy pace, and then into 'Crossroads'. Dom played them both straight out of the 'blues-woman done paid her dues' mould, then took the pace down and the emotion up for Rory Block's 'Lovin' Whiskey'.

That set, Jake was on fire. He wasn't note-perfect, but he pushed the limits of inventiveness, and the crowd began to cheer him on. Lotte now leaned against one of the thick iron pillars, rapt, all the emotional stress of her journey fallen away. I guessed Annika had helped her wash away the grime and sweat, leaving true love to transcend the crapness of life.

Then it was time to play 'Bell Bottom Blues'. We welcomed Jürgen onto the stage, sang a verse of 'Happy Birthday', then kicked into the intro. Jürgen behaved himself, playing gentle fills around Dom's vocal until it was time for his solo. The solo was a neat improvisation, different from what he'd rehearsed with us, but it ended when and where it was supposed to. Naturally, it was received with enthusiastic whistles and calls for an encore. We finished to plenty of applause, but Jürgen didn't try to outstay what we'd agreed.

Which brought us to the final number of the first set — 'Whiskey in the Jar', our own version. Neale's fiddle intro got some puzzled looks and then some broad grins. I didn't know how much the crowd picked up on the lyrics of the verses, but they threw themselves into the chorus.

And then we were done. More applause, and when it began to die down, a slurred voice called out to "Play another *trinken* song" accompanied by desultory calls of "*Zugabe!*" — encore — and the odd "*Ja!*" That triggered a bout of foot stomping and a creditable attempt by four drunks to sing "Mush a-ring, dum-a-do, dum-a-da…"

It all petered out, but it nagged at me, and I rushed off to find paper and pen because I'd had an idea for a song. I needed to find peace and quiet, though, so I wandered about Jürgen's house, trying to escape the music and the crowds. I bumped into Jürgen as he exited his computer room.

"Hi, Kai. You look lost. Can I help?"

I smiled. "Thanks. I'm looking for somewhere quiet to write down an idea for a song where I won't get interrupted."

"Sure thing. You can go in there." He pointed at the computer room.

"Are you sure?"

"Yes. Everyone knows it is *verboten*…"

"Forbidden, yes. I know what *verboten* means. I think even Jamie knows what *verboten* means. But your English is much better than you let on. If you're doing it to make us poor English—and Irish—feel better about our abysmal language skills, then go ahead. I promise we won't take offense."

He grinned. "No one will disturb you. Don't touch anything, please. I hope it's a good song."

Inside, only the light from the screensaver relieved the gloom. It suited me, though, and I sat in a high-backed gaming chair that wouldn't have been out of place in a starship weapons control room. I settled down in the comfortable seat, and the song flowed easily from my pen.

I got the chorus down first…

Play me another drinking song
Keep it simple so I can sing along
Love songs only cause me pain
So drain your glass let's sing again

The verses came easily. They were all about 'drinking to get drunk' and 'drinking to forget'.

I was deep in thought when the door opened. I didn't turn

around because I was struggling to fit too many ideas into not enough syllables and not break the metre. I ignored a giggle and a shush, which didn't register beyond sounding vaguely familiar, more rustlings and laughter, and then the sound of a zipper.

I really should have said something at that point. Coughed perhaps. But I'd just figured out that I could rhyme 'worse' with 'verse', and how 'memory being worse' could be followed by 'something, something, singing la, la, la to the verse'.

I got it down, over the whispering, and then I caught a phrase.

"Oh, Lotte."

Oh, shit. I'd left it too late.

I didn't look.

It was none of my business. Jake and Lotte were adults. If they wanted to sneak into Jürgen's soundproof computer room for a shag, then fine. I'd sit here until they were done, finishing my song. Their amorous sighs and sensuous gasps and erotic panting would all pass me by.

I mostly succeeded.

Then began the furniture squeaks, somewhat erratic at first, quickly becoming more regular as Jake found a rhythm. I tried not to imagine what was going on, but that was never going to happen. At least I'd got the song down on paper because I really couldn't have concentrated any longer.

And then I realised I needed a pee. Quite soon. Really soon. But Jake was doing very well for someone who'd been bottling up lust for two days — a perfect gentleman, as they say, in waiting for Lotte.

But I had to go. Had to. As quietly as I could, I got out of the chair and stood up. The sounds continued unchanged. I was undetected.

I turned slowly and, keeping my face to the wall, sidled on cat feet around the perimeter of the computer room towards the door. Behind me, Lotte was starting to get louder, and my time was running out.

I touched my hand to the door handle and turned. It squeaked, but Jake and Lotte's extended moans of ultimate ecstasy drowned it out. The door opened, spilling soft light into the room, and I was out.

I didn't mean to look back; I just turned to close the door behind me. I guess Orpheus must have said much the same thing.

The sofa they'd chosen was illuminated by the soft light from the doorway. Jake lay spent, with his face buried between her breasts. Lotte, though, stared past Jake's head right back at me, blinking in the light.

I blushed and bolted to find a toilet, wondering if I'd been recognised but mostly hoping I'd get to the loo in time.

*

I FOUND NEALE in the crypt at the bar, drinking neat orange juice. Maybe it was a diabetes thing.

I thrust my scribbled notes in front of him. "It's a song."

He looked at it disdainfully. "It's a bloody mess. And it's not a song; it's just some lyrics."

"Don't get picky, Neale. I've got a tune in my head too."

"So it's your song?"

"Of course it's my song. I need your help though. You write dots fast."

"Yeah, because fiddle players are musicians. Unlike drummers."

I didn't rise to the bait. Neale knew full well I could read drum notation. Bugger was winding me up.

"Can you get something down for the band in the next few minutes? I'd really like to get a first version out into the set tonight."

"The difficult, we might do at once, eh Kai? But the impossible takes a few minutes longer. What's the rush?"

I told him about the inspiration for the song. The drunken call at the end of the set.

"Ah, you want to impress Matthias, do you?"

"Matthias?"

"Jürgen's boyfriend."

I hadn't recognised him. Blame it on the poor light.

But that was Neale's sparring done. He picked up Jake's acoustic guitar and got me singing my tune. In about five minutes, he'd wrapped some chords around my melody—nothing fancy, but that was the point—it *was* a drinking song.

"It's a good song, Kai, and this audience will probably love it. But your voice is not right for it. Too pure."

Back to that again. Shit. "Well, why don't *you* sing it? If I'm too angelic, I'm sure you can provide rough Irish drunk."

He took a sip at his orange juice, about as ostentatiously as it was possible to sip a non-alcoholic drink.

"In a pinch, I can fake it," he said. "But those are bloody tricky words to fit around your tune. Did you write it on speed?"

"Writing it was another story. I'll tell it you some day. It had a happy ending for me at least. I hope it has a happy ending for the others."

He raised an eyebrow. "Keep your secrets, you coy bugger. I'll need to go learn these words, else the song's not going in. Can I leave it to you to clear it with the band?"

I nodded agreement.

"And, Kai, we need to have a band talk about Jake and Lotte. How the fuck did this happen? What's Bettine going to say? Has she called the police?"

"So what? Lotte's an adult." And never mind that I'd already thought the same.

"Oh, if only real life was as simple as that. Bettine is a *cailleach* — or would be, if she had the fortune to be Irish. She's a woman who could make trouble for us. But never mind. Now's not the time. Go find the band and tell them what you've done."

He frowned, turned, and walked away, shaking his head. Whether about my lyrics or Lotte's flight, I wasn't sure. I don't know what he meant by a *cailleach* — from the context I'd guess a powerful woman or a witch. But he was right about Bettine. Now that he'd said it, I realised my anxiety was nothing to do with Lotte and everything to do with her mother's possible reaction.

I went back upstairs and found Dom. She was chatting in entirely passable German to Annika and Matthias. I hung around on the edge of their circle, waiting for a moment to speak to Dom about my new song.

She turned. "What's up, Kai?"

"A new song — for the next set, if you're up for it…"

"Tell me more — " she began, but then Matthias cut across.

"What sort of song?" There was a glint in his eye.

I glinted right back. "*Ein Trinklied.*"

"Drinking song! High five! High five!"

And why not? We high-fived, and Matthias called out: "Hey, guys! Kai just wrote a drinking song. For meeeee!"

He was tipsy, not stupid drunk, but drunk enough to kiss me—a slobbery, drunken kiss and only vaguely near my lips. But I stiffened, and Matthias instantly sensed he'd transgressed.

"*Es tut mir leid, Kai.*" And then in English, "Forgive me, Kai."

So I smiled and said it didn't matter. Which, after my initial surprise, it didn't. I tucked the feeling into a little-used folder in my brain labelled 'things I've learned about myself'.

*

IN THE END, we played the drinking song as a duet. We'd had precious little time to practice, so we did it first up after the break while it was still fresh. Neale played the guitar and sang, and I sang unison with him. He'd not learned the words but had spent the time copying them in large print onto paper, and we used a music stand.

Matthias worked out the chorus quickly, as did almost everybody by the end. We got calls for "*Zugabe!*" straightaway so everyone could sing the chorus, at least the way I'd written it.

> *Play me another drinking song*
> *Keep it simple so I can sing along*
> *Love songs only cause me pain*
> *So drain your glass, let's sing again*

Two highlights. About three songs in, we did 'Hall of Fallen Angels'.

*There's a place that no one speaks of at the end of Meet-
ing Street
Where the faithless and the loveless and the heartless
lovers greet
It's the place where last-chance losers come to live their
hopeless dreams
Where guilt walks masked as innocence, and nothing's
as it seems*

*The past mistakes we left behind, reopened and laid
bare
It's the Hall of Fallen Angels, and I was welcomed
there*

When it came to the end of the first verse, I was really nervous singing the words, wondering who Dom was going to call to
sing verse two. Perhaps she was playing it safe, or perhaps it was
an impish inspiration, but she called us both. Neale and I did another unison duet while she harmonised "oo" beneath our melody.

Shivers down my spine.

And later, Jürgen's sax spot.

He joined us to massive cheering. Matthias and his friends
were well-lubricated by then, but Jürgen had been taking it easy
with the drink. He was relaxed, and his sax playing flowed. It got
me wondering whether… Well, I'd given soul music a bit of a
wide berth in my musical upbringing, but adding Jürgen's
mournful sax to 'Blue for No Reason' put the song in a new light.
I wondered about finding a sax player back in England. The

thought, *a whole horn section*, also waved briefly, but I shushed it.

Our self-penned 'Cross, Don't Cross' had its second outing, and Jürgen's crowd got the message quickly enough. Dom started to prowl around the crypt, taking the radio mic up first to Matthias and then to Annika to flirt. Whether or not she'd primed them both, they both flirted right back, totally camp and self-mocking, finger-tracing great crosses provocatively back at her.

We took an encore of 'Rolling and Tumbling', which we'd played in the first set, but it could stand a second outing. The final applause was generous but not over the top, and we were happy to be done. Happier still not to have to load the van and head off into the night.

*

THE PARTY LASTED long. I caught up with Jamie, and we toured Jürgen's friends freely. For Jamie's sake, we majored on the English-speaking and the female. There was a moment when I could have reunited with orange fedora guy, and an imp of mischief even suggested saying *Fender Precision* and gluing him to Jamie, who wasn't averse to talking bass guitars.

But I bade the imp begone because Jamie had been pretty good if you discounted his ongoing grumbles about being crushed by gear avalanches in the back of the van. And it wouldn't have been fair to orange fedora guy, either, who I knew better now, and liked. He'd given me his business card, even — in case I was ever in Berlin and wanted to buy that Telecaster. So we shuffled past with our backs to him and encountered a very pretty lass, Alina, and introduced ourselves to her. Fair-haired, blue-eyed, and petite. Very much Jamie's type. She spoke English well and didn't mind us joining her on Jürgen's balcony, where she'd been watching the city lights.

Jamie didn't notice when I left him, and I don't think Alina did either. By some good fortune, Jamie appeared to be her type. For all he's my brother, and I got all the interesting genes, he's nevertheless a decent guy, able to conduct an intelligent conversation. Especially when I gave him a head start.

Left to my own devices, I gravitated back down to the crypt. There, I found Jürgen and Matthias sitting with Dom and Annika. They were part of a larger group, several of whom I recognised from Jürgen's screensaver. They sat on beanbags and sofas, talking about everything under the sun. A couple of girls scooted apart to let me join them, introducing themselves as Klara (on my left) and Mareike (on my right). The beanbag was a bit small, and Klara was a bit precarious, so I put an arm around her shoulder. Just in case. She didn't seem to mind.

Somebody's arm brushed my cheek, and a bottle of beer appeared over my shoulder. I looked up and behind me at Lotte, doing the rounds with Jake close by. I shoved aside my last mental picture of the two of them and smiled my thanks. They smiled back but didn't stay.

At some point, Mareike left, but then Jake and Lotte returned with more beers. Jake sat on the vacated beanbag, his legs spread, with Lotte settling in front of him on the floor, relaxing back against his thighs. Jake leaned forward and rested his arms over her shoulders, hands clasped upon her collarbone.

Klara asked me how I'd learned to play the drums and whether it was difficult. So, I started telling her about how learning to move your hands and feet independently, and she asked me to show her. I shifted around on our beanbag and opened my legs in a broad vee, and she tucked her butt firmly inside my thighs. I told her to rest her toes on my feet and took her hands in mine. Tuning into what the sound system was playing, an old Smokey Robinson love ballad, I found the bass beat with my right foot. Her toes relaxed into the motion. Then I added snare on beats two and four with my left hand holding hers. So far, so good. Klara let me guide her hand and her toes to find the rhythm. I added in the right hand, crosswise, to pick up the ride cymbal, and that was where Klara's synchronisation broke down. She collapsed, laughing, on the floor, and I slipped down beside her.

Someone handed me another beer…

*

I WOKE IN the dark, feeling cold, lying on my side on a beanbag. The main lights were off, though a few LEDs glowed in blue and in red. I could just about make out the space of the crypt and snoring but not much else. The party was over. I needed a pee.

I tried to stand, which was when I realised my legs weren't helping because I ended up rolling off the beanbag and sliding onto the floor.

Fuck. I was too drunk to stand, and I was going to piss myself. How embarrassing was that?

I reached down. I'd got something wrapped around my legs—a duvet or a sleeping bag—and I managed to remove it. Able to stand now, though a little unsteady on my feet, I made my way to the bathroom.

The door opened easily, and I clenched my eyes shut at the bright light streaming out. I knew the toilet must be somewhere in front of me, so I stumbled forward.

And my right hand met warm, bare flesh. I opened one eye.

"Hello, Kai."

I opened the other eye. The light hurt, and my head definitely ached, but I recognised the face. "Hello, Dom. I need a piss."

"You should really knock. I'm bathing."

I opened my eyes wider, ignoring the ache. Dom held a flannel in her hand and was down to bra and panties. "Sorry."

But then I didn't know what to do.

"Do you need help, Kai?"

I nodded. I could do that.

She steered me to the toilet and popped the seat down. I tried to undo my belt because I knew that was important. She brushed my hands away, undid my belt and unzipped, then lowered my trousers and underwear. She coaxed me down onto the seat.

"Look 'way," I said, and she did so.

She was my *best* friend, I thought, as I stared at her navel.

"If you don't mind," Dom said. "I'll finish my washing."

"Go 'head."

There wasn't very much room. I didn't have many choices where to look while she faced the washbasin and stripped to complete her wash and then towelled herself dry. She dressed again in a plain white T-shirt-and-panty combo. It might have been the same T-shirt she'd worn after the shower at the campsite forever ago.

"Let's get you back to your sleeping bag, shall we, Kai?"

"Mmm."

She helped me haul myself up, dress again, and we stepped

out into the darkness.

I remembered a name. "Klara. Wha' happen' to Klara?"

"You were playing drums together. Then you both fell on the floor and started laughing. You spent a while talking about I-don't-know-what and drank two or three more beers. You finally fell asleep, so we put your sleeping bag over you. Klara left about half an hour later when the party broke up. I think she was disappointed you didn't say goodbye."

She helped me into my sleeping bag. It was nice and warm, and I could feel the tired climbing up towards my eyes.

"Night, Dom. Love you, frien'."

"Sleep well, Kai. Sweet dreams."

She bent close and kissed my cheek, but I was already dreaming.

Chapter Sixteen

Monday, October 3, 2016
A Quiet Day in Berlin

DAWN NEVER CAME to a crypt. But someone had turned on some lights when I next woke, considerably more sober and still in my sweaty stage clothes. I got up and looked around.

The body count was way more than just the band. It seemed Jürgen had turned the crypt into a dormitory for any of his friends who'd been too drunk or tired to get home.

But the band was all present. Jake and Lotte lay curled up together, and I felt happy for them, even as my mind turned over options for what we would do about them. I'd assumed she'd left home to become an item with Jake. But on what evidence? That Jake's spirit had gone walkabout since leaving Aachen, chan-nelled via smartphone messages with—obvious now—Lotte?

That Lotte had nursed a crush on Jake from their gaming days, based on his witty conversation and his unfailingly chivalrous and noble spirit? Could I convince myself it was more innocent than that? Perhaps she'd absconded for a day trip to Berlin, a quickie with Jake, and would soon be heading back to Aachen and Bettine. No problem.

Wishful thinking, I told myself, as I looked at the entwined lovers. Lotte's right arm lay across Jake's naked chest, and his left arm covered it, hand upon her shoulder. His eyes opened and met mine. His expression became defensive. We'd acquired a passenger.

Roll with it, Kai. I smiled.

"Morning, Jake. All's well. Catch up with you after I've showered. Okay?"

He relaxed and smiled back. "Okay. Thanks."

A queue had already formed for the shower.

Annika stood by the door and smiled at me. "Good morning. Did you sleep well?"

No hint of mockery there; I took her enquiry at face value and smiled back. "Yes, thank you. I hadn't realised how tired I was."

"Your brother was telling me about your tour. You must be exhausted."

Jamie had abandoned Alina? Or she'd abandoned him? Shame. I reminded myself it was just a party, not a dating holiday. I was seeing potential relationships everywhere.

"Yes. I was thinking of taking a long shower," I answered.

"Don't. Jürgen has something better in mind. Have you ever tried a German sauna?"

"No."

"Then you must come. You must all come. You will feel so much better for it."

She leaned closer and sniffed. Mischief sparkled. "Actually, Kai, do take a shower. But make it a quick one, or we'll be here all day."

The bathroom door opened then, and Lars stepped out. My heart lurched.

The ones that we have left behind, the first loves we now wrong…

"Hi, Kai," he said, grinning. "Good party, huh? You sleep well?"

Annika gave me the briefest of smiles and ducked into the bathroom. Thanks, Annika.

"Yes, thanks. Uh, is there any breakfast around?"

"Sure. Upstairs. I'll see you there."

"Yeah. See you soon, Lars."

Soon? Not 'see you later'?

When I got back to the crypt, the band had all surfaced and gathered on a couple of sofas. Lotte had tucked herself under Jake's arm. When I mentioned Jürgen's idea of the sauna, she perked up.

"*Prima!* Yes. That is a wonderful idea. I will go. Jake, you must come."

Well, that was one easy convert. Jake nodded vigorously.

Jamie thought a moment and said, "Yeah. It's something to do, and we've got some free days. I'll give it a go. Dom?"

Dom gave him a most curious look. Then she glanced at me and seemed to come to a decision.

"Yes, Jamie. I will go. It will be good for us, I think."

Neale was sceptical. "Is this another bloody gherkin deal?"

Lotte looked puzzled, of course, not getting the reference.

"Gherkins," I offered. "He doesn't like pickles."

She laughed. A wicked laugh, if I was any judge, and there was a twinkle in her eye as she said, "No. There will be no gherkins, Neale."

"You should tell them, Lotte," said Dom. "It is only fair."

Lotte pouted in disappointment but then nodded, agreeing. "Yes. You are right. German saunas are the best in the world, naturally. To be the best for your whole body, it is forbidden to wear clothes in the sauna."

Jake looked crestfallen. "Oh. I thought we would be together."

"But of course," she answered. "We will all be together. In a German sauna, everyone is together."

"But..."

"Yes. Together. And naked."

*

IN GERMANY, NAKEDNESS was normal. The rest of the world was abnormal. So said the German nation. And—courtesy of Gizem's organisational skills—here we were, trapped in a small convoy of taxis with a bunch of German health nuts, determined to prove their point.

Trapped? Not true. Or not entirely true. After Lotte's revelation we'd argued ourselves out of the idea. Then we'd argued ourselves back in, several times back and forth, finishing with a final I-will-if-you-will round of bravado.

"I don't understand you English," Lotte complained. "It's

not a pissing contest. Just do it, and don't get upset about it."

"It's like their insane drinking laws," Dom agreed. "Everything is forbidden in their country, so when they find freedom, they can't handle it."

*

JÜRGEN'S PREFERRED SPA was a few kilometres out of town on the northern bank of the Spree. It was part of a private hotel, with grounds where one could — in summer — take a walk down to the Spree, still *au naturel* if desired. A very pleasant idea, but summer was long past. The warmth of the sauna was a far more attractive proposition than a skinny-dip in the Spree. If that was even safe.

We all trooped in and paid our day membership — Jürgen was a full member. He gave us a quick reminder of sauna etiquette. It boiled down to: take off your bathrobe before entering the sauna, don't stare, don't sit directly on the seats (use a towel to sit on). Outside, you could slip your bathrobe back on if you wanted. Or not.

It was like standing on the top diving board. You could jump in and splash or dive with as much grace as could be mustered. But there was no way back.

I fixed my gaze on a point on the wall, a lot of pink (and brown, and yellow) blobs in my peripheral vision moved about, taking off or putting on clothes. They might be old or young, saggy or taut. And, of course, male or female. That was of no concern. They were just blobs, accompanied by a backdrop of chatter, as one would find in a café, minus the clink of cups and plates. I'd hung my clothes neatly in a locker and now stood at the sauna entrance in a soft, white terrycloth robe.

I undid the belt, let the robe fall open. Tugging the left sleeve, I let the robe slide down off my shoulder and arm, then the right arm, and caught the robe before it landed on the floor, grasping a last moment of modesty.

This is normal. It's the rest of the world that is freaky. Act like you're German. Stop covering yourself and feel the breeze. Walk over to the wall, hang the robe on a hook. Turn.

I turned. A well-tanned blob came into view. Flick. Focus. Male. Matthias.

"Hi, Kai. It's fine; you look fine."

"I didn't think you were supposed to look."

"You are not supposed to stare. That's all. You look, then you let your gaze move on. May I demonstrate?"

He swiftly glanced down the length of my body, neither furtive nor lingering but courteous and appreciative, finishing with a gentle smile. It was like the Look, but also not. There was no feeling of being X-rayed, nor of being judged on that X-ray. It was more like being a work of art. 'Kai. Self-portrait. Oil on canvas, 2016'.

"Like I said," Matthias continued. "If you look, do it like that, and no one will be offended."

I took him at his word. "Since you are so kind as to offer. I accept."

So, I took in his brown eyes, moved past stubbly chin, to chest…and on. I saw…exactly what I expected to see. He was as trim as I'd expect Jürgen's partner to be.

"Are you going in? Or are you just going to stare at my toes."

"Huh?" I was miles away and had been staring, but Matthias didn't seem to mind.

"You've come all this way, Kai. Pick up your towel and step inside."

When I entered the sauna, the heat was way more than I'd expected. I was actually more concerned about breathing than about the glistening bodies arrayed on the tiered benches.

It passed, and Matthias left me at one of the benches where our party had gathered. I made a mental note to thank him later. He'd done much to put me at ease about being naked.

Annika looked up as I approached and beckoned me to sit next to her. "How are you feeling?"

"Hot."

"Of course. But this is your first visit to a sauna, isn't it? You need to stay hydrated."

"I'm okay. Getting used to the heat. Uh, Annika, is it okay to say to someone that they look good?"

"It depends on how you say it. Did someone say it to you, or are you asking about saying it to someone else?"

"Uh, Matthias…"

"Matthias would have meant it as a sincere compliment. He would not have been making a pass at you. Matthias is not that sort of person. He and Jürgen have been together for several years, and they are very happy together. Besides, to make a pass here is not good manners."

"So it was meant as a compliment?"

"Were you hoping otherwise?" — but there was mirth in her voice — "No, I am sure it was a sincere compliment. And he has a good eye. You do look good."

"As do you. Diet and exercise."

"And good genes from my parents."

And then a voice came from behind me. "Hallo, Kai."

I turned and found myself staring straight at elfin breasts. When looked up, it took a couple of moments to recognise the face.

"Alina?"

She grinned. "You remember me! Yes, you are right."

I did indeed remember. But I asked what she doing here. Did none of them work? Had they all called in sick?

She laughed. "Today is German Unity Day."

Ah, a public holiday, so no one was working.

"Where is your brother? Jamie?"

Direct. *No, Stop seeing relationships everywhere, Kai. She's a nice girl, making polite conversation.*

"He'll come soon if he's not already here."

I hoped it was true, that Jamie hadn't bottled out in the changing room, and when he did arrive, he'd be downright pleased to see her. I wondered what to say to her in the meantime. I couldn't keep telling everyone "You look good" (naked implied). It was probably the sort of thing only foreigners said. Or what Germans said to foreigners to put them at ease.

But Alina got in first, asking me what I did when I wasn't playing drums, and I told her I didn't have a proper job, having not long finished college. Three years wasn't long. But I admitted to doing voice work, which she said *was* a proper job. And she was something in IT — a project manager, I thought she said — having done a business degree in the Netherlands under the Erasmus exchange programme. She dropped the name Joni, and I assumed that was her partner until she mentioned his recent fourth birthday party, and I twigged Joni was her son. I suggested she didn't look old enough. She laughed again and admitted to being twenty-seven.

I spotted Jamie heading towards us and waved. He waved back, and I was relieved to see him smile when Alina turned to him and waved also.

"Is there room for a little one?" Jamie asked, even though there obviously wasn't.

"It's okay. You can have my seat," I said. "I just spotted Neale coming in, and he's looking absolutely terrified. I'll go over and reassure him."

"You? You think you're the right person to put him at ease?"

What was the etiquette of punching your tactless brother in the face while naked? I wondered. I shrugged it off, deciding Jamie was probably nervous himself.

Before I reached Neale, Jürgen intercepted him and steered him into a little group with Matthias, Lars, Mareike, and Gizem, plus others. That left me high and dry, so I found another free bench and sat down on my towel.

I wondered about Gizem. I'd seen her around at the party, watched how she'd roamed, one moment on the move, another attaching herself to this group or that. Checking that everyone was having a good time, excusing herself, and moving on again. We'd spoken, briefly, and I'd seen that same knack, the ability to draw people out, that I'd seen with Dom. Now, though, she looked more relaxed. I would have expected her to stay clothed, if I'd thought about it, while on duty. But on reflection, I was pretty sure she could command any situation, clothed or naked. She turned, revealing a large dragon tattoo covering much of her back. I wondered what the etiquette was about admiring somebody's tattoo.

And Lars. I wasn't sure if he'd seen me. It would have been nice to have caught his eye. Regardless, I'd have gone over, if only to look at Gizem's tattoo, but there wasn't room. Somebody — it might have been Klara — had mentioned that Lars was gay. Which I'd pretty much worked out anyway. From one or two things he'd alluded to, I'd guessed he wasn't in a relationship. I couldn't remember if Klara had confirmed that also.

But Klara wasn't here, which was a shame. She was fun. *Perhaps a little less beer, Kai, next time, and you might remember where you'd got to.*

With no one to talk to, there was little to do save look around, again, not staring but taking it in and moving on. After a while, the abnormal became normal; I suppose it always must do sooner or later. I tuned out the sexual nature of the bodies in the sauna, which was strange but also exhilarating. The penises and the breasts stopped being the focus of attention, no longer things that divided us into male and female, no longer separate, no longer add-ons to sexless shop dummies. They blended, instead, into the unity of each body, neither more nor less than eyes, or hair, or belly.

I experienced a moment of transcendence. A phrase came to me. *I am fearfully and wonderfully made.* Yes, I was. And yes, so were each of the people here today. I saw the beauty of the human form, clothing us in uniqueness, and I loved it in every one of its manifestations.

I found I could look, really look, at each person and not stare, like seeing the total composition for the first time.

I didn't know how long I sat there in stillness, drinking in the wholeness of everyone. I became aware that someone had sat down next to me and turned to face them.

Dom, looking curiously at me, waiting for me to speak.

"They're beautiful," I said to her. "Every one of them. The young ones and the old ones. The ones whose heads are blotchy and balding. The white and the black and the brown and the yellow and the coffee. You're beautiful, too, Dom, but I couldn't say right now that you're any more beautiful than that pensioner two benches to our right."

"You are right. They are all beautiful, but how often do we stop and notice them, the ones who do not meet society's ideal?"

"I never have, until now."

But her interruption had broken the spell. My perspective changed, and I was aware once again of *Dom*. The heat of desire piled on the heat of the sauna. I felt my cheeks redden. Redden more.

Panic. Surely, she could *see* my embarrassment. She would *know*. What I felt. What I was thinking. I stood, far too abruptly, now feeling very odd. Dizzy.

"Excuse me," I croaked. "It's too hot."

"Let me help you. I think you are dehydrating. Have you drunk enough water this morning?"

I didn't know, shook my head, and let her guide me to the cool outside. She made me sit, then fetched me a glass of water.

"Drink this."

I downed it, spilling some on myself. Clumsy. More embarrassment.

Dom was watching me closely; she fetched another glass of water and drank one herself. "Do you feel better now?'

"Yes. A little."

"It would also help to take a shower. A warm shower, not cold, not hot. Can you do that on your own without fainting?"

I nodded.

"Then I will go back and remind the guys it is time to come out."

I stood in the shower, letting it wash away my sweat. Over the following minutes, the rest of the band joined me, along with Jürgen and his friends. He led us to a poolside café, where we sat in bathrobes or on towels, drinking herbal teas, fruit juices, and mineral water. Everyone talked in whispers, if at all, as though after getting rid of all the toxins—and did I actually believe that?—we were letting stillness soak in to replace them.

We lingered. Matthias announced he was going to get a massage, and three or four others followed suit, including Lars and the other girl from the beanbag, Mareike. Others chose to go for a walk outside or take a swim in the pool. Annika shed her robe and swam twenty lengths or so in a well-practised crawl. I followed a few lengths later but not with any hope of emulating her; she was powerful and fast and graceful as a dolphin.

I spent a pleasant hour recapturing some of the transcendence I'd felt in the sauna and even Dom's company. I was disappointed when Jürgen announced that it was time to go. How odd it seemed to pull a T-shirt over my head, how strangely uncomfortable to feel it so tight against my skin. And how weird that, reclothed and wrapped in mystery, my new friends looked more alluring, not less.

*

GIZEM SMILED ME an *It'll be fine*, patted my hand, and took the last seat in the BMW. It pulled away, crunching over the gravel drive towards the exit. There was one taxi remaining, a Mercedes, which rolled into position next to me. Us.

"Hello, Kai."

The meeting with Lars that I'd been avoiding had arrived. And I didn't have a shred of a plan for what to do or what to say.

"Hello. Broken any walls recently?"

"I could ask you the same question. But first, thank you for not running away. It would have been easy to swap places in the taxi queue, but …"

"I didn't dare. Gizem cornered me. She told me I'd wonder for the rest of my life what might have happened if I didn't speak to you today. Now, she said."

"So here we are, the two of us, sharing the last taxi to Berlin. We have half an hour to discover if we want more than that half an hour."

It was a good question.

"How," I began, "do we pick up from last night? When we were interrupted, I felt that I'd just been hit by a thunderbolt. But then a load of other stuff happened, and our paths didn't seem to cross, after that. I thought maybe I'd just imagined it. The thunderbolt."

"I came looking for you between the sets. But you'd vanished. I thought you were hiding from me."

"I was writing a song."

"Ah, yes. The famous 'Drinking Song'. What was the line? *'I'm not drinking to get drunk; I'm only drinking to forget'*. Which turned out eerily prophetic."

"Coincidence."

And then a rare impulse of openness hit me.

"Maybe more than that. There's…history."

"Don't tell me. Not until you're ready."

"I won't. I mean, I will. Tell you when I'm ready."

The taxi slowed, halted. The cars in front weren't moving.

"What's the hold up?" I began, but at the same moment, Lars spoke:

"I felt it, too, Kai. The thing you called the thunderbolt. It hasn't faded."

I tried to imagine how that might have felt. "How did you sleep?"

"Badly. And then at the sauna, Gizem caught me staring at you. I was hoping you into coming over, but then Neale arrived, and the opportunity had gone."

"Oh. I did look over at you too. Well, not at you. Fuck it! Yes, I did look at you. And later on. Just the view of your backside, before you put your dressing gown on to go for your massage."

The taxi jerked forward—whatever the holdup had been, it had cleared.

"What now?" Lars asked.

"I was thinking the same thing. What now? In practical terms, you could at least join me for lunch. I'll be meeting the band for lunch, but I don't know where yet."

"Well, I can suggest a couple of cafés near the Alexanderplatz. Nothing expensive—"

"That's good. We're on a tight budget. Give me the details, and I'll message the guys…"

*

WE ARRANGED TO meet for a light lunch at an American-style sandwich bar as Lars had suggested. Quite a few of Jürgen's friends rolled-up, too, and we ended up split across several tables, some in the open, some inside. I drifted gently along, my spirit still sitting beside the pool at the spa, only my body sharing a table with Lotte and Jake. And Lars. Occasionally, they asked me to translate a word that Lotte did not know, which served to check that I was still alive.

We still needed to have that conference about what to do with Lotte, but that would wait till we had all the band together.

Which was when I realised…

"Shit! Where's Jamie?"

Lotte came to my rescue. "Did he not say anything? Forgive me, I did not realise. Jake and I shared a taxi with Jamie and Alina. We stopped the taxi at *Jannowitzbrücke* to let them catch the U-Bahn."

"Them?"

"Alina and Jamie. Jamie was going with Alina. To her apartment."

"Why? No, forget I asked."

Did Jamie know Alina had a kid?

I immediately tried calling, but Jamie wasn't answering his phone.

Jürgen sat at the next table, but he declined to give me Alina's Handy number. He was polite but firm about not divulging her mobile information.

"I'm sorry," he said. "If Jamie isn't answering, it's because he's busy and doesn't want to be disturbed. So don't ask me to go behind his back and give you Alina's number. They are both adults, and you should grant them privacy."

I wasn't happy, and I was sure my face showed it. But he was right even though it did leave us in an awkward position, not knowing when Jamie would rejoin us. I wasn't sure Jamie had enough German to find his way back to us, and I told Jürgen as much.

"It is far worse than that. Alina is a sorceress and the daughter of a sorceress back seven generations. Her kind bewilders men, then enslaves them. Doubtless, she will imprison him in her enchanted castle deep in the *Grunewald* for one hundred years, and you will never see him again."

He was winding me up. I took a deep breath and changed the subject.

"Okay. I get the point. I'll stop worrying. So, two things. We were planning to move on to a campsite tonight, but without Jamie, we can't leave as he doesn't know the address. Can we crash in your crypt again, please?"

"Yes, naturally. And the other thing?"

"We'd like to look around the Berlin sights today. What do you suggest?"

"I suggest you ask Lars."

*

AN AFTERNOON SPENT wandering around the Brandenburger Tor and the Reichstag — the Brandenburg Gate and the parliament building — was a very pleasant, if chilly, way to get to know Berlin. Then, over to the *Museuminsel* for an introductory visit to the

Altes Museum. Lars was a good guide.

About four o'clock, I got a text.

JAMIE: *With Alina and Joni. Where is campsite? Will meet you there 2nite.*

KAI: *Campsite cancelled. Staying chez Jurgen 2nite. Have fun.*

I couldn't be bothered to find Jürgen's *umlaut* on my phone. I didn't think Jamie would miss it.

When we got hungry, we undid all the good work of the spa and found a pizza restaurant. Over pepperoni, beef, and onions, I finally broached the question.

"Jake, Lotte. I think we need some frank discussion about your plans."

Jake's expression hardened, preparing for war. Lotte's right hand gripped Jake's arm as though she were hanging from a cliff edge.

"I'm with Jake," she muttered.

"I guessed," I answered, capitulating without a shot being fired. "It's all very well deciding to stay with Jake. The question is how we make it work. I mean, we're driving down to München in a day or so. There's bugger-all room in the van as it is. Do we gaffa tape you to the roof?"

Jake delivered an emphatic "No!"

I rolled my eyes.

"Oh. You were joking."

"Yes, Jake. You know it's against band policy —"

"Stop it," Dom interrupted. "Your humour isn't helping."

"It's helping *me*," I retorted. "I can't see how we're going to make this work, and I'm trying very hard not to get angry."

Lotte placed her hand on mine. "Then let me speak. Jake and I have talked this over."

She glanced at Jake for reassurance. He nodded.

"I spend all my time helping my mother run the bar. I don't go out much. So, I have saved money of my own. I can take the bus or the train."

"On your own?"

"If I must. But I hope Jake will come with me."

"Yes, I'll come. Of course."

"It'll be expensive," I said.

Lotte laughed. "No. This is Germany. Trains and buses are cheaper than you think."

"Fair enough. Okay, so we're going back to England at the end of the tour. Have you thought of what happens then?"

"I go with Jake."

"You have your passport with you?"

"Yes. Jake and I planned this."

Okay. So that just left the elephant in the room.

"And your mother?"

"She treated me like shit! She can kiss my ass!"

Oh. Not a good state of play between mother and daughter, then.

"Ahhh…do you think she will try to stop you?"

"How? I am an adult."

"I don't know. Could she call the police? Claim you were kidnapped, that sort of thing?"

"You did not kidnap me. I waited two days before I left. Lots of people saw me working at the bar long after you left. So no, she cannot stop me. Even, I resigned my job as bartender in writing. Very formal. No love-and-kisses."

There didn't seem to be anything else to say, after that, there wasn't anything Bettine could do to stop her daughter. Legally. But Bettine didn't seem the kind of woman who'd forgive and forget.

There was one other thing on Lotte's mind.

"Kai, I hope we can be friends."

She spoke hesitantly, with a querying note to her voice. But I got it. She wanted to be friends, not only with me but with all of us. No. It was more than that. She was asking to be admitted into the band.

"Yeah, we're friends. Ever since we fetched mineral water together, I dare to say."

"Thank you." She smiled at last. "Your advice was good."

Jake watched us, puzzled, suspicion in his eyes, gaze flicking between us as we spoke.

"It's okay, Jake. Lotte and I are clearing the air between us. Promising not to scratch each other's eyes out, that sort of thing. Same goes for the whole band."

"So, Lotte can stay?"

"Of course, you big lump. She's *in*."

"Uh…"

"Yeah, Jake. Lotte can stay. She's one of us. Not that I'm the boss here. I'm just the gopher who has to make it all work. And I'm *not* bitter about it."

But I was seriously skewed. Jake plus Lotte. And whatever was going on with Jamie plus Alina (not forgetting Joni). Leaving Dom, Neale, and me. Having made a start on Jake and Jamie, did the fates have some plan in store for that odd little trio?

I leaned back, distancing myself from thoughts of an unknowable future, and turned to my left, where our guide sat, silent, taking everything in.

*

"WE CAN JUST catch their first set, if we leave now."

"Yeah, Lars. I'm game. Anyone else?" I asked.

"Thank you, but no," Dom replied. "I am a bit tired. I will return to Jürgen's place."

"Okay. Get some rest, then. We'll see you back at the basement."

Lotte had made up her mind. "We'll come, yes, Jake?"

"Neale?"

"I'm always up for the craic."

No surprise.

*

RICKY AND THE Sunsets played a mix of sixties and seventies soul in English, plus their own material in English and German.

The band wore matching shiny mid-blue suits and ties, but each of them had a little trademark extra. A bow tie instead of a straight tie. A beret for the sax player — oh, and a caricature French onion-seller stripy shirt. The trumpet player was blinged to the max with gold-plated chains and medallions. The bassist wore a double-breasted jacket, and the rest of them, variations on hats, cravats, and spats.

Ricky wore the same cloth but cut as an evening jacket, with tails and sequinned lapels. Understated it was not.

They were already playing Sam Cooke's 'A Change is Gonna Come' when we arrived, but the girl on the door assured us they'd only just started and were down to play two one-hour sets.

Ricky's voice was on a par with Clay's and very comfortable across a full tenor range. Plus, he had two decent backing vocalists, a baritone and bass doubling on keyboards and guitar respectively.

The first few songs were more sixties soul covers, from well-known Stax/Atlantic/Motown artists. As Ricky linked from one track to the next, he proved he was also a showman, inserting little snippets of soul history, gilded with outrageous lies about being buddies with every artist or mentoring them through their careers, despite many of these icons having died long before he was born.

"You would not believe it," Lars told us in the silence between numbers, "but Ricky teaches woodwork in a local school."

"Well, well," boomed Ricky from the stage in an entirely passable Southern drawl. "It sounds like we have some fellow Americans in the audience."

"I'm Irish," yelled Neale. "And these guys are my band. They're English, but you can't blame them for that. We've come to size up the competition."

"Then you've come a long way, friend," Ricky answered, unfazed. "Step up to the microphone, sir, and let us talk as one superstar to another."

Neale swaggered onto the stage, where he bowed theatrically to Ricky and then to Ricky's audience.

"Your name, sir?"

"Neale. And I'm from Dublin."

"And your band?"

"John Doe's Blues."

"Good name, Neale. Been together long?"

"It seems like forever but perhaps that's just this tour. But we're almost done. Gigs in Munich on Thursday, then Regensburg, and back to Berlin on Saturday. Where are we playing on Saturday, Kai?"

Oh shit! What was the name?

"Club—club something or other," I called back. Then it came to me. "Club Mojo."

Just in time. Ricky was done with Neale.

"Well, folks, that's wonderful. Neale and his band, John Doe's Blues, at the Club Mojo. Fantastic venue, played there myself back in nineteen sixty three. Private gig for the late, great John F. Kennedy after his famous speech. Give them a big hand everybody, and get along there if you can."

Then it was horns *ba-dap-daa, ba-dap-dap* into 'Hold on, I'm Comin', and Neale sat down next to me.

"Well, you can stick that on your social media, Kai."

"I'm ahead of you. I'm following them already, and I've got a couple of tweets out. Got a photo of you. Looks like you're sharing a mic and singing."

"Let's have a look—nah! You've not caught my best side."

"Which side would that be?" I asked innocently.

He held up a warning finger. "None of your damned English lip, y'hear."

With the audience now well warmed up, Ricky took the Sunsets into fresh territory with a song I couldn't place called 'Do You

Want Crying?'. The slow pace and beautiful horns underpinned a completely over-the-top vocal that somehow managed to stay just outside comedy.

I leaned over to Lars. "I've heard this before, but I can't place it."

He grinned. "Imagine it speeded up without the horns. No?"

I gave up.

"Katrina and the Waves mean anything to you?"

Right. "Kick me, Lars. I should have known that. They were big in Germany?"

He nodded. "So-so, I think. I remember when they won Eurovision. I was quite young though."

Lotte arrived at our table. "Come," she began, "You have to help me. Jake doesn't want to dance. He says it's embarrassing for him."

Jake embarrassed? What about *me*?

"We must help Lotte," Lars said.

He was already on his feet, and Lotte had dragged Neale up. We weren't the only ones dancing, by any means, and no one was paying us any great attention. So, I danced. Half-heartedly, but I danced.

Lotte gave it her all, in her element—lively, graceful, balanced, poised. Jake did his best, but without a guitar around his neck, he was rooted to the spot. Gradually, he relaxed and let Lotte guide him. I had my own worries because neither Lars nor Neale were remotely inhibited about dancing, and I was swept up into a little trio.

There was safety behind a drum kit. You were where you were, and no one could budge you from that. But on the other hand, no one got to be a good drummer without the whole body being a part of what was going on. I'd learned that playing was all about movement and balance, letting the rhythms flow through arms and legs, hands and head, everywhere, using the body's natural momentum to do the work.

Dancing was like that too.

How had I not realised that until this moment?

I wasn't sure what Lars or Neale made of what I was doing. They had their own styles. I'd seen Neale 'dance' at the Club Lorelei, of course, but that had been drunken prancing. Now he was using his heritage 'properly', if that wasn't too analytical. Or condescending.

And Lars? Lars was a jiver, if that was the right word. He spotted some of Lotte's moves and coaxed her away from Jake for a minute, and they showed us some steps. Then he turned and came for me.

Put like that, it sounded scary, and that was how I felt. I was still finding my feet on my own, and now, Lars was going to get me jiving?

But Lotte had made it look easy enough. So why not? Lotte had returned to Jake, and Neale was in a world of his own.

So, I caught the hand that Lars was offering.

Chapter Seventeen

Tuesday, October 4, 2016
Still in Berlin

BACK IN THE crypt, and it was odd. The gear was packed and waiting to be loaded into the van, but it would be tomorrow before we did that. A guitar — Jake's acoustic — propped on one of the sofas served as sole reminder that we *were* a band. I'd picked it up at one point, strummed a few chords. But the muse wasn't with me, nor with anyone else, and the guitar went back on the sofa.

Jürgen had stopped by to see us but hadn't stayed. Perhaps he'd been checking that we *were* getting ready to leave. Our welcome was wearing thin, and who could blame him?

Jake and Lotte took themselves off to a secluded corner and began to fuss with cushions and beanbags and sleeping bags. The rest of us took the hint and found our own private spaces to settle down.

The night was long and, as far as I recalled in the morning, dreamless. Nobody stirred, nobody woke me. No midnight meetings disturbed my slumbers.

The next morning, it was raining. I sat in Jürgen's breakfast room, picking at croissants and cold meats, drinking strong coffee. Matthias appeared and sat next to me.

"Hi, Kai," he began. "Do you know what you're doing today?"

"Waiting for Jamie. Then we're off. Jürgen has been very kind to let us stay, but we mustn't impose ourselves any longer."

"Are you planning to stay in Berlin another day?"

"Possibly. We've got to get down to München tomorrow, but there's space at the *Campingplätz* tonight, if we want it. I don't have any better ideas."

"Okay. Then I have a message for you. Do you remember Lars?"

"Of course. The Danish guy. He's very earnest." I didn't mention the dancing.

Matthias smiled at my description. "Yes. That is Lars. He asked me to invite you over to the Stasi Museum this afternoon. He offered to show you round."

"Me?"

"All of you."

"I'll ask the guys."

"You should go. It will help you understand the stains in German history. But do something fun beforehand, as the Stasi Museum can be a bit heavy. Do some shopping, perhaps."

"I…don't have a lot of money."

That fazed Matthias. "Then try Checkpoint Charlie or the new Reichstag building."

"I'll think about it."

"So, what shall I tell Lars, Kai? He's waiting for your answer. Actually, here's his number. You can tell him yourself."

I wondered whether to mention that I didn't need his phone number, as we were friends on Twitter. But then, why hadn't he just DM'd me? Neale piped up while I was still thinking. I hadn't heard him enter the breakfast room.

"Tell him we'll go," Neale said. "I'd like to see some of them places. The Irish know something about repression, after all."

We had to wait for Jamie before we could do anything. But he showed up a little after nine o'clock as we were loading up the van. Alone.

I was all set to give him a blast for fucking us about, but he had a strange air about him. He appeared from nowhere and began loading the van with us as though he'd popped off to the loo for a moment, and here he was back again.

"Y' okay, Jamie?"

"Yeah. Thank you."

His voice was light, ethereal. He wasn't all there, by my reckoning, clearly having left his soul in a castle deep in the *Grunewald*.

"Anything else? Anything you'd like to mention?"

"No. I'm thinking things over."

"Anything I can help with?"

"No. Look, I'm fine, Kai. Just…"

"Just what?"

"Move on. Just move along. There's nothing to see."

*

SO WE VISITED the Tiergarten for a pleasant autumn stroll that—fortunately—demanded nothing of me, for my mind was elsewhere.

I called Lars.

I told him we were famished, and would he suggest somewhere to meet for lunch because I would really, really welcome his company.

Lars's company? The Danish guy I'd called earnest? An administrator at the Stasi Museum? Earnest was okay. And I couldn't deny that he was—as the French put it—*très sympa*, which is a lot better than *okay*.

The jury was still out on the jiving, mostly because my limbs were a bit tender. Apparently, being a drummer does not give one a free pass on the aches and pains of too much dancing.

Lars was already at the chosen café when we arrived and stood to greet us. Yes, he was rather formal. Yes, he did shake hands with us, one by one—though Dominique did hug him, too, and he was fine with that.

But he relaxed, and over that beer, we picked up where we'd left off. At least, one of the places we'd left off. That morning, alongside all the other stuff happening in my head, I'd been reflecting on my meetings with Lars. Each one had a strange, episodic quality, as though it had its own purpose. Maybe they just seemed to be cut off without warning. Last night, dancing to Ricky and the Sunsets—when the set ended, we'd checked the time and worried about getting back too late to chez Jürgen. With Lars having to get up early for work, there'd not been a proper goodbye.

I picked a different tangent and asked him about his family.

"My father was Danish, of course, but my mother, who was German, brought me back to Berlin when he died. I was fifteen."

"He died? How… No, none of my business. I'm sorry."

"It's okay. It was messy. They were divorcing at the time, and he had a heart attack. Out of the blue. He was forty-two. So young…"

"So, you've been here how long?"

"Eleven years."

I did the sums. Lars was twenty-six?

"I'm twenty-seven next month. You had a calculating expression on your face. We didn't just leave. There was the estate to settle under the laws of Denmark and Germany. My mother took his death very hard."

"Even though they were divorcing?"

"Yes. At some point, they had forgotten that they loved each other. But when he died, my mother remembered very well."

*

FROM THE CAFÉ, we went to the Stasi Museum. 'We' was now just Lars and me. Dom decided to visit the art museum, and Neale, Jamie, Jake, and Lotte all tagged along. We agreed to meet later back at the café.

So, the Stasi Museum. Neighbour spying on neighbour. Children turned against their parents, informing on them. Where else had I seen that? Oh, yes. Orwell's *1984*. But it had really happened in East Germany. On a massive scale. Plus, all the other mechanisms of spying on the West and the Berlin Wall and all its tragedy, and we had a microcosm of a whole country divided.

Lars was incredibly knowledgeable. He was a bit of a facts nut—I already said he was earnest—but he also told some breathtakingly human stories. Courage and cowardice, success and failure. He'd gleaned them from the archives, I suppose, but he had the knack of telling them from the heart.

This museum had its artefacts, its exhibits—machines for spying on a whole population on an industrial scale. It would be so much easier, today, of course. But they didn't have computers then. Instead, they had huge card indices and files and dossiers.

"It's because of the stories, Kai."

I'd just asked Lars what the attraction was, working here. Well, no. What I'd actually asked him was why he worked here. With a bit too much emphasis on the 'here'. But he'd chosen to ignore my tactlessness and answered the question I should have asked.

"Somebody has to keep those stories alive. Who said 'those who cannot remember the past are condemned to repeat it'?"

"The internet. Or at least, the internet knows."

He looked miffed. I was babbling, suffering foot-in-mouth disease every time I spoke. Why was I doing that to poor Lars? He didn't deserve my condescension or my irrelevant flippancy.

"I'm sorry," I said. "I'm not myself today. A short night's sleep, and my mouth is running wild. I can do better. I promise."

Lars was gracious. "Of course. I was saying that I try to keep alive the remembrance of what happened here in my mother's country."

A moment of brilliant intuition. At least, that was my opinion. "Your mother was *East* German? And she married a Dane?

How did that happen?"

And then I did a bit more arithmetic. "Wait…you were born the year the wall fell, yes?"

He chuckled. "The day. The *day* the wall fell, I was born."

That explained a lot. But…

"So your mother married a Dane before the wall fell. Ergo, she escaped?"

"Yes. On a Danish ship."

"And your father was…"

"One of the sailors who smuggled her on board."

"That's…beautiful."

"I think so. I hope so."

"Surely…"

"Then why did they start their divorce?" he said, finishing my thought. "My mother doesn't talk about the subject. Perhaps there was never love, only gratitude, sex, and the pressure to bring up a child in security.

"Excuse me. I'm only guessing. I should not have mentioned that. It was a private matter between the two of them."

We moved on to other exhibits. I didn't recall them though, my mind full of pictures of a terrified young woman hiding in a cargo hold while East German guards searched the ship with sniffer dogs.

I felt a gentle touch on my arm.

"Are you all right?" Lars asked. "I don't think you've heard a word I've been saying these last minutes."

"I'm sorry," I said, apologizing again. "I was thinking. Wondering about your mother and what it must have been like for her, escaping."

"She sometimes spoke of it. Down in the bilges of the boat, hiding in the darkness, half-submerged in foul seawater where the stink of piss and oil and diesel masked her from the dogs. It was not good air down there, and she came close to dying. Anywhere else, though, and the dogs would have found her."

His voice was low but intense. I wondered if I should remove his hand from my arm.

"She had to duck under the water when the guards—soldiers—searched the bilges. The dogs wouldn't enter, but the guards stomped around, shining their torches everywhere. The engines were throbbing, so she could barely hear the boots clattering on the walkways. There was so much oil and diesel about that she didn't dare open her eyes. Her lungs were on fire, and her head was swimming with fumes and consumed with pain until she felt she would die if she didn't take a breath."

"What happened?" I whispered, captured by his narrative. I'd lain my hand on top of his and pressed it tight against my arm.

"She came up for air. She was about half a metre from a guard, right behind him. At the same moment she drew breath, the guard vomited into the bilge water, dropping his torch as he did so. His fellows had to guide him out. But my mother had ducked back under the water, and they never saw her. When she came back up again, the soldiers had gone."

"And then?"

"The guards had secured the hatch from the outside, and she couldn't get out. So she sat shivering, covered in oil and vomit, with a splitting headache from the fumes, sure she was going to die. But about ten minutes later, the engines picked up speed, and the ship began to move. About five minutes after that, my father came down, released the hatch, and carried her out."

"And they both lived happily ever after…"

Damn my mouth! Speaking the first stupid thought that came into my head. Lars jerked his hand out from under mine, and we looked at each other for a long moment. Of course I didn't know what was going through his head right then, but I missed the warmth of his hand and the…companionship…we'd felt.

"Sorry," we said together. But the moment had passed, and we didn't rejoin hands.

*

I WAS VERY quiet on the U-Bahn. The bleakness of the Stasi Museum had stuck with me, despite Lars's wonderful stories. I had a lot to digest—experiences and emotions.

We'd met up at the café, more or less at the agreed time. Everyone else was pretty buoyant, so I let them bubble together. Meanwhile I was processing my…interactions…with Lars. In particular, the moments before we parted.

"Thank you for spending your afternoon with me," he'd said. "It was special. As were all the times we've spent together these last few days. You're a unique person…"

I imagined I looked at him with either a sad or a shocked expression. I know I answered without a shred of tact.

"Please don't call me that. I'm not unique, I'm not special, and I don't want you to think of me in that way."

Because I knew exactly what he was saying, and I was afraid of it. His hand on my arm…

I had enjoyed the sensation. Under his touch, I'd let my mind roll back to the sauna and a vivid memory of Lars. A Greek god would be the obvious metaphor. Perhaps an overused metaphor and overflattering to Lars, who had a touch of chubbiness around the waist; nevertheless, in my opinion, his backside deserved to be captured in marble.

Lars had answered with more self-control. "I'm sorry. I hope I've not offended you. I thought the attraction was mutual. You seemed to be enjoying our time together at least."

"You're mistaken, Lars — oh, fuck it, no! That's not it. I mean, yes, I really enjoyed our time together. Chatting with you in Jürgen's kitchen. I love the way your mind works. Your stories this afternoon. You tell them with such passion. And your jiving… confident, graceful. I wish I could have done your dancing credit…"

"You could learn. I would teach you."

"I know you would. And you would be a fabulous teacher. But when you said the word 'attraction', that was the thing I choked on."

"Do you know why?" he asked, his voice gentle. "What does attraction mean to you?'

"Sex. What else?"

"Maybe…interest? Would it help if I said I was interested in you, very interested, because you are a fascinating person, and there's so much that we share, and some areas of difference that I would love us to explore? We could maybe let the sex thing sort itself out over time?"

"I don't see how that would work. I mean, wouldn't you be wanting it and just pretending it didn't matter? That's not fair on you."

"Some people are worth it. But have I got you all wrong,

Kai? There was that girl — Klara. You were getting quite close with her."

I shook my head.

"Dom, then? You prefer girls? I was not sure. You keep that part of you hidden."

The truth was, I didn't know how to handle my feelings for either of them. It wasn't so simple as preferring girls or not. I could as easily summon up a memory, a vision of Dom, equally nude and equally beautiful. Equally sexually attractive. But some element of that brief sauna moment of transcendence remained. The physicalities simply define how to express desire. Or love. Or both. But not where that feeling might be bestowed, that is, on whom or when.

I'd dodged. "Perhaps. Perhaps not."

"Then we can be friends? Just not *special* friends?"

"Please don't pressure me, Lars. I like you for all the reasons I've already mentioned, and more. You're fun on Twitter. You're a fascinating person in the flesh."

I shouldn't have said that. Damn my subconscious. "I mean, yes, we're already friends. But I can't see myself in a…relationship with you."

"I see. Then I will learn to content myself with your friendship. Okay?"

And there he'd stood, all hopes dashed, sad puppy-eyes, not meaning a word of what he'd said but being very brave because that was a fuck of a lot less humiliating than being honest.

And I wouldn't be bullied by sad puppy-eyes into changing my mind, so I'd stood motionless while a part of me longed to hug him tight, and another part of me balked at the very idea of anything more physical than a polite handshake, and all of me felt like a total shit.

"We're coming back to Berlin for our last gig on Saturday. I hope I'll see you then."

"Yes, you'll see me then," he'd whispered. "I'll be there. The Club Mojo."

"I've got to go. I've got to say goodbye. Or '*Tschüss*'."

He didn't say anything. Only when I'd finally found the inner hardness to turn away did he speak in a hoarse whisper that did nothing to hide the pain.

"Don't disappear from my life, Kai. Please, don't be a stranger. *Tschüss*."

*

I HADN'T LOOKED back. I'd kept on walking and let the U-Bahn swallow me. I'd let the escalator take me deep into the bowels of the earth which was exactly the right place for Kai the Shit.

"What's wrong?" Dom had been quietly asking me the same thing a few times while trying not to draw attention to either of us.

"It's the museum. It's got to me."

She looked at me then as if at someone being pig-headed and eye-rollingly stupid. "We'll talk later."

Implied — when you're ready to beam back from Planet Stupid, Kai.

Berlin didn't have a Circle Line, but my head did, and I didn't know how many times I went around it.

*You're a very special person…*his hand on my arm…*you prefer girls?…* A vision of Dom, equally nude…*You'll see me then…*a whisper that didn't hide the pain… *Don't disappear from my life, Kai.*

You have my friendship, Lars. What more can I give you?

He'd not said it. But the word was there. Lurking.

Love.

Excepting my parents, no one had ever used that word to me. Lars's unspoken word was a chain wrapping around my throat, binding my hands, winding around my chest. Tightening. Tightening. The word stole my choice, robbed me of my freedom. *Don't do this to me, Lars. I…*

What about me?

Who do I love?

Dom. Nobody. Myself. Lars.

Lars. Myself. Dom.

Nobody.

No.

Body.

Like a Greek…

… god…

…ess

Until the U-Bahn finally halted, and we each fetched up on the platform like six shipwrecked mariners. Out onto the street and into the early-winter Berlin day.

*

THE CAMPSITE WAS my fault.

There were around ten *Campingplätze* in and around Berlin and three or four near to the Wannsee. Naturally, only one of them accepted tents. Naturally, it was the grottiest site.

We'd left Jürgen's place late. Once it had become clear that we were leaving, Jürgen had thawed, and we'd had a final round of coffee and cakes. When we departed, six of us impossibly squeezed into the van, the light was gone.

So, we put up the tents in the dark, using torches and van lights to illuminate our pitch. It was cold, with a mist trying to be a drizzle — or vice versa. The tent went up without a hitch, but…

We were now indeed six. I'd planned for four, and the tent would take four in a pinch. I discounted Jamie's two-close-friends tent, which was for an emergency only. When Dom had joined us, it was still fine because at least one person would have to sleep in the van. I'd no intention of leaving the van unoccupied, given its piss-poor security.

Now add Lotte, and two people had to go in the van. Dom and I had taken that on the first night; it had been pretty cold, and I'd been grateful for Dom's warmth next to me. This time, Jake and Lotte were quickest to volunteer, beating me to the punch. The van could have taken three, but…

I didn't go there. The van was no four-poster bed, but it was the poor best option for two lovers seeking privacy. Leaving aside the prospect of playing gooseberry to Jake and Lotte, any third occupant would have to find their own warmth on the front seat. The van geometry didn't permit any three-way arrangements.

No thanks.

So it was four in the tent, which was going to be cosy. Perhaps warmer. But comfortable? I doubted it. The drizzle had turned to rain, so everything would have to stay in the tent. The one bright spot was that the *Campingplatz* had a restaurant. We had a chance to fill our bellies and drink a beer or two before bedtime.

We were the only guests, but the boss was willing to open the kitchen, provided we were happy to choose from the bar food menu, which was all microwavable food from the chiller.

We hung up our jackets and coats to dry and settled in a booth to get warm. We filled our bellies and ordered beers, postponing any return to our tent, certainly while the rain drummed hard against the window. Then we ordered another round of drinks. A little voice whispered in my brain that we'd regret it later, but the lashing rain drowned it out. Ha! Pun intended. It was going to be a jolly evening. Perhaps I *was* becoming a bit tipsy, but…

Jamie looked glum. I took a trip to the bathroom, and when I returned, I settled next to him, opening a little gap with the others. Dom's head turned a fraction as I sat down, but she turned back to the others and rejoined their conversation. We had a temporary island of refuge.

"What's up, bruv? You look like the goat just ate your turnip."

He didn't say a word. Something was going on in that head of his though. I'd have to wait for it to come out.

"I had a wonderful day, yesterday, Kai."

I nodded, willing him to continue.

"Go on," I encouraged, as nothing else seemed forthcoming.

"You remember that fair-haired girl from the party? We were all chatting, and then you got bored and left us. I thought she was really interesting though."

"Tall girl. Very mannish. Flat-chested and stubble on her chin. That the one?"

"No!" He sounded aggrieved, then twigged. "Oh, right. Kai-joke. Your usual crap timing."

"Yep. So you spent the next day with Alina. With Joni too. I got your text, remember?"

At that, his face lit up. "Of course. Yeah, we picked up Joni from the childminder and went out to the park. He's a lovely lad. He's four years old and full of energy. He talks, you know."

"Yes, Jamie. Most kids do at that age."

He pouted. "I know that. I meant he talks a little bit of English."

"Well, that's nice. It's a shame you don't speak much German."

The grin returned. "I'm learning. A little bit. Back at her apartment, he had a playtime, and dinner, and we got him changed for bed. Alina was telling him a bedtime story. In German, of course. But then Joni asked *me* to tell him a story."

I nodded. "So you read to him? In German?"

"Yeah, and he laughed at my pronunciation and told me how to say the words. He made me repeat them back to him. And Alina was laughing too. But after we turned the lights off, the kid wouldn't go to sleep—he kept coming out of his bedroom. The light was too bright, or he was thirsty, or there was too much noise, or he was having a bad dream."

"Kids do that. Mum says *we* did, and I've no reason to doubt her. It's part of making sure mums and dads don't get a moment's peace to make more kids. Natural selection at work."

Jamie smiled ruefully at that.

"Oh. You and Alina?"

"No! It wasn't like that. We were talking over wine and

nibbles. About the day. Playing in the park with Joni and back at the apartment. She told me a lot about herself too. And I told her about me. She's really easy to talk to. And before I knew it, it was midnight. I asked her to call a taxi, but…"

"She offered to put you up, instead. You slept on the sofa? Or did you choose the floor at the foot of her bed? Sir Jamie, the no-ball knight!"

"No. I slept with her. In her bed."

My jaw needed closing. I didn't think we were that close, my brother and I. Not since our parents had stopped bathing us together.

"So you…and she…"

"Yeah. Several times." Defiant—and proud.

"I didn't need to know that."

"I…needed to tell someone. You."

"Thanks, brother. I'll try to expunge the image from my brain."

"Was it wrong?"

Why was I suddenly Jamie's conscience? Jamie wasn't in any other relationship as far as I knew. He'd broken up with what's-her-name, Louise, a good six months ago. Since then, I hadn't seen any unexplained underwear around the house he shared. At least, nothing that implicated him.

"Depends entirely on what you do about it, Jamie. If you both wanted a one-night stand, then there's nothing more to say. If she's looking for a new daddy for Joni, and you're running for the hills, then you're a cad, and she'd be within her rights to come after you with a shotgu—"

I stopped then. But it was too late. Kai's big mouth had

struck again.

"Do you mean that?" he asked. "Or is this another crap Kai-joke?"

"Forget it. Everything I've said today has come out wrong. She sounds a really interesting person, and there's something special there, isn't there? Something more than a one-night stand. If you both feel it, and I think you do, then give it time. Finish the tour, but stay in touch with her. Don't be a stranger. See what develops, and let the rest sort itself out over time."

Don't be a stranger. Lars's exact words to me. Now my words to Jamie.

Shut up, conscience. The cases are not the same.

Oh?

Just…just — this is Jamie we're talking about. Okay?

We changed the subject. Or at least, I did. Jamie had stopped talking and was looking thoughtful. Dom reckoned that whatever we'd been talking about was now finished and brought us back into the group.

We chatted about this and that for an hour and experimented with some random singing. Dom tried to get us to work on harmonies, but our timing was all shot. Still, Lotte wasn't afraid to join in, singing the melody in unison with Dom. Her voice didn't have a lot of power, but she could certainly pitch her notes accurately.

Jamie, though. was barely with us. What was going on in that head of his? Had I blown our relationship with my tactless utterances? Would Lars ever trust me again? *Jamie.* Would *Jamie* ever trust me again? It was getting harder to think straight, unfortunately. I tried to push brother Joni out of my head, but he wouldn't go. Jamie, I mean. Joni was his son. Ah…Alina's son.

The barman, AKA the campsite boss, was getting a little fed up with our singing. He came over and asked if we'd like to order any more drinks. He mentioned our bar bill, which sounded a bit high for my liking, but I couldn't deny that I'd had three or four whiskies. There were the empty glasses to prove it.

My legs still worked, which, for a moment, I'd feared they wouldn't. I took my turn in the bathroom like everyone else. Whether we'd make it through the night without a wee was any-one's guess. But the rain was pissing down as hard as ever. I wouldn't want to leave the tent if I could possibly stay warm and dry inside, even if my bladder swelled to the size of a tennis ball. And no, I didn't have the faintest idea of what the normal size is for a tennis ball. Bladder.

Outside, the rain soaked through my coat in about ten paces. 'Warm and dry' was starting to look unlikely. Then my foot slipped in the mud, and I went down on my arse. That wasn't fun—I landed on something hard and sharp that hurt a lot, even through the mud and muscle. My eyes watered, and for a mo-ment, I was painfully sober. I could feel the water soaking through my jeans and tried to push myself back onto my feet. My right hand shot out, and I landed on my side. They—not excluding Dom—all started laughing at my pratfall. Thanks, guys.

"Hey. Help me up when you've finished cackling, you bas-tards."

They got me up on my feet. Jamie, bless him, actually had the decency to ask if I was all right. I tried a step. It hurt, but it didn't feel like I'd broken anything. I limped back to the tent about ten paces behind everyone else, sucking air between my teeth on every painful step.

When I caught up, they'd all clustered around the front of the tent, not going in.

"What's up?" I asked, finally taking an interest in the part of the universe that wasn't throbbing with pain.

'Up' was the flysheet. Somebody hadn't pegged it down right, and one corner had lifted up, now rain-plastered over the ridge. We didn't have a dry porch anymore, the inner wall of the tent now soaked where the flysheet had blown free. There was no sign of the errant tent peg in the dark, so we had to sacrifice a peg from the main guy. Fine, as long as the wind didn't get up in the night.

Inside, the water had pooled underneath the leak, soaking Neale's sleeping bag. But some had trickled around the edge of the tent, and nobody's kit had wholly escaped.

"Get in, you stupid bugger, and close the fucking door."

Stupid bugger was me, standing dumbly outside in my wet jeans with mud all over my arse. Four whiskies inside me, I had no idea how I was going to get to my own sleeping bag without dripping all over everyone else on the way. Neale bundled up his own useless sleeping bag and pushed past me, radiating anger fit to fry an egg. He set off in the direction of the van in search of any spare clothing, leaving a space by the doorway.

"Take your jeans off outside — they're soaked through anyway — and leave them there. Then come inside and dry yourself."

Easy for Jamie to say. Not easy for me to do. Particularly the bit where, with my jeans down around my ankles, I had to sit and put weight on my bruised backside. From that position, I began the struggle to unlace my shoes. I wanted to bring my shoes and jeans inside, but the jeans were wet through. Jamie made me leave them outside, with the legs knotted around the guy rope so they wouldn't blow away.

"Jeans are a killer," said Jamie, which made me smile. It was something the scoutmaster used to say to anyone who dared bring jeans to camp. Most of us tried it, at least once, because camping trousers are dull and jeans are cool. I never did because Jamie had warned me. Jamie had been a patrol leader, and I, two years younger, was a plain oik. The scoutmaster was wise; Jamie was never *my* patrol leader. Most of Jamie's bossiness landed on his own oiks. So we got on—mostly by avoiding each other—but we covered each other's backs and learned to enjoy life outdoors. That could be a lot of fun in a mixed troop of young teens, away from parental prying. So long as you avoided hypothermia-inducing jeans, flying mallets, sharp blades, dead sheep in the water supply, and the dares and hazings of your fellow scouts. Happy days.

Then Neale returned, minus sleeping bag, but with a couple of extra layers.

So. Four in the tent. Three sleeping bags. Two degrees above zero. One torch. I might be exaggerating about the temperature, but it felt that way to me in my underwear, and Neale was not much warmer.

"I will say it, in case the men are too embarrassed," Dom began. "We need to lie together to keep warm. Take off your wet clothes. Put on dry clothes if you have them. Then two of us will curl up together either side of Neale."

"Who…" asked Jamie.

"Jamie, you and I will keep Neale warm between us. Kai,

you're on your own by the door, but Jamie will lend you his excellent sleeping bag. You should keep warm enough."

Oh.

Chapter Eighteen

Wednesday, October 5, 2016
Crossroads Blues Club

WE MADE IT through to the dawn. I remembered far too much of the night, which was perishing cold and wet throughout.

Jamie, Neale, and Dom must have got off to sleep in minutes. They were a warm, snoring huddle, and I longed to be part of it. But the logic said that, to avoid touching the walls, only three people could be part of that huddle. The fourth person ought to be the guy with the best sleeping bag. That was Jamie. So why had Dom picked me for the solo spot?

Because you were drunk as a skunk, and you'd have to get up in the night to piss, puke, or both.

Too shimple, shurely. I worried about what the real reason was. And I worried about Jamie and whether he'd do the right thing about Alina and Joni—and what that right thing might be. And I worried about Lars and about Dom—meaning I worried about myself and what my feelings for each of them said about me. And I worried about the tent wall that was not now in any sense waterproof. I worried about the water that was still drip-dripping off the tent wall and pooling close to my feet. And I worried about feeling cold and left out of that huddle and about my bruised backside, which was still giving me a lot of grief. I worried that it was still raining and blowing hard out there.

And I worried that I'd have to get up for a pee.

I was definitely going to have to get up. Definitely. Luke-warm as it was in Jamie's sleeping bag, it'd be colder and wetter out there, and I wasn't looking forward to venturing out.

Resentful, I climbed out of my sleeping bag before my bladder stretched to basketball size. I stripped off my dry clothes and pulled on my muddy wet pants and T-shirt. Much as I did not want to die of hypothermia in wet clothes, I even more didn't want to get lost while wandering around the campsite naked.

The wash block was a hundred metres away, and it had been lit up when we'd left it. But the rain hid it, and of course, my torch was too puny to pierce the night. So, I set off, squelching through mud in already-soggy trainers, in what I hoped was the right direction. I passed the van, resisted the impulse to peer inside, and followed the roadway to the main block, shivering and wishing I'd put another layer on.

I found the wash block open and was able to do what needed to be done. And then I had an inspiration, though it might have been the whisky. I'd have a shower, get myself warm again, and wash out the mud while I was at it.

The water started cold, and I jumped back, nearly tumbling on my arse again. But it warmed up, and I stepped under it, letting it wash over my skin. The heat began to drive out the chill and soothe the pain in my backside. I stood for long minutes, wringing the mud from my clothes and enjoying the water running warm across my skin. Then, the water chilled again as the hot water tank drained, and the last warmth disappeared down the plughole.

Ow!

I leaped out of that shower faster than I'd have believed possible, given my recent injury. Lacking a towel, I brushed off what water I could with my hands.

Still, I was a lot warmer than I had been, and my clothes were mud-free. I slapped them against the wall to drive out as much water as I could, dressed, and headed back into the rain. The warmth didn't last long, but I passed the van without breaking into shivers and found the tent, properly zipped, as I'd left it.

The huddle was still there, snoring. I no longer felt quite so jealous *because I'd had a warm shower*. So there!

But the pool of water had grown larger. I mopped at it with my wet T-shirt and wrung it out several times until I'd dumped the worst of the pool outside.

"Are ye okay, Kai?" asked a wide-awake Irish voice.

"We've got a leak, Neale. I'm sorting it out. Get back to sleep. I can manage."

"Okay. You need to put some clothes on. You'll freeze."

"I have one—just one—dry T-shirt. And I have one wet T-shirt, which I am currently using to mop out the tent. Mister Wet T-shirt must not meet Mister Dry T-shirt, else they will turn into the Wet T-shirt Twins, and I will indeed fucking freeze. So, thank you very much for your advice, but my four-whisky wisdom is that stark bollock naked is my best option."

"Uh. Forget I spoke. I'll get back to sleep. Goodnight, Kai."

"That's probably best. Goodnight, Neale."

After that little episode, I lay awake some more. not quite so cold as I had been—or at least with a placebo warmth from the memory of the shower. But the other worries still remained and stayed dancing around my head for most of the night. From time to time, I mopped out the worst of the leak.

Dawn finally arrived, and I finally dozed off. I woke again aware that something was missing—a beautiful silence, the absence of rain. My feet were cold, though, and wet because I'd given in to sleep and had stopped mopping.

But no one had hypothermia. Neale was fine, very fine for someone who'd spent the night in a cold, leaky tent without a sleeping bag. Shortly, we all discovered the shower block had hot water again. We had some wet clothes and Neale's sodden sleeping bag, sure, but there was a launderette and a dryer, and To Hell With The Expense.

Ditto with the breakfast, and if, in the end, what we'd spent wasn't far short of what a B & B would have cost, then to hell with that expense too. While the launderette was doing its thing, and we were all filling our faces with toast and jam, washed down with coffee, we had a band meeting. We solemnly and unanimously agreed to cancel all remaining camping and book B & Bs for the rest of the tour. THWTE.

The next stop was Munich. At least, that was the big plan. The detailed plan was far more complex, with a lot of to-ings and fro-ings. Neale ferried Jake and Lotte to a railway station while the rest of us broke camp and did our best to dry out the tent. Oh, and we found the lost tent peg. When Neale arrived back, we loaded the van and…had another coffee.

It should have taken five minutes. Fifteen, at the most.

"We have to get moving, guys."

And everyone agreed that we should, and we sipped some more coffee, and let the warmth spread out to our fingertips.

And then someone else said, "We have to get moving, guys."

Three hundred miles, near enough, but we'd not driven a single one, and it would soon be noon. We didn't have to do it all today. The next gig was on Thursday. So, we could drive for a few hours, pull in at a likely looking motel, and finish the journey tomorrow.

Then Dom got angry.

"What's happened to you? You've turned into zombies! For fuck's sake, let us go!"

"Okay, Dom, don't get riled," said Neale. "I was just finishing my coffee—"

Dom slapped Neale's cup out of his hand, sending it flying. The mug shattered on the tiled floor and hot coffee sprayed everywhere.

Silence.

The barman looked up, surprised. "*Was ist da los*?" he called. "What is going on?"

"An accident," I replied. "He dropped his coffee. He's very sorry."

Neale still sat with his mouth open. "What the fuck was that for? We've got plenty of time."

"*You* have…" she began.

Then she began again. "I am very sorry, Neale. I lost my cool. I am still…distressed after last night. I did not sleep well. Please forgive me."

Neale nodded, his mouth still open in shock. "Uh, yes. Of course."

The barman came over, carrying a mop. He looked annoyed but not throw-us-out annoyed.

"Another one?" he asked.

"No, thanks…" I replied and pulled out my credit card. We were done.

He waved his hand as if to say not to worry about the broken cup but showed me the bill for the coffees we'd drunk. I added a tip, which I hoped made up for the breakage.

And we still took a good five minutes in the loo.

*

FOUR IN THE van. It was pretty comfortable, all things considered. We still had a wet tent in the back, dripping on the floor, hopefully not anywhere near electrics. Barring disaster, we wouldn't need it again, but it was borrowed from a good friend. I wanted to get it dried out as much as possible so it wouldn't get mouldy when we put it away.

Jamie had taken the back seat with Neale at the wheel, leaving me in the middle seat and Dom next to me by the passenger door. We were driving through forest, the Wannsee now behind us. Berlin too.

I found myself pondering Dom's warning about Berlin. 'A dark side to Berlin…' she'd said. No. I didn't think so anyway.

Berlin had changed us, I couldn't argue with that, but not in a dark way, surely. But then, what about Dom's angry outburst? Did she want to get away from Berlin so much? Or was it something else?

I could ask her, but she had her eyes closed, asleep...or feigning sleep. Anyway, too public. But Dom was right. We'd been turning into zombies. Two nights without a gig, and we'd lost our fire.

No. Not lost it, but our energies had focused elsewhere. Sleep and sex. Jake and Jamie leading us astray. Though a comfortable bed would be welcome...

...and someone to share it with?

But Jamie had put on a track by Kyla Brox, and in the space of two bars, I was beating out rhythms on my thighs. Right now, a good night's sleep was the start, middle, and end of my physical needs. That, and...

Dammit, I *have* to play a gig.

"Me too."

"Aren't you asleep, Dom? Did you hear me?" A stupid question. Of course she wasn't asleep, and I do sometimes mutter.

"No. But I thought I heard you. You want to play again, to beat the drum and to sing."

"Too right. Beat some skin and sing."

"That sounds like you're ready to raise some hell."

"Yep. I got the fight back in my soul."

Though I didn't think I wanted to fight anybody unless my subconscious was trying to tell me something about my bandmates. A gig was what we all wanted — that was agreed. But I did want to sing too.

There was something else I needed to know. Why Dom's

anger? Why the hurry when we had plenty of time?

"Dom, you said 'zombie' before."

"Yes, and I regret it. I was angry with you."

An apology but no explanation of why. It seemed like Dom had peered into each of our souls, but Dom was a mystery to me, to us all. At best, she'd given us some distant family history. A story about working in a department store in Paris. But the recent past? Nothing. And the future? She'd skilfully avoided our questions about her plans post-tour. But that last outburst…

I needed to know.

"You said we had time but… What were you going to say?"

"Nothing. Nothing at all. I was angry and tired."

Anger and tiredness. An easy excuse for hasty words not meant to be spoken. They might even have been true words, but if so, Dom wasn't saying.

Neale interrupted. "Do any of you good people need a pit stop? There's a service station coming up."

"No, thanks. Where are we though?"

"Not like you, Kai, to not know where we are. We're getting close to Leipzig. I'd like to keep going, though, if everyone can wait. There's another service station on the far side of Leipzig in about forty miles — that's about sixty-five kilometres in euros."

"Sounds good. How far do you think we'll get today?"

"Well, the roads are pretty good. We might get to Nürnberg by the time the light goes. If Dom's okay to drive a bit, we could make it all the way to Munich by seven."

"I'm okay to drive, Neale. We can try. Jamie?"

"Yeah. Go for it. But we should tell Jake and Lotte. I've not heard from them."

"Have you called them?" I asked and got a withering look in return.

"I've tried. They're not answering."

"Okay."

I bit back my impulse to tell him to keep trying. Jamie could be bloody quick with the sarky response.

*

"WAKE UP, KAI. Wake up."

Dom's voice.

I opened my eyes, but I already knew we were stopped. Silence. We weren't on the autobahn, nor even close. No cars. Maybe a distant hum.

And daylight still, so I couldn't have been asleep all that long. We were on a quiet country road, long and straight, with trees and farmland.

"What's up?" I asked.

"We don't know," Dom replied. "Neale just turned off the autobahn without warning. He took an unmarked turn and stopped us here. Hasn't answered any questions except to say, "Kai knows.""

I twisted around to face Neale, who was sucking orange juice from a carton in his hand. He removed the straw from his mouth, but didn't look at me. "Tell them, Kai. I'm fine, but we have to stop while I get my shit together. Tell them why."

Ah. The penny dropped.

"Neale is having a low. A 'hypo'. Is that right?"

He nodded.

"He's diabetic."

"Ah" from Dom and "What?" from Jamie.

So, I explained for Jamie's benefit at least. As closely as I could remember Neale's words, I echoed what he'd told me. He kept quiet while I spoke, sucking on his orange juice but occasionally nodding confirmation.

"And you didn't tell us?" Jamie's tone was distinctly aggrieved.

"It's because…" I began, but Neale interrupted me.

"I'll make my own apologies, thank you, Kai. You've done a good job of explaining the situation, but no one says sorry on my behalf."

I nodded. It was mostly true.

"Kai found me out, and I promised I'd tell the rest of you. I was waiting for the right moment, but the wrong moment happened first. I'm sorry."

"You didn't trust us," Jamie replied.

Dom stomped on that. "No, Jamie, that is not true. And you are not being fair. There is much that each of us has not told the others. It does not mean that we do not trust one another. Perhaps we, too, are waiting for the right moment. The moment when someone needs to know, or when someone needs to tell. You have not told us about your time with Alina."

"That's my business. You don't need to know."

"Exactly. We do not need to know, and you do not need to tell us. So let Neale speak."

Neale nodded his thanks to Dom, then began.

"It's always hard to know what to tell people if you have diabetes. People don't understand diabetes, and they don't feel safe with what they don't understand. So, like many diabetics, I choose not to talk about my condition. My control is good — if it weren't, I'd have had to give up my licence. But today, I was angry with Dom for slapping the coffee out of my hand and didn't check my blood sugar before driving. So, I got a hypo. But I spotted the signs early, got off the motorway, and I'm dealing with it. I'm going to wait twenty minutes, then I'll do a blood test, and then we'll drive on."

Jamie wasn't happy. "We're running late. Your diabetes is making us late, so it does matter."

"I will drive," said Dom. "Neale, you will rest for an hour or two. There will be a rest stop soon, right, Kai?" — and after I nodded — "And we will all want to stop and have something to eat, and Neale will take his blood test and take insulin or whatever so that he is able to drive again. You will teach us all how to help you in case you have another attack."

"I won't have another attack; I promise you."

"Shut the fuck up, my dear friend Neale. I am sure you will not. But you will teach us anyway because that is the only condition under which I will let you drive."

Dom reached across me — *cross me* — and deftly removed the keys from the ignition. She jangled them for a moment, just out of his reach, grinning.

"I have always wanted a reason to do this…" She dropped the keys down the neck of her T-shirt between her breasts.

The bulky keys refused to slide down but lodged in sight. "*Merde*," Dom whispered, then pushed with her index finger, and the keys disappeared, leaving red abrasions in their wake.

"Oww. Not the effect I was hoping for…"

But Neale was grinning too. "Okay, Dom. I agree to all your

conditions. Now carefully fish them keys out from your boobs and drive us out of here."

*

WE'D BEEN EATING for a while when Dom's phone rang.

She swallowed and answered, then said to us, "It's Lotte."

"'Allo, Lotte," Dom continued. "Where are you, my dear?"

Squawks.

"You are *where*? Oh. Yes."

More squawks.

"They're in Prague. With Lotte's uncle."

I had a good map, complete with the main railway lines. "Why the fuck are they in Prague? It's not on the main line to Munich; it's not even the right country —"

"Shhh!" — to me, then: "Say again, Lotte. There's interference."

Crackles, followed by squawks.

"She wants to know if we can get to Prague by seven hours tonight. Can we?"

I did some calculations. Decided not to ask the question 'why', nodded, then added, "Tell her we're already beyond Leipzig, so we'd have to backtrack a bit. The best route would be to turn around and drive north-east, back past Leipzig, and take the autobahn."

"We can do it though?"

"Yes. I'm guessing they're not stranded, robbed, waylaid, or otherwise incommoded, but have got us a gig. In Prague."

"*Oui*." And to Lotte: "Yes, we can do it. How much?"

Indecipherable noises.

"How much is ten thousand Koruna?"

What was that site for exchange rates? Google 'exchange rate calculator', yes, that was the one. Come on, you bastard internet, move…

"About three hundred and seventy euros. Go for it, guys?"

I collected nods from around the table. It was better than nothing by a long way.

"Lotte, the guys say 'yes'. Tell your uncle we'll do it. Text me the details. *Tschüss.*"

More miles, then. At least it was only Europe we were touring, not somewhere huge, like Russia.

Back on the road, we had to head south first to the next junction, where we could turn around and head north. As we drove, Lotte's information dribbled in, bit by bit: Satnav coordinates. A street address and the name of the club—the Crossroads Blues and Jazz Club. Accommodation provided—no details. Arrive seven, but play for two hours between nine and midnight. Drinks at our expense. But then the next text was: *Jake says Czech beer is dirt cheap but tastes like gnat's piss.*

I doubted that would stop us from pouring it down our necks.

"This one?" called Dom.

It was our exit. Two minutes later, we were no longer travelling south. We were headed back north on our way to Prague.

*

PRAGUE WAS A wonderful city, boasting…

Actually, I didn't know much about Prague at all, and I wasn't going to download a guidebook on my data allowance. We had no map, and the sun had set by the time we entered the sub-urbs, so we trusted the satnav.

I did see what might have been some pretty silhouettes of old buildings against the already-dark sky and tower blocks that looked like offices, judging from the neon signs on the outside. The morning would reveal if it was a city of tastefully blended architectural styles, or a former-communist eyesore in concrete, swamping the last remnants of mediaeval twee-ness.

Neale was driving—we'd had several driver changes along the way—and making caustic comments about the Czechs, their driving skills, and their cars.

"It's all bloody Škodas! What chance have you got of finding your own car after a night on the stout? Where's originality, crea-tivity, and class?"

"They don't do stout here, and I think you mean, 'Why aren't there any BMWs?'"

"Well, you could put it like that, Jamie. I did see a VW—don't you dare cut me up, ye little shite-bag—but if that's as high as their aspiration reaches, then the country's going down the pan. Anyways, it had a D plate on it, so it was a German tourist come to brag in a Beamer-free zone."

In one hundred yards, turn right…

"That won't work, ye damn-fool robot, it's no entry."

Around the block again, and we were there. At the Cross-roads Blues and Jazz Club. But it wasn't what I was expecting. It seemed to be a sports hall or social hall, with banners for soccer clubs and sewing circles jostling one another, all cable-tied to the mesh fencing surround.

Straightaway, we spotted Lotte and Jake standing on the

pavement, waving like lunatics as they recognised the van. I looked at my watch—seven-thirty—not too bad, but we were going to have to get a move on.

Inside, it was obviously a community hall. Noticeboards carried posters and flyers for even more clubs—Karate, drama, volleyball, model railway, cross-stitch. A hundred other notices in Czech hung on the walls without any recognisable words or pictures to help me. Beyond the foyer, we passed into an already-busy bar area and to the main hall. The main hall, a huge cavern, had varnished wooden floors with a volleyball court marked out in red tape and other courts in a rainbow of colours. And at the far end, a stage with proper lights, curtains, and room to spread out.

Oh, and a backdrop of a fairy-tale landscape, complete with castle, left over from some amateur dramatic production.

Yay!

Then came a great booming sound from behind us.

We turned to a huge bear of a man, grinning and with arms outstretched in greeting. My ears tuned in to his speech, and I realised this was Lotte's uncle.

"... you will excuse my English, please. I am Peter."—which he pronounced *Payter*—"Welcome to the Crossroads Blues and Jazz Club. Welcome! Welcome!"

Dom picked up the metaphorical baton. "We are so pleased to meet you. But we are surprised also. We had not expected to get a gig at such short notice."

Peter shrugged. "I did not expect either, but schedule band cancel yesterday. Their singer was infect. The throat. Not singing."

"A shame," Dom replied. "We are happy to help out. So, you will have a good audience tonight?"

"I think, yes. Many people visit club. Good crowd. Old guys like me. Young kids like nephew Lotte. Niece. Drink beer, everyone sing blues. Good time."

"Okay. We'll get set up, then. When do you want us to play?"

"Two sets times one hour. Nine and ten-and-half. Close bar at twelve. Everyone gone by one, latest two."

"Lotte said there would be accommodation. Where do we sleep?"

"I find places. With friends of me. Tell you after you play."

Uh-oh. That sounded a little…informal. But there wasn't much we could do about it now.

"You don't think we should try a B & B?" I ventured.

Peter looked alarmed. "No, no! Spend money on hotels, wise is not! You have come far, you are guests. Our hospitality is your place."

So that was that.

The next hour was a rush of dragging in equipment, setting it up, and running a soundcheck. Meanwhile, a handful of volunteers set out tables and chairs on the hall floor, turning the place into a blues club. The harsh fluorescents shut off, and a guy in a black leather jacket climbed up a ladder to swivel some of the stage lighting around. Better — now the place had a bit of atmosphere. With a few coloured filters, it looked pretty decent.

The guy who'd done the lighting came over and introduced himself as Pavel. Thirty-ish, with rosy cheeks and a round face beneath hair just beginning to recede, he smiled with easy warmth and a confidence that immediately put me at ease.

"I do lights and sound. You can use our PA," he said.

I almost argued. Perhaps Pavel saw storm clouds brewing.

"Listen. You can trust me," he said. "I know this room; you don't. I know what makes it ring and how to make it stop. I know how it changes when the audience comes in and how to adjust. If you want to use your own mics, that's fine. If your singer wants to walk out into the audience, I can handle that. If you can give me a set list, I can make you sound like…" He paused and looked at us, gauging what sort of band we might be.

"…like Beth Hart."

I looked him right back.

"You're cocky, Pavel. I've been thinking Bonnie Raitt, but I'll take Beth Hart if you can deliver."

"I know Bonnie Raitt. But let me listen to soundcheck. Get a feel of band. Irina!"

Irina? His sidekick. Wife? At any rate, she looked about Pavel's age, and she wore a leather jacket like his over a Led Zep tee. But where he was round, she was rake-thin, as though she ran marathons before breakfast. The two of them got to work, adding microphones to our backline. My drum kit got four!

"We are saving up for more microphones," Irina apologised as she knelt to fix up the bass drum mic. "I would add more if I had them. But good drum mics are not cheap in Czech Republic."

"Nor in England," I sympathised. But four microphones for a drum kit… I'd never had my kit mic'd. Not even with one mic. Never. I wondered whether I'd died and gone to drummer heaven.

Which was when I saw Pavel had given Jake his own vocal

mic. Alas, no. I was not in heaven. Jake only got a live mic in the other place.

"Uh, Irina…" I began.

"Later," she answered. "Pavel is calling me."

And she was gone. I'd have to catch her quickly and have a quick word… But then it was soundcheck time.

It was funny how, after a couple of nights without a gig, we'd already slipped. We weren't tight, not as together as we'd been at Jürgen's party. I was dog-tired, and I hadn't been driving, so how Dom and Neale felt I didn't know.

But we had foldback speakers! And there was Pavel asking me what mix I wanted — which was a tad more bass and a lot more of Dom's vocals. And Dom got her own foldback mix too.

"Can I get down off the stage?" she called.

"Sure. We've got a feedback eliminator wired in. Give it a try."

So she dropped off the stage, singing 'Three Hundred Pounds of Joy', an old Howlin' Wolf song. It was a lot of fun, but, well, no way was Dom three hundred pounds of big momma. A hundred and thirty. Max.

Keep your mind on the drums, Kai.

She prowled the hall, learning where she could go — which was most of the way to the back until the time delay started to get noticeable — and where she couldn't, which was out to the sides. She came back with a great big grin on her face until she got back to the stage.

It was the first time I'd seen her lose her poise. The stage was a bit too high for her to push herself back up. For a moment, she looked around for some other way up, but there weren't any steps. Then Neale put his fiddle down, crossed the stage to her, and reached down to haul her up.

By that time, she'd stopped singing, and we'd all lost the plot. Complete shambles of an ending.

"Sorry, guys. I don't know what happened there. I think I'm a bit tired."

As were we all.

"Soundcheck over?" called Pavel.

"Yeah. Are you okay with that?"

"Sure, Kai. I can mix you good. Can you give me set list?"

"Give us ten minutes, please, Pavel."

But it took us less than that. As soon as we sat down, Dom pulled out the set lists from Jürgen's party.

"You can play that. I need to sleep. Fifteen minutes."

It was twenty to nine.

I spent the next quarter of an hour scribbling arrangements—if that wasn't too grandiose a term—against each of the songs in the set so Pavel would know how many verses and choruses each song had and who took solos. Which would be Jake and Neale only; there were no drum solos nor were there any bass solos. We weren't that kind of band.

In the short time I'd been working on the set list, the hall had pretty much filled. So, Peter had come up with the goods—a bunch of eager punters, ready to be entertained.

Two minutes to take it across to Pavel. He picked it up, glanced down it, and nodded.

"Got it. I can do this. Now you've got about three minutes to get on stage. The audience is waiting."

"Oh shit! I'm not even changed."

Backstage, Jamie had woken Dom, who looked a bit less like death warmed up after her sleep.

"Two minutes, guys," I called. "And I need to change."

"*Deux minutes? Oh, merde alors! Moi aussi. Tournez-vous.* Look away."

After the Berlin sauna, a bit of bare skin shouldn't have mattered. In any case, I was sure Jamie, Jake, and Neale were good lads and didn't stare at Dom. Perhaps it was because we were now in another country where the mores were unknown.

Whatever. For a brief moment, I stood in naught but pants, my Keith Moon T-shirt ready to pull on. Dom had her back to me, removing a blouse from its hanger. For five seconds, if that, my gaze lingered a moment on her back. I followed the lines and shadows of flesh over muscle from her neck to her derrière. In that moment, she turned and saw me. First, she held my eye with her own, and then, she walked her gaze over me from head to toe. My cheeks grew hot, but when she met my eyes once more, I didn't look away but kept my gaze locked with hers, trying not to be ashamed of what I was feeling. She nodded as if she had read my mind and understood my deepest thoughts. Then she Mona-Lisa'd me with a most enigmatic smile and buttoned up her shirt as though she had all the time in the world.

But she knew what I hadn't let even myself truly acknowledge. Until now. And I knew that whatever I felt, for that moment, she'd felt it too.

Hastily, I threw my T-shirt on and my jeans. In Prague, the mores were unknown.

"Come on, Kai. Come on, guys. Let's go."

We climbed the stairs and stood huddled behind the fantasy

castle, waiting for Peter's signal.

The arrangement was that we'd all troop on together, save for Dom, and strike up a groove led off by Jake. Then, Peter would announce 'Dom and the Blues' — or some other mangling of our name — and she'd stride on and kick into 'Rolling and Tumbling'.

Peter gave us the nod, and we all made our way to our instruments. There was barely enough light to see, but nobody tripped, nobody twisted any ankles or knocked anything over. I sat on my drum stool with no more than a slight twinge from my recovering backside. Peter had told us to start straight in.

The audience hushed. Somebody whistled loud and harsh, and then it was quiet once more. I checked; Jamie and Jake had strapped on their guitars — we were all ready. Another of those whistles shrilled, and another. Somebody shouted something I couldn't make out. In Czech, of course. It sounded quite angry, but maybe that was the way Czech sounded. Another whistle followed. And another shout. Definitely angry.

Maybe, I thought, gigs were supposed to be like the trains in Europe. We were a minute or so late going on — that could have been the height of rudeness here, and the crowd was letting us know we'd fallen short.

Well, nothing I could do about that without a time machine, but I could kick off the groove. Sticks high, beat four…

tock, tock, tock, tock

And we were in. Four bars of Jake's guitar on its own, then adding nice, steady rhythm on bass and drums, with Jake's guitar line still carrying the melody over the top. Standard twelve-bar structure, nothing fancy. Then Peter strode on from behind the castle, moved to the front, and Pavel gave him the centre spot.

Peter glanced back, but we'd already taken it right down so he could do his announcement.

It was in Czech, but I caught the name 'Dom and the Blues' — oh well — and 'English blues band', so that was okay. But they were whistling constantly now, with some angry shouts.

Peter called something back at the heckler, all the while shaking his head. Finally, he shrugged his shoulders, called out, with some force, what could only have been, "Please welcome to the stage Jan Does Blues Band, featuring Dominique." He left the stage, saying, "Ignore them. Troublemakers. They will give up as soon as you start playing."

But I could see the fear and the lie in his eyes.

Still, some modest applause followed, and Dom strode on. She wore the same costume as for our first gig — the two-piece pin-stripe suit and tie, complete with fedora. That got a few whistles, nicer ones mostly.

But Peter had gone on talking a couple of bars too long, and though she'd tried to spin it out, Dom reached her mic a good six bars too early to start singing. Six bars in which the bad whistles came back and the angry shouting too. We weren't popular, and we didn't have a fucking clue what we'd done wrong.

Dom gave it her all. And we gave her everything we could in support. Jake played a cracking solo, with Neale harmonising around the guitar line, and Jamie and I were as tight a rhythm section as you've ever heard. But we finished to stony silence. And then the whistles and shouting started again.

I'd never played to a reaction like that. None of us had. I felt like I'd held out my hand in friendship and been punched in the guts for my trouble. If it had been me out front, I'd have hightailed it for the van and driven the hell out of there, all the way back to Germany. Or even England.

But Dom took it on the chin. She scanned the crowd and pointed to someone.

"You there. Yes, you, sir. Talk with me, please. Come up here where we can talk like civilised people, without all this noise. Tell me what we have done to offend you; because I swear to you, we are here in friendship. It is not our intention to anger you. How can we make amends?"

And then she said it again in French and in German.

She said it with her arms opened outwards, palms towards the audience. Her body language echoed the puzzlement and the desire for reconciliation of her words. And this big guy, biker-big, trucker-big, shambled up from the audience, clambered up onto the stage, and towered over her.

He didn't look happy.

"Thank you," Dom said. "Are we okay to talk in English? I speak French and German also, if that's better. Or Flemish, but I don't suppose anyone else here speaks Flemish."

"English is good."

"Fine. Now you already know my name. Dominique. What's your name?"

"They call me Štefan."

"Hi, Štefan. Pleased to meet you."

And she reached to shake his hand. After a moment, Štefan clasped her hand in his and shook it reluctantly, but he shook it.

"Štefan, the band and I have come a long way to play blues for you guys. Now we're here, you're not happy. What have we done to offend you? How can we make amends?"

That was the gist of it, and if Štefan didn't quite get it the first time, and Dom had to explain in different words, then forgive me if I skip the fine details. The gist of Štefan's reply?

"Well, you weren't the band that was supposed to play tonight. It was the house band, the Crossroads Blues Brothers" — I had to smile — "and they're our friends."

"Yes, I heard about that. I heard that one of them was ill, and we stepped in to fill the gap."

"Well, that's a total lie," Štefan shot back. "That was what we had heard, but people kept asking who was ill and asking if it was serious. About half an hour ago, Antonín — the singer — finally tweeted that nobody was ill, but he'd been *told* they couldn't play tonight. He'd been told not to say anything about it. Antonín wasn't happy telling lies, and he finally admitted what had happened. People were not happy. Word got around. It is not fair. What do you say? You know how it is when immigrants come and steal our jobs."

That got a laugh.

Well, he hadn't named names, but it was pretty obvious who it must have been — Peter, surely. But was it his own idea? Or had Lotte sweet-talked him into it? This was going to be awkward…

"I see… Štefan, I promise you that I did not know about that. I swear to you we did not ask for this gig, nor bully anyone into changing the line-up. We were on our way to Munich, and we were completely surprised by the offer of this gig. We turned around and drove to Prague in good faith. Now we're here, what do you want us to do?"

That took him by surprise. "Uh, I don't know. It is not right that the Crossroads Blues Brothers do not play."

"I agree. But we have come a long way, thinking that we were helping, and that we would be welcome. Shall we not play?"

He thought a bit. "No. That is not right either. You have come far. But what to *do*? There is no right thing to do."

"It is hard to know what to do. But listen, Štefan, we are being paid for this gig. I speak only for myself, but I will not touch the money. I would still like to sing for you, if you like? But no money. Give it to the Crossroads Blues Brothers."

Štefan muttered something.

"I'm sorry? I didn't catch that."

"I said they have already been paid."

"Oh. Then they will be paid twice. That is more than fair."

"No. That is not right either."

"Then I give the money to you. If you want us to play for you, we will. But no money. You use it to pay for another guest band. Or you give it to charity."

Dom turned to us. "Do you agree, guys?"

Well, there was a time to be noble and a time to be…noble. That money would have helped cover the loss we were going to make on this tour, but it was tainted money now.

"I agree," I called. And everyone else answered similarly.

"So what do you want us to do, Štefan?"

He didn't hesitate. "You play."

And to the audience, Dom asked, "Do you agree too? This is your club."

She'd done it. Dom had turned them around. They were cheering and applauding now, not bring-the-house-down cheering but at-least-give-them-a-chance cheering. She gave Štefan a big hug, and he went bright red. Rather hastily, he disengaged and clambered off the stage. Girlfriend waiting?

"You are a good man, Štefan. Okay, guys. What's next?"

"Crossroads."

Very appropriate and not at all planned.

Dom turned back, whispered to Neale for a moment, and took some deep breaths while we played the intro. Neale came in on the fiddle and played melody over the top of the first verse. I didn't suppose the audience could see it, but Dom was shaking. *I don't blame you, Dom*, That must have been pretty stressful.

Verse two, she came in fine though. Did I catch a hint of a quaver in her voice on the first couple of notes? No, she was fine. The audience was with us now, and there was no life like a rock'n'roll life.

*

AT THE END of the first set, we all had pretty much the same idea, which was to have a word with Peter.

But where he'd gone to, no one knew. We asked Pavel, Štefan, several people. No one had seen him leave, but leave he had.

Then Jake spoke up. "Where's Lotte?"

"Have you checked the bar?"

"Of course I've checked the bar, Kai. Hell, I've even checked the ladies' toilet. She wasn't there."

"Oh?"

"I got someone to go in and check. She said it was empty, so when she left, I checked. It was empty."

"Anything on your phone?" Dom asked.

"Nothing."

"Are you sure?" I asked. "The coverage isn't very good in here. Lots of metal…" I waved my arm around — lots of steel girders and corrugated sheet metal to block RF. I'd got about one bar on my own phone.

Jake marched outside, followed by the rest of us. Within twenty seconds of stepping outside, his phone binged, and Jake got busy with his thumb.

"She's gone off with Uncle Peter for a talk. In his car. She says they're driving to his home and not to worry. It's not far, and she'll be back for the second set."

"Why drive home?" I asked. "I mean, why go anywhere. They could just as easily talk here, in the car park."

"I don't know. She doesn't say."

"But she says 'don't worry'?"

"Yes."

"And you trust that?"

"I suppose so. I mean, he's her uncle."

So naïve, Jake. Yeah, he was her uncle. Family. But sometimes, family was the thing you shouldn't trust. However, I wasn't going to be the one to burst his bubble and fill his heart with dread. Call me a coward — I preferred the term 'realistic optimist'. For now, I was willing myself to believe the best of Uncle Peter despite his recent ill-conceived plotting.

So we left it there. Everyone else turned to go back inside.

"I'll catch you up, guys. I think I'll take a short walk in the fresh air."

*

I'D NOT GONE far when I heard footsteps on the cobbles.

"Would you mind if I joined you, Kai?'

"It's a free country, Dom. And…yes, I'd enjoy your company."

I paused to let her catch up. We fell into step and strolled in easy silence. Dom broke it first.

"A pound for your thoughts…"

"The going rate is a penny. I don't think mine are worth half that though."

"So, a penny, then. And they are worth far more."

Crazy thoughts. Dom. Lotte. Jake. Jamie. Alina. Neale.

Well, that was threepence at my rates.

"Why does everything have to be about sex, Dom?"

"What?"

"Why does everything have to be about sex?"

"Does it?"

"Don't play word games," I answered. "Please. I planned this as a simple Germany tour by an ordinary blues band. But it's got all twisted up. Everywhere you look, there's hormones sizzling."

I could have done with some sizzling just then. It was October, and it was fucking freezing 'cause we'd left the gig in just our stage clothes.

"Yours, too, I think."

"What?" It took me a moment to make the connection. "No. Not me. I don't do that stuff."

She stared right back at me. "Have you forgotten Berlin so quickly?"

"Klara? She was fun. I liked her a lot, but we didn't fuck or anything. We were two adults horsing around."

"I didn't mean Klara. I think you know who I meant. He would be good for you. If you dare to let yourself be yourself."

"I'm happy with who I am."

"Who are you, Kai?"

"Why do you care?" I shot back.

"You don't have to sound so angry. I am your friend. I care for you because that is what people do."

I didn't say anything. Then her brow furrowed.

"That is not your experience, is it?" she said. "What happened to you?"

I should have stonewalled her. But she wasn't someone you could stonewall, not forever. And maybe, just maybe, I wanted to tell someone who wasn't my brother.

"I'm Kai."

It was a beginning.

"I wasn't always Kai, but that person lived a long time ago. That person...was loved, very much, by their mother. But then...she...the mother...went away."

"She died?"

"*Stop*! I never said that...*that* word."

Anger rose.

"She didn't want to leave me. Any of us."

"Leave Jamie, you mean?"

"Yes. And Dad. Why would anyone ever leave the people they love?"

"Perhaps she had no choice."

"That's not fair."

"Tell me about it."

Odd. Upset as I was, the rising intonation didn't seem right.

Almost as if…

"Please, tell me about it."

So I did. Condensed. Held at arm's length where it couldn't hurt. Dad going off the rails. Booze. Losing his job. Jamie and me — two lost teens. Spinning, diving. Crashing. Jamie following Dad down the neck of a bottle. I…

"And then Cassie showed up."

"Who was Cassie?"

"An old flame of Dad's, I think. Childhood sweetheart. She *saved* us."

"You sound bitter."

"Maybe I didn't want to be saved. At least, not by Cassie."

"And Jamie? Your Dad?"

"She made Dad…not happy, but healed. Mostly."

"That is good, isn't it?"

"But she wasn't Mum." I spat out the words. "And they were…" I couldn't say it.

"Lovers?"

"That wasn't the way I would have put it. They were noisy about it too."

Dom rolled her eyes, and my traitor mouth smiled. "They are just people. That is what people do."

"Not me. Not like that."

She ignored me. "He wasn't being disloyal. People grieve for what they have lost. Then they have to heal. Because they have their lives to live."

I heard an almost-sob, and through my own tears, I saw one of hers roll down her cheek.

"And that was when you chose a different path for

yourself?" she asked. "Or did that come later?"

"Later. The path to Kai was never that simple. But there was a moment. Jamie was a part of it. Some of the other kids, talking about me, loudly, so I could hear. About my looks, and about who would ever want to f—ever want *me*.

"And so, when I got home, Jamie saw straightaway that something was wrong, and I told him everything they'd said. And he just sat there and thought, and after a while, he said two things. "First, he said, 'Don't let them put you in one of their boxes'. "Then, he said, 'If you don't like the boxes on offer, *make* one that's just right for yourself'."

Dom laughed. But it was a dawn-is-breaking laugh, not cruel. "You called him your 'rock' the first time we spoke. I begin to see why."

"Yes. He is my rock. He has never let me down. He wasn't the only one who helped me on my journey to Kai, but he was the first. The first kind words."

"And after that?"

Now it was my turn to chuckle through tears. "A lot of looking at boxes. Trying some too. But not too many because there were exams looming, and good GCSEs were one way out of Marden Combe."

"You did okay?"

"Sort of. My school reports called me bright but not academic. Anyway, I fucked around for a year, trapped into A levels that bored me shitless. Then I realised I wanted to do music, not some soulless office job, and I quit school to study it. Which led to—"

"The Clayton Paul Blues Band. Right."

"I'm sorry, Dom. I didn't mean to dump my whole life story on you with repeats. But you did ask."

She was smiling, but her lip was quivering too.

"It is all right," she said, her voice soft. "It is all right. Come to me."

And we stood there, embracing on a lonely street in a suburb of Prague on a cold October night, me in my sweat-frosty Keith Moon T-shirt and Dom in her pinstripe and fedora. She was warm and soft, and my tears streamed down onto her shoulder.

"Let it go, Kai." And one of her tears plinked warm onto my neck. "Let it go and learn to live because the future is such an empty place alone."

"Would you be…" I began, but then I stopped.

"I am on a different journey. You have your own friends to walk with you. Some you have known for a while, and some you have only just met."

"Hmm?"

She pushed me away, not roughly, but firmly. Fuck, it was cold all of a sudden.

"Hear me, Kai! Don't be so bloody obtuse. You and Lars. You click. Don't you dare walk away. Don't you fucking dare."

*

THERE WAS NO sign of Lotte when we got back. Jake stood by the front door, scanning the street for any cars. If he even noticed Dom and me huddling together when we appeared, he said nothing.

We warmed ourselves in the bar with a glass of *svařák*, which is the local mulled wine. It sparkled outwards to my fingers and toes, defrosting them instantly. By English standards, it was winter, and I'd gone out in my sweaty drummer T-shirt. What had I been thinking? Damn, I'd been lucky Dom had been with me.

Jake appeared. "She's still not here. I've got to go and look for her."

"What?" I asked.

"I've got to go look for her. I can't just sit here and do nothing."

I started to say something, but Dom got in first.

"Jake. Tell us what you are worried about."

"She should be here. That's what I'm worried about."

"Yes, she should. But there are good reasons why she might not be. She said not to worry, so why are you worrying? People are late. Traffic, usually. Or she hasn't noticed the time. We don't go hunting for someone every time they are five minutes late. We would never get anything done. Besides, where would you go?"

"To Uncle Peter's house."

"Do you know where it is?"

"Uh…"

"So, you can't find it. And even if you could, she won't be there. She will be on the road, in Uncle Peter's car, heading back here while you are getting lost in Prague."

"But…"

"But we have a show to put on. The audience was quite hard to win over. But we did it."

"You did it," Jake said.

"And you all helped by staying calm while I talked to them. We owe them, and we honour that debt by playing a second set that is at least as good as the first."

"I suppose so…"

"Are you all with me, guys?"

"Yes," we all answered in our best marine corps sir-yes-sir style.

"Then let us go."

*

BUT JAKE WASN'T on board, his head somewhere else. His rhythm work was passable, and then he missed his entry on his first solo. He recovered, but it jarred. Then he concluded with a weird fretboard run that left everything hanging, unresolved.

That brought Dom in on the wrong note, and though she corrected herself within a bar, no one could miss the fluff. The audience applause at the end was distinctly muted. Nobody was fooled by Dom's quip about 'free-form jazz chording'.

So, we were on an uphill grade for the next couple of songs while Jake got his act together. I couldn't speak for the others, but I was too tense, waiting for the next glitch.

Four songs in, Jake found his groove and played guitar that I could honestly call blistering.

Next after that, Dom called out, "'Three Hundred Pounds, guys'." It wasn't supposed to be in the set, but we had sound-checked with it. I hoped Pavel would roll with it—Dom had decided it was time to prowl.

Time for Dom to prowl; time for Dom to flirt. We were supposed to be professional when Dom roamed and keep eyes front, but she was good to watch. I took the beat down, nice and easy while I watched her, making bets with myself on whom she'd pick. Another Karin, perhaps? But tonight, she only flirted with the guys. Perhaps she'd checked out on attitudes in Prague.

Perhaps she was just being cautious.

One of these days, she was going to dislodge some old geezer's hairpiece and cause a riot, but not tonight. She played it to perfection and even found someone who could sing the hook line in tune.

Then back she strode. For one awful, heart-stopping moment, I thought she was going to fluff getting back on stage again. The strength in her arms faded and an undignified flounder looked inevitable. Somehow, she turned it into a floor roll, finishing up propped on her elbows, facing the audience. I pictured a huge, saucy grin on her face as she crooned the hook line, deep and sexy.

Where did you learn your tricks, Dom? How many ships have foundered on your rocks?

And she'd done it in suit, shirt, and tie, not a glimpse of flesh showing.

*

I DIDN'T SPOT the moment when Lotte reappeared.

What I spotted was the moment when Jake noticed Lotte because he missed his cue. Again. When I glanced up, his mouth was hanging open, and I turned to where his head was pointing. Lotte stood right there, an odd expression on her face, but I wasn't going to miss my cues…

…And Neale came in on fiddle to cover for Jake's statue moment. Okay, we were rockin', even if Pavel had been a little late getting the level up. It didn't matter too much by then, as the audience was back on our side. We were on the home straight of the last three numbers.

For Jake was playing as if his heart was set to burst, with a chemistry that was born to the moment, notes now cascading off the fretboard like fireworks, hauling back, sonic embers lost, dying in the night, a poignant underpinning of Dom's closing high-C heartbreak howl.

Dom's fedora was gone. The tie had come off, too, and her shirt was at three buttons undone. Beads of sweat glistened like diamonds on her cheeks in the spotlights, testaments to the intensity of the show closer. Her hair tumbled medusa-wild as she leaned on the mic stand, letting the applause swirl round her.

"Thank you, Prague. Thank you, Crossroads Blues and Jazz Club."

Then Uncle Peter appeared from nowhere, striding onto the stage, thanking us in English and Czech, hands raised high over his head, clapping.

"Let us hear it for the band," he called and conjured with the audience volume one last time. "Thank you, Dom. Thank you, guys."

We took our bows and were happy enough that there was no call for an encore. Happy to troop past the fairy-tale castle, job done, and into the calm and cool of the backstage.

"Thanks," I told Dom. "Thanks for getting us all through that."

"What else could I do?"

Put like that, nothing. But Dom had stopped listening, closing her eyes and leaning back against the wall. She looked tired but more than gig tired. Tour tired. The driving was taking it out of all of us, but Dom and Neale were taking the brunt of it.

Which was when the backstage door burst open, and Lotte

stormed in, closely followed by…Lotte?

No. Bettine. Lotte's mother—sprung from a busted pentacle and pursued by Lotte—made a beeline for Jake, trailing smoke and sulphur.

"You bastard. You fucked my daughter for the last time! I'll cut off your dick!"

She was bloody terrifying in her rage, and Jake saw doom approaching too late to run. He mewled, a sad little squawk of hopelessness, and hugged his guitar as her arm swung and slapped hard on his cheek.

"Bettine! No!" yelled Peter, following.

Jake flew backwards and collided with the sofa, which saved him from a cracked skull. His beloved Strat slid out of his grasp towards the floor. I got to it just in time, save for the *tiniest* dink. I wasn't callous; my priorities were fine—this was what musicians did for one another.

Bettine raised her arm for the death blow, but Lotte finally caught up. She pushed past and plastered herself atop Jake, her knee catching poor Jake in the groin. His gasp of pain proved he was still alive.

Lotte moved her leg but otherwise continued to press him down. His moans grew faint; I suspected Jake might not be able to breathe.

"I won't let her kill you," Lotte declared.

Or cut your cock off either. Hopefully that had been an idle threat…

'Her' hovered above them both, looking for a clear shot at Jake.

"Bettine! Leave him alone. You promised." Peter lumbered

forward, out of breath.

"Oh, fuck off, little brother. Go play outside," she responded.

"You will not kill this young man," Peter said. "Not today. Not ever, I hope. I hope, one day, you will even talk as friends."

Bettine snarled, still looking for an opening, but Peter kept talking.

"Lotte is my niece and my god-daughter, and I understand her better than you do. She has grown up. She is making her own decisions now. You must let her live her life, with her friends. And when she chooses a young man to love, you must respect her choice."

"But he is a rapist. He will get her pregnant. And then, he will run away."

"*Are* you pregnant, Lotte?"

Lotte raised herself a little—Jake gulped oxygen—and looked back over her shoulder. "Fuck, no! Does she think I'm too stupid to take a pill?"

Less than tactful in the light of what Neale had told me about Bettine's own story.

But then, Lotte pushed herself away from Jake and faced her mother. If Bettine had been terrifying in her rage, her daughter transformed that fury, turning it into defiant adamant, against which Bettine's anger beat powerlessly. Unable to dominate, Bettine took a pace back.

Lotte stepped forward into the space. "Bettine, I'm going to England with Jake. I told you in my letter. I told you again at Uncle Peter's. I thought you'd accepted that. So, I agreed you could come and meet him. But now…you've attacked the man I love.

You've tried to protect me from your old mistakes—not mine—but you ended up trying to control me. You lied to me and betrayed me. This is where it ends. I will not be controlled by you. Do not ever attempt to see me again."

Shit! Never? Lotte hated her mother that much? I didn't get on with my dad too well since Cassie, but to never want to see him again?

Bettine's anger crumpled in the space of a second. She sank to her knees, her face buried in her hands, and began to sob.

"Aber… aber…ich liebe dich, Lotte. Wie kannst du mich zurückweisen?"

That's not love, Bettine. It's control. And your daughter isn't rejecting you; she's leading her own life. Your tears are sham. Lotte's not fooled by your 'love'. Look at her face.

"Uncle Peter?"

"Yes, Lotte."

"Can you take her home?"

"I can do that. What will you do?"

"I don't know Prague. Can you find us a motel?"

"I know a hotel near the station that may have rooms. I will call a taxi."

Then Neale spoke up. "I thought you had arranged rooms for us to stay—with your friends from the blues club."

Peter shook his head. "Not anymore."

"Why not?"

Peter said nothing, but his shoulders drooped in shame.

"Because he's been caught in a lie," Jamie explained. "He's lost the trust and the friendship of these people."

"I wanted to help Lotte. And Jake too. I wanted to see if I

could make things better between Lotte and Bettine, so I called her up"—he gestured at the tear-stained Bettine—"and she suggested—"

"Don't lie, Peter," Bettine interrupted. "You suggested the plan."

"Yes," he sighed. "But not this…this brawl. That was not my plan. Jamie is right. I did lie to the band. And then they didn't keep quiet as they'd been paid to do. I had to tell more lies. My reputation is destroyed. Perhaps the club will forgive me. But I think they will find a new promoter."

"So what do we do?" asked Neale.

"I will try to find you a hotel. And I will call taxis if you need."

"We'll need at least one taxi," Lotte agreed. "There are too many to fit in the van."

"You are not coming to stay…" Peter began, then realised the tactlessness of what he had said. "No, of course not. I will look after Bettine. Give me a few minutes."

*

IN THE END, it was two taxis. Peter found rooms in three separate hotels. Lotte and Jake went off in the first taxi. Then Jamie and I had an argument about the van and security.

"We need to keep watch over the gear," I insisted. "I'll sleep in the van."

"Like fuck, you will," he argued. "You've already spent too many nights in there. I'll do it. Or do you think I'll just leave it on the street and sleep in the hotel?"

Yes. Despite everything, I did think just that. What kind of a control freak was I becoming?

"No, Jamie. It's not that."

"Then what is it? Do you think you have something to prove? That you can take anything I can take? That you're harder than big brother?"

I shook my head.

"No, Kai, that's right." His voice held a gentleness I'd rarely heard. "You've got nothing to prove. You've been fantastic on this tour. You've organised us, cajoled us, led us by your example. But you're wearing yourself out, and it's time you let the rest of us take on the load. This is something I'm going to do. Understood?"

Damn. He'd outmanoeuvred me.

"Okay. I'll do it your way."

"Good. And there is something only you can do. Help Dom. She's been working hard too. She's pretty shattered. You're the best person to help her right now."

I'd not given a thought to Dom, still leaning against the wall. She'd not spoken a word since coming off stage and through Bettine's little drama, not that I could remember. That wasn't like her. I'd have expected her to be the peacemaker.

But she'd heard Jamie and me and struggled back to alertness, blinking rapidly to stop her eyes closing again. "Yes. That would be good. Help me, Kai. I am too tired."

Still, Dom did muck in as we loaded the van, though Jamie made sure she didn't do any heavy lifting. The first taxi arrived while we were still packing, so we sent Lotte and Jake off to their hotel.

Neale and Jamie stayed with us until the second taxi came. Dom stumbled as she climbed in but caught herself. As we pulled away, I could see Neale and Jamie in the van, both looking anxious. After a few moments, the van started up and followed us as far as the first intersection, then disappeared off to the left.

At the Hotel Splendide, I paid the taxi driver, who was happy to take euros in cash. He unloaded Dom's bag and mine from the boot, carried them as far as the lobby, and dumped them on the floor. I struggled to wake Dom, but the driver helped me get her out of the car and walk her into the lobby. I had no idea what the Czech was for thank you, but he smiled at my English and left us. I'd obviously been ripped off on the euros.

Behind the façade, the Hotel Splendide was shabby, with faint echoes of grandeur. A surly clerk sat at the reception desk, his breath foul with the odour of stale cigarettes and fingers stained with nicotine. Behind him, a portable television was tuned into some sort of talent show, currently featuring a trio of girl singers dressed mostly in sequins. The lowered volume didn't do enough to hide that they couldn't hold a tune. The clerk didn't seem to mind, though, because—sequins notwithstanding—plenty of skin was visible.

And this hotel was full? But it was a *dive*. How bad could the others have been? Or were they out of Peter's budget? He'd paid for the hotels, but honouring our pledge to the audience, he'd not paid us for the gig.

As the hotel didn't have a lift, I sat Dom on a grubby sofa, carried the bags up to the landing of the first floor, and came back for her. I got her up the next two flights and into the room, where she managed to stumble over to the bed and tumble onto it. Then I returned for the bags, which hadn't been stolen in the interim.

The room, when I finally got to look it over, was clean

enough. And warm.

Dom sat up on the bed, peeling off her clothes. Just as well, I decided — she'd been more than a bit sweaty.

"Are you feeling better?" I asked.

"Help me, Kai."

I looked more closely. She was struggling with the buttons of her blouse and couldn't undo them, her fingers just not working.

"Let me do that for you."

She looked blank.

"*Je t'aiderai, Dominique.* I will help you."

I moved my hands slowly, keeping them where she could see them, and popped the buttons one by one.

"I'm going to remove your blouse, okay?" I repeated it in French because she didn't seem to understand English. Was she drugged? I tried to remember the stories I'd heard about date rape and the drugs involved. Didn't they also cause loss of coordination?

"*Oui,*" she agreed, and I slid the blouse off over her arms.

I rummaged in Dom's bag and found her pyjamas — a thick, warm T-shirt-and-pants set. I held them out to her.

She looked up, and I was relieved to see she was more awake and alert.

"Thank you," she said. "Leave them on the bed, please. I want to take a shower."

"Will you be all right? I mean, you were acting pretty tired back then."

"I am fine. No, not fine, but a shower and a warm bed and a good sleep will do most of what can be done."

Most of what can be done?

But then she was up off the bed—too quickly, for she staggered a little.

"Let me take your arm," she said.

I helped her into the bathroom and sat her on the toilet while I sorted out the controls. Whatever the hotel's other faults, the shower ran comfortably hot. When I turned back, Dom was struggling with her bra.

"Let me help you," I offered.

"*Oui.*"

My own T-shirt was getting splashed. Between this and the Berlin campsite, I was about to run out of clean, dry clothes. Fuck it. My T-shirt came off and then everything else.

I placed my clothes in a neat pile just outside the door, then helped Dom into the shower, and tried to recapture the way I'd felt in the sauna in Berlin. It helped.

Dom held tight to the shower rail, while I bathed her from head to foot. It was about as sexual as a nurse handling a patient, which was to say not at all. And that was probably exactly how she'd viewed me, when I'd gotten drunk as a skunk after the gig in Berlin.

When she was done, I towelled her dry and led her back to the bed, where I helped her into T-shirt and pants. I tucked her into bed and returned to the bathroom to finish my own shower.

I stood a long while under the spray, while my mind processed what I'd seen—perhaps a dozen tiny scars, some covered by make-up, others artfully concealed where they'd never be seen, save in the intimacy of a bedroom or a shower. There was no doubt in my mind that, at some time, Dominique had received considerable and excellent—which meant expensive—cosmetic surgery.

She was asleep when I returned, the duvet pulled up to her chin, her face relaxed and peaceful. So I put my own pyjamas on and climbed in next to her. I'd left the bathroom light on, a sliver of light shining through the almost-closed door. The light let me see the contours of her cheeks, the line of her nose, a wisp of hair that lay across her face. Carefully, so as not to disturb her, I sat up again and crossed my legs, like in school assemblies.

I sat there for long minutes, drinking in her serene beauty. I didn't want to move, didn't want that moment to stop. I might have sat there all night, watching her as new parents watch over their day-old child.

I was back in the sauna, in that moment of transcendence where fleshly desire had been set aside, each human being seen as their unique self. Unique, she lay sleeping, wrapped in her own glorious identity. I rested motionless, unconscious of any notion of my own self, absorbed in Dom.

Transcendence was ever fragile—that wisp of hair fluttered as she exhaled, settled against her cheek, which twitched, twitched again.

I dared to reach out and gently smooth the stray hair back into place. The twitching stopped, and I let myself stroke her hair, straightening more strands, blessed by its softness beneath my hand.

Enough. I didn't wish to wake her. She wasn't some plaything or pet. She was tired and needed rest. Yet I dared lean over to place the softest of kisses upon her brow. She did not stir.

"Sleep well, sweet friend."

I lay down then, turning my back on the light and Dom. Tiredness flooded over me. I slept.

Chapter Nineteen

Thursday, October 6, 2016

Arrival in Munich — The Jazzkeller

IF I DREAMED, none disturbed me. When I awoke, the bed was empty beside me, and pale light struggled through the curtains into the room.

"Dom?"

No answer.

"Dom?" — louder.

"I am in here."

Bathroom. Door closed. Washing sounds.

"What's the time?" I called.

"Eight o'clock. Time to get up. If we are quick, there is breakfast downstairs. I have had a text from Neale. They will meet us at eight forty-five. Jake and Lotte are making their own way to the station to catch the train to München."

She emerged from the bathroom dressed for the new day.

"Have I got time for a shower?"

"Your choice. Breakfast or shower. Not both. And only if you actually get out of bed."

"Very funny, dear friend. The night has performed wonders on you."

She laughed and twitched the duvet off the bed and onto the floor. "Indeed, you have, O faithful knight."

"Hey, it's cold."

"Don't be a chicken. Be quick; the shower is lovely and hot. I will drink coffee downstairs and wait for you. The longer you take, the fewer the croissants I will leave."

"Well, you've certainly perked up!"

Her smile vanished. "Yes, I am sorry I caused you trouble."

"No. No trouble. You've been pushing yourself. You told *me* to be careful. You be careful too. And remember, I'll always look after you if you let me."

I thought I'd spoken too much. Dom looked serious for a moment, then nodded.

"I understand. You are truly faithful. I wish…" She paused.

"What?"

"Many things. I do not think any of them will happen. Do not worry. But hurry, now. Get your shower. Come to me downstairs."

*

THE CLOCK SHOWED eight forty-five, but there was no sign of Neale and Jamie. So, we sat, bill paid, bags at our feet, finishing off the last fragments of croissant and jam, sipping coffee at leisure.

"I wasn't asleep last night, Kai. At least, not completely."

"Oh."

"I felt you stroking my hair."

"Straightened it. That was all."

"And the kiss?"

"You felt that?"

"No. Call it a lucky guess."

"Ah."

"I felt the love. I felt you guarding me."

"Yes. That's how it was."

"Yesterday was a hard day. I cannot always be strong. Thank you for being my strength, when I needed it."

"But you're better now?"

"Yes."

The comforting lie.

Why can you not be open with me, Dom? Have I not bared my own soul to you? What will it take for you to do the same to me?

"You seemed so…drained."

"Yes. It is passed. There is no need to speak of it anymore. But I wanted to thank you."

"That's okay."

"There is one other thing."

"Yes?"

"You…desire me."

I nodded. There didn't seem a lot of point in denying it. "Yes."

And now I'd said it too. It was out in the open.

"Do you plan to do something about it? Or are you going to let the swan glide past?"

"Is that a Belgian idiom?"

"It is a Dom idiom. Now, answer the question."

"That depends on the swan, surely."

"The swan is within your reach."

"I would have hoped for more enthusiasm from the swan."

"The swan is mute. It needs no words."

"Too clever, Dom. Are you sure you're Belgian?"

"My father was English. Again, you dodge. You need to make some decisions. One day—maybe sooner, maybe later—we all run out of time."

My heart's desire—I just had to say a word…

And heavy footsteps came towards us with a cheery greeting from Jamie.

"Morning, Dom. Morning, Kai. Sleep well? Looks like it. Hey, you look sprightly, Dom, after last night. You were pretty wasted—what was that all about?"

"Just tired. But I'm fine now."

"If you say so. Anyway, we're outside, ready to go. Nothing stolen. But that van is fucking freezing. I don't know how you managed it with your cheap sleeping bags, but I threw on a couple of extra layers, and it was okay."

Dom gave me a look that said *I'm not letting you off the hook.* And I didn't know whether to kill Jamie or to thank him.

*

BEHIND THE WHEEL, Neale was looking good too. I didn't think any of us had actually slept more than six hours. But as my dad would say, "You can do that sort of thing when you're young."

Still, Neale was an old guy. At least, from where I was standing, he was an old guy. Witness his behaviour around Bettine in the fuse cupboard. Shit! That was almost a whole week ago. So much water under the bridge already.

With a swan, gliding downstream…

"Ah, and look at the two of yez. Slept the sleep of the sinless, yeh have."

I laughed. "Top 'o the morning to you, too, Neale. You look ready to drive us to the moon."

Neale grinned but then turned earnest. "I'm okay. I'm doing my insulin properly. I'll get you all to Munich in one piece. The moon though? I've always wanted to go there. But they'll have to sort out the problem with the bars first."

"Huh?"

"There's no atmosphere."

"Argh! That's awful."

"Ach. Ye've no sense of humour, yez English. Get in, will yeh."

"And stop the cod-Irish accent," I said, joking. "You're just putting it on for effect."

He didn't answer.

I checked Dom. A ride in the front seat would do her good. "Is it my turn in the back?"

"Over ye go…"

And thus we travelled—out through the suburbs of Prague and on to the E50 and the long, long road to München. Two hundred plus miles. Three hundred and fifty kilometres. Take your pick. The wheels on the bus go round and round…

An hour and half later, we took ten minutes to stretch our legs, change drivers, and set off again. The only consolation was that this was the last long haul until the long drive back at the end of the tour. We'd go from München back up to Berlin in two easy stages with a gig along the way.

Highlights of the journey were few. A shabby road sign marked the border crossing into Germany. The Danube crossing, and what we saw of Regensburg, was picturesque. I wondered if we'd get some time when we came back to Regensburg on Friday to actually walk around the town a bit. At that moment, it felt like I'd seen nothing but the inside of the van, a hotel room, and a community hall since forever. It counted for nothing, the two days we'd spent bumming around Berlin with Jürgen, Annika, Alina…

Lars.

I took my phone out south of Regensburg and started to write an email to Lars. Conscience had been nagging away all through the long miles. Dom had made it clear that she was open to…something. My desire? But what was that? A one-night stand—the very thing I'd berated Jamie for? Did I want a simple physical relationship? If 'simple' was the right word when Dom was involved. And…mixed signals. She'd also told me Lars and I were made for each other.

I found my thoughts bounding all over the place, but mostly to a café and to a museum, and to a curly-haired half-Dane/half-German guy five years my senior. Lars, in whose company I'd been rapt over a couple of days and more and from whom I'd fled when he'd said, "Don't disappear from my life, Kai. Please, don't be a stranger. *Tschüss.*"

I'd tapped out a sentence. It had the word 'sorry' in it, but the rest of it didn't make any sense, neither in English nor when I deleted it and tried to say the same thing in German. Sorry I'd run away? Sorry I'd offended him? You said sorry if you'd do something different next time — if there was a next time — and if you could figure out what you'd do different that wasn't worse or scarier. Or both.

Will I see you on Saturday?

No. Try: *Will you be at the gig on Saturday?*

But he'd said he would be. And if he'd changed his mind, did I really want to know?

Missing you — was I? Deleted, just in case.

I needed something safe. Last night's gig, I suppose. In ninety-two characters: *Hostile crowd. Dirty work at the crossroads. Dom turned them round. Slept with her later.*

No. I wouldn't have written that. Never.

Why do you love me? I don't deserve you.

I nearly hit send on that one, but whatever he'd meant, he'd never used the L-word. So I scrapped the first bit and decided to translate the second part into German. That was the right language, surely.

Bugger. What was 'to deserve' in German? *Verdienen.* But didn't that also mean 'to earn'? I didn't want to say 'I don't earn you.' He'd frown and wonder what kind of a stupid idiot I was. Wrong tack. Start again from scratch with a positive. Something I *do* want… Maybe: '*Verstehen*'. I want to understand you. So stop pissing around, Kai, and get the first bit down…

Ich will dich

My very best German for Lars.

"Kai…"

Delete.

I looked up at Dom, watching me.

"Are you going to send something?"

"I was just browsing Regensburg." I locked my phone and put it in my pocket.

"Yes. It is very pretty. It is better to watch the real thing though."

"Fair point. Did you discuss with Neale when we'd take a break? I'm feeling hungry."

"There's a service station soon. We'll be in Munich before the light goes, don't worry. Oh, and one other thing; have you found our accommodation for tonight?"

"I've found two possibles. I'm waiting to hear back from them."

Which was sort of true. I hadn't actually sent the emails that I was waiting to hear the replies to. I'd been off in messed-up-head-land. I took out my phone again and unlocked it, tilting so Dom couldn't see. Send/Receive All.

"No replies yet."

Well, there wouldn't be. There they went: Three email(s) sent.

Three?

Shitshitshit.

I've had a lot of practice keeping my emotions off my face. I didn't think it'd deserted me.

"Are you all right, Kai? You look a little pale."

Well, bugger that for a hypothesis.

"It's nothing. I…it…it's a bit surprising I've not heard. If we can stop soon, I'd like to call them, to make sure they've got my messages. It's too noisy in the van."

*

WHEN WE STOPPED at the service station, I called the hotels. A good, old-fashioned phone call. Happily, one of them did have the rooms we needed at a decent rate. I hadn't learned Bavarian German in school, and the mental exercise was a welcome distraction. A distraction from what? From worrying what Lars was going to think of the not-deleted email I'd sent — and what he might say in return. And I had sent it, incomplete and unsigned. I checked what I'd actually written, and it was a textbook example of how German word order can utterly torpedo an innocent remark. *Ich will dich…*

I want you.

At least, that was the literal meaning. In practice. Though, the way Germans use it…

I want to fuck you.

Unambiguous. He'd made it bell-clear he was after my mind. My sparkling wit, my sense of humour, for God's sake. I'd run away from the best offer I'd ever had. And now, out of the blue, I'd told him: *I want to fuck you.* No fine nuance there. Well done, Kai.

We rolled off the autobahn and joined the Munich road network. After Berlin, we were all braced for another endless traffic jam. We did encounter a couple of hold-ups, but nothing caused us more than a ten-minute delay.

Another town, another club. The *Jazzkeller.* The Jazz Cellar. Even Jamie could work that one out, once he saw it written out. I'd been calling it the 'Yazz-keller', of course. It had once been some sort of warehouse, I guessed. There'd been a cellar, even, but someone had ripped out the upper floor, creating a cathedral-like space. A low stage occupied one end, and at the other, a bar. Rows of long benches neatly packed the floor space.

Neale nodded, approving. "It's a proper Bierkeller, this." He pointed to the huge beer glasses in evidence around the hall. "How big d'ye think those are?"

"A couple of litres?" I guessed.

"What's that in fuckin' pints?"

"Three and a half, I think. Were you planning to order one?"

His eyes brightened at that, but then he frowned.

"Ach, I'm fuckin' driving. Not a bloody drop for me, then, yeh bloody spoilsport."

"I could drive…"

Why did I say that? Some sort of quixotic impulse to let Neale relax, I supposed.

"Ach, is there anything Kai the Wonder cannot do?"

He cackled. Then: "Drive my bloody van, that's what. Over my dead body. Over my fuckin' dead body will you drive that van. Not until y've got a proper licence."

I must have looked offended because he put his arm around my shoulder and breathed in my face.

"Fer Chrissake, lighten up, Kai. Y'need to let y'hair down. Get laid. Y'still a virgin?"

"None of your fucking business, Neale. Just as your own sexual antics are none of my business. You don't judge me; I don't judge you. Happy to keep it that way?"

"Oh, sure I am."

He changed the subject. "So, are you going to get one of

them big steins of beer and drink the lot?"

"Not before I play drums, no way. And not after, or I'll be pissing all night."

That set him off cackling again.

"Oh, and don't call them steins. Only tourists call them that. You ask for *eine Mass Bier, bitte*—a mass, a 'measure', of beer, please. And I remember now; they're designed for just a litre but bigger because there has to be room for the head. Munich has strict laws about that kind of thing."

"A mass of beer? Then I can tell the priest that I partook of mass while in Germany, and perhaps he'll reduce my penance—"

"Penance? I hadn't really thought of you as a devout Catholic, Neale. Do you do confession, then?"

"And what would a God-fearing soul like myself have to confess, Kai?" He winked. "None of your fuckin' business, just like we agreed."

Just banter. I winked back.

*

MOST OF THE benches in the *Jazzkeller* had been filled by eight. A friendly crowd, enjoying their beer, listening to the music on the sound system. When we'd first arrived, they'd been playing what Neale parochially referred to as 'oompah music' to a tiny clientele. An hour later, when we'd set up the gear, the manager had given the signal for us to do the soundcheck. Soundcheck done, the sound system had come back on, now playing bland American rock.

The audience had grown steadily in that hour or so, and there wasn't a single empty table. I guess there'd been a shift change because there were a lot more waiters around. Everyone carried armfuls of beer, never less than four or five and occasionally eight or ten. I said waiters…

"Bloody hell, Kai, they don't dress like that in the Barrel Organ."

"So why am I now — your partner-in-crime, Neale? Discussing the dirndl-clad waitresses in a far-off land?"

"A dirndl, you call it?"

"A traditional German costume."

"D'you think I could persuade Magda to wear one?"

Magda was, I presumed, one of the barmaids in the Barrel Organ.

"Who's Magda, then? Your sweetheart?"

"Ach, no. But she's got the tits for it."

"That doesn't particularly help. Another clue?"

He indicated 'short' with a gesture of his hand.

Okay, so now I knew who Magda was. "Ah, the landlady herself. I think you'll find she's Polish, and they don't wear the dirndl."

"But she'd look bloody good in one. She's got the —"

"Yes, you already said. I'll tell her you said so."

"If there's any telling to be done, I'll do it myself, thank you very much. I'm old enough to do me own telling and any other services that might be required. All I said was that —"

We were interrupted at that moment by the sound system switching back to oompah music. But not just any oompah music. This was 'Ein Prosit der Gemütlichkeit', a song that is special in Munich and across Bavaria. Everyone stood up, raised their steins, their *Mass*, high, and started singing, "Ein Prosit…". Neale and me included. And Jamie and Dom. Very Bavarian. Very jolly.

We sang it twice. That made it ten times already.

"Getting to know the words, Neale?"

They weren't difficult. Just '*Ein Prosit, ein Prosit der Gemüt-lichkeit*', sung twice, with the second- time melody a minor variation on the first.

"I know the fucking words, Kai. It's a bloody earworm, and it's going to haunt me fucking dreams for days. And I could play the tune blindfold with one arm behind me back."

"We may have to."

He didn't say anything. Nor did I. There was an elephant in the room. A seriously large pachyderm.

Yeah, the gear was on stage, ready to go. Yeah, there was a good audience, drinking and waiting to be entertained. There was just one problem.

No Jake and no Lotte.

Eight-o-fucking-clock, and we don't have a guitarist.

Not a peep. We'd all tried calling them. Straight to voicemail, every time. They weren't connected to the network.

They weren't lost. They weren't dead. At least, we didn't think so. We knew exactly what the problem was. We had internet — this wasn't the twentieth century. There'd been a derailment on the line. A goods train, nobody hurt. But the line was blocked, and the train from Prague was on the wrong side of the blockage.

And then, about an hour ago, we'd had a text from Lotte.

Waiting for bus. DB says one hour for buses to get here. Then one hour to get to München.

DB? It took me a moment. Deutsche Bahn. The train company. So, two hours. Plus, however long it took to get from the central station to here. Say half an hour by taxi. We were going to have to play at least half our first set without a guitarist.

Well, unless…

We had Neale, who, though not currently the possessor of a guitar, was a guitarist—by his own admission at our first meeting in the famed Barrel Organ. Not just any guitarist, but Jake's former guitar teacher to boot. And we had Jake's guitar. So, we could have guitar. Or we could have fiddle. Just not both together. There'd been some frantic working out what we absolutely had to have guitar on, some scribbling of chords. For everything else, we'd manage.

We hoped.

Quarter to eight, we'd had another text. The buses had arrived at the middle-of-nowhere station where the train had been diverted.

So now we were waiting for the text to tell us they were actually on a bus.

Why was nothing simple with this band, this tour?

*

TEN PAST NINE. On stage.

They were on their way. They got on the bus later than hoped, but the bus was making good time. Swings and roundabouts; 9:30 was a tad optimistic.

First up—'House of the Rising Sun'. Everybody knew it, including the band. It was about as safe as we could get. Just three of us on stage—Jamie, Neale, and me. Neale brought us in on the fiddle, nice and slow, and we added the bass and drums on the second verse.

A drunk sat at one of the tables near the front, head down on the table, a *Mass* of beer in front of her. Half way through instrumental verse two, she looked up, stared about wildly, and called out, "*Was… Wo bin ich?*"

'Where am I?' Good question, darling. She staggered to her feet, getting a laugh from the audience. And then she started to sing.

The German was terrible, neither scanning nor rhyming nor even making sense. It was the best we could cobble together — well, that Dom and I could cobble together — in the time we had. Dom straightened up, hapless drunk no longer, and now everyone could see the microphone, no longer half-hidden by the sleeves of her jacket.

Dom grinned as she sang and slipped in a shout of 'Hallo, München' at the end of her verse. Light-footed, she sprang up onto the stage to join us over a four-bar repeat of the last line.

Dom took us through five verses of 'Rising Sun' — now switching to English — with Neale, a fucking show-off git, improvising around her vocal line. Sometimes, show-off git was exactly what you needed though.

So where were Jake and Lotte? No idea. My phone vibrated in my pocket against my butt sometime in that first song, but there was no time to wrestle it out and read any message. We could only keep going.

Song two was a weird gamble. Neale plugged his violin into a long chain of guitar effects — compression, parametric equaliser, chorus and overdrive or some such — transforming the fiddle to a heavy blues electric guitar. Sort of.

The 'Sky is Crying' is what came out. A slow, tortured blues that let Dom do her best Etta James. Somehow, it worked, though it hurt my ears.

Two down, and number three was 'Blues with a Feeling'. Neale picked up Jake's Strat and strapped it on. So far, Neale had stayed with the fiddle, the guitar an unknown quantity, but we were letting him find his way with this one. Jamie would pick up most of the work on the bass, while Neale just played chords, plus whatever fills he felt confident throwing in. Dom sang it with soul bleeding.

Four. 'It Serves You Right to Suffer.' The old John Lee Hooker song brought back memories of Jake's painful rendition the night Clay quit the band. But tonight, Neale was in his element. Yeah, this *was* the guy who helped teach Jake to play guitar. This was blistering, paint-stripping power in slow blues. Dom picked up the vocal and prowled the stage. She drove down to the bottom of her vocal range, then flew high in a Daltrey-esque scream, into which Neale's guitar blended. Her voice dropped away, and Neale's solo teetered around the madness and the anguish of woman-treated-you-so-bad. Serves you right to suffer, yeah.

Five.

Five was 'I Come from the Blues'.

The opening chorus and first two verses took us down into the darkness. Neale played some eerie fiddle obbligato around Dom's vocals, and then we hit the first upbeat chorus.

> *Where did I come from? I come from the blues*
> *Where am I going? Wherever I choose*
> *Where is my hope, if not in my friends?*

Where is my future? Around the next bend.

So then, into verses three and four:

But I have a friend in these blues, set me free
There's Muddy, and Etta, all Howlin' for me
The pain doesn't go, but sometimes it fades.
The darkness recedes, there's a light in the shade.

The blues never leaves me, it's deep down inside
It laughs when I laugh, as it cried when I cried
The blues is the singer, and I am its song
I come from the blues; it survives when I'm gone.

And then Dom yelled "VERSE" as we were about to drop into the final chorus, and there was a godawful graunch as Jamie dive-bombed down the fretboard from an *A* to an *F* and Dom's singing:

And sometimes I wonder 'bout what might have been
If things had been diff'rent, what might I have seen
What lovers and friends, what highs and what lows?
I peer in the mirror and ask what it knows.

Totally improvised? Nothing *we've* rehearsed, at any rate.

Don't ask me that question, it seems to reply
You don't need to know, so don't ask me why
Just play what life deals you, the cards in your hand

Play the next blues song and sing with the band

And softly, "Take us out, guys," and Jamie got to play his *A* for the exit chorus.

And what was that about? Parked for later.

Six.

We didn't have a six. Not a proper six, at any rate. I looked at my watch, and it was 9:30. Where the fuck were they?

Neale took a moment to tune the fiddle. If this were a car, we'd be running on fumes because this wasn't blues. It was a con—a pure fiddle tune called 'Soldier's Joy', which Neale explained to the audience went back to the American Civil War. The title referred to the opium the soldiers used to take to deaden the pain of their wounds. The explanation was met with total silence.

"Ah, fuck it. Just listen to the tune."

Neale had taught Jamie a quick bassline, and I added a basic beat, doing my best to emulate a bodhrán. Three times through, though, and it was getting a little tedious. But Neale gave the nod, and he switched into '*Ein Prosit der Gemütlichkeit*', which baffled the audience for the first verse because they just weren't expecting it. Jamie's mangled German didn't help, but then, they got the second verse and…

Then we segued back into 'Soldier's Joy', and I caught sight of a little group of punters, arms straight lined by their sides, legs blurring and shoes clattering in faux-Riverdance style.

Oh God. What have we done?

The wheels were about to come off. We had no plan after this. From blues to Riverdance—what have we come to? Perhaps we should roll with it and become a folk-dance band. The dancers were enjoying it, at least, especially one black-haired girl, pogoing wildly, tresses whipping left and right...

"It's Lotte!" I called, on-mic, to the puzzlement of all.

Somehow, I avoid adding "We're saved," which we might not be because I couldn't see Jake. But then he appeared climbing up the steps onto the stage, where he grabbed his guitar.

Neale called, "C", which must be the key. But Jake had worked it out from watching Jamie's fingers on the bass. He was in with some choppy chords, and—bloody Norah—we had a band. By the skin of our teeth, we had a band.

And Dom was dancing like some crazy dervish. Somewhere, she'd found my tambourine which, thankfully, she was beating in sync with my snare.

*

WE SNAPPED BACK into blues so fast it should have taken our fingers off. The remaining half hour of the first set was an anticlimax, being a workmanlike blues and soul set. In that context, I should confess that we wrapped the set up with a rendition of '*Ein Prosit*'.

I could get to dislike that song.

We trotted off stage, looking for a table to sit at. Lotte danced over, and it was hugs all around. Warm, lingering hugs; even Jamie and Jake did hugs with only a hint of embarrassment. It had been a pretty lousy journey for Jake and Lotte, for all that they'd been together, supporting each other. I was pleased that Lotte felt like she was an integral part of the band, rather than a WAG added on.

But then, after a five-minute huddle with Dom, Lotte asked the band if she could join as a backing singer. And I opened my mouth without thinking.

"Lotte, you know there's more to being a backup than singing along with the melody?"

She looked hurt. "Yes, Dom said I'd have to learn to sing different lines."

"That's hard. Backing singers are often technically better singers than the lead vocalist. They have to adapt when the lead goes off script. Please don't be offended, but you've got a way to go."

"Yes. I know that. Dom says I've got good pitch."

"Yes, that is true," Dom said. "You know that, Kai. Lotte was singing with us at the *Campingplätz* near Berlin. You must remember. She picked up the melodies no trouble."

Hmm. I mostly remembered. I'd had a few drinks.

My butt twinged, reminding me of recent folly…

"So, I can learn to harmonise, I'm sure."

Dom stared at me. Everyone stared at me.

"Dammit! You're all looking at me like I'm Darth Vader, and I just killed Tinkerbell and Santa Claus. I'm just saying that it takes a lot of hard work to be a backing vocalist, and I'm not sure someone can just step up and do it…"

A long silence followed. I counted the number of times I'd just said 'just' and realised how defensive that sounded.

"Forget it, then. I'm sorry I asked." Lotte's voice broke, and a tear appeared, began to roll down her cheek. Angrily, she wiped it away. Jake put his arm around her, but she pushed him away.

"I am sorry," she said. "I promised myself I would not cry if any of you said no. I knew how much I wanted to do this, how much it would hurt if you said no. But I did not believe you would say no. Kai, I respect your decision, and I hope we can still be friends. I dared…I dreamed…"

Another tear. She stood, brushed the tear away, and turned to go. "I need a few minutes outside in the night air. Alone, Jake. I will return soon when…I am feeling better…"

On my left, Jake stared after Lotte. Next to him, Jamie rolled his eyes up to heaven and kept them there. Neale gazed into the oracle of his drink, shaking his head from side to side. Past the empty space…

Dom? I wasn't sure I wanted Dom to meet my gaze…

Dom shook her head at me. "You and I need to have a little walk together."

*

WE DIDN'T SEE Lotte when we left. She must have gone another way. By rights, there should have been a trail of hot tears burning craters into the pavement behind her.

"Oh, Kai."

"I really am Darth Vader, aren't I? And I did just kill Tinkerbell."

Dom raised her eyebrows. "Sometimes, you get too weird. But Lotte, she will get over it. She is strong."

"So this is about me. You want me to change my mind. I'll do it."

"That would be nice. But your heart and your head do not yet agree. You are doing it to please me. Or you are doing it to please Jake and the rest of the band."

I considered. "Yes. Those are still good reasons."

"Why did you say no though?"

"I didn't think I had."

"It certainly wasn't a yes. Or even a why-don't-we-give-you-a-try-out? Is she going to be perfect? Probably not."

"Still…she's not ready."

"None of us is ready. The four of you had two weeks' practice together before you came out. We've been together as a band one week. How can we possibly be ready?"

She was right. We'd lurched from near-disaster to near-disaster. Snatching victory, or sometimes just a stalemate, by the skin of our teeth.

"We've been lucky?" I asked her.

"Yes. You're all decent musicians. Good amateurs. And you are lucky."

I must have looked hurt.

"I don't mean to insult you, but it's true. Even pro bands practice solidly for months before a tour. We're still learning songs as we go. We have a good atmosphere at our gigs, but we're living on the edge of catastrophe. If you listen hard, you hear the weaknesses. We have not recorded our gigs, and they will live bright in our memories because of that, and they will never tarnish against reality."

"Are you saying we're no good? That we might as well let Lotte join because she's no worse than we are?" My voice was angry, and I did not want to be angry with Dom.

"No. That is not what I mean. Napoléon wanted his generals to be lucky, above all else. And you are lucky."

"It didn't help him at Waterloo…"

"No. One day, luck runs out for all of us…"

She paused, just a moment, then continued. "But we are

riding a stream of luck. Every gig is different. There are challenges, different challenges every night. And we overcome them."

"Yes," I whispered. "Yes, we do. But I wish…"

"What? That we could have just one ordinary gig? Where everything goes to plan?"

She knows my heart.

"Yes. That is what I wish."

"I promise you; it will not come true. Or if it does, you will not like it. Life is change. This tour—it is new every night. It is exciting. It makes me feel alive."

"Look, Dom, haven't we had enough excitement for tonight though? Can we just play the gig?"

"Yes. But life is risk. Life is for living. And while we live, let us *live*!"

"YOLO?"

"Yes. Something like that. And Lotte deserves a part in that."

I thought about that for a bit. "Let's go back. I've got some serious dirt to eat."

*

I APOLOGISED TO Lotte, tears in my own eyes. I borrowed quite a lot of Dom's wise words, wondering the while where she'd found that much wisdom.

Lotte knew that I meant it, that it wasn't my arm being twisted, that I'd had my Damascus moment because she threw her arms around me and sobbed her thanks. And I—I relaxed into her hug and felt her tears damp on my cheek, mingling with mine.

We had a spare microphone but no stand, so Lotte ended up holding the mic at the start of the second set. I just hoped she wouldn't fiddle with it when she wasn't singing or there'd be ugly handling noises coming over the PA.

The rules were simple. She could sing melody in any chorus where she knew the words. When she was singing, she was to hold the mic an inch — sorry, Lotte, two-to-three centimetres — from her mouth.

And so, we changed again. Dom brought Lotte front stage for a number — 'Lovin' Whiskey' — and they sang together, sharing the spotlight. We weren't a simple blues band anymore. Soul had crept in, and I wondered once more where we could get some horns. And Jürgen, of course, at least for our final Berlin gig, but I was thinking long-term.

Beyond the music, visually, the two girls were eye-catching. No, that didn't do them justice. Nor would comparing them to, say, Abba's Anni-Frid and Agnetha. There was a sparkle, a sexiness, of course. But Dom projected 'sisters-together', and Lotte played along. It didn't stop the boys from staring one iota, but some of the girls paid a lot of attention too.

For example, after the show, while we were breaking down the kit. I watched as a tall, skinny African girl buttonholed Dom. The girl wore her hair close-cropped, bleached blond, and sported a rainbow two-piece suit. Yet another of Dom's friends? But she looked like she was asking Dom for something, and Dom was shaking her head, her regret evident.

Then the girl looked straight at me, and for a moment, her eyes filled with hunger. Then it was gone, switched off.

*

OUR HOTEL HAD a garage, where we locked the van. There was

no bar, but the night porter was quite happy to sell us beer anyway, and he let us take them up to our rooms on the second floor. They'd put us in a big family room with a double and two singles, plus a twin room a couple of doors down. We ended up in the family room, sitting on the beds and on the floor with a crate of Paulaner.

Dom called a band meeting. Or it just happened. Whatever — it seemed the right thing to do. Kind of a recognition of Lotte joining. Plus, a 'what do we do about travelling?'

Jamie was out of it; he fell asleep. I leaned over and removed the beer bottle from his hand. He didn't stir.

"We are all tired," Dom began. "But I believe we can get through the last gigs. It is a short drive back to Regensburg tomorrow, easy. The drive back to Berlin will be longer, but we have the strength *spécial*, the hunger to return."

She looked at us, one by one. When she turned to me, I felt a little thrill, deep inside.

Berlin.

For a moment, Dom was Galadriel looking into my heart. *There, all dreams end, and there, courage will find your heart's desire.*

But that's you, Dom. And you're here…

Her gaze had moved on though.

Who knew what the others felt, what secrets bubbled up in each, but she paused longer when she came to Lotte.

"Lotte, heute Abend bist du eine Sängerin geworden."

"Ja, vielleicht."

"Ich fühle du hast eine Menge Potential. Du wirst bestimmt noch sehr viel besser."

"What're they saying?" Neale whispered to me.

"That Lotte became a singer this night, and she'll definitely get stronger," I whispered back.

"Exactly. Thank you," Dom broke in, obviously overhearing us. "Lotte has potential, and we should help her reach that potential in the next two days. I will teach her."

"How?" I blurted. "I mean, she's travelling with Jake. There's no room in the van."

"You are right. We will need to make room in the van for Lotte to be with me, so one or two will have to travel separately. Neale must stay with the van to drive. One of the train riders should be a German speaker."

The logic was inescapable. Shit.

Chapter Twenty

Friday, October 7, 2016
Regensburg, the Daubhaus

I DECIDED TO travel alone. I could have asked Jamie to come with me, but the van would take five, so why inflict an extra train fare? And I'd have had to nursemaid Jamie across Germany.

Dammit, that sounded patronising. He was learning a bit of German, though—without Alina—rather half-heartedly.

That aside, I'd travel alone through choice. I've always liked it, sorting myself out, going where I please. The indignity was in being asked, in being kicked out of the van.

On the positive side, I'd slept well the night before. Jake and Lotte had taken the twin room while the rest of us spread about the double and the two single beds. And I'd enjoyed a decent breakfast. I'd wrapped up warm against the cold autumn air in a thick puffer jacket. I called my goodbyes, but they were all sitting in the van already, and only Jake could see me to wave back.

The van drove off into the morning traffic. I didn't watch them go. I didn't think about all the fun they'd be having, singing their hearts out on the way to Regensburg while Dom began to turn Lotte into a singer. Damn.

Yeah, damn.

Damn the lot of them. Damn Lotte for daring to sing better than a strangled bat. Damn Jake for falling for her hot little bod. Damn Jamie for falling asleep when he could have volunteered to come with me. Damn Dom for being so logical and a lovely person and…achingly beautiful and… deliciously, intriguingly…*flexi*. And most especially, damn Neale for not having a proper six-seater tour bus complete with roadies in the boot.

Right. That got rid of a bucketful of poison I could do without.

Now, if I caught the S-Bahn, I'd have just enough time to get to the central station and catch the next train to Regensburg…

But…I didn't. *What the hell. I'll look around Munich. It can't do any harm.*

I wound up at the *Frauenkirche*, the cathedral, which was the tallest building around and only five minutes from the main station. I wandered around the exterior for ten minutes, or so. Then I headed inside because a chill wind was cutting through my jacket.

Warmth returned in the quiet, peaceful interior, silence echoing around infinite columns as was the way with cathedrals. I let the silence reach into me, calming, soothing, relaxing.

My phone beeped, and I called out in surprise, a choked-off

"Shi—" that made half a dozen people turn round.

"Sorry," I whispered "*Entschuldig—*"

Better not to have said anything.

"*Englische Touristen…*" someone muttered.

Yes, the bloody English abroad. Making a spectacle of themselves. Swearing in our churches.

So. Single beep. Text or email. Who?

Ah. Lars.

Thank you, Lars, for making me swear in church. So what did you have to say for yourself?

LARS: *Where are you?*

KAI: *In a church.*

LARS: *I do not think so. Selfie, please.*

KAI: *In a church, I said. Are you crazy?*

I walked outside and took a selfie of me against the cathedral front because Lars wouldn't believe me.

He didn't mention my email to him. Nor did he didn't mention my being a total shit when I'd parted from him. And he didn't mention the days that had elapsed—how he'd been feeling after I'd rejected him.

No. It went back further than that.

I want you, I'd written. Subject—auxiliary verb—direct object. Without the infinitive, the meaning reverts to just plain 'I want you'. No frills, no finesse, no ambiguity. Truth will out.

The phone vibrated, bringing me back to Lars's reply.

LARS: *Thanks. You look good!'*

KAI: *Bollocks, Lars. Do you understand me?'*

A shocked smiley came right back. Plus, *haha.*

And then, while I was still pondering how to respond, the phone jangled. I didn't need to see the caller. I *knew.*

"Hi, Lars."

"Hi, Kai. How are you?"

"I'm fine. Listen, about that email I sent…"

"I'm a Dane, Kai. German too. But in this matter, I am a Dane."

"What's that got to do with anything?"

"And you're English. Which means you're a shit linguist, and you're incapable of communicating emotion, even in your own language. And I—because I am a Dane—I am a shit-hot linguist. Better than these Germans. I am also smart and forgiving. Oh, and I am astonishingly humble."

Humble. Damn it—he was.

"My email…" I started.

"I read the words, but I know the heart."

The thing I both feared and desired.

Change the subject.

"Aren't you at work?"

"Yes, naturally. But it is quiet. Nobody comes to the Stasi Museum early on Friday morning."

"So you're calling me on work time? The Stasi will have you shot!"

"No such luck. The Stasi didn't show up this morning. To

their own museum. Can you believe it? It is Friday today, and that means it is casual Friday. Dress how you want. Hey, it's better than that, Kai. I declare that today is officially Fraternise with Western Fascists Friday. Don't tell a soul, but I even heard a rumour that the Wall has come down, if you can believe such a thing."

I laughed.

"It's good to hear you laugh, Kai."

"Anything else I can do for you, Lars?"

There was a long pause. I wondered if the connection had failed.

"Just be my friend, Kai. Until you're ready to be something more."

"I am," I answered. And then, "I will be. When I see you in Berlin."

Long pause. I hoped he'd understood.

"Thanks… Oh, shit. Sorry, I must go. Someone has just come in. *Tschüss*, Kai."

"*Tschüss*, Lars."

And he was gone.

The next train to Regensburg left in fifty minutes. While I waited, the train for Berlin pulled in at the next platform. For two pins, I'd have jumped right on board.

I didn't hear from Lars again. I guessed the Stasi Museum had gotten busy after all. Weird thought—the Stasi *had* just showed up and had shot him for fraternising with a decadent Westerner… I laughed again. All was well with the world. And I, I had a date for tomorrow in Berlin.

*

I FOUND THE guys busking and giving out leaflets near Regensburg station. Lotte and Dom were front and centre, not pushing it but working a couple of songs out. People walked past or stopped and listened. Or looked. Why wouldn't they?

Neale handed me a leaflet—one that we'd made back in England and had finally gotten around to using. It didn't make much sense. The picture was a collage of black-and-white photos of old bluesmen, something Jamie had painstakingly put together on his computer. The name, though, jarred.

"Who the hell is John Doe's Blues?" I asked him, though I was smiling. "And which one of the girls is John Doe?"

"I know. It makes no sense now. It seemed like a good name back in the Barrel Organ."

"Hmm. I thought you'd all parked your brains outside that day."

"I resent that remark. Still, it's got the name of the bar where we're playing, and it's the right date. So, what else would we do with them all? Take them back to England?"

"Fair enough," I agreed. "Where's Jamie? With the van?"

"Yeah. Parked a couple of streets over there." Neale pointed off to the north.

"How was the journey?"

"Dull, but easy. We were wondering what kept you."

"I took a slow train."

"That doesn't sound very German."

"Not every train in Germany is an express. The one Jake and Lotte caught wasn't."

Neale didn't look convinced, but he didn't pursue the topic either. Damn though. I didn't tell lies, but I'd spun a porky there. What business was it of Neale's why I'd not taken the planned train? I should have told him to mind his own fucking business, which was what I felt. But I was too nice on the outside.

"I'll go and say hi to Jamie," I continued. "Get him out of the van and into the fresh air."

*

THE VAN WASN'T hard to find. It looked battered and unloved in the middle of a long line of pristine German automobiles, with its broken wing mirror still held together with gaffa tape. Dirt had turned the van from white to grey, wherein someone had scrawled *putz mich*. Clean me. Ha ha. You could just about read the number plate, and I wondered if I should wipe it down. Illegible plates were surely as illegal in Germany as in England.

Jamie was staring at his phone, wearing a sour face. I tapped on the window, and he wound the glass down.

"What's the matter," I asked. "Neale put one of your strings out of tune?"

"Yeah, but he won't tell me which one. The old ones are the best, eh? But no. Bigger problem. Well, no, not a problem, but a disappointment. I got a call from Alina. Joni has got the shits, poor kid. And Alina doesn't want to leave him to come to the gig tomorrow. She says it's not fair to the babysitter."

"Oh. Bummer."

"Yeah."

"Want some company?"

"Since it's you, come aboard." He shifted across the bench

seat, and I tucked up next to him.

"Arm." I'd decided it was going to be an arm talk.

He put his arm across my shoulders. We sat in silence for a while. A long while.

"Tell me it's none of my business," he finally asked, "but are you all right?"

I thought about that for a long while more, tucked beneath Jamie's arm, warm and safe. Just like in the old days, Jamie seemed to be happy to wait.

I weighed things up. Some things were fine. Some weren't. "Yeah. Mostly."

"Not getting stressed out?"

"Nope. Should I be?"

"I can think of a few things that mightn't be, y'know?"

"They're fine."

"Good."

There was another long pause.

"There was one thing…" Jamie said.

"That's fine too."

"Are we talking about the same thing?"

"I have no idea. But it's okay."

"I mean, you and Lars."

I let him wait. It was an opportunity to reflect.

"And you and Dom," he continued. "You don't really seem to be able to choose."

"I'm getting there. Don't worry."

"Right. Well, I just want to say…I mean, we're all grown-ups. And I'm…on your side, Kai. Whatever you decide. I'm with you. Wherever you are on the rainbow."

Damn, but there was a tear in my eye. This was Jamie, and it was an arm talk. I let it roll.

"Even if Dad doesn't like it. You can move out if he and Cassie are difficult. Come in with me for a while."

And a lump in my throat.

"Thank you, Jamie. I hope it won't come to that. But I appreciate the offer. I don't want to crowd you though."

"That's okay too."

"That's my line."

We both laughed.

More time passed.

"Do you remember when we were small…" Jamie asked

"What?"

"You used to curl up with your head on my shoulder."

"Hmm."

"Like you're doing now."

"Hmm. I remember it being a lot more comfortable. You've got bonier, Jamie."

"And you haven't…"

"… says the master of the bleeding obvious. Because I'd get crazy-bored spending as much time in the gym as you do. But perhaps Alina likes her men scrawny."

"Scrawny? You go too far, kid."

"Huh? She could play xylophone on your ribs. Osteophone, if you want to be picky. Never mind. So if you're not going to see the luscious Alina tomorrow, what are your plans?"

"I'm coming back."

I sat up then, and never mind the arm talk rules "Blimey. You made your mind up quick. So the lusciousness *has* reeled you in—"

"Oh, fuck off, Kai. It's not about sex…"

Arm talk. Plus, eyebrows.

"…It's about being part of something. A family."

I smiled, then, and stretched out my arm for Jamie. He nodded and settled close in. Not easy, given he was a good few inches taller, but we've always managed to work it out.

"And you're happy…" I managed to not end on a rising note.

"Yeah. I guess I'm as surprised as anybody. But, yes. Alina and I click, and Joni… Joni is funny and charming and innocent, though other times he can be very wise and serious."

"Then I'm pleased for you, Jamie. Really pleased. And just a little bit jealous."

"You could find family in your future too."

"I don't think I was put together that way. A family is for other people."

"Just because our own family is fucked up doesn't mean we can't make something better for ourselves."

I gave Jamie a little squeeze across the shoulders.

"I think you'll be a good stepdad. And a dad in your own right, too, I hope."

"Thanks, Kai. I'd like that. And…I hope you'll find what you're looking for."

"If I can work out what that is."

"Completeness. The person who helps you become who you were made to be."

Deep, but… I nodded. It helped. It helped a lot.

"That's how you think of Alina?"

"Yes. I've thought about it a lot."

"Then that'll do me."

*

SPOTLIGHTS FADED TO black. Applause.

I couldn't remember much about the gig. I couldn't remember the audience, not in any detail. Some of it was down to the lighting. The club had a lighting guy who knew his stuff; he knew the blues, and he had a great sense of intuition. He had spots set up to pick each of us out, so I saw a lot of Dom in eye-catching silhouette, and Lotte too. The downside was I couldn't see much of the audience at all. Damned lights in my eyes.

I could hear, no problem. I could hear all the cues, and I'm pretty sure I picked up on them, and the guys picked up on what I was playing. And I sang in the right places — the right notes, the right words, the right order. And the audience applauded. I think it was a good gig. But…I couldn't remember it with any clarity.

I went through a phase whenever Mum or Dad asked how my day had gone where I'd say, "Fine." That was the Regensburg gig. Fine. No disasters, no salvaging a victory from the jaws of defeat. Dom's prophecy coming true…

No. It wasn't that. It was that whole day, following my chat with Jamie. I remembered very little of Regensburg, the pretty town on the river that, on the way down, I'd claimed I'd so wanted to see. It had become no more than a way station on the journey back to Berlin, a town and a gig on the far side of which lay…

Answers.

Life. Of a new and exciting kind.

*

SO WE LOADED up. Doors closed, everything in place, ready to head off.

"Final check?" Dom called.

I offered to go with her, and then, "Neale, why don't you run Jamie, Jake, and Lotte over to the hotel and come back for us?"

Dom's suggestion made sense. We could wait in the warmth, while they did the round trip.

We ran a final check—nothing but a set list and one of my drumsticks. Nobody but myself to blame for that one. Then the barmaid made us a coffee while we waited. On the house. Claudia was a good sort.

"That's lucky for us," I told Dom. "My jacket's in the van."

Dom nodded then did a double take. "Shit, me too."

"Not to worry. Neale will be back soon."

But one by one, the customers left, and Neale didn't show. Claudia collected the glasses and stacked them in the dishwasher. She picked up our coffee cups, and they went in after the glasses. She flicked off the lights—not all of them, but enough to get the message across.

Nothing on our phones. No texts, no emails. But then, my battery was pretty much flat, so I switched it off. Dom's had more power, but she couldn't get a response from anyone.

Claudia came over, wearing a thick coat. "I have to lock up. You'll have to leave. Have you got somewhere to go to?"

I named the hotel where we were staying.

"It is too far to walk. You should call a taxi."

Looking embarrassed, Dom answered, "We don't have our

wallets with us. The guys should have been back to collect us ages ago."

"Well, they're not here. What are you going to do?"

"We'll find another hotel."

"Do you want me to come with you? You've got no money."

"It's all right. The guys will have our wallets with us in the morning."

*

IT WASN'T ALL right. The first hotel we found asked us for a credit card. Dom offered her watch as security. It was a decent watch, but...

Nein.

We were out on the street and thence to another hotel about fifty metres on. We tailgated a guest using his keycard to get in. At the reception, the night porter was on the phone.

The phone went down. Frost looked us over. "No rooms. Sorry."

We pleaded. Dom's watch came out. But they didn't want bums in their beds. Too much hassle. Management policy. Whatever. We were out, again.

We went to the station to find a taxi, but the last train had long gone. The station was all closed up, and why would there be any waiting taxis?

We looked for the police. I wondered if we could get arrested and spend the night in the cells. How? Assault a policeman? German police go armed. We could end up dead...

The problem never arose though. We didn't find a policeman. At least, not one that would stop for us — though a police car did drive past quite fast. We waved and shouted, but they were twenty metres away, cruising down the main road, and we were shrouded in the darkness of a side street.

We were both shivering.

"We have to get out of this cold," Dom said.

I nodded. "One last try at a hotel?"

"Have you got an idea, then?"

"Yes. I think so."

We found a hotel a notch down from the other two, but that was okay. I wasn't looking for four stars. The night porter let us in. Maybe he wasn't part of the No Vagrants cartel. Maybe he was influenced by Dom's glamour. Maybe he was just a decent human being.

He was young, and I hoped that would make a difference.

Yes, there was a room. And we had our passports with us—thanks to our encounter with the law in Köln—without which, no room.

No, the hotel didn't take PayPal. Only credit cards. And cash.

"*Aber, haben* Sie *— selbst — ein Paypal Konto?*" I asked, hoping he did, indeed, have a PayPal account himself.

"*Ja...*" he answered, not seeing where I was going.

And then the light went on in his head. Yes, he could accept a transfer to his personal account. Yes, I could use his computer to transfer funds.

Saved.

*

THE HEATING HAD long gone off in the room, but the bed looked huge and very warm.

"Would it help if we hugged a bit?" I suggested. "To get warm."

"Only to get warm?"

I didn't answer. Which was itself an answer.

She hugged me anyway. Or because.

She was warm and gentle, and I wanted her very much.

"You are very tense, Kai. Relax."

I tried to relax. Forget the body; feel her warmth. But I couldn't. There wasn't much more than a T-shirt and a blouse between us.

"What do you really want?" she asked me.

This was it. The point of no return.

I want…

"I want you…to tell me about yourself."

She tensed, and a gap opened up between us.

I took a pace back and looked her square in the eye. "People love you. You touch people's lives, and you change them. You've changed us—the band—and you've changed me. That's a good thing."

"Go on." —Wary.

"I've poured out my soul to you. There's something about you that makes it easy. Or at least possible. Sometimes it feels less like pouring and more like bleeding, but I can't help myself because it's so good to get some of that hidden crap out into the light. But it's all one way."

I let the words hang.

"Let me see your soul," I said.

"It's not…"

"It's not pretty? Neither is mine, but it didn't bother you. You plunged your hands into it, found a load of shit I didn't need, and I'm glad to see the back of it."

"I am glad also."

"Well then, let me do something for you."

Now, she stepped back, but her fingertips lingered on mine. A tear formed and then another. Somewhere, she found a shy, crooked smile, which broke my heart.

"There is nothing you can do for me, Kai. But you asked, and that is everything."

Though I cradled her through the night, and her tears wet my cheeks, she said not a word, save only "Love Lars and be happy together."

Chapter Twenty-One

Saturday, October 8, 2016
Berlin — Club Mojo

BELLIES EMPTY AND rumbling — our budget hotel didn't do breakfast — we made our way back to the club. It wasn't open, of course, but it was our only rendezvous. The van was already there, with Jamie and Neale in the front seat in sleeping bags. We banged on the windows, stupidly happy to see them, stirring from slumber and then relief flooding their faces as they recognised us.

After we'd got the "thank God's" and the "what the fuck's" out the way, we managed to piece together the chain of calamities that had stranded Dom and me. Neale had suffered a hypo; his blood sugars had fallen too low to drive safely. They'd texted us, but of course, my phone was dead. Dom's?

"Bande de connards!"

"Who's that? The phone company?"

"Now they send me a text, saying my credit card was bad, and I am blocked. *Connards*! Fuckwits! I will use another." She turned away, fanning cards from her wallet and muttering.

And Neale. "We didn't realise you had no money. Not at first. We assumed you'd get our texts and find a hotel. But when I'd sorted my hypo and went to check the van, I saw your jackets."

"Yeah," said Jamie. "He came tearing back inside and dragged me to the van, and we came back here. We must have missed you by ten minutes, no more. We drove around for a while but couldn't find you. We parked where you found us because we guessed you'd show up, too—eventually."

If we didn't die of cold first, that was. But I didn't say it. I couldn't see what else they could have done. Water under the bridge. With ice.

"Can we get some coffee now?" I asked. "And some hot breakfast? We passed a couple of cafés…"

Neale locked the van, and we headed for the nearest café, maybe seventy metres down the street, and ordered coffees and food.

But…Dom's credit card was bad? She'd not batted an eyelid at coughing up for the radio mic. She'd picked up a few tabs, here and there—quite a few things, when I thought about it. So, was she now pushing beyond her limit?

Before I could think about that too deeply, Jamie took me on one side.

"Quick word, Kai?"

I swallowed my coffee; the hot breakfast was still in the kitchen. "Sure. I've got time."

He led me outside, leaving Neale and Dom to puzzle over what could possibly be private after so many days in one another's company.

He came straight to the point. "I want you to meet Alina. This afternoon, in Berlin."

"Why?"

"Because I've been thinking about what you said. I want you to tell me what you think of her."

"Why does my opinion count for anything?"

"It does. There's no why about it. You're just wise. Okay?"

"I thought I was a nine-times fuckwit who puts the wrong fuel in vans."

He grinned. "Yeah. And you let Dom go off with strangers. But you're also astonishingly wise. Which is why I want you to come with me on the train up to Berlin."

"You want me along to make sure you don't get lost. Truth?"

"Yeah. That. And I wonder if there's anyone you want to call in Berlin."

"No."

He looked surprised. "Lars?"

"He's working." Damn, I answered far too quickly.

Jamie nodded. "Shame."

But it was what it was, so we went back inside and told Dom and Neale what we were doing and why. Dom smiled as if she'd planned it herself, and Neale said there'd be more room in the van for the rest of the band. And that was decided.

"We'll pick up a day bag from the van, then, and head off," said Jamie.

"What about breakfast?" I was still hungry.

Jamie looked at his watch. "Hurry, then. I don't want to miss the train."

I nearly got indigestion, bolting my breakfast, and almost lost it trotting back to the van.

*

WE KNEW THERE was something wrong the moment we saw the van.

"Fuck! The bloody door is open." Neale was a couple of seconds ahead of us.

Yet when we reached the van, puffing and panting, everything looked to be there.

Almost. Nobody would steal a PA in broad daylight. But…a guitar…

Jake's guitar. His beloved Strat.

I'd seen it packed in there when we'd closed the back doors last night.

"Nothing else taken?" asked Dom.

"As far as I can tell," I said after a quick check. "The front doors haven't been opened. Those bloody back doors, though—"

"Your bass, Jamie?"

"I can see it. Wedged a bit too deep to be easily nicked."

"Then there's nothing you two can do that I can't do just as well," Dom said. "Neale and I will call the police, though I don't suppose there's anything they can do either, except make us late for the gig."

"But—" I protested.

"I said there's nothing you can do," she repeated. "So, get started, or you'll miss your train. And don't worry about us. We'll sort something out. And I'll tell poor Jake what has happened."

*

WE CAUGHT THE train by the skin of our teeth.

All the way to the station, though, and on the train…

What had gone wrong? Had someone forced the door? I didn't think so. Had we forgotten to bungee it shut? Had it swung open, or had someone been trying their luck? Had someone recognised the van from the gig? That would have been strange karma, to have been burgled by a fan…

I didn't know the answers, and it bugged me. It had happened again. *Fuckfuckfuck.* I'd let my guard down in a moment of weakness, and some bastard had struck. All those freezing-cold nights, sleeping in the van for nothing. Some fucker had ripped us off in broad daylight.

Around and around and around it all went, imaginings of the million punishments I'd inflict on them — if I ever caught the bastards — spinning futilely in my head.

"Don't beat yourself up, Kai. It wasn't your fault."

"What? No, *I* forgot."

"Bollocks. Utter bollocks. We *all* forgot, so we're equally to blame. That's how it works."

"Jake loved that guitar."

"Yeah, he did. But get over it. It's just a fucking plank."

And little by little, I did start to let it all go.

There were texts, of course, to remind us. A little buzz from my back pocket.

NEALE: *Dom just told Jake. Gutted.*

And later:

DOM: *On the way. No surprise. The cops won't do anything.*

Cops, eh? Lazy buggers.

KAI: *What about a guitar for Jake?*

DOM: *Need ideas. The music shop here is closed till lunchtime, and we have to get moving now, or we won't get to Berlin in time.*

That told me everything I needed to know about the shop owners who were most likely gigging musicians, playing a club as we'd been doing. Getting back late from wherever they'd been playing, getting some sleep. Yeah, I could see why they might not open too early on a Saturday morning. Guitar nerds, eh?

Guitar nerds…

Orange fedora guy.

I rummaged in my wallet between the receipts I meticulously kept but never looked at, and there was his business card. A bit crumpled, but his name was clear—Helge Klein—and he owned a guitar store in Berlin.

KAI: *Here's a number. Get Jake to call him. He's heard Jake play, knows what Jake likes. He'll find Jake the *right* guitar if anyone can.*

*

WE CHANGED TRAINS at Nuremberg, with barely time to grab a couple of sandwiches at a kiosk. We shouldn't have bothered; we were riding an ICE train, smooth, quiet, and well-provisioned with food, drink, and Wi-Fi:

SIMON: *Hello Kai, How are you getting on?*

KAI: *Not so bad.*

SIMON: *No platitudes. Straight answers only. You know the rules.*

KAI: *Köln was shit. Gigs been getting better since then.*

SIMON: *Not *totally* shit, but yes, I found the second set, which was utter crap. Who is that twat on the fiddle?*

KAI: *Neale. He's calmed down. And got better.*

SIMON: *I should bloody hope so. Your singer though. She's special. How did you find her?*

KAI: *Muzomart. She's from Belgium.*

SIMON: *Where's she to? is the question. Tell me you're bringing her back to Marden Combe.*

That was indeed the question. She'd dodged every time I'd tried to pin her down. And tonight, I needed to get some straight answers.

KAI: *I wish I could.*

SIMON: *That's a no, then. What else do you know about her?*

KAI: *She's bi.*

SIMON: *I saw clips of Fulda. Of course she's bi. And how are you?*

Straight answers only.

KAI: *All I can say, within the rules, is I have a date tonight. I hope I don't screw it up.*

KAI: *Not the bi lady, BYA*

Silence.

More silence. Bloody hell, had I finally managed to render Simon speechless?

SIMON: *Jeff is crying. Do you know that? Sending good thoughts. You won't screw up.*

KAI: *Thx*

SIMON: *<3<3 from both of us. I'm crying too.*

Dammit. I was…

*

HELLO, BERLIN.

Somehow, you had become an old friend. I knew you, now. Not your skyline, nor yet the apartments backing onto your railway lines. Nothing so definable as a smell or an architecture. Nothing about the way the Berliners—no, that was JFK's misnomer—anyway, the way the people of Berlin dressed. Something too subtle that I could say, "That's it," such as the different way they drove, the same as how Midlanders and Londoners drove differently.

Likely, my own mind was playing tricks. Psychic Kai, anticipating a pivotal moment that might never happen and overlaying it onto the way the Berlin pigeons were flying. Psychic bollocks.

But I felt comfortable in Berlin as we arrived in the central train station. It helped, steering Jamie through the signs that still baffled him, listening to him mangle basic words but also feeling a little twinge of pride in his willingness to try.

After five stops on the U-Bahn and a seven-minute walk, we arrived at an apartment door on the second floor of a low-rise block.

Jamie raised his finger to buzz. "You'll love Joni," he mentioned, only for the fifteenth time that day.

"I'm sure I will," I reassured him.

Alina opened the door.

I hoped someday someone would open the door to me and look at me the way Alina did at Jamie.

"How's Joni doing?" Jamie asked.

Alina laughed. "He's fine. Come in. And come in, Kai. It is good to see you. Both of you."

Jamie got a quick kiss. I shook her hand, polite and friendly both. Then I heard a stampeding elephant, and Joni burst out of his room, shouting, "Jamie" at the top of his voice.

He crashed into Jamie's arms, laughing and babbling, I know not what. Two seconds after that, he was leading Jamie back to his playroom, and they were gone.

"He looks fit enough," I suggested.

Alina chuckled. "Yes. Today, he has more energy. Yesterday was not so good. He had a temperature, thirty-nine degrees, tired, and miserable. *Und der Dünnschiß.*"

Alina's expression was all the translation I needed. Diarrhoea. Or, as Jamie had put it, 'the shits'.

Alina showed me around the rest of her apartment. It comprised a single large area with a TV, a pile of toys, sofa, table for two, and a kitchen area. Doors led off to bedrooms, a bathroom, and a balcony. Basic, but nicely decorated and — pile of toys notwithstanding — well-kept.

"It's nice," I told her. "Tasteful. And you look after it."

"Thank you."

I helped her make coffee, by which I mean I got in the way while she made coffee. In the background, I could hear somebody making aeroplane noises and somebody else laughing. That must have been when I started grinning.

Alina poured a couple of cups. "I will make a fresh coffee for Jamie later. I think he will be busy for a while."

"You know, Alina, this is a side of Jamie I've not seen before."

"Really? He is so good with Joni. I thought he must have a nephew or a niece."

"No. Well, yes, one of our cousins has a couple of kids. But we hardly see them. And I've never seen Jamie get excited about their kids."

"Well, he is good with Joni. Genuine, I am sure."

"Yeah, Jamie wears his heart on his sleeve."

She looked puzzled.

"It means he easily shows his true emotions. And I think he

is very…fond of you. He speaks highly of you. He was very keen for me to meet you."

"And I was keen to meet you again. I wanted to apologise for last Monday. I thought Jamie had agreed his plans with you."

"No need to apologise," I said. "It was fine."

"But you stayed with Jürgen an extra night. Was he okay about that?"

"Mostly. We kept out of the way, went tourist for the day."

"Yes. I heard about that. You met up with that guy, Lars, at the museum. Jamie told me."

"Oh."

"And that is working out well?"

"I hope so. I'm looking forward to seeing Lars at the gig to-night."

"And after that?"

I took a deep breath. "Yes, I hope I will see Lars again."

Alina put her hand on my knee. "I don't know Lars very well, but the word is he is a good person. It is good that you are friends. And more than friends?"

"Too soon to say. You, though…" I nodded in the direction of the playroom, trying to make it a question.

"Yes," she agreed. "I think Jamie has made a decision. One which pleases me very much. I must ask though. Did you speak to him? About me?"

"Yeah. I called him a cad."

"What is a cad? I know Computer Aided Design, but that is not what you mean."

I laughed. "A cad is somebody—a man—who takes ad-vantage of a woman and then leaves her."

"Takes advantage?"

"Has sex with her. Usually gets her pregnant too. Then runs away. It's a staple of British literature of a long-gone time."

"And what do you call a woman who takes advantage of a man?"

I must have looked puzzled.

"I wondered if I was a cad, too, Kai."

"You? With Jamie?"

"No." She laughed. "When *I* invited *him* back, all either of us wanted was a one-night stand. But I changed my mind. We *each* changed our minds. No, this is about before Jamie. I was thinking of what happened with Joni's father."

"He ran away?"

"No. *I* ran away. My choice. I wanted a baby. But I didn't want a man as well. At least, not that man, not then."

"That doesn't make you a cad, Alina."

"It seems to me a cad is another word for a selfish person. Someone who makes their life the way they want and uses other people to make it happen."

"We all do that."

"Well, I did it once. But I don't want to do it with Jamie. I'm not saying that because he's your brother. He has a real innocence—listen to him now, playing with Joni. I love him for it. I can't believe that no other woman has seen it in him and"—she clenched her fists around imagined lapels—"grabbed tight hold of him."

*

WE SPENT AN hour with Alina and Joni. Enough time to walk with them down to the nearby park. I wanted to give Jamie and Alina some minutes together, so I tried playing with Joni, pushing him high on the swings, listening to his joyous squeals. To me, it felt false, and I couldn't find my own child-heart to meet him. He got bored after a few minutes and went back to Jamie and Alina, saying he was cold and wanted to return home.

So, we said goodbye to Alina and Joni.

"Will we see you at the gig?" I asked.

"I don't think so," she replied. "Joni is not quite right yet, so I don't want to leave him with a babysitter."

Jamie pantomimed disappointed. His reward was the first of several farewell hugs with Alina.

"I'll see you again, Alina. I promise."

"That will be nice. Make it soon."

"Christmas. I could come over at Christmas."

Joni joined them in a three-way hug.

Alina bent down and told him that Jamie was going back to England but would visit again at Christmas.

Joni looked puzzled and then hurt. He had no concept of how far England was, and Christmas probably seemed forever for him to wait.

It tore my heartstrings because Joni started crying, and then Jamie was promising to read him a story over Skype from his far-off island in the North Sea. Joni decided it would have to be a story every night, and Jamie looked set to agree. But Alina put her foot down, gently but definitely, and settled Joni with an almost-promise to read a story every week.

"Off you go, now," Alina told us. "Thank you for coming to

see us, both of you. But you have a gig to go to."

She gave me a peck on the cheek and Jamie his last hug and kiss of the visit.

As we left, Alina's "Love you" still hanging in the air, Jamie called back to her a creditable "*Ich liebe dich.*" He'd been working quite hard on his pronunciation quite hard.

Back on the U-Bahn, I congratulated him.

"Yeah," he said. "And I meant that bit about coming back. Christmas seems a fuck of a long time to wait though."

*

WE WAITED IN a coffee bar near the Club Mojo for the rest of the band to turn up. Jamie fished for compliments about Alina.

"She's a lovely woman," I said. "I was only ribbing you about the flat chest and the stubble. And Joni's a great kid. What else do you want me to say?"

"Why me though? She could have her pick—"

"It's because you're—" I wasn't sure 'innocent' would go down well. "—genuine. She sees that and admires you for it."

"But I'm nothing special."

"Alina sees something in you that you don't realise you have. Trust her."

At about five-thirty, I got a DM from Jake—a DM, not a text. Jake had set up residence in the twenty-first century: *C u in 30 mins*

I asked the question that I should have been worrying about all day: *What r u doing about a guitar?*

Sorted

That was helpful. Typical laconic Jake. But if he said it was sorted, it was sorted. Maybe Orange Fed—no, Helge—maybe

Helge had found him a replacement. Or maybe Jürgen—or Dom—had a friend willing to loan a guitar.

Jamie and I finished off our coffees and walked the hundred and fifty metres to the Club Mojo. We found the manager, who pointed to some stairs leading down to the basement.

Empty.

I breathed a sigh of relief. We were safe from my final nightmare—being double-booked with another band. It was the one disaster that hadn't happened to us—though Prague had been close—out of all the calamities I'd been imagining. And if another band did show up now, well, we'd be in place.

With the stage cleared, the basement was pretty much ready for us to set up. We piddled around with chairs and tables. Jamie tore down some old set lists. I found a beer bottle that the cleaners had missed and placed it on the bar. But that was it. We waited. After six hours on the train together, Jamie and I didn't have anything left to say to each other.

Some twenty minutes later, I heard noises above and then the sounds of footsteps coming from the dark stairs.

The figure who emerged carrying a guitar wasn't Jake, nor Neale. Certainly not Dominique or Lotte.

Shit!

"Hey! *Wer ist da*? Who's there?" I called. Who the fuck are *you*, strolling in here with your guitar like you owned the place?

"Kai. Have you forgotten me already?"

No. No way would I forget that voice. It went with a slightly chubby waist and curly hair and a tightening in my throat.

"Lars?"

"Hi, Kai. Good to see you."

He put down the guitar, laying it on one of the tables. In the dim light, I could make out Fender markings on the case.

"Whose guitar is this?" I asked. I'd begun to feel warm, though the basement was rather chilly.

"I don't know. Jake gave it to me to carry down. I thought it was his."

"Uh-huh. Jake's guitar got stolen."

"I didn't know. I'm sorry."

I'd run out of things to say about the guitar, mostly because at that moment, I no longer gave a flying fuck about any guitar. I reached out my right hand towards him. Yep, he was definitely the cause of the sensation of heat. Left hand followed, and Lars clasped my hands in his own.

"I'm sorry I was so rude to you," I heard myself saying. There seemed to be a lot of buzzing happening, starting in my hands and flowing up into my head and my chest and all over.

"I understand. It's all right now. It is forgiven and forgotten."

"Yes. We start from this moment."

I held him tight as he held me. Then as one, we drew back and looked each other in the eye. No words, but heart spoke to heart:

Is this what you want?

Yes. This is very much what I want.

The gentlest of kisses. The one we would always remember.

*

CLUB MOJO WAS heaving, thanks to a serious social media push by Jürgen and co. Jürgen had shown up, of course, with sax as requested.

And he'd brought along a trumpet player (Erich) and a trombonist (Silke).

"Oh, bloody hell, Dom!" I asked, glancing at Jürgen. "What are you up to?"

"It's okay, Kai. The guys were fine with it."

"You mean Jake, Lotte, and Neale…"

"Why, yes, we talked it through on the road. Jürgen called us, suggesting it. We voted. Everyone said yes."

"You've got them twisted round your little finger. Whatever happened to that simple little blues band that left England?"

"It grew up. But…you were never simple."

"Any more growing planned? Bring in a few backing singers, a little three-piece groupette from Detroit? No, let's make that a full-blown gospel choir—"

"Why are you so upset, Kai?" Lars asked.

I didn't have an answer for him. Was it a change too many when I'd so recently thrown my own life onto the roulette table?

So, I tried laughing, and it felt better than being angry and upset. "Never mind, Dom, never mind. Bring it on. I trust you."

"Thank you," she replied. "You are my lucky band."

Now, Club Mojo was truly heaving. We'd soundchecked with Erich and Silke—who were actually a husband-and-wife team—and with Jürgen on the same numbers we'd done with him before. Whoever was on the sound system had put on a bunch of stuff from the Stax/Atlantic back catalogue. Dammit, why *shouldn't* we play rhythm and blues?

*

THE LIGHTS WENT down…

…and came up again. And we were…

Neale, *Der hot Geiger*, bringer of catgut wildness and eerie tenor vocals, stage right.

Jake, *Der Mann in Rot*, gangling Strat fiend, master of blister, also stage right.

Jamie, bass thunderer and my right-hand man, confusingly stage left.

Kai, beater of skins and brass, the still point at the centre of all mayhem.

Lotte, newly hatched songbird, sister-together, centre stage.

Dom, *chanteuse*, blues-lady, binder-of-all and sister-together, stage everywhere at once.

We were John Doe's Blues, for one night only the best band in the whole fucking world, and I'd fight anyone who said differ-ent.

We were *in*.

'Rolling and Tumbling' — what else? Whoo!

*

AT THE END of the first set, I headed straight for Lars.

"How was it?"

"*Nicht schlecht.*"

"Not bad, my arse. It was brilliant."

"So why did you ask me? Of course it was brilliant. You trusted Dom, and she held it together. The brass section was ex-cellent, in particular."

"Indeed, it was," said a warm, resonant voice from behind me that I couldn't place. But I'd heard before. I turned around.

Minus the shiny suit and tie, I struggled to make the connection. Lars was quicker.

"It's Ricky."

Of course. That mock Southern drawl.

"I…I didn't expect to see you here. Ricky," I said. "I'd have thought you'd have your own gig on a Saturday night."

"So I should." His smile was pained. "But the gig was cancelled. The venue was shut down at very short notice. I'm told it failed a safety inspection."

"I'm sorry to hear that. It that a thing in Germany, then?"

"If it is, it's not common. But I didn't interrupt you just to moan about losing a gig. I want to tell you — as one superstar to another — that you are one talented bunch of musicians."

I had to smile. Not just because of the compliment, but — aside from that 'as one superstar' phrase — Ricky had lapsed into his native English accent, which I placed somewhere near Birmingham.

"I'll not keep you," Ricky said. "You have others wanting to speak to you. But you, personally, are a first-class drummer, and it would be an honour to work with you should our paths cross again."

He flipped a card from his jacket pocket and held it out for me to take. "Stay in touch."

Ricky nodded, turned, and was gone. I closed my mouth, my farewell too late.

At a tap on my shoulder, I pocketed Ricky's card and turned to a grinning Annika.

"That was really good, Kai. I think you have gotten better on this tour, even since Sunday."

I barely blushed. "Thank you. I'm sure you're right. Dom keeps pushing us. Or we push ourselves to get better for Dom."

She glanced between Lars and me, and her eyes twinkled. "Excuse me, I must go. Matthias owes me some money. A little wager…"

I looked at Lars, and he shrugged his shoulders.

"We're holding hands," he explained. "It's a giveaway."

I released his hand.

"Too late for that." He chuckled. "Berlin gossip is the only thing that travels faster than light."

I kissed Lars and left him to go mingle. The crowd ebbed and flowed, and I let it take me to Dom. I had a question I needed to ask her. Two questions. About Jake's guitar, all the financial ups and downs, the credit cards that had let her down but always another one that saw us through. And the one that had bugged us all. Why us?

I'd been looking for the right moment, and it had never been the right one. Something she'd said, though, had niggled. It had been in Köln, when we'd been trying to put together the set list for that disaster of a second set. Dom had suggested 'I Come from the Blues'. But it was one of Clay's songs. I was sure no one had mentioned it to her, and the only footage of it had been on our old website, which Clay had nuked before we even met her. Which meant Dom already knew of Clay's band before the whole shenanigans started. Perhaps she even knew Clay personally. So now, right moment or not, I'd ask her.

The crowd washed me up close to Dom and a short-haired girl who looked familiar, both of them standing at the corner leading to the Ladies.

The girl was saying, *"Tu es sûre? Demain, c'est tout fini, et tu iras à Digne –"*

"Non, Karin. Je vais seulement à Zurich – Ah, Kai, hello." Dom had spotted me. "Do you remember Karin?"

Karin turned around, and of course, I recognised her straightaway. The girl from the Gaelic Club who'd flirted with Dom.

"Oh, yes," I said. "You were in Fulda. And you helped us load up afterwards. You were with – what's his name – Giulio? Am I right?"

She looked pleased. "And Dom came to stay with us. Yes."

Oh, yes. My other fuckwittery – letting Dom go off with strangers. Except they weren't strangers, and jealous Kai had more than half suspected that Dom had gone off for a jolly three-some.

But I was no longer jealous. That whole episode had stopped mattering to me when I'd overheard her conversation with Karin just now. The only thing that mattered, suddenly very much, was that Dom would leave us tomorrow, *demain*, and I didn't much care if she was going to Digne or to Zurich.

"You've come a long way, Karin," I said. "Fulda is a long drive."

"Ah, yes. But I wanted to see Dom this one time more. While she was…in Germany."

"And Giulio couldn't come?"

"No. He is working."

"Oh, well. Another time perhaps. Back in Paris –"

She blinked. "Yes. I'm sorry. Will you excuse me?"

And she disappeared through the ladies' room door.

"Did I say something wrong?"

Dom shook her head. "How could you know? She and Giulio, they are having…difficulties."

"Oh. I'm sorry. Anyway, while we've got a moment, I wanted to ask you about Jake's guitar. Jake loves it, I can tell. And he's playing it really well for a guitar that was hanging in a shop this morning. How—"

"It was your contact. He came up with the goods. And it wasn't particularly expensive either. I offered to buy it, but Jake said no, even as a loan, until the insurance comes through. If it does."

"You'd have bought it for him?"

"Yes. But he declined. Your friend Helge had it waiting for him, along with two or three others. It's the one he thought would best suit Jake's style. You should have seen Jake's face when he picked it up, played the first few runs on it. I shall remember it for…"

She stopped. Choked with emotion.

"It's okay, Dom. I felt the same when I saw him reunite with Lotte. There's an innocent joy in Jake, seeing good things happen to him. I've welled up once or twice on Jake's behalf. You okay though?"

"Yes. I'm fine."

"You're sure?"

"Yes. Like English children say—cross my heart."

She crossed her heart—the same bold gesture she'd used in Fulda, flirting with Karin.

I nodded, acknowledging her gesture. "We're playing that tonight."

"Of course. It's appropriate. At least for some of us."

"I suppose so. Will you be out flirting?"

"Probably. Does that bother you, Kai?"

"Not anymore. While you've got it, flaunt it."

"*Ah, oui…* Do you have any regrets?"

"What about? You and me?"

"Yes. Of course. *I* do."

"Me too. But it's stopped hurting. I'll live. Lars…"

"Yes, I am glad that you have Lars. Look after each other, won't you?"

Was that another tear in her eye?

And then she was all business again. "Come on; it's time for the second set."

And it was too late for "Why us?"

Bugger.

*

THE SECOND SET kicked off with 'Blue for No Reason'. We had another guest spot, with Jürgen and his horn section playing sweet and soulful and Lotte taking the vocals on her own. She was settling in, and damn if I didn't believe she could lead the band if it came to it.

Then, we played another couple of real blues and soul numbers, including 'I Come from the Blues', which Dom took, finding that rich, butterscotch timbre. I accompanied with laid-back drums on that one, adding brushes and a lazy shuffle beat through the dark journey and out into the final chorus of hope…

Where did I come from? I come from the blues
Where am I going? Wherever I choose
Where is my hope, if not in my friends?
Where is my future? Around the next bend.

…before switching into the faintly ridiculous part of the set—all jigs and reels and treacherous molls named Jenny, with 'Drinking Song'.

And then back to serious. I include 'Cross, Don't Cross' in that, despite all Dom's egregious flirting, for the sake of her poignant, improvised end lines:

Don't cross me, cross to me
Cross boundaries, cross me bold
Cross my heart… hope to die
Cross me once, before I get old

'Hall of Fallen Angels' was another stand-out in that set with lots of rich harmonies and subtle horn underpinning from Erich and Silke. Goosebumps. 'The Sky is Crying', with Jake's weeping guitar…

And then, we finished with more uptempo songs—'Crossroads', 'Three Hundred Pounds of Joy' and an improvised 'Baby, Where Did Our Love Go?' complete with mock Supremes: Dom, Lotte, and Silke, still toting her trombone.

The lights dimmed…

And a single spot shone.

Dom turned to us and said, "No backing on this one, guys" and then to the audience, "Thank you, Berlin. This is the last number. It's been a wonderful time here in Oz. But now our tour is over, and it's time to go home to Kansas. It's been a whirlwind for us all. We've made a lot of friends here…"

She looked over her shoulder at us. A lump the size of Denmark lodged in my throat. Dammit, I was tearing up.

"… and memories that we'll carry with us always, I'm sure. I should give out medals to Lion and Tin Man, to Scarecrow, and even one for Toto. But instead, this is my own thank you to my brilliant, lucky band."

And then, I heard the quiver in her voice.

Somewhere, over the rainbow…

Her voice was wobbling as I'd never heard it before, and she was straining hard not to screw up her finale. She held it, silhouetted there in a single spotlight, her voice growing stronger, still tinged with the heartache of every lover's goodbye.

I could only see her from behind until, in a brief moment between verses, she turned around. For a moment, tear tracks on her cheek glistened in the spotlight. Then she faced the audience again.

She carried it off, entirely a cappella. A long moment of total silence followed at the end. Then she gave a little bow, and the audience knew it was over, that they could breathe once more. Literally. I swear I heard a collective sigh as they all breathed out. A guy who'd been sitting at the table right in front of her, rapt, for the whole gig, finally closed his mouth and began clapping furiously. With that signal, the rest of us joined in.

Dom beckoned for us all to join her. Slow to extract myself from the drum kit, I found myself at the end of the line next to Neale. He already had his right arm round Dom's waist, and he flung his left arm out to welcome me into the line. I marvelled that I hadn't killed him, and then I settled next to him. Who knew what the future would bring, but it was getting less likely that I would delete him from my friends.

Dom shifted her left hand from Neale's waist and rested it on my upper arm for a moment. She squeezed gently. *Thank you.* I reached, found her shoulder, and squeezed back.

'Over the Rainbow' was the last song we played. So clear in my memory.

We left the stage.

*

LARS CAME UP to me then.

I didn't—couldn't—speak to him. It was sinking in how much had come to an end.

The band had already split up. Yes, that quickly.

Dom had gone to sit at a table with Karin. She had a shot glass in her hand, a clear, colourless liquid therein, and their heads were close. It might be lovers talk, idle gossip, or a dastardly plan to lace Superman's coffee with Kryptonite.

Jake and Lotte had split away too. Jake wiped down his new Strat while Lotte coiled cables from his guitar rig. She'd not got the trick of rolling the cable as she formed each coil, so it didn't lie flat. Jake put the guitar down and crossed over to her. He stood behind her, reached around her, and took her hands in his, showing her how to give the cable the little half twist with the thumb to make it coil flat. They stayed in that curious embrace long after Lotte had learned the trick.

Neale and Jamie stood at the bar together but weren't

connected. Jamie had a beer in one hand and talked earnestly into his mobile phone in the other. Neale drank mineral water, alone in the crowd.

"What are your plans?" Lars asked. "Do you have hotel rooms booked?"

I nodded.

"But are you going to use them? I mean, Jake and Lotte might. But Jamie must be talking to Alina right now. Dom is in deep with Karin. So, I wondered if you and I…"

He left the sentence hanging. I found my voice, which didn't quite break.

"I'd like that. I would so like that, but it seems wrong to abandon the others—and Neale on his own, at that—after all we've done together. It feels like we—like I would be the one breaking the band apart."

"It has already happened. You cannot stop it. I am not sure that if the boss of Sony walked through the door with a recording contract in his hand, you could get everyone back together. I do not know if she intended to do so, but Dom ended the band when she sang 'Over the Rainbow'."

He was right. I'd seen it, but now I understood how the forces that had held the band together were now pulling it apart. Had pulled it apart.

In which case, accepting Lars's offer of a night of passion or tenderness—I was up for either—might be the last opportunity for a while to spend some time with Lars. At least, until I could afford to return here again. I'd put quite a lot on my credit card, and I was afraid to work out how long it might take to pay off.

I took a deep breath. "Then I'd better start breaking down

the gear."

I reached over and touched Lars's hand. I didn't have any cables I could show him how to coil, but…

"Lars, it seems to be a thing tonight, so how would you like to learn how to dismantle a drum kit?"

Chapter Twenty-Two

Sunday, October 9, 2016
The Drive to Calais

AND THEN IT changed.

I was most of the way through packing the drum kit into its many cases when Neale and Jamie appeared, looking concerned. Jamie got straight to the point.

"Neale is out of insulin."

"Oh? It sounds bad. How bad is it?"

"It means I need to get back to England as soon as possible. I'm not going to die, but I do need to get back to my fridge, where I've got some spare."

"Can't you get some here?"

"It's a Sunday already. I don't know how the system works here. I guess I'd have to go to a hospital. It's going to be a pain, a real fucking pain. I reckon it'll be faster if we drive back."

"And are you okay to drive?"

"If we start now, yes. I'll be fine."

"Can I just say 'oh shit'? How did you come to run out of insulin? Didn't you bring any spare?"

"Yeah, but when I looked, it was actually out of date. It'd been sitting under some other stuff in the fridge, and when I noticed it, I misread the date. So, I can't trust it."

"Shit. Let's round up the guys."

*

IT WASN'T THE farewell I'd have wanted, but that was how the cards had fallen.

The goodbye with Dom had crept up on us, and none of us had prepared for it. I'd kind of imagined us all going back to the hotel, everybody together, sharing our experiences of the tour, then a good night's sleep and drive off in the morning, fresh.

I could not accept that it was better this way. Short, sharp farewells all around. A too-brief hug for each of us. A not-at-all-electric kiss for me.

"Good choice," she whispered so only I could hear. "You and Lars. And the swan glides past."

"Thank you—" I began, but she glided across to Lotte and kissed her and whispered something private…

…and so it went for each of the others.

"It is time," she said. "You should all go. I will remember this tour as long as…always."

Jamie had something in his eye. Neale looked grim, but that was his diabetes clock ticking. I wondered about pretending I had something in my eye too. Hell, no. I let the tears roll. It wasn't British to show emotion, but my heart had decided to show Dom she was special.

"Chin up, guys," said Jake, the last person I'd have expected to try to jolly us up. "We've got a million memories to take back, Dom. Thank you for making this a once-in-a-lifetime tour. I'll never forget you."

And that finally broke Dom's composure. Her own tears flowed, and a second round of hugs followed, the kisses not at all mechanical.

I didn't know what Lars and Karin felt, out on the fringes, but Lotte was weeping too. Lotte had got as close to Dom as anyone in the last couple of days as Dom crash-mentored her singing.

I'd had my own goodbye with Lars, not so fraught as that with Dom, because I knew I'd be seeing him again soon.

*

TEN HOURS TO the coast, according to the satnav, and it was all on Neale. But nobody could drive ten hours straight, diabetic or not. We'd need stops. Twelve hours, plus. As none of us were drivers, we hadn't thought about it properly before leaving England. We'd had a vague idea that we'd drive back in short hops, with Iron Man Neale taking a five-minute nap every couple of hours. In reality, it would be early evening before we got back to England, and only with luck would we be back home before midnight.

"The insulin isn't completely useless," he'd admitted when I'd tackled him privately about the length of the drive. "It's just not as effective once it goes out of date. I've injected a couple of times with it already, and it has some effect. Just not full strength."

I was navigating, and the others had fallen asleep. Jake and Lotte lay together, entwined on the back bench. Jamie's head rested against the door frame, supported by a rolled-up towel as a makeshift pillow.

Though I was navigating, my mind was off doing weird, distracting stuff. Pictures of Dom and images of Lars rolled around in my head, alternating memories of each goodbye. After a while, they blurred into one composite memory, which was a little disturbing but not entirely surprising, given the emotional entanglement I had with each. And those memories swirled again to superimpose themselves over images out of a Bogart movie — streetlight haloes and posed silhouettes photographed in the grainy black and white of night.

"Penny for your thoughts," said Neale as he flicked the wipers over the light spray on the windscreen.

"Thinking of Dom," I admitted. "I'll miss her."

"Yes. Me too. But I'd have to be blind not to see that you and she had a…chemistry. Early on. I really thought the two of you would get together. She seemed to find plenty of reasons to cosy up with you. But you ended up with Lars.

"Could've gone either way, I suppose. I'm not judging, I'm not going to criticise anybody, not with my record on love and marriage. I'm divorced — did I say? She got the kids and a bloody large whack of my month's takings to support them all."

"I wondered why you were eager to leave old England behind. Bailiff trouble?"

"None o' your fuckin' business, Kai." But he said it with a smile on his face. "Yeah. Fuckin' bailiffs."

A kilometre passed, or ten. I had other things on my mind than counting.

"Where did Dom come from? Where's she going?"

"Eh? Was that a rhetorical question, Neale? Or were you asking me?"

"Well, it's bloody strange. Yes, we found her through muzomart, but what went before? I mean, no one gets that good without a lot of gigging experience. Where was that? She's got the demos but no CV. I've tried searching for 'Dominique' plus 'singer' plus 'Belgium' and all the variations I can think of. And I know you well enough to bet that you've done the same."

I nodded, even though Neale still watched the road. "Yeah. You know me that well. There's nothing. I had a look for singer recognition services, something clever that Google might do to tell you who a singer was from a clip of their voice. But that's still the stuff of PhDs. If she's been performing under another name, we're never going to find her."

And if she's also had cosmetic surgery to change her appearance… I kept the thought to myself. Neale wouldn't understand.

"So you never asked her," he said. "Why not? You were close to her."

"True." I pondered. "I can't remember a moment when it would have been the right thing to ask."

"Me neither, and I'm a gabby Irishman with no tact. I wanted to ask, but… I'd like to say she controlled every conversation, but it was more subtle."

"Yeah, you're right. No conversation was ever about her. At least, none of any depth."

We both fell silent. A kilometre passed under our wheels.

And another.

We had her phone number so we could stay in touch. So why not just call her and ask?

"She's gone."

"What?" asked Neale.

"She's been messing with my head. The final song. The goodbyes. She's planted the idea deep in my brain that she's gone. Gone for good. I could phone her. Or DM her. Or go back to muzomart."

"Why don't you, then?"

My phone was already in my hand. But my thumb wouldn't move. I willed it to, but it wasn't in an obedient mood.

"I'll call her tomorrow. It's too late to call her now."

"Right. She'd not thank you. Nor would Karin."

"You think they're snuggled up together, Neale?"

"Don't you?"

"I guess. It doesn't bug me. Not much. Not now. We had our chance, and we both turned it down."

"You're fuckin' daft. A woman that sexy, and you turn her down? And for Lars?"

"Yes. Change the subject before I call you out on your fake sexist remarks."

"Ah, you're no fun to wind up," Neale said. "You see through all my tricks. So yes, she's gone. And it all seems like a dream already. Those gigs—all that new material we kept shoving in. How? Where did it all come from? From us? I'm an okay musician, but I know my limits. This was way beyond. I was playing out of my skin. Way out. And I think you were too. We all were. Dom carried us to a place we couldn't have gone, unaided.

And she got us out of some tight spots."

"You mean Prague?"

"Yeah. And others. The gear, I guess. No. That was your doing. That bloody campsite in the rain. She organised us, stopped us freezing to death."

"You make her sound like a guardian angel."

"Yeah," Neale said. "She was that."

"Do you mean that devout-Irish-Catholic-literally? Or are you speaking metaphorically?"

"I wish I knew. She was so fuckin' talented it was unreal. She might well have checked her harp in with Saint Peter and gone slumming it with the first band going nowhere that posted an ad on muzomart."

More kilometres rolled under our wheels.

"Did you consider," I asked, "that she might have come from the other place? To show us a glimpse of what could be, and then leave us with only a memory to torment us the rest of our lives?"

"Jesus, Mary, and all the saints! Are you serious?" The van lurched as he said it.

Jamie stirred and grunted, 'Whafuck?" and went back to sleep.

"Could be. I bet she's the ghost of Billie Holiday or Janis Joplin, sent back to earth for a week to strut her stuff and sing the blues."

"Ten days, Kai. Not a week. Ten brilliant fuckin' days I won't ever forget if I live to be twenty-nine."

"Fifty-nine."

"Whatever."

"Ten unforgettable days it is, then." I turned to him. "But were they real? Did we all die instead in a pile-up ten days ago? Have our own ghosts been touring since then in some fantasy world? And now we're done, and we think we're driving back to England. Are we condemned to drive this autobahn for eternity? Because that's what hell is, at least for us."

He gaped at me.

"Watch the road, Neale."

He faced front again, and then he laughed. "You had me going there. I bow to the master of wind-up merchants. You've had your revenge. Now stop weirding me out."

A sign caught my eye. "There's a *Raststätte* coming up. Do you need a break?"

He nodded.

We pulled off the autobahn and followed the signs to the car park. Neale brought the van to a halt, letting it coast the last few metres. Nobody stirred.

"You can get some rest now," I said. "Switch off."

But he didn't. Instead, he looked at me. "I can't do this alone. You know that, don't you. I need to keep driving, but I also need to sleep."

I took a deep breath. "Yeah. And we have to keep moving — sleep or no sleep — else your insulin won't last."

He slid out from behind the steering wheel. I arched up, and he passed behind me while I squeezed past and down and into the driving seat.

"You said 'over my dead body', Neale."

He ignored me. "Get used to the controls. Spend a minute or two learning the clutch. Find the biting point."

I did as he suggested. The van moved forward with a bit of a jerk, but that was okay; nobody woke.

"Set up the mirrors."

"Ah…one of them's buggered."

He grinned. "Bloody French. Wrecking my van."

"Couldn't possibly have been your fault, could it? Forgetting to set the hand-brake—"

"None o' your lip, kid! Ready?"

Though illegal in so many ways, we had to do it for Neale's sake. Well, no. We could have taken him to hospital, pleaded with the doctors to give him insulin. Which, of course, they would have done. But how long would it have taken? Nobody wanted to hang around Germany, wrangling with forms we didn't understand, at the mercy of someone else's bureaucracy. We'd muddle through. So very British.

I let out the clutch, and without too much of a lurch, we were on our way again.

*

JAMIE WAS THE first to wake and notice.

Neale had coached me through the first few kilometres, helping me get used to driving on the 'wrong' side of the road. Then he'd announced, "You're doing fine. I'm going to rest my eyes."

Shortly after that, his breathing had slowed, and his snore joined the frog chorus. Half an hour passed, and we were all still alive and un-wrecked. An hour, and I was feeling pretty confident.

About that hour mark, though, Jamie woke and—as the

penny dropped—swore, and I had to shush him, explain what was happening, and why it was an almost-sensible choice. But Jake and Lotte woke then, and I had to yell at them all.

"For fuck's sake, let me drive," I whisper-shouted. "Neale's knackered, and I'm doing my best not to kill us all."

Silence you could cut with a knife.

Fifteen minutes of near-total silence later, it became too much to concentrate on driving, and I pulled over onto the hard shoulder. I climbed out, trying to massage my spinning eyeballs back into their sockets.

Neale stirred. So they shouted at him. He let it wash over him, and when they'd finished, he spoke.

"Look, you're all fuckin' right, okay? It was a stupid thing to do. Don't blame Kai though. It's my fault. Let's see where the nearest town is and if it's got an A&E."

"Can you get us to Hannover?" I asked. "It's about thirty kilometres. It's a big city with lots of hospitals. For sure, one of them will have an A&E."

"I guess so."

*

GOD BLESS SAINT Tim Berners-Lee, Creator of the Internet. By the time we reached the outskirts of Hannover, we knew exactly which hospital to go to, and we'd even found a couple of blogs posting encouragement and tips on what to expect.

As we drove through Hannover, Jake spoke up.

"Neale, can you take us to the station?"

"What?"

"Lotte and I, we've had enough of riding in the back of the

van. We've checked, and we can get a train from Hannover all the way back to England. Cologne, Brussels, and then the Eurostar."

"But—" Neale started.

"No. They're right," I said. "It's a shitty deal in the back. And by the magic of the interweb, we know that German hospitals do give out insulin, so the only problem is how long we'll have to wait to get you sorted out."

"Thanks, Kai," Jake said. "Yeah, I've got to be back at work on Monday. Lotte's going to travel with me."

We diverted to the station, pulling up at the drop-off a little after four in the morning. The five of us made a lonely group, clustered on the pavement. Lotte wore her heavy coat and woollen hat. With her backpack on, she looked as I remembered her from Jürgen's party. Jake had a holdall in one hand and his new guitar case in the other.

"Take care of my stuff," he said. Then he put his luggage down on the pavement and hugged me. "You're a fuckin' great drummer, Kai. Magic tour."

"You too, Jake. Safe journey."

And Lotte.

"Have a good trip, Lotte," I wished her as we hugged.

"You, too, Kai. *Tschüss*," she replied and kissed my cheek.

"*Tschüss*," I agreed. "Look after Jake."

They turned and started to walk into the station.

"Wait!" Jamie called, and Jake and Lotte turned around. "I'm coming with you. Can you wait?"

He looked at me, guilt written on his face. "I have to go too."

I sighed.

"I wish I could stay with you," he continued, "but—"

"You've got work on Monday too. Sure. Go."

He climbed back into the van and emerged a couple of minutes later with his own bag.

"Passport?" I asked.

He rolled his eyes, fished out the burgundy rectangle from his coat, and waved it in my face.

Another parting as the band disintegrated a little more. Three figures walked off towards the booking office.

I turned, and Neale was watching me, pensive.

"I'm staying," I assured him.

He nodded his thanks. "Jamie doesn't deserve you."

"He's all right. If we'd needed him, he'd have stayed too."

*

ON THE DRIVE to the hospital, I had Kafka-esqe visions of nightmare waits in corridors. Of waiting rooms full of bleeding drunks. Of being ignored or simply being forgotten because we were English, not part of the system.

There were corridors. There were one or two drunks. Inevitable. This was the spillover of a Saturday night in a large city. But we weren't ignored, nor forgotten, and the system bent and accommodated us.

Neale wasn't covered by health insurance, not even the free insurance that was the right of every EU citizen. His own fault, but Neale wasn't the sort of person who did the necessary paperwork ahead of time. So, there was a charge, and I remembered Neale's 'bailiff trouble'.

"Oh fuck! Sorry, darling," he said to the young woman who'd, moments ago, presented him with the bill and now looked shocked at the British Tourist.

He pushed the insulin back across the table. "I'll manage with what I've got."

"No, you won't," I interrupted. My poor card groaned.

The insulin came with a thick wad of paperwork. I struggled a bit with the unfamiliar vocabulary but found what I was looking for near the bottom of page two.

"I think this means you can claim it back when you get back to the UK."

"I'll pay you back when I get the money," he promised.

It was a sincere promise, I was sure. If it had been over a bar bill, then I was sure I'd never see the money again. In this matter, however, Neale would be an honourable man.

*

THE SUN HADN'T yet risen, but I felt hungry.

"Shall we get some breakfast?"

"No. Let's get out of Hannover and get some miles under our belt."

"Don't try to be a hero."

"And don't you mother-hen me, Kai. I'm feeling rested and ready. I'll let you know when I need a rest."

I dozed while Neale took us out of Hannover and back onto the road to Calais.

About ninety minutes later, Neale pulled off the autobahn and rested half an hour — a proper sleep. And then repeated the cycle, dozing or at least resting his eyes. Once, after I caught his eyes closing when he was behind the wheel and yelled at him, he slept for two hours at a service station. The sun was up by then, and we were both pretty tired.

We didn't speak much on the journey. We wondered how Jake, Lotte, and Jamie were getting on, but we'd had texts from them at Köln and again at Brussels. They were speeding ahead of us, well on their way to England.

Finally, about noon, we left Germany, knowing their train would be past the channel. But that was okay. We were moving. Or we were still, and the world turned beneath us. Around Antwerp, it started to rain, but that was okay, too, because Calais was now only two hundred kilometres away.

Somewhere on that part of the journey, we must have passed the rest stop where we'd met Dom. I didn't notice. I was dozing at the time.

And then we were in France and past Dunkerque and—by now it was getting dark—into Calais.

*

DRIVING OFF THE boat felt good. The crossing had taken an hour and a half, and Neale and I had slept through most of that. We joined the line of cars heading through Immigration and Customs.

And then a bearded guy in a peaked cap and a hi-vis jacket walked over to us and tapped on the window. Transport Police? Customs? I didn't know. Neale wound the window down.

"See that building?" the man asked, pointing to a large shed. Neale nodded.

"That's where you're going."

"Something wrong?"

"They'll tell you what to do when you get there."

Neale shrugged and put the van back into gear.

When we got there, the signage gave it away. Customs. Two customs officers were waiting and directed us to a vacant bay. We got out and stood on the concrete floor, looking around, wondering what would happen. A couple of vehicles sat in other bays; their doors were open, and luggage lay spread over the floor.

One of the officers addressed Neale. "Where've you come from?"

"Germany."

"You're Irish?"

"And proud of it."

"And you?" He meant me.

"British."

"Just the two of you?"

"Yes."

"Nobody else?"

"No."

"There's a lot of gear in there for two of you."

"There were more of us in Germany. They came back a different route."

"Which route?"

"Eurostar."

"Better give us names."

"Jake. Jamie. Lotte."

"Full names, please."

Neale obliged, except that neither of us knew Lotte's surname. Then they got us to unpack everything. They told us to put it into piles according to the owner. There was a hat left over. Dom's fedora. Oh. We hadn't mentioned Dom. I claimed it.

"Nice hat."

"Thanks."

"You were a bit slow to claim it."

"It was a present" — kept as close to the truth as possible — "from a girl who sang with us. But she wasn't part of the band. We met her out there."

"Let me see the hat."

I handed it over. He ran his hands over it, then ran a finger around inside the hatband and inside the lining. He gave it back.

"Anybody else you've forgotten?"

"Nobody else."

They clustered round Jake's pile. Not a lot to it, apart from Jake's amp and accessories, his sleeping bag, and one other small bag, tucked in the back of his amp.

That was when I remembered Jake, Jamie, and Neale at the campsite in Köln. They'd been smoking something. Cannabis in some form, I supposed.

An officer picked up the bag, hefted it, sniffed it, and carried it across to the table.

"We'll come back to that," he announced.

Then they started on Jamie's pile. They found nothing save a soft porn magazine, also tucked into the back of his amp. The customs man flicked through it.

"Standard wank-mag. Nothing illegal," he commented, his voice bored and contemptuous. He placed it back in the amp.

Lotte's pile was tiny — her mic, the one that Dom had given her, and a make-up bag. The customs men opened both. Neither contained anything of interest.

"Whose is this lot? With the drums."

"That's all mine," I answered.

"Okay. Tell me what's in each box."

He began to pick up my toolbox.

"No!" I screamed. "Put it down."

The officer smiled, relishing my discomfort, and lifted it off the ground anyway.

The box exploded. The catch flew open, and my tools and spares spewed out. A plastic box containing screws and bolts landed on a corner and shattered. Hundreds of tiny pieces of iron-mongery lay scattered across fifty square feet of floor. A tin sprang open and a couple of dozen glass fuses joined the mess of components on the concrete.

"You—" I bit back the word I'd been going to say. "I tried to warn you not to. I could see the catch wasn't latched properly."

He had the grace to look apologetic at the scatter of tools and components on the floor but made no move to clear up the debris.

"I'm going to pick this lot up if you don't mind. If anyone has a dustpan and brush, that would be very helpful."

Nobody offered. I started to pick up the pieces.

One of the other officers returned with Jake's bag. I ignored him.

"This bag's been used to keep drugs in, but there's nothing there now. It'd be a waste of time to prosecute."

The officer who'd dropped my tools had more braid on his uniform. "You heard that. You're lucky. Load up your van and sod off."

I nodded and carried on scrabbling for my lost screws. Stupid bastard!

*

NEALE BREATHED A sigh of relief as we drove out of the shed. "That was priceless. The disappointment on that officer's face when the toolbox flew open. He was convinced you'd got drugs in there."

"I wasn't looking at his face. The bastard. I'm not sure I got them all."

"Got what?"

"The screws. The fuses. A few other components."

"Small price to pay. We got through okay."

"Well, why wouldn't we? Jake had finished off whatever was in the bag."

Neale didn't say anything.

A light went on in my head. Finally. "You had some stuff."

"Yeah. In the bag with my insulin. Jake's. Did you notice they went for his pile first?"

"So?"

"Think about it."

I did. I didn't like what popped out. "Not a random search, you're thinking, Neale."

"Ah, what they call 'intelligence-led'."

"A tip-off."

"Yeah. The last spiteful act of a mother."

Bitch.

*

SKIP MOST OF the rest of our journey back to Marden Combe. Suffice to mention that it involved a lot of moving slowly along the M25. But we drove up outside Jamie's house while the lights were still on.

Jamie answered the door. He lowered his gaze when he saw me, not wanting to look me in the eye.

"We're just dropping stuff off," I said. "Then we'll be on our way."

"Fine. How was your journey?"

"Is. We're still travelling. It's been long, but the van has done its stuff. Meet up for a drink later in the week, and I'll tell you about it. Your journey?"

"Yeah. Okay. Lotte made sure we went to the right counters and platforms. We were fine."

We unloaded his amp and the other gear without saying much else. But then, as Neale and I were leaving, Jamie finally faced me.

"Look. I'm sorry that you had to do that journey without me, but I didn't know —"

"Yeah. You have to be at work in the morning. Well, that's your priority, your decision."

"Don't be so judgemental. I can't afford to lose my job. It's a small town — where would I find another?"

"Fair point. Nobody's condemning you," I said. "And if you're not simply being polite, I'd very much like to meet up later in the week for that drink."

"The Barrel Organ?"

"You're so going to have to change your ways. But okay. Sure."

At Jake's place, the lights were off, so I scribbled a note to say we were back safely and pushed it through the letter box. The flap was sprung like a bear trap, and it clanged shut. I didn't lose any fingers.

A couple of minutes later, my phone buzzed. A DM.

Come back round if u can. Slow getting 2 dor. Jake.'

Lotte answered the door, wearing one of Jake's jumpers over a nightie. "Kai! Neale!" She buzzed with excitement to see us. "Come in. We're both still up."

We stepped through into the hallway and caught a wave and a 'Hi!' from Jake, emerging from the bathroom to join us.

Lotte resumed. "You look so tired. I'm sorry. You had a shitty trip, didn't you?"

Neale grinned, hollow-eyed. "Yeah, it was a crap journey. But you did the right thing. One time, I had to pull over on the motorway and close my eyes. The cops woke me up, asked if I was all right. If they'd found the two of you in the back, we'd have been up shit creek, and I don't know what else."

"I didn't know that—" I said.

"You were fast asleep too. I didn't want to disturb you."

Lotte wanted to make us coffee and call out for a takeaway, but I said we were here to drop off Jake's gear and had to leave.

Her face fell at that, and I felt bad. But it didn't take a psychic to foresee Neale and me both falling asleep over a biryani.

Lotte pushed her disappointment aside. "Yes. Do not worry. I understand how tired you must be. It would be nice if you could come round for dinner soon. I want to make friends now we are in England."

Jake was nodding agreement. Dammit, I'd make some friends, too, as long as we were back in England.

It took a bit of fussing to get Jake's amp and effects together. But not too much. We'd been awake enough to repack the van sensibly from the neat piles on the customs shed floor.

From Jake's, we continued to my dad's house. The porch light was on. A note inside the door read:

Hope you had a good holiday, Kai dear. Try not to make too much noise when you come in as your father has to get up early for work. You can leave everything in the lounge so as not to be banging about on the stairs. Love, Cassie. XX

Fair enough, and we got to it.

"Neale, are you going to be all right?" I asked as we stood in the lounge, surrounded by my drum kit and the PA, as well as the tent and a large bag of laundry.

"I could use a quick coffee before I go."

"Sure."

But he didn't make a big thing of it. It really was quick, no conversation, and then he got up to go.

"Thanks for the coffee, Kai. And thanks for sticking with me all the way home. You're a good friend. But I'd best be on my way."

"Are you sure you're okay to drive? And you've got your own gear to unload."

"I'll be fine. Don't worry about me. I'm the hired help, like I said."

I protested, and he snorted amusement back at me.

"See you soon, Kai. Next time you need a fiddle player. Or a plumber."

I closed the door after he'd driven off and sat quietly with the last of my own coffee.

It was odd. In the stories, you followed the quest to the very end. But I wouldn't see that—the moment where Neale, too, rested his head against his own pillow. Then the story of our tour would have come to an end, and it peeved me that the last action wasn't going to be mine.

But things don't ever end that neatly in the real world. The tale would be over tomorrow when I got the PA stacked away in the garage.

No, that might not be the end of the tale either. The band—minus Dom—was now in England. In Berlin, Lotte had taken up the mantle of singer, at least in part. We had the recording studio booked, over in Oxford. So maybe this was just Chapter One…

Chapter Twenty-Three

Wiedersehen

YOU COULD PLAN everything but not your heart. Your brain could plan whatever it likes, but your heart would always have other ideas. Sometimes better ideas. Or at least different ones. And the outlook from the one I'd picked was better than the outlook from the back bedroom in my dad's house. Urban, not suburban.

Yeah, I moved out. I left Marden Combe. I talked it over with Simon first, of course, listened to every word of my own advice. I wasn't sure he said a word, but I still heard the happy tears in his voice. That probably wouldn't make a lot of sense to anyone who hadn't had a mentor.

Jamie, though, had been the first to make the break. He didn't wait till Christmas. He flew to Berlin for a weekend a fortnight after we got back. Uh, yeah. We cancelled the recording session in Oxford. A month later, Jamie quit his job and moved over to be with Alina and Joni. He was now looking for work and swotting hard on his German.

About the time of Jamie's first flight, I had an email from Lars. He wanted to visit. He had some idea that I would show him London. Or Birmingham. Or Stratford.

And that, he'd said, would avoid the tricky question of having a 'friend' come to stay at my dad's place. It would still be too much scrutiny. My business. Not theirs.

Instead, I went with Jamie, who'd flown back to pack his worldly goods to ship to Alina in Germany. I met up with Lars and stayed the night. And another night. A week later, I returned to Marden Combe to pick up a couple of suitcases of my belongings, including basic recording gear, so I could at least do some voiceover work. Now, I was settled in Berlin, lining up job interviews and missing my drum kit but not much else.

So that was two out. Three, if you counted Clay, currently on tour with his soul band. But there was still work for the escape committee to do.

I kept in close touch with Lotte. She was missing Germany, if not her mother, and it seemed Jake's circle of friends was a bit limited. I floated the idea of them moving to Berlin, only to discover I was pushing an open door. Lotte said they talked funny in Berlin, but it wouldn't be too bad. She could do bar work anywhere, but they couldn't rent a place just on her earnings. Jake's job was the sticking point; the good news was that he'd started looking.

I hadn't yet worked out how to get Neale to Berlin.

I wonder if the Germans needed plumbers?

*

SPRINGTIME IN BERLIN was the perfect time to enjoy a stroll along the boulevard Unter den Linden — and to enjoy a coffee under those linden trees after a shitty winter. Lars and I had done both already.

Over the last months things had been falling into place. Now that I was determined to settle, everyone had stopped speaking English to me, and I was realising how much German I still had to learn. It still felt like drowning, sometimes, but it was good enough for me to get a job.

Also, and not unrelated, I had a drum kit. Not my Marden Combe drum kit; I couldn't see how that would fit in Lars's apartment. I had a *new* drum kit.

I'd bought it with my wages from working in a music store, doing drum sales in the basement, of course. This music shop's bread-and-butter was guitars, and that happened at street level. But that was fine. The drum level was my domain, where I didn't have to listen to endless renditions of 'Stairway to Heaven' or 'Smoke on the Water'. Anyone who managed to find their way down was already a potential customer, so selling wasn't difficult, even in German.

When it got quiet, I'd go upstairs to see how business was with Helge. Whenever it got really quiet, he'd leave me in charge and spend an hour or two in the basement luthier workshop, working on repairs or improving the used stock. Having an assistant suited Helge very nicely because if there was one thing he liked more than playing guitars, it was fixing them and setting them up. Life has been good at Orange Fedora Guitars and Drums.

But: the kit.

The kit was really lovely, ex-demo, and with a staff discount on top. Electronic, so I could practise at home wearing earphones without disturbing the neighbours.

Lars helped me put the kit together. Because he was my drum roadie, as well as everything else.

"Play it," he said when it was all set up. "You've been missing it, I know."

So I did, a bit tentatively at first. It wasn't that I hadn't been playing quite a bit since starting my job, but this was Lars's apartment, and the neighbours…

The neighbours weren't going to hear a thing. I knew that with my head, but it was still hard to feel in my bones.

I told Lars to clear off because getting to know a new kit wasn't anybody's idea of a spectator sport, and I loved him too much to put him through that much boredom.

Love? I still wasn't sure what that meant, or if I was using the word right. The tale Lars had told me about his mother's escape still haunted me, and whether it was really for love or just gratitude and sex. Because Lars offered me my lifeline out of Marden Combe, and I was grateful for that. But I liked to think that hadn't been on my mind or his when we'd met in Jürgen's kitchen, when we'd discovered we were two people who simply clicked. And found new ways to click. I had no idea that I'd enjoy dancing as much as I do. I was still nowhere near Lars's level, of course, but getting there.

Amidst all those thoughts, I became aware of how my body

was settling into the feel of the kit. It felt part of me, as my old kit had been part of me. I kept playing, shuffling at random through a thumb-drive of some newer favourites and old blues tracks.

Crossroads.

It Serves You Right to Suffer.

Midnight in Harlem.

And that broke me.

Dom's voice sang out from one of the demo tracks she'd sent us. I kept going, kept playing while the tears rolled down my cheeks. But that was fine. They were my memories, and I would a million times have rather had them than not. If it was time for some of them to come out and get a little airing, then it was time.

I let the track run through to the end, then stopped the playback and put my sticks down.

I sat there for several minutes, thinking, remembering. Lars came in, treading softly, not wishing to break my concentration, watching me, trying to gauge my mood. I turned around, not wiping the tears away.

"What's the matter?" he asked, soft and concerned.

I smiled. "I'm fine. And now I know I'm ready to play again."

"That's good." He nodded towards my Handy, as I was now getting used to calling my smartphone. "You going to call Ricky?"

"Yes, I'm taking his offer. I'm ready to be a Sunset. At least, while Jonas is recovering from his operations."

Ricky's drummer, Jonas, had suffered a skiing accident, a bad one, though his helmet had protected him from any head injuries. He'd broken a hip, his right knee had been shattered, and there were torn ligaments. All very repairable, but while he'd be out of hospital next week, he wouldn't be fit to gig for a few months. So, Ricky had made good on his promise and called me.

So what of John Doe's Blues? Jamie was here in Berlin. Lotte and Jake would be moving over next month.

I couldn't talk for the others, but for me, it was all a bit raw still. I didn't want to try to recreate what we'd had because, without Dom, we couldn't. And I thought we were all wise enough not to try.

In any case, Jake and Lotte were doing their own thing. Jake had switched to acoustic guitar, and they were setting up as a folk/blues duo, which suited Lotte's softer voice better. They'd sent some tracks, and I thought it was the right choice for them.

Jamie said he'd be in if everyone else wanted to do something together, but I think he meant a one-off rather than as a gigging band.

And what of Dom? I'd tried calling. The number had rung out the first few times, and I left voicemails. A week later, the number came up unknown.

At first, I scanned the music papers and online gossip forums every day. Then weekly. With her talent, how could she not have been discovered?

She had to be somewhere in Paris. *Dominique. Where are you?*

*

IN THE END, it was a total fluke. I wasn't the best at doing laundry, and one of my suitcases had been sitting in the corner of the bedroom in Lars's apartment, making me feel very guilty because I'd stuffed a bunch of dirty clothing in there. The rest of the bedroom was pretty neat, though Lars had dropped a strong hint that morning as he left for work.

I caved in.

It wasn't too bad, except for the black plastic bag with my jeans from the tour. The pair that had got muddy when I was drunk and slipped over onto my arse. The pair that I'd then sluiced the mud off of — badly — in the shower. I had half a mind to chuck them, but then a euro coin fell out of a pocket. I went through all of them to see if there was anything else worth salvaging.

And there it was. The credit card slip from the music shop in Fulda. It wasn't in the best of condition, screwed up and water damaged. I unrolled it, and there was Dom's signature and name, still legible. Her real name.

Juliette Robard. Not Dominique.

I didn't have much to go on. But I found her, as Juliette, on SoundCloud, the picture, like her, but not like her. Her face had an asymmetry that wasn't comfortable to look at, her nose larger than I remembered and crooked. I almost thought it was a mistake, but the voice was her voice, and the songs were the songs she'd sent us. And some others I'd not heard. They made me weep; they were so awesome.

But the picture drew me back to those tiny scars I'd seen in Prague. It was obvious, now. Juliette Robard had turned herself into Dominique with the help of a surgeon. A very good surgeon, who wouldn't have come cheap. How could she have afforded that on a department store sales-girl salary?

There weren't many honest options.

And still, I had no way to contact her directly — until, an hour later, I found her Facebook page. A "shrine" page.

Dominique—I should say Juliette, but she will always be Dominique—was dead. A brain tumour? At least, that was what one friend posted. Something inoperable, but my mind stopped functioning at that point. I wept.

A whole bunch of little things clicked. The credit cards. She'd been spending like there was no tomorrow because, for her, there *was* no tomorrow. She'd timed it almost perfectly, but her credit line had started to fray in the last day or so. That momentary flare-up at the Wannsee campsite— "We've got plenty of time," Neale had said. And her reply: "*You* have." Little things, indeed, taken separately. And, of course, Dom had been telling the truth about Zurich, but I hadn't understood. Not Digne, but Dignitas.

She'd known what was waiting for her only a few weeks down the line, and she'd wanted one last adventure. If things had been different, if there'd been no disease, she would have gone on to stardom. But then, our paths would never have intersected.

*

I'VE BEEN BACK since then—to her shrine. I've read it all, and I didn't think anyone knew about her last tour. Karin hadn't posted there, nor Giulio. Maybe they didn't do Facebook. I've thought about posting something myself, but what would I say? "Hey, you folks, you knew her for twenty years, but we were the people she chose to spend her last days with." I didn't think so. Let them enjoy their memories, but I preferred mine.

How had she funded that makeover? Did she have her hand in the till at the department store? I couldn't believe it. So much else about her rang true.

I had a theory…

Actually, I had lots of theories because I had a crazy imagination that weirded even me out sometimes. Neale would vouch for that. But there was this one that was my favourite. One of my favourites.

Picture this crime boss who had a stash of cash he needed to launder, and he came across Juliette on SoundCloud. Her voice really knocked him out, but he knew that, with her looks, she'd never be a star. So, he approached her—like, Juliette was Doctor Faustus, and he was Mephistopheles—and made his pitch. M would fund the surgery, the best that wads of cash could buy, and in return, she'd sign an ironclad contract to pay him 30 percent of everything she earned. Ever. Juliette became a star, and M's money got laundered. Job done.

And before the ink was dry, M whisked her off to a surgeon happy to work for cash. I was still working on the surgeon's backstory there. So, the surgery happened, and she was recording her demos, and M was about to launch her career when they discovered she had an inoperable tumour that was going to kill her. Bang went M's investment. Nothing he could do. And besides, M had fallen in love with Juliette. It wasn't Juliette's fault. Nobody deliberately contracted a terminal disease to wriggle out of a contract. So there was no incentive to rub her out. Or maybe she realised that, although M loved her, he *was* going to eliminate her, painfully and messily. Because M was an evil creep. So, she escaped with a couple of cards funded with M's credit and decided to have that last adventure. With us as her conduit to a painless death at a time of her choosing.

It fit.

But it was a wind up. The only merit was that it was more exciting than Juliette just having a wealthy family who paid for the cosmetic surgery.

Had we been nothing more than her bucket list? Or was there something more than that? I liked to think so. I looked at my life now, and I was truly grateful. Dom had given far more than she got, and the more I reflected, the more it seemed she knew what she was doing.

Neale had called her a guardian angel. We were where we were. I could wonder uselessly about the details. But this I did know.

She'd kept her side of the bargain.

Chapter Twenty-Four

The Swan

"TODAY IS GERMAN Unity Day, Kai."

It'd been a whole year since I'd heard anyone speak the phrase. But then, it had been Alina speaking; now, it was my Lars from the other side of the bed.

"And so?"

And so, all kinds of memories took it upon themselves to surface.

"Do you remember…" I began, but I choked up.

Lars rolled over onto his side and kissed me softly on the cheek. "Dom. Yes, I remember her. Fondly, for the most part."

I smiled at that, thinking of how, as Lars and I were learning to trust each other, he'd confessed a mix of anger and jealousy that Dom had been trying to seduce me. He'd been fighting a ton of anguish, and I loved him for how he'd conducted himself.

I pushed him back and stretched up to kiss him on the lips.

And that was when my Handy rang.

"Answer it," he said. "I'll wait for my kiss."

I made a face at him.

International number. I didn't recognise the prefix, but I was pretty sure it wasn't a scam nation, else I'd have taken that kiss.

"Hallo?"

"Hallo, is that Kai?" A woman's voice, accented. But one that sounded familiar. The short-haired girl. K-something…

"Karin?"

A chuckle. "Yes, you remember. Thank you. Are you happy to talk? To me?"

"Yes?" Why wouldn't I be?

"This is difficult; I am sorry. But I made a promise to…Dominique. Not quite a year ago. On her last day. A promise I did not wish to keep, but I could not refuse."

"When you went together to Zurich. To Dignitas." I didn't make it a question. I knew.

"You know that much, then? What else?"

"I know she was really Juliette Robard. And she had some sort of inoperable condition."

"Yes. Once, she was Juliette Robard. But she became Dominique. I loved both."

Ouch! That was her *deadname*. Sorry, Dom, sorrysorrysorry.

"But I thought you and Giulio…"

"It is possible to love more than one person at the same time. It was not always easy. You of all people must understand that."

With Lars sitting opposite me, I couldn't really deny it. How much was he picking up? A question for later.

"So, you called me. Why now?"

"It was not easy. Dom gave me her phone with all your numbers on it. But your number did not work."

True. I'd let it go when I decided my future was in Germany with Lars.

"I had tried and failed," she continued. "I thought I could leave it there. But my conscience would not let me alone. I tried calling Jamie. No response. Eventually, I tried Neale. I persuaded him to give me your number. He said you'd probably tell me to fuck off, but he did give it to me."

"Why…" No, it didn't matter. "What was your promise to Dom?"

"Will you meet me in Zurich? Two weeks from now? We can talk properly. Bring the band, if they wish to come. To say good-bye. To let her go."

*

ROSE PETALS TUMBLED from my hands. They fluttered briefly, but the waves took them without exception. Physics was cruel. They swirled and then were lost in the wake of the cruiser.

"We should have hired a boat just for ourselves," I said. "Without the constant diesel sound or smell when I'm trying to remember her."

"She told me the van was noisy and smelly. I think she'd appreciate the similarity."

Karin was right, of course. And so I smiled, remembering the miles and the music. Only Neale was missing. Alina and Lars had been invited but declined for their own reasons.

"I'm only the hired help," Neale had said. "I'll make my remembrance of her in my own way. You can let me know when you're out on the water."

When we returned to shore an hour later, the rattle of the anchor chain was the last echo of my own chains falling away.

*

KARIN HAD BOOKED a restaurant overlooking the lake.

The waiter led us out to the terrace, furnished in black-lacquered wrought-iron, to a circular table set for five with labelled places. Karin sat on my left, then Jamie, Lotte, and to my right, Jake.

Once we were all seated, the waiter poured wine for each of us. Then Karin rose.

"Thank you," she began, "and welcome to my country, my city. We've come together to remember our friend Dominique. I knew her for more than twenty years. We met at a school in Brussels, popular with diplomats. You only knew her for a few days, but even that short time changed all of your lives. And that was Dominique in a nutshell. A whirlwind. A life-changer. Let us raise a glass and toast her memory. To Dominique:"

"Dominique," we chorused. The wine was sharp and fresh on my tongue, and I asked what it was, mostly to get a conversation started.

"It's a local wine," Karin replied, while Jamie started a conversation with Lotte. "We don't export it—well, maybe a tiny amount to Germany. I like it, but Dom was always scathing about it. Her mother's influence, I think. She was Belgian, but she had French pretensions, especially for their wine and their food,"

"I remember she said her father was English."

"Yes. They both worked in Brussels. He was a diplomat of some sort; she was a translator. Dom never said how they met. They were there for fifteen years, perhaps a little more. Then they split up. It was quite acrimonious. They fought bitterly over custody of their only child. But she wasn't really a child; she was fourteen and very determined."

"I can believe it."

Karin continued. "She was her mother's girl, though, still Juliette, mimicking her mother's phrasing: *'He will not take you to England, Juliette – I promise – and over my dead body will you ever live in Marden Combe with him...'*"

Oh.

Suddenly, there was silence. Karin saw the shock on my face instantly. Then she looked around at each one of us, even Lotte, who'd spent a few months in Marden Combe with Jake before they'd returned to Germany. All of us sat there with our mouths hanging open.

Karin wasn't stupid. "I see. That explains a lot. Juliette would never have gone against her mother, but Dom was not Juliette. I don't think she ever saw her father after he went home — he died about five years later — but I can imagine her wondering what her life might have been if she had followed him instead of staying with her mother."

We could have been her band...

Looking around the table, I knew everyone else was thinking exactly the same thing.

Jamie broke the silence. "It's like that movie, *Sliding Doors*, where Gwyneth Paltrow has two choices. One looks bad and turns out good, and the other looks good but turns out bad. Uh, I'm not telling this very well."

"I love that movie," Lotte picked up. "But it's not Paltrow's choice. It's somebody else's action, and that splits into two alternate timelines. Oh, and Paltrow's character is called Helen…"

That triggered a memory of sitting in the van, just after Dom had joined us, thinking of Faustian bargains and singing with our 'Helen of Troy'.

But then, somehow, the conversation twisted, and twisted again, and Juliette had gone to university in Paris. A year later, when Karin had followed in her footsteps, she'd found Juliette teetering on the edge of becoming Dom. Childhood friends had become ardent lovers.

And Dom had dropped out. She could have followed a conventional career, but she'd found her voice and was making good money in the clubs and bars of Paris, topped up with commissions earned in a very upmarket Paris department store. Plus, a trust fund her father had set up, which paid for cosmetic surgery. So, no mysterious M.

The main course arrived, and the talk died down, somewhat, while we tackled our steaks and Zurich sliced veal. I wasn't sure what Neale would have made of the food, but there were no gherkins in sight. The waiter brought more drinks, and despite Karin's best efforts to promote Swiss wines, I found myself joining Jamie in drinking sparkling water. Yeah, me, sparkling water.

And in that alternate timeline, did Dom drop out of Cambridge? Did she return to Marden Combe and fetch up in the Cherry Tree LGBT plus community?

I tuned in again as Karin came up to date. She'd drifted apart from Dom, moved to Florence, and hooked up with Giulio.

After the meal, we ordered coffee, awakening memories of the campsite in Berlin when Dom had knocked Neale's coffee out of his hand, and we'd got the first hints that Dom didn't have much time left.

"Did she get a diagnosis?" Jamie asked.

By then, we'd left the table and were leaning on the terrace railing, watching the evening lights reflect and sparkle on the waters of the lake.

"She did," Karin replied. "But she did not share it with me, nor anyone else. I just knew it was something rare and terminal. She had to tell Dignitas, of course."

"And you went with her." I made it a statement.

"Yes. It was the hardest thing I've ever done, but she had no one else. I was with her all the way, as far as they would let me go. I hate that she was alone at the very end—"

Karin choked up then. There were tears in her eyes, and why would there not be, so close to the anniversary of Dom's passage over the rainbow? Tears in my own eyes too.

Everyone's eyes.

Then, a final toast, and it was time to go. Trains did not wait for dry eyes. But there was time to hug Karin.

Thank you, Karin.

Goodbye, Dom.

*

BUT IT WASN'T quite goodbye.

We'd taken a taxi to the station, where we said our farewells. As we turned towards our platform, Karin touched my elbow.

"This is for you alone," she whispered and passed me a small, slightly worn envelope with my name written in Dom's hand. "Now, go."

It went into my pocket and stayed there for the whole of the train journey. I didn't want any sort of inquiry about it. That Dom had written me a note told me most of what I wanted to know. There'd be answers to at least some of the questions I'd asked in our bed in the Regensburg hotel.

In my own mind, I was settled though. We had the link with Marden Combe. Never mind the connection from Clay to Dom, evidenced by her mentioning 'I Come from the Blues'. Never mind whether Dom saw potential in Clay's band, even without Clay. Forget the speculation that she wanted one last adventure, one last challenge, before Zurich. Scratch any thought that I was part of that challenge, even though she'd called me 'striking'. Dom knew her *Sliding Doors* moment and wanted a glimpse of her other timeline.

*

IT WAS STILL two hours before sunrise when I began my walk back from Berlin's central train station towards the apartment that Lars and I shared. It was hardly any distance from the station to the River Spree and the elegant bridge, the Moltkebrücke, that spans it.

The bridge parapet was lower than I'd have liked, too low to rest my elbows on it. Never mind. I removed the letter from my pocket and held it under one of the lamps, making sure it was Dom's handwriting. It was.

And, opening it, what then?

It wouldn't bring Dom back. Perhaps Dom would write that she wished we had been intimate, perhaps even that she'd loved me. And how would that knowledge change me? And how would it change my relationship with Lars? That was the rub. Knowledge wasn't neutral.

Very well.

For a moment, I was back in Köln, standing on another bridge, letting out the poison of my ambition.

And then, a voice from right behind me spoke in German, but my brain was elsewhere.

"What?" I said and turned around.

"Oh, English. Are you okay?"

Ah. A policewoman and, farther back, her partner.

Caught in the act?

"Sure," I replied, trying to sound calm.

"You're not upset?"

"No."

She glanced down at the envelope I was holding. "Is it…bad news? Do you need to talk to someone?"

"No?"

I was missing something. And then I finally realised what was going on.

"I'm fine," I said. "I have no plans to jump. Honestly. Life is good."

"You are sure? If you're uncomfortable talking to the police, I can call someone else to talk with you."

And she looked down at the letter again, doubt still evident on her face.

What's mute, white, and floats on a river?

"A swan," I said.

"What?"

I'd puzzled her.

It would have been easier if the letter had been square, but it was only one extra fold, and in a few moments, Dom's letter was a tiny, origami swan.

I held it up in the light so she could see it clearly, sitting in my right hand. "This is the past."

With my left hand, I pointed to the far end of the bridge, roughly in the direction of home and Lars. "That way is the future."

I opened my right hand and watched the swan tumble down, down towards the water, where the gentle current swept it under the arch.

"I choose the future," I said.

At that, she smiled, convinced.

"I should fine you," she said. "For littering."

"You should," I agreed. "Let's walk over to the other side. If we see it, you can fine me."

"If I see you walk into the future, I won't," she replied.

"Deal."

I'm still walking.

Appendix

Original Songs

Cross, Don't Cross

Alone in the night, thinking of what
If I were not so formed we would not
Be strangers, but closer than
Threads in a loom
Don't cross me, cross to me
Cross the street to my room

Alone in my mind, alone in my heart
Wondering why love should force us apart
Two bodies, no closer than
Sun and the moon.
Don't cross me, cross to me
Cross my heart, sing my tune

Heat of the day, cool of the night
Alternate faces, nature to fight
'Gainst nature, far closer than
Lover do hold
Don't cross me, cross to me
Cross boundaries, cross me bold

Cross my heart, hope to die
Cross me once, before I get old

Whiskey in the Jar

As I was going over the fair Kilgarry Mountain
I met with Captain Farrell and his money he was counting
I first produced my pistol and then I produced my rapier
Saying stand and deliver, for you were a bold deceiver

Mush a ring um do dum-a da
Whack fol the daddy o
Whack fol the daddy o
There's whiskey in the jar

I counted out his money and it made a pretty penny
I put it in my pocket and I took it home to Jenny
(Jenny) I sighed and I swore that I'd be faithful to him ever
He knew I was a beauty but not that I was clever

(Jenny) I led him to our chamber, first for play and then for sleeping
He dreamt of gold and jewels, he'd spend on drink, and not be
keeping
He slept—I drew his charges, and filled them up with water
And sent to Captain Farrell to be ready for the slaughter

'Twas early the next morning when I arose to travel
Up stepped a band of footmen and likewise Captain Farrell
I drew forth my pistol for I saw that they were many
But I couldn't shoot the water and a widow was my Jenny

(Jenny) And then came Captain Farrell to the room where I'd been
staying

His shirt a-splashed with scarlet from the man that he'd been slaying
But I was gone with gold and jewels; for England I was sailing
In London will I live a Lady's life with wealth unfailing

(Jenny) And no more shall I see the fair Kilgarry Mountain
My cycle have I missed and now the months I am a-countin'
My child will know no father, and my greed it was the reason
And though I gulled two men, it was myself I was deceiving

Drinking Song

Sitting in a bar — it's late and I should be home
The band is cranking it out and I'm all alone
In the middle of a crowd of couples all holding hands
There's no place for a man just looking for a one-night stand

Play me another drinking song
Keep it simple so I can sing along
Love songs only cause me pain
So drain your glass let's sing again

The barman tells me, "Son, ain't you had enough?
If you drink up now, you'll have time to catch your bus"
So I ask for another beer, light a cigarette
I'm not drinking to get drunk, I'm only drinking to forget

Play me another drinking song
Keep it simple so I can sing along
Love songs only cause me pain
So drain your glass let's sing again

(Guitar Solo)

((spoken) 2 3 and)
Play me another drinking song
Keep it simple so I can sing along
Love songs only cause me pain
So drain your glass let's sing again

A touch on my shoulder "Are you looking for some company?

You look like a lonely man, come sit by me
Tell me about your problems, I'll tell you mine
Order a beer and I'll have a glass of wine

((spoken) While the band can)
Play me another drinking song
Keep it simple so I can sing along
Love songs only cause me pain
So drain your glass let's sing again

So we talk, neither listens, the band is playing too loud
We dance to the music and sway along with the crowd
My memory is bad and it seems that hers is worse
As we sing to the chorus and la-la-la to the verse

((spoken) All together now)
Play me another drinking song
Keep it simple so I can sing along
Love songs only cause me pain
So drain your glass let's sing again

(repeat)

The Hall of Fallen Angels

There's a place that no one speaks of at the end of Meeting Street
Where the faithless and the loveless and the heartless lovers greet
It's the place where last-chance losers come to live their hopeless
dreams
Where guilt walks masked as innocence, and nothing's as it seems
The past mistakes we left behind, reopened and laid bare
It's the Hall of Fallen Angels and I was welcomed there

Dark angel calls to angel and two hearts forbidden beat
As one, and one draws closer, and passions flame and heat
In secret rooms we threw off caution, and played our fantasies
And I crept home and filled my once love's ears with hollow lies
The new mistakes we're building, which you and I now share
In the Hall of Fallen Angels, in the bed of I-don't-care

The ones that we have left behind, the first loves we now wrong
With lies that sound so sweet, but taste so bitter on the tongue
A stolen hour at noon-time spent in passion on a quilt
The room keys shine like gold but all they open up is gilt
The futures that we hoped for have turned to dark and cold
In the Hall of Fallen Angels, where we count the love we stole

I've Got the Blues, I Ain't Worried

I've got the blues, I ain't worried
I seen the last of my ol' man
My last dollar in his pocket
And a suitcase in his hand

Headin' down the road to Memphis
Headin' down the lonesome track
He's a leavin' me with nuthin'
And it's nuthin' I'll take back

So I followed close behind him
He never stopped to look behind
But he waited at the crossroads
There was evil in his mind.

They say he shouldn't a' hit a woman
They say she shouldn't a' hit him first
They say she shouldn't a' used a breadknife
They say the two of us was cursed.

So when you get to where you're goin'
Jus' keep walkin' t'ward your fate
In that place where it ain't snowin'
'Tain't Saint Peter at that gate.
I don't wish I never killed you
Though the hangman waits for me
Soon I'll be walkin' just behind you
For the rest of eternity.

I Come from the Blues

Where did I come from? I come from the blues.
Where am I going? I'm going to lose.
Where is my future? I'm sure I have none
Where is my hope? My hope is all gone.

My momma, she loved me, but she loved to fight.
My daddy, he left her, and vanished from sight.
So who can I trust to love me and care?
I'm searching for someone, but nobody's there

I'm standing alone, and around me is night
The darkness, it closes, it blots out the light
I'm sinking, I'm drowning, I can't reach the shore
I'm locked in my head, I can't open the door

(repeat opening chorus)

But I have a friend in these blues, set me free
There's Muddy, and Etta, all Howlin' for me
The pain doesn't go, but sometimes it fades.
The darkness recedes, there's a light in the shade.

The blues never leaves me, it's deep down inside
It laughs when I laugh, as it cried when I cried.
The blues is the singer, and I am its song
I come from the blues, it survives when I'm gone

Where did I come from? I come from the blues

Where am I going? Wherever I choose
Where is my hope, if not in my friends?
Where is my future? Around the next bend.

Author's Note and Acknowledgements

Where did I come from? I come from the Blues.

Where do stories come from? Muses, of course. By which, I mean the people we've known and the times we share. This story? Some of it came from real life, specifically my experiences of playing bass guitar in a ramshackle college band. A couple of years after graduating, we toured Germany twice in the days before the internet. Some of the incidents in the book were taken from things that happened, perhaps slightly differently. I'll tell you for free that the exploding toolbox incident really happened—and it was *my* toolbox.

The first jottings emerged years later, when I was struck by the notion of writing a love story that worked, regardless of the (not stated) gender of the protagonist. What drove me was a single scene—Dom and Kai (at that time called Stevie) who, having become separated from the band, search the back streets for shelter.

That notion didn't really fit with my other published novel—*Expiration Day*—and my then editor was keen for me to produce a sequel to that, so the idea went on hold for a year or two.

It took about a year to get to first draft, with life's usual interruptions interleaved, of which the Brexit vote was a significant one. The story served as my remembrance of my country's having been a part of something brighter, better.

Bit by bit, the story evolved, as did my understanding of the LGBTQ+ rainbow. Gender-ambiguous Stevie became non-binary Kai. And this is where I drop my first 'thank you'—to Emma Osborne, who was my sensitivity reader and teacher, who guided me as I developed Kai's character, steering me away from a number of pitfalls.

My next thank-yous are for my beta readers and crit partners: for fellow author, fellow musician and lifelong friend, Howard Whitehouse, who—perhaps wisely—managed to bail out of the band before the Germany tours. He was the first person to whom I showed the novel, and he encouraged me to keep working on it.

Howard, in turn, introduced me to Laura Sorrese Lefkow, which led to us doing deep chapter-by-chapter critiques of each other's work. Laura has excellent intuition for what works on the page, so most of her suggestions went in, in some form or another. As I write, I have fingers firmly crossed for Laura's own novel, agented, and on query with publishers.

And thank you to Hilke Kurzke, from my BSFA novel crit group, whose advice on German language and culture was invaluable. My schoolboy German was nowhere near as good as I thought it was, and she put me right. But I also learned from her that English is practically the second language in Berlin. So, when the novel finally got accepted by NineStar Press, getting rid of the German wasn't the pain point that it might have been. If language errors remain, they're Kai's fault, and I take full responsibility for them.

Thanks also to my other editors: Jeanette Spohn (who advised me to reset the story into the near-present), Raquel Brown, and Georgia Holmes—you all helped refine and improve elements of the tale.

And of course, my no-longer-ramshackle college band—Ken Wood and the Mixers—some of whom appear thinly disguised either here or in Expiration Day, and whose exploits inspired parts of this tale. Ken, Frank, Andy, Steve, Ketch, Terry, Hoss, Rex—and roadie Chris. So many memories from the fifteen years we were playing together. Thank you.

And so, to the present.

Working with Elizabetta McKay—my editor at NineStar—has been immensely positive. Challenging, of course, but that's her job, to coax me to think deeper about what the novel could become, helping me lift the blinkers. And I loved her little notes in the margin ("I can't stop laughing") that made the editing process feel like she was sitting at the next desk. Elizabetta 'got' Teardown, 'got' Kai, and that shone through the whole collaboration. Thank you.

So here we are, nine years on from *Teardown*'s inception, and it's a real book. There's also real music to go with it, and it's been such fun to record demos for the original songs in the book. They're demos, as I couldn't get the real John Doe's Blues to record them for me. I do hope they'll give you something for your imagination to build on. And if you get inspired to form your own band, and maybe cover one of the songs, that would be brilliant. You'll find the demos over on my website—williamcampbellpowell.com.

Kai wished 'someone would write a book about people like me'. So, I did. Kai's journey is just one of many journeys. Whoever you are, whatever journey you may be on, I hope Kai's tale will encourage you to hold firm to your course and to support those on different journeys through the difficult times in which we live.

Lastly, I must express my gratitude to my family, and especially to my wife, Avis, ever patient, loving, and forbearing. Thank you.

About the Author

William lives in a small Buckinghamshire village in England. By night, he writes contemporary, speculative, historical, crime and other fiction. His debut novel, *Expiration Day,* was published by Tor Teen in 2014 and won the 2015 Hal Clement Award for "Excellence in Children's Science Fiction Literature". His short fiction has appeared in Metastellar, DreamForge and other excellent 'zines. By day, William writes software for a living, and in the twilight, he sings tenor, plays guitar, and writes songs.

Email
contact@williamcampbellpowell.com

X
@willcampowell

Website
www.williamcampbellpowell.com

Instagram
@willcampowell

BlueSky
@willcampowell.bsky.social

Connect with NineStar Press

Website: NineStarPress.com

Facebook: NineStarPress

X: @ninestarpress

Instagram: NineStarPress

BlueSky: NineStarPress

Threads: @ninestarpress

www.ingramcontent.com/pod-product-compliance
Lightning Source LLC
Chambersburg PA
CBHW060304100726
47907CB00002B/269